PERDITION HOUSE

PERDITION HOUSE

A BAY TANNER MYSTERY

KATHRYN R. WALL

Kathryn R. Wall

BellaRosaBooks

PERDITION HOUSE

ISBN 978-1-933523-16-3
2009 Reprint Edition by Bella Rosa Books

Previously Published in the U.S.A. by St. Martin's Press, LLC.
First Hardcover Edition: June 2003; ISBN 0-312-31385-3
First Paperback Edition: May 2004; ISBN 0-312-99824-4

Printed in the United States of America on acid-free paper.

Book design by Bella Rosa Books

BellaRosaBooks and logo are trademarks of Bella Rosa Books

10   9   8   7   6   5   4   3   2   1

For Norman,
again and always.

PERDITION HOUSE

CHAPTER ONE

I had no idea when we set up our informal inquiry agency that one of the first clients my father and I would have would be one of my own shirttail relations. Life is strange that way sometimes, or so I've found.

Mercer Mary Prescott had the relationship down pat, from each third- and fourth-cousin-by-marriage twice removed, back through an incredible tangle of ancestors, all the way to our mutual great, great-something grandmothers who were half-sisters. At least I think that's how it went. She lost me somewhere after the second *great*, and I decided then and there I'd just take her word for it.

It was certainly hard to believe, looking at her through the glass partition that rainy afternoon in mid-November, that we could be related by any but the most tenuous of blood connections. Huddled in the too-big orange jumpsuit that leached any remaining color from her already sallow skin, Mercer Mary Prescott resembled nothing so much as a bedraggled owl. Muddy brown eyes, magnified by a pair of functional, drugstore glasses mended on the left temple with grungy adhesive tape, made brief contact with my own bright green ones, then slid guiltily away. Poker-straight hair—dirty blonde in both senses of the word— was pulled back with a thick rubber band into a drooping ponytail, and her nails, on surprisingly long, tapered fingers, were bitten down to the skin.

She did have a sweet smile, or so it seemed in the one, brief flash I'd seen of it when I first strode into the visitors' room at the Beaufort County Jail. The effect was ruined, however, by the yellowing, purplish bruise mottling the left side of her narrow chin. Mercer Mary Prescott had said little beyond her recitation of our common lineage, an attempt to explain, no doubt, why she used her one allotted telephone call to reach my father. About her injury she remained stubbornly mute.

"Look, Mercer," I said as she attacked her already shredded fingers, "I don't understand what else you expect me to do. I've called a local attorney, a friend of my father's, and he should be here soon. If bail is granted, I'm sure the Judge and I would be happy to help you out. You being family and all," I added with a touch of sarcasm that seemed completely lost on the child.

"Oh, no, Cousin Lydia, please!" It was the first sign of animation I'd seen out of her since she'd stopped spouting her genealogical mumbo-jumbo. "I won't mind it here, truly I won't! I'll probably have a cell to myself, and the food is bound to be good. I've been in worse places."

"Recently?" I blurted out, then mentally kicked myself.

What is your problem? I demanded silently and could find no reasonable explanation for this instinctive antagonism toward my newly met cousin.

"And no one calls me Lydia any more," I plunged on, consciously softening my tone, "at least not since my mother died. It's 'Bay' now."

Somewhere in elementary school I had abandoned the burden of Lydia Baynard Simpson for the sleek simplicity of *Bay*. The *Tanner* was added after a short, love-at-first-sight courtship led to nearly a decade and a half of solid marital bliss, cut short over a year ago by my husband's yet unsolved murder. Dealing with Rob's death was a daily exercise in self-control and acceptance. Some days the pain receded to a dull ache just behind my breastbone. On others . . .

Mercer sat quietly, her chin dropped so low I found myself staring at the crooked part on the top of her head.

"So why did you call us then? And what are you in for, anyway?"

Maybe I would have to revise my generous offer of bail money if she'd been accused of an ax murder or something equally reprehensible. Besides, I was getting tired of badgering her. The dull afternoon was fast fading into twilight, and I didn't relish the thought of navigating the narrow, two-lane road back to Hilton Head Island on such a rainy, miserable night. I wanted out of there, family duty be damned.

"Mercer?" I tried hard for patience. "What did you do?"

"Vagrancy," she finally mumbled into her chest.

"Vagrancy? You mean you were sleeping in the street or on a park bench or something like that? Why? Where are your parents, for God's sake?"

I didn't get an answer to any of my questions, at least not then.

"Time's up, ladies." The guard was a deputy I didn't recognize, even though my brother-in-law, Sergeant Red Tanner, had introduced me over the years to many of his colleagues in the Beaufort County Sheriff's Department. This guy probably worked for the city police, who, now that I thought about it, no doubt had jurisdiction. Our county was still peaceful enough that everyone shared the same jail.

I bristled a little at his remark until I registered his soft brown eyes and realized he had meant no disrespect. Mercer Mary Prescott might look like trailer trash, but our great, great-whatever grandmothers had been half-sisters, and I would demand she be treated accordingly. "Miss Prescott's attorney will be along shortly," I informed him. "He'll want to speak to his client."

"No problem, ma'am," the deputy said, as Mercer and I both rose in our chairs. I felt a rush of relief that mine was on the right side of the partition.

"I'll wait around and see about your bail," I said, looking down on my newfound relative. At just under six feet I towered over the diminutive young woman, who couldn't have been much over five feet three inches even if she stood up straight.

"Not much chance of that, ma'am," the deputy interjected, "beggin' your pardon. Judge Pinckney's up in Columbia today at some conference, and he isn't expected back until tomorrow."

Being the daughter of retired Judge Talbot Simpson, I've kind of gotten used to throwing his weight around. Crippled by a series of debilitating strokes, my father has been confined to a wheelchair for the past several years. Despite an almost pathological fear of being pitied which has kept him housebound as well, his power remains undimmed in local jurisprudence circles. There isn't a member of the northern Beaufort County bar or bench who hasn't at one time or another shared whiskey and cigars around his poker table, or shucked oysters on our back dock, or fidgeted through one of my mother's interminable formal dinner parties. The same went for law enforcement. If my father couldn't ultimately bust Mercer Mary Prescott out of jail with a couple of judiciously placed phone calls, I'd be very much surprised.

"We'll see about that," I began, but Mercer cut me off.

"It's okay, really, Cousin . . . Bay. Tomorrow will be fine. I really don't mind staying here tonight. I don't want to be a burden to anyone." She looked almost panicked at the thought of getting out of jail.

What did this poor, bedraggled child think?—that I would spring her from the slammer and toss her back out into the street? Had I made *that* bad an impression?

"Let's wait and see what Law Merriweather has to say," I replied, certain my father's old friend could arrange it somehow so I could just pay her fine and whisk Cousin Mercer back to Presqu'isle. Lavinia Smalls, my father's housekeeper-companion and the woman who, for better or worse, had been primarily responsible for rearing me, would bluster and shake an accusing brown finger at me, complaining about unexpected guests in the old antebellum mansion where I grew up. But in the end she would attack this problem as she did most others—with food and herbal tea and a deep compassion for those in need.

I could dump this problem on Lavinia and my father and retreat back to my beach house on Hilton Head with only a slightly muddy conscience.

Mercer Mary Prescott nodded, apparently used to taking as an order any suggestion made by someone who spoke with the least degree of authority. "Thank you," I saw her mouth over her shoulder as the deputy led her away. Even he seemed to recognize her frailty, guiding her by a hand placed gently under her scrawny elbow.

I wove my way down the halls and out into the gloomy darkness settling over the covered walkway outside the jail. The wind had switched around to the northeast, coming straight in off the ocean now, forcing me to zip up the battered leather aviator jacket I had pulled from Rob's closet. As I shoved my hands into the deep, warm pockets, I promised myself I would get his things cleaned out. Soon.

The fingers of my right hand fondled the loose cigarette, the last of my daily allotment of ten. Trying to quit was a mountain I was only partly sure I wanted to climb, but every exercise in self-control was another foothold up the slope. I inhaled a lungful of damp night air and peeled the foil from a piece of nicotine-replacement gum. I grimaced at the sharp peppery taste, then tucked it against the inside of my cheek. As I waited for the familiar comfort of nicotine hitting my needy bloodstream, I wondered who had left that long, ugly bruise on Cousin Mercer Mary Prescott. And why.

The old house lay shrouded in mist, the light from its windows muted in the steady, dreary downpour, as we emerged from the long avenue of live oaks which had once been the main drive up to the plantation great house. The magnificent trees, whose dark leaves and gray clumps of Spanish moss usually provided a welcome canopy against the oppressive heat of the South Carolina Lowcountry, now dripped heavily from the assault of two straight days of relentless rain.

I spared a glance at Mercer, huddled in the bucket seat of my BMW, as I negotiated the squishy mud road in my low-slung sports car. I am firmly convinced that many of these same pot-holes I was weaving my way around have existed since horses and carriages first picked their way up to Presqu'isle a hundred and fifty years before.

My cousin had been strangely quiet on the short drive from the jailhouse to the Judge's home on St. Helena. She'd shown little emotion when Law Merriweather emerged from a brief con-ference, which had included the expected phone call from my father, to announce that she would be released into our custody until such time as Judge Pinckney returned.

Mercer Mary Prescott disappointed me by her lack of response to her first view of the ancestral homestead, a house most viewed as one of the finest examples of antebellum architecture on the South Carolina-Georgia coast. Built high off the ground on an arched foundation of lime-and-oyster shell tabby, the split central staircase and wide, columned verandah gave the solid old place a touch of elegance without the ostentation so typical in other structures of the period. Its location on a spit of land jutting out into St. Helena Sound had given my Huguenot ancestors the inspiration for its name: Presqu'isle, French for peninsula.

I pulled up into the circular drive at the foot of the steps and turned to Mercer. "Legend has it this is pretty close to the spot where Francisco Gardillo first waded ashore and claimed the island for Spain," I said, hoping to engage her in what appeared to be the only subject in which she had any interest. "It was August—"

"The eighteenth," she provided without looking at me, her voice so low I could barely hear her, "in 1520. St. Helen's Day, which is why he named the island St. Helena. In her honor."

"Right."

I whipped open the door and reached for Mercer's battered duffel bag jammed behind her seat on the rear floor, but she beat me to it. It was the one thing about which she exhibited any real emotion, insisting on carrying it herself. It would be a relief to get the thing out of my car. Hopefully the sour odor of unwashed socks and overripe fruit wouldn't linger on the upholstery.

Lavinia must have been watching for us. As we dashed through the rain and up the steps, the heavy oak door swung open, spilling welcoming light out onto the dark recesses of the verandah. Mercer, following my lead, wiped off her scruffy Keds on the welcome mat before stepping gratefully into the wide, center hall.

I tried to see the place through her newcomer's eyes: the sweeping staircase, its oak banisters gleaming, as it curved gently to the upper story and its many bedrooms; the heart pine floor scattered with genuine Persian rugs; the glass-fronted cabinets displaying my mother's precious antiques. I had no real emotional attachment, either to the house or to its contents, the museum-like sterility of it having contributed to my less than idyllic childhood. But I had to admit to a fleeting flash of pride watching Mercer's dull brown eyes take in all that splendor as she stood dripping in the front hall.

"Come along, child," Lavinia commanded in that voice that brooked no opposition. "We need to get you out of those wet things."

Recognizing an irresistible force when she encountered one, Mercer allowed Lavinia Smalls to relieve her of the drab green duffel bag, then followed meekly up the stairs.

"The Judge is waiting for you in his study," Lavinia called over her shoulder to me. "And don't give him a cigar. He's already had one today. Dinner will be ready in half an hour."

"Yes, ma'am," I answered meekly.

Lavinia Smalls had been a permanent fixture in my life for as long as I could remember. She and my late mother had maintained an oddly formal relationship, always excruciatingly polite, referring to each other as *Mrs. Simpson* and *Mrs. Smalls,* despite the fact that each knew the other intimately, warts and all. Amidst the chaos that was my early life at Presqu'isle, I don't think I would have survived without Lavinia's calm, unflinching presence and staunch defense against my mother's erratic behavior.

I turned toward the rear of the house and went to join my father.

After his second stroke left him partially paralyzed, we had turned his former study into a bedroom suite, complete with wheelchair-accessible bathroom and a ramp to the back verandah so he could wheel himself outside on fine days. The view out across the Sound was magnificent, and the wide lawn rolled down to a narrow salt marsh which provided a communal gathering place for all manner of wading and shore birds. It was one of the most peaceful spots in the whole of the Lowcountry. I had done some of my best thinking out there, curled up in a weathered rocker, gazing out toward the sea.

I felt the warmth at about the same time I smelled the sweet, fruity smoke drifting out of the Judge's room. Lavinia must have laid a fire in the narrow, brick-fronted hearth. Although almost every room in the house, including the kitchen and the bedrooms, had working fireplaces, we rarely had occasion to use them except on stormy November nights like this one.

My father's wheelchair sat in front of the flickering fire, and for a moment I thought he might have fallen asleep. His full head of thick, white hair bent forward, as if he dozed, but I quickly realized by the motion of his one good hand that he was reading. Probably one of his legal thrillers, I thought, maneuvering around him to plop myself down in one of the wing chairs to the side of the hearth. He devoured them as fast as I could pick them up from the East Bay Book Emporium or the library, whichever could promise faster service.

But the papers spread out across the plaid lap robe covering his withered legs were not a bound, hardcover book. They were standard letter-size pages once held together by a length of coarse, brown twine now curled in a heap on the floor. They appeared to have been written in a formal, dainty hand.

"Tea still warm?" I asked, indicating the blue-flowered pot resting on the butler's table near his elbow.

"Should be. Pour me one too, will you, sweetheart?"

I retrieved another cup and saucer from the sideboard and poured, one finger resting lightly against the lid of the pot, as I had been instructed. Some of the most harrowing moments of my young life had been spent in attempting to master these maidenly skills under the ever-critical eye of my socially prominent mother. Emmaline Baynard Simpson would never have been convinced that my master's degrees in accounting and finance were as important to my future as how to pour properly from a centuries-old teapot into equally delicate and ancient, thin-handled cups.

And who's to say she was wrong? Widowed and childless at thirty-eight years old, I had little to show for my hard-won career, except a financial security which would allow me to do nothing for the rest of my life, if that's what I decided. In the months following Rob's murder I had expended all my energies on recovering from the injury to my left shoulder, mutilated by a flaming piece of debris when his plane exploded before my eyes, and to coming to terms with spending the rest of my life without him. By the time I recovered—physically, anyway—I found I'd lost interest in the accounting practice I shared with the sons of two of Charleston's old families. My *unofficial* job as Rob's financial consultant and sounding board in his quest to rid the state of drug dealers had, of course, ended with his death.

I set my father's tea cup on the side table next to his good right arm. He grunted his thanks, his attention once again caught by the papers in his lap.

So I was basically unemployed. But through an odd concurrence of circumstances and luck, both good and bad, I had recently been involved in some nasty situations I had been able to help resolve. Thus the formation of Simpson & Tanner, Inquiry Agents, an informal confederation among my father, me, and a young computer hacker named Erik Whiteside from Charlotte. We figured our individual areas of expertise, when combined and focused on a problem the authorities either couldn't or wouldn't address, would enable us to offer unique solutions. We didn't plan on advertising or even hanging out a shingle. We'd just let the word slide around town that we were available and see what turned up.

Not exactly what my mother had in mind while she was rapping my knuckles for dribbling tea on the Hepplewhite table, but then children so seldom turn out the way they're supposed to. Or so I've observed.

"So what's she like?" the Judge asked, trying to collate the loose pages in his lap with only one hand. "Damn!" he growled as some of them slid from his grasp onto the floor.

I knelt and gathered them up, straightening the edges in true obsessive-compulsive style. Bringing order out of chaos is what I had done for a living. Rob had always joked that I could tolerate six inches of dust on the furniture so long as the magazines were stacked precisely on top of each other, and the pages of the newspapers were returned to numerical order and refolded neatly.

"Kind of a mess," I said, collecting the rest of the loose sheets from his lap and carrying them with me back to my chair. "Mother would have made her use the back door. What's all this?"

My father shot me a look of disapproval.

"An old family genealogy, done by one of your great-aunts, I think, in the twenties or thirties. I had Vinnie dig it out of the attic after . . . What is the young woman's name again?"

I smiled at his use of Lavinia's nickname. He was the only one she allowed to use it with impunity.

"Mercer Mary Prescott. She prefers all three."

"Interesting. There's a Mercer in there." The Judge waved his hand toward the stack of papers I was unconsciously straightening in my lap. "Why'd you bring her here?"

"What else was I supposed to do with her? You're the one that wanted her sprung. I sure as hell wasn't taking her back to Hilton Head with me."

The Judge arched a shaggy white eyebrow at me and ignored the outburst. "What did she do?"

"Didn't Law tell you? She got picked up for vagrancy. He said they found her going through the garbage cans out back of the Fig Tree."

My father flinched, imagining, I supposed, what his political cronies would make of one of Judge Talbot Simpson's relatives scavenging in the refuse containers behind their favorite restaurant in downtown Beaufort.

"If she was in that bad a shape, why didn't the silly child just call us? It would have saved everyone a whole lot of trouble. Does she think we would have turned her away?"

"I really wasn't sure what my reception might be, Uncle Talbot."

Mercer Mary Prescott looked vastly different from my first view of her through the bulletproof glass in the county jail. Her shining hair, still damp from the shower, hung softly around her well-scrubbed face, covering the stark ugliness of the fading bruise. She'd spoken from the doorway, and, as she sidled self-consciously into the room, I had a moment to wonder where Lavinia had been storing the Northwestern sweatshirt and faded, rolled-up jeans I'd obviously outgrown a lifetime ago. Although they still hung off Mercer's painfully thin shoulders and hips, they were a vast improvement over her own ragged khakis and army fatigue jacket which had borne similar odors to her duffel bag.

In short, she looked quite presentable. Which is why I was stunned to hear the cry that burst from my father's lips as his teacup trembled momentarily in his shaking hand, then shattered into a dozen delicate fragments against the heart pine floor.

CHAPTER
TWO

It had been an accident, his hand brushing against the butler's table as he turned his wheelchair. That and nothing more. It was the Judge's story, and he stuck to it.

I knew he was lying. Something about Mercer Mary Prescott— her voice, her sudden appearance in the doorway, *something*—had spooked him, forcing that bark of alarm and the tremor which had sent the Royal Doulton teacup flying.

He recovered quickly. By the time I returned with a clean rag and a dustpan, my father and my newfound cousin were seated companionably in front of the fire exchanging curricula vitae. Mercer, unfamiliar with the Judge's legendary cross-examination techniques, no doubt thought she was volunteering information.

"Fascinating!" I heard him say with enough fervor that *I* almost believed in his sincerity, even though I knew full well he had not one shred of interest in all this kinship business. Lord knows I had heard him expounding to my mother often enough on the stupidity of worrying about whose ancestors arrived before whose.

Still, his feigned regard seemed to be having an amazing effect on Cousin Mercer. As I blotted up the spilled tea and gently gathered the remains of the cup and saucer from the second-best set of china, I saw some of the wariness leave her eyes, watched as she began to open, like a tightly-closed rosebud brought in from the cold.

Another fire crackled brightly in the usually cold and formal dining room as we took our places around the solid mahogany table. With all the leaves removed, it made a comfortable seating arrangement for the four of us. If Cousin Mercer was surprised to find Lavinia joining us, taking her place at the foot of the table after setting the steaming tureen of chicken and dumplings on the hot pad before her, she made no sign. Normally we three would have dived into this comfort food amid the warm coziness of the kitchen with the clutter of its preparation scattered around us, something Emmaline would never have countenanced. But tonight we had company, even if my half fifth cousin didn't merit the good silver and china.

"So who figures out all this stuff?" I asked while Lavinia ladled the hearty stew into wide soup bowls. "I mean, what is a half fifth cousin, anyway?"

Mercer tried not to shovel her food, but she was obviously having a hard time remembering her manners. To judge by her scrawny frame, this was probably the first decent meal she'd had in Lord knows how long. My questions at least forced her to pause occasionally to wipe her narrow lips with the damask napkin. And to take a breath.

"I do it on a computer program. You just put in the names—the children, and their parents, and their parents, like that—and then it tells you how everybody's related to everybody else. It's like I told you before. Our third-great grandmothers were half sisters."

I wondered when and where she had gained access to a computer terminal long enough to do all this entering.

"Did you work from a genealogy someone else had already prepared, or did you do the research yourself?" The Judge was, as usual, reading my mind.

"Would you like some more, dear?" Lavinia asked, interrupting the clatter of Mercer's spoon against the now empty bowl.

"If it's not too much trouble, Mrs. Smalls, ma'am," she replied, holding her dish out by two hands like some hungry waif in a Dickens novel. "It's absolutely wonderful."

"I'm glad you're enjoying it." There was no surer way into the guarded heart of our Lavinia than by wolfing down her cooking.

By the time we'd polished off half an apple pie and helped Lavinia set the kitchen to rights, we'd managed to wheedle pretty much the whole sad story of Mercer's life out of her. Pregnant at fifteen, Mercer's mother had been unable to decide which of her many "suitors" her father should force into matrimony, so she declined them all. To the evident dismay of her strait-laced family and the general condemnation of her small town in upstate Georgia, she had given birth to an acknowledged bastard daughter. She'd apparently been a good mother, showering her child with affection while defiantly finishing high school, despite the stigma which, even in the enlightened seventies, still attached to illegitimacy in scattered pockets of rural America.

"My grandparents stood by us," Mercer said as we settled once more in the Judge's study. "At least at first."

I hauled in a few more logs from the porch and coaxed the dying embers back to life. Rain still pounded against the slate tiles on the hipped roof, although the wind seemed to have dropped a little.

"My mom got a job right after she graduated. Nana Mary— that's my grandmother—said she was saving to go on to college. I guess I was about six when she went out to work one day and never came back."

The Judge and I exchanged startled glances. Lavinia deposited the tea tray, then excused herself. She would make up a guestroom for Mercer Mary, and, if I knew my old friend, do up all the dirty laundry in the musty carryall. I could tell she'd been uncomfortable listening to the intimate details of the young woman's life. Intensely private herself, Lavinia had as little curiosity about her fellow creatures as any woman I've ever known.

"My grandparents left me with friends and went looking for her. I remember they stayed away a long time, days really, but eventually they came back without her. After a while, I sort of got used to the idea of her being gone. Then Grandpa got sick, and Nana Mary had to take care of him, so I went to live with a foster family," Mercer continued. "They were real nice. They had lots of kids they took in, so it was my chance to see what it was like having brothers and sisters. That's where I learned how to use the computer. And play the piano, too."

My father's eyes lit up, then shot me an unspoken apology. It had been a great disappointment to both my parents that not one jot of their musical talent had filtered down to their only child. I had loved listening on those rare evenings when my mother would take her place at the baby grand and my father would gently remove his violin from its battered black case. Try as they might to force any semblance of music from my uncoordinated fingers, I proved totally hopeless. I have a pleasant singing voice, but that's the extent of my contribution to the performing arts.

"And do you still play?" the Judge asked hopefully.

"I haven't in some time," Mercer replied. "Why, do you have a piano?"

"In the morning room. Follow me."

I led her across the hall and into the small parlor which had been exclusively my mother's. She had personally haunted the auction houses in search of the claw-footed Empire furniture and had sent to England for the pale yellow silk adorning the walls. By the time she'd finished, the room matched perfectly a description she'd unearthed in an old diary she'd found in the attic. Although the piano took up an inordinate amount of space, she always insisted it be there, in her favorite room, among the rest of her favorite things.

I propped open the lid as Mercer seated herself at the bench. "What a beautiful cover," she remarked, running her hand across the delicate needlepoint. "Did you . . . ?"

"Good God, no!" I laughed, lifting several music books down from the top of the bookcase. "I have no domestic talents whatsoever. Can't even sew on a button. My mother worked that, as well as all the seats on the chairs in the dining room. Very medieval of her, don't you think?"

"I think they're lovely," she said in a tone that accused me of being an ungrateful wretch for failing to appreciate the beauty I had grown up with.

She was probably right. "I'll be across the hall. Begin whenever you're ready." I pulled a low footstool over to use as a doorstop. "He likes Mozart," I added, the nastiness of earlier in the afternoon creeping back into my voice. I expected her repertoire probably ran to Clint Black and LeAnn Rimes.

After a couple of false starts—totally understandable, I supposed, for someone who hadn't played in a while—Mercer Mary Prescott made me eat those thoughts. The hauntingly beautiful strains of the Piano Concerto No. 21—popularized as "The Theme from *Elvira Madigan*"—drifted into the warm cocoon of the Judge's study.

The joy on his face brought unaccustomed tears to my eyes, and I had to look away before he caught me. It's hard to think of your parents as old and frail and not all that far from death, even when they are. My mother's passing, though a shock, had been quick and clean, and a long time ago.

Mercer moved on into something else equally soft and soothing, although I couldn't put a name to it. We sat like that for some time, rain beating above us, the fire hissing beside us, my father's eyes closed in rapture at this unexpected gift of music once again in the old house. It was inevitable, I suppose, that something—or someone—would spoil it.

The stately grandfather clock in the parlor had chimed out midnight before the last of the sheriff's deputies finally left, Cousin Mercer Mary Prescott in tow. She still wore the hand-me-down clothes along with an old flannel jacket Lavinia had resurrected from the hall closet.

Mercer had clung to her duffel bag up to the last minute when a wide-shouldered officer forced it out of her determined grip. After a cursory search, the deputy thrust it at me as I hovered in the middle of what I had loudly proclaimed to be a Gestapo-like raid on the sanctity of my father's house.

"Do something!" I'd shouted at the Judge as he sat calmly in his wheelchair in the entry hall while Mercer Mary was handcuffed and led out into the rain.

"Be quiet, Bay!" he ordered gruffly. "They have a warrant. There's no way we can stop them."

"Then find someone who can!"

I'd tried frantically to reach my brother-in-law, Sergeant Red Tanner, when the ominous knock interrupted our peaceful evening, but he wasn't on duty, and there was no answer at his apartment. Ditto Law Merriweather who had arranged Mercer's release just a few hours before. I left messages everywhere I could think of, but neither of them had called back in time to prevent the deputies from marching my cousin away into the night.

The calm resignation on Mercer's face when the cold, steel cuffs had snapped into place around her pitifully thin wrists had enraged me to the point of incoherence. "What's the point of having all these damned powerful friends if you can't find them when you need them?"

I took my frustration out on the scruffy duffel bag, aiming a kick that sent it skidding across the highly polished floor. Instantly I regretted the action, retrieving the carryall and sliding it under the hall table out of harm's way. Mercer had been so protective of it, so determined to keep it with her, it must contain something precious to her. The least I could do was keep it safe until we got her out of this mess.

"It was a federal warrant, daughter," the Judge said in a voice at once exasperated and weary. "Trespassing and destruction of federal property, and failure to appear. It had to have been issued by the U.S. Attorney's office in Charleston or Columbia, and there's no way we're going to learn anything more tonight. Tomorrow we can get Law over there and find out what the fool child has gotten herself mixed up in. In the meantime, I suggest you go to bed."

He activated the controls on his motorized wheelchair and steered himself toward the study. Lavinia appeared in the doorway, waiting as always to assist him. The look she shot me said more than words about what she thought of the turmoil I had brought into the house in the person of Mercer Mary Prescott.

"Goodnight, Daddy," I called after him as I sank down onto the bottom step of the staircase and wished I had the energy to drive back to Hilton Head. Although Lavinia kept my old room ready for me at any time, I much preferred sleeping in my own bed at the beach house.

I made the tour of the downstairs, checking windows and doors and turning off lights. Lavinia had already scattered the ashes in the fireplaces. In the hollow stillness broken only by the precise, rhythmic ticking of the grandfather clock, I realized the rain had stopped beating a tattoo on the slate roof. Hopefully the wind had finally switched away from the northeast, and we could look forward to a return of the sun.

I paused, one hand on the banister, as I spied Mercer Mary Prescott's duffel bag stuffed forlornly between the legs of the oak console table. On impulse, I pulled it out and carried it with me up to my room. Unwilling to chance doing irreparable harm to the ruffled white counterpane that covered my four-poster bed, I squatted cross-legged on the rag rug under the window. With a silent apology to my half fifth cousin and only a slight twinge of remorse, I dumped the contents out on the floor in front of me.

Her clothes were inexpensive, but clean now, thanks to Lavinia: a couple of changes of underwear, a white cotton bra, jeans, T-shirts, and some khaki shorts. No cosmetics—which didn't surprise me—a curling iron, an ornate, silver-backed hairbrush and a ring holding three keys, which did.

What does a homeless person need with keys? I wondered.

I leafed through the dog-eared paperbacks—a couple of romance novels along with several local histories and guidebooks. The obviously much-handled genealogy was stuffed into an over-sized, brown mailing envelope devoid of a return address. A couple of dollars' worth of stamps had been canceled in Honea Path, a tiny village in the upstate somewhere between Anderson and Greenville, if I remembered correctly. It had been addressed in a spidery, shaky hand to my cousin, in care of the Herbert-Hanson Clinic in Columbia.

My fingers unconsciously tapped and straightened the edges of the papers in my lap. They didn't appear to be in any order, at least none I could discern from a casual glance. Organizing them was going to take more energy than I had left to invest at nearly two o'clock in the morning at the end of what had already been a weird and frustrating day.

I tried once more to make out the date on the envelope, twisting and turning it underneath the candlestick lamp on the bureau, but all I could be reasonably sure of was it had been sent on the 20-something of a month ending in *b-e-r*.

I decided to hang it up and get some sleep. By early the follow-ing morning you could be sure my father would have an opening salvo mapped out in the campaign to bust Cousin Mercer Mary Prescott free from the feds, and I would, as usual, be his point man and legs.

I folded my clothes neatly over the back of the bentwood rocker and crawled naked between scratchy sheets. That sweet breath of salt-laden air mingled with the familiar laundry detergent Lavinia had been using for more than thirty years always brought my childhood vividly into focus. I shook those gloomy thoughts away, shivering, and pulled the worn, hand-worked quilt up around my shoulders. Its warmth felt good against the damp chill seeping in from outside.

Wrapped in this soft cocoon of nostalgia, I had almost drifted off when a random thought sent me shooting straight up in the wide bed. I had suddenly remembered about the Herbert-Hanson in Columbia.

It was the state's premier mental hospital.

CHAPTER
THREE

Lawton Merriweather always reminded me of how my father looked before the strokes had bent and worn him. Nearly as tall as I, and never seen in public without a suit coat and a tie, regardless of the weather, for me Law epitomized courtly Southern manhood.

"Bay, darlin', we do seem destined to meet under tryin' circumstances, do we not?" The snowy-haired attorney brushed my cheek with thin, dry lips, and held open the door of the Fig Tree so I could precede him.

"You should drop around for poker more often," I replied as we made our way through the low-ceilinged bar toward the seating area that faced the river. Even though last night's storms had been swept out to sea, the sun had yet to make a complete breakthrough, so we avoided my usual spot on the covered porch and settled for a table inside, as far away from the ubiquitous overhead televisions as we could get. "How's Miss Melie doing these days?" I asked.

Lawton Merriweather's wife, Amelia, had been battling crippling arthritis for almost as long as I could remember.

"Some good, some not so." Law pulled out my chair as Gilly Falconer, the proprietress of the local hangout, set two steaming mugs of tea down in front of us. "Mornin', Gilly," Law said, squeezing her arm as he passed around to the other side of the table and seated himself. "How you been keepin'?"

"Tol'rable. Hey, Lydia. Anything else, or are you two just gonna set around takin' up valuable space I could be using to make a few bucks?"

Gilly's café-au-lait face split into the lopsided grin I'd first encountered when some of my underage friends and I had tried to sneak into the bar on a busy Saturday night. She'd literally chased us out the door with a straw broom, hooting and laughing at our terror and humiliation.

"Depends on how long-winded the counselor here is," I replied. "Could be we'll still be around to order lunch."

"Holler if you need me," Gilly called as she marched back toward the bar, her long gray-and-black braid swinging jauntily behind her.

"So, what's the scoop on my shirttail cousin?" I asked as I stirred one packet of sweetener into the strong tea and blew gently across the top of the cup. "What's it going to take to get her out of jail?"

"More juice than I've got, I'm afraid."

I looked up, startled both by Law Merriweather's quick admission of defeat as well as his terminology. *Juice* sounded alien, anachronistic somehow, riding on his slow, cultured drawl. I didn't know what to say.

"The federal boys don't have much use for us small-town players, Bay. Actually, you might have better luck, what with your connections in Columbia. Any of Rob's friends still around there?"

I busied myself with lighting my first cigarette of the day to postpone answering. I blew the smoke over my shoulder, away from Law, as images of my dead husband's boyish face flashed behind my partially closed eyes.

"I'm not exactly at the top of their hit parade, if you recall," I said, remembering the unreturned calls, the endless conferences which seemed to occupy my husband's former associates whenever I tried to reach them. Perhaps the fact that I had hounded them all unmercifully for the better part of a year had something to do with it, but I would never relent until the men who had planted the bomb on Rob's plane were brought to justice.

"Sometimes politics is an ugly business," Lawton Merriweather remarked, reaching to pat my hand reassuringly. "That drug task force Rob headed up for the Attorney General's office did some fine work. There are a lot of kids out there who won't have a chance to mess up their lives thanks to him. You should be proud."

"I am," I said, swallowing the last slug of tepid tea. "I just don't understand why they can't put the bastards who killed him in jail. Everyone knows who they are."

"Knowin' and provin' . . ." He left the rest unspoken.

"So what shall I tell the Judge?" It seemed an appropriate time to change the subject before the grief and frustration which had nearly paralyzed me since Rob's death crept back to smother me again. Besides, I had my own guilty knowledge about my husband's murderers, information I couldn't share without endangering everyone—and everything—I held dear.

Law signaled Gilly for refills and waited silently until one of the other waiters had delivered fresh cups. "Best I can ascertain, your cousin was arrested last month along with a group of protesters at the Savannah River Site. The group's organizers bailed everyone out, but Miss Prescott and several others failed to appear for their hearing, and federal bench warrants were issued. After you took her home last night, our folks finally got around to running a check, and her name popped up on the federal 'want' list."

"Hold on," I said, my head spinning. "What was she doing out at SRS? Isn't that the old nuclear facility up by Barnwell? I thought that closed down years ago."

Early lunch customers had begun to drift into the dining area, and Law lowered his already soft voice so I had to lean in to catch his response. "Oh, no, it's still operating. Of course, not on the scale it once was. As I recall, back in the sixties and seventies, it was a top-secret bomb factory. I think they produced plutonium and some of the other radioactive components for nuclear warheads. Now I believe it's just a storage facility. Although it seems to me I did hear something recently about their being in the running for some new Department of Energy project."

"So what interest could a child like Mercer have in an outdated bomb plant?"

"You'll have to ask her that, Bay. All I could learn is that some antinuclear group is worried about the potential for catastrophe from the proposed transportation of fissionable materials and staged a well-orchestrated demonstration. They were arrested for trespassing on restricted-access federal property. None of them would have been sentenced to more than a fine, I'm sure. And the organization would probably have paid that, too." He paused to smile acknowledgment at a group who hailed him as they passed into the bar, turned back to me. "I can't understand why your cousin would have done something so foolish as to fail to appear. She may be looking at jail time now."

"Is there a chance she could be allowed bail a second time?" I asked, sure this is what the Judge would want me to do. Despite his strange reaction at his first sight of my cousin in the study last night, I knew he felt a responsibility for the waiflike vagrant with the bruises on her chin.

"She's being transported to Columbia sometime today to appear before a federal magistrate. I don't think you can do anything until that takes place." Law Merriweather shook back the cuff of his perfectly starched white shirt and consulted his gleaming Patek-Philippe. "Sorry to run out on you, honey, but I have to see a client over on Hilton Head at one o'clock."

Law removed a gold Mont Blanc pen from his breast pocket and scribbled something on the back of one of his elegant parchment business cards. "This is the name of an attorney friend of mine up in the capital. You have the Judge give him a ring. I'm sure he'll be happy to represent you on behalf of Miss Prescott. Use my name."

Law leaned down to drop a fatherly kiss on my forehead. "Thank you," I said as he patted my shoulder and made his way to the front of the building, stopping every couple of tables to greet clients and colleagues.

I shook my head sadly and contemplated his retreating back. I knew he hated admitting how powerless he was to grease the wheels and make Mercer Mary Prescott's problems go away. Just like my father, he had grown used to being a force, albeit in a relatively small arena, and would take it as a personal affront that he had been unable to bend the feds to his will. Even pushing eighty, the two of them continued to believe nothing had changed since the days when they had moved from their aristocratic upbringing into their rightful places as the movers and shakers of our little slice of paradise on the South Carolina coast.

Men, I thought, revisiting a familiar theme, as Gilly Falconer dropped into the chair Law had just vacated. She pulled one of her odious black cheroots from the pocket of her stained smock and used my lighter to set it aflame.

"You want somethin' to eat?" she asked, fanning away the foul-smelling smoke with a plump hand.

My stomach had been rumbling ever since I'd sat down, but I was leery of substituting food for nicotine in my quest to quit smoking. I'd used the rehabilitation of my left shoulder to hone myself down into the best physical shape of my thirty-eight years, and I didn't want to have to start all over again.

"No thanks," I said, ignoring the tantalizing smells eddying around me as the staff served up heaping plates of burgers, fries, chicken fingers, and crab cakes.

"So what happened with Little Orphan Annie?"

"Who?" I asked, eyeing Gilly quizzically.

"The waif, the vagrant I found rustling up lunch in my garbage cans yesterday. I hear she's one of yours."

"A distant cousin," I admitted, amazed that the story had already reached the streets of Beaufort. "Fallen on hard times. She's left town now."

"But not under her own power, or so I hear."

Although everyone knew Gilly Falconer loved her gossip, she was being unusually bitchy on the subject of Mercer Mary Prescott.

"She's got her troubles," I replied vaguely, and the normally pleasant woman across from me snorted. "What's got the wind up your skirts about it?" I snapped, with a little more asperity than I'd intended.

"Makes me look bad," Gilly replied, crushing out her cigarillo in the metal ashtray. "Child was hungry, why didn't she just come in and ask? She coulda washed dishes or swept up or somethin'. Hell, I prob'ly woulda fed her just to see a little flesh form on those skinny bones of hers."

"I'm sure no one blames you, Gilly," I said with a smile. I should have known it was something like that, not any malicious pleasure in another's misfortune. "Think how the Judge feels."

"Related on your mama's side, ain't she?"

"How'd you know that?"

"Got the look of the Baynards, 'specially around the eyes. Didn't you notice it? Lord, but it's a good thing your mama ain't around. Think of what the garden club ladies woulda made outta this! No offense," she added quickly, apparently responding to the scowl on my face.

It was okay for *me* to bash my late mother's obsession with rank and status, but it somehow didn't sit well to hear it coming from someone I thought of as a friend.

"Anyway, I just wanted you and your daddy to know I wouldn't have turned her away if'n she'd asked," Gilly said as she rose and tugged the straining hem of the smock over her well-rounded rear end.

"I know that," I said and meant it. "So does the Judge."

"And I didn't turn her in, neither," she added, wagging a brown finger at me. "You tell him that, too. And eat something, will ya? That child's a good example of what you could turn into if you're not careful."

I looked from the pack of Marlboros to Gilly Falconer's stern face to the parade of college kids hefting loaded trays out from the kitchen. "Oh, what the hell," I said, shrugging, "bring me a cheeseburger, medium. And fries," I called to Gilly's back as she bustled away before I could change my mind.

And just to prove I was in complete control of the situation, I lit another cigarette.

A light breeze rippled through the tall oaks and pines overhanging the two-lane highway, allowing the late afternoon sun to cast dappled patterns across the hood of my car. In the welcome warmth following three days of cold and damp, it was almost enough to mesmerize me, so that every few moments I had to snap my attention back to the road. The temperature hadn't risen enough to entice me into letting down the top on my seafoam-green Z3, but the rush of air through the windows felt wonderful against my face. The dank odor, rising like a miasma from the pluff mud off to my left, had always seemed to me the sweetest smell of my native Lowcountry, and I drank it in gratefully.

I had timed my return trip to Hilton Head perfectly, just missing the parade of long, yellow school buses, and running about half an hour ahead of the evening rush. Traffic was slowed a little by construction, a result of the successful campaign to convince us of the hazards of this lovely, winding road and move us to approve a sales tax increase in order to widen it to four lanes. Already hundreds of trees along its once scenic boundaries had paid the price of this "progress," and I could sense Taco Bell and Wal-Mart hovering just over the horizon. Despite repeated assertions to the contrary by our local politicians, the developers seemed to be winning the war against the preservationists.

I had spent the early part of the afternoon closeted with the Judge as we made arrangements with Law Merriweather's attorney friend in Columbia to represent Mercer Mary Prescott. As an indigent person, she could have had a court-appointed lawyer, but my father wouldn't hear of that. I still couldn't figure out where all this sudden familial duty stuff had come from, and he obviously had no intention of enlightening me. In a pattern well established since my childhood, he'd tell me what he thought I needed to know when he was damned good and ready, and not before.

As I rolled across the second of the two bridges which give access to Hilton Head Island, I determined to put the whole strange episode out of my head. The forced confinement of the past few rainy days had made me edgy. I needed a couple of hours of hard exertion, like a good singles match or a long run on the beach. But both would prove difficult with evening closing in rapidly.

And why can't we have daylight savings time all year 'round? I wondered as I smiled up at the security guard who waved me through the checkpoint and into Port Royal Plantation. I skirted the golf course, admiring the huge mounds of bronze and yellow mums along the cart path before pulling into my own driveway just as the outside security lights clicked on in the deepening dusk.

And stopped dead in the driveway, my finger poised over the button of the garage door opener.

The house itself was dark. Beyond the glow of the sodium vapor lamp placed strategically to illuminate the exterior, the windows loomed blankly, dull and opaque. Off to the left, pulled up among the boles of the loblolly pines, a dented blue Hyundai squatted on the pine straw.

So Dolores Santiago, my part-time housekeeper and full-time friend, was still there. This, too, was strange. Dolores usually left me something simple to warm up for dinner, then hurried home to prepare the evening meal for her husband and three teenaged children. Having been almost as close as I to the near-disasters of the past few months, I knew she would never have allowed me to walk into a dark and empty house. Neither would she herself sit alone without the comfort of a glowing lamp.

The all-too familiar prickling of fear touched cold fingers along the back of my neck. The primal part of my brain sent urgent flight messages I had to force myself to ignore. I eased the gearshift into PARK and cut the engine. Through the open windows I strained to distinguish any unnatural noises above the soft whisper of the breeze through the live oaks and the muted sigh of the ocean just a few yards away over the dune. Shielded from its neighbors by the towering trees dripping long beards of Spanish moss, the house confronted me, silent and somehow menacing. Once again I cursed the isolation which had been one of its initial charms.

And cursed myself for my refusal to carry a cell phone. I hated the damned things. But the aggravation of being accessible every waking minute seemed insignificant now in the face of being unable to call for help at moments like this. I could almost hear the voice of Red, my sheriff's deputy brother-in-law, reminding me of the futility of having a carry permit for a nine-millimeter Glock when I insisted on keeping the weapon tucked safely away in the floor safe in my bedroom.

Shaking off the idea that I was behaving like one of the stupid heroines in the gothic novels I'd devoured as a teenager, I slipped out of the car. In my head I could hear a fourteen-year-old me shouting, *Don't go in there, you idiot! He's waiting for you!*

In my hard-soled loafers I moved as silently as I could up the wooden stairs to my front door, key in hand, telling myself all the while that there was probably a perfectly rational explanation for the lights' being off, and that I was going to feel like a fool for all this creeping around. Dolores might simply have sat down to take a well-deserved rest and dozed off. Or her ancient car wouldn't start, so she'd called one of the kids to come pick her up and, in her haste, had forgotten to switch on the lights.

I eased open the screen door and froze, all thoughts of rational explanation vanishing like smoke in the wind. The heavy oak panel was ajar. Not wide open, just a crack, as if someone had intended to close it and not pushed quite hard enough to engage the latch.

Visions of bright orange flames exploded behind my eyes, engulfing me in a waking nightmare of noise and light, smoke and sirens. Images flashed across my mind, the remembered agony of pain and loss, mind-numbing fear, and the sickly smell of my own smoldering flesh. The ugly scars across my shoulder burned as if the wounds were newly made.

It seemed like hours, but could have been only a few moments before the distant sounds finally penetrated the grip of my panic attack and registered on my quivering consciousness: a low moaning, punctuated by the plaintive mewing of the cat.

I pushed through the door, screaming, "Dolores!" as I ran.

CHAPTER FOUR

I found her, crumpled and twisted, in the hallway which leads to the three bedrooms and their matching baths, to the right off the foyer. Mr. Bones, the battered tomcat who'd once inadvertently saved my life, prowled back and forth in the confined space, alternating between loud yowls of protest and attempts to coax Dolores back to consciousness by rubbing his scarred head against her still, olive face.

I flipped on the light, then dropped to my knees beside her tiny form. My heart resumed beating when I detected the steady rise and fall of her chest, then stopped again at the sight of the hideous gash along her left temple. Blood had run freely down the side of her face, congealing in the slight creases of her neck before disappearing under the neckband of the pink Salty Dog sweatshirt her kids had given her on her last birthday.

She moaned in obvious pain, the sound finally snapping me out of my stunned immobility. "Don't move!" I ordered, squeezing her thin, cold fingers and sprinting to the kitchen phone.

The 911 operator assured me help was even then being dispatched and instructed me to keep Dolores warm until they arrived. Under no circumstances should I attempt to move her. I pulled the hand-crocheted afghan from the back of the white sofa in the great room and rushed back into the hallway.

As I gently draped the heavy cover over her motionless body, I suddenly realized her left leg was bent under her at a strange angle. "Dear God, what happened here?" I asked the silence, unable to see an overturned stool or stepladder, anything that might have accounted for a fall severe enough to have caused this much damage.

Afraid to touch her in case I might aggravate any other unseen injuries, I curled myself into the space between the wall and her outflung arm and gently stroked her hand. "It'll be okay," I murmured, not certain whether I was reassuring Dolores or myself. "Don't worry," I said, over and over, unable to take my own advice.

The paramedics found the three of us huddled there in the hallway. I think one of them had to move me physically out of the way. Clutching the unusually docile cat to my chest, I backed into the great room. Two-way radios crackled, and uniformed men dashed in and out of my front door. A steady stream of equipment—kits and bags and needles, an air cast, and, finally, a stretcher—paraded by as Mr. Bones and I watched in helpless silence. Then, swathed in gauze and nearly invisible beneath a canopy of tubes and IV pouches, my broken friend was wheeled down the steps and into the dark maw of the waiting ambulance.

If anyone asked me if I wanted to go with her, I don't remember it. What did register, with a gut-wrenching flash of *déja vu*, was the sight of my neighbors, their faces once again flushed from the strobe of the flashing red lights, parting at the end of my driveway to allow an emergency vehicle to speed off into the night.

It took a few moments for me to realize that not all of the invaders had departed. The woman, her solid hips straining against the seams of her khaki trousers, regarded me solemnly from sympathetic black eyes set deep in a pleasant brown face. The deputy sheriff's badge rode proud and high on an impressive shelf of bosom. It, too, pushed against the confines of its restraining uniform. The other one—taller, skinnier, and whey-faced—looked about twelve years old. And vaguely familiar.

"Sorry, ma'am," he said in a languid drawl which conjured up images of chrome-laden pickup trucks with Confederate flags proudly displayed in the back windows, "but we need to ask you a few questions. I'm Daggett, and this here's Deputy Bell."

His voice apparently broke the spell which had held Mr. Bones silent and quiescent in my arms. With a yelp of protest, the cat wriggled out of my grasp, pushing off with his back feet and leaving three long, ugly scratches across the back of my hand. I watched in numb fascination as blood began oozing from the cuts.

"You wanna get somethin' on that right away," Deputy Bell said in voice as soft and small as she herself was large. "Never know where cats's bin."

I smiled my appreciation, noticing by the gold, engraved identification bar that her first name was *Charity*.

"If you could just tell us what happened here, ma'am," her partner interrupted. "The paramedics said the Mexican woman'd been attacked. You know anythin' about that?"

"Guatemalan," I said, smearing the blood from the cat scratches absently along the leg of my khaki slacks where it mingled with the drying splotches from Dolores's wounds. "She's Guatemalan. From San Luis. Just across the border from Belize."

"Look, lady, it don't matter where she came from. All I'm interested in is who tried to take her out."

"Back off, Tommy, will ya?" Charity Bell said quietly as my face blanched, and I felt my knees trembling beneath me. "Can't you tell she's had a shock?"

"What do you mean, take her out? No one would try to kill Dolores, that's just crazy! She fell! Any moron can see that!" The anger stiffened my legs as well as my resolve. "I remember you now," I continued, moving up to stand toe-to-toe with the smug deputy. Even in my flat shoes I had him by at least an inch. "You're the smart-ass I had the run-in with outside the cemetery a couple of months ago, aren't you? Tried to conduct an illegal search of my bag without probable cause. You would have done it, too, if my brother-in-law hadn't come along and run you off. I don't have to tell you squat! You get the hell out of my house!"

"Ma'am, please take it easy." Again Charity Bell tried to play peacemaker, but her partner was having none of it.

"That was no fall," he said around clenched teeth. I could feel the effort it cost him not to scream right back in my face. "Someone whacked that woman upside her head, then pushed her down and broke her leg. And this ain't just your house no more. It's a crime scene. Now you're gonna talk to me whether you like it or not."

"Maybe it would be best if we got Sergeant Tanner over here, Tommy. Maybe she'd feel better talkin' with him."

"And maybe I don't give a damn what she wants," Daggett began when we all jumped at the sound of the screen door banging shut.

"Bay? What's going on here?" the familiar voice called from the foyer.

Relief flooded through me, and I felt the quivers of delayed reaction begin once again in my knees. The image of Dolores's face, crusted with her own blood, rose up to fill my vision as I bolted from the room.

When Red Tanner finally caught up with me, I was huddled on

the cold tile floor in the master bathroom tossing my cookies into the spotless white toilet.

Hector Santiago, his dirt-roughened hands dangling helplessly between the knees of his stained work pants, seemed bewildered by the bustle and glare of the emergency room. He leaned forward over his elbows, his back hunched, staring at the green tiled floor. In an equally uncomfortable fiberglass chair next to him, his seventeen-year-old daughter, Angelina, spoke softly in lilting Spanish. Her hand made circular motions across his shoulder, soothing and calming her father whose agitation had threatened to erupt several times during our long wait for a report on Dolores's condition. Though I understood only a few words of his rapid Spanish, I could sense that most of that anger was directed at me. Across the room Angelina's brothers, Roberto and Alejandro, slouched in that peculiarly graceful manner of teenaged boys who seem to be all legs.

I glanced up toward the reception desk where Red chatted easily with one of the young nurses on duty. In his civvies—well-worn jeans, a faded Marine Corps sweatshirt, and scuffed Topsiders—he looked even more like my late husband than he did in his stiff, khaki uniform. Although Red was younger and slightly shorter, there were times, like now, when the resemblance cut straight into my heart.

I swallowed hard and crossed to Angie. "I'll be right outside if you need me," I said, tilting my head toward the brightly lit parking lot as I patted my pockets in search of a lighter.

I stepped on the mat that activated the automatic doors, and through the soft *whoosh* of their opening I heard a man's voice say, "Are you the Santiago family?"

I turned back, and my eyes caught Red's. With a brief shake of his head he stopped me in mid-stride. I watched as Hector and his children gathered around a weary-looking doctor in scrubs just pulling the surgical cap from his grizzled head. My brother-in-law made shooing motions with his hand and sidled up to the perimeter of the group.

I pulled the lighter from the tangle of junk at the bottom of my bag and stepped out into the night.

● ● ●

When Red joined me, three cigarettes and a couple of miles of pacing later, his face told me just about all I needed to know.

"How bad?" I asked.

"She's got a concussion," he answered, looking me squarely in the eye. "It may affect her memory of what happened. The cut on her forehead was deep and needed a lot of stitches. The worst part is her leg."

"Her leg?"

"Yeah. There are several bones broken, some of them pretty smashed up. She's going to need a lot of surgery, maybe some pins eventually."

"Dear God," I said, sinking slowly onto the wooden bench outside the ER doors. "I need to talk to Hector about the cost, the bills . . ."

"Leave it for now." This time Red's eyes slid away from the question in mine. "Wait here," he said, "I'll go get the car."

I watched his retreating back, my mind filled with images of the woman who had been first my nurse, then my companion, and finally my friend. She had nurtured my spirit as well as my mangled body in those early days after the explosion which blew my husband's plane out of the sky and scarred my back and my heart with the indelible memory of it. I had been quite prepared then to die myself. But Dolores wouldn't let me. She helped me to bathe, insisted in her quiet way that I get up and dress every day, and refused to let me dwell on the wrenching grief and loss. She coaxed me to eat, tempting me with Lowcountry favorites she learned how to prepare from a dog-eared cookbook and with spicy delicacies from her native Guatemala. She brushed my hair in long, soothing strokes and told me tales in halting English about the beauty of her land and the poverty of her childhood. She talked of her children, of her love and hopes for them, and of her faith in a benevolent God. And always she held out the promise of tomorrow—a new day, a fresh start. Less pain, more healing. A clearer understanding.

Dolores Santiago saved my life.

And because of me she lay just beyond these doors, in unimaginable pain, her body smashed and broken. I didn't know why, but it had to be *because of me.*

No wonder Hector hated me. I hated myself.

CHAPTER FIVE

Red had left his lovingly restored Ford Bronco in the visitors' parking lot which gave me enough time to get myself under control.

How like him not to take advantage of his position and pull up close to the building, I thought, as he wheeled up in front of the ER. There were so many traits he shared with Rob: A wry, understated sense of humor. A passionate hatred of injustice. A deep-seated love for their native Lowcountry and its proud heritage.

Red reached across to swing the door open, and I climbed up into the modest forerunner of today's massive SUVs.

"You hungry?" he asked as I fastened the antiquated lap belt across my waist.

I glanced at my watch, surprised to find it was past ten o'clock. "I don't know," I replied honestly. "I haven't had a chance to think about it. No, I guess not," I added after a moment's contemplation of his question.

"Well, *I* am," he said, easing the Bronco out onto Beach City Road. "Want to stop for a bite?"

"There's probably nothing open this time of night."

The local restaurants tend to shut down early after tourist season officially ends on Labor Day.

"I'm sure we can find something."

"Thanks, but I think I'd just like to head on home. It's been a long day. I could fix you something, though, if you're really starving."

Red's laugh helped dispel some of the gloom I felt hovering over me. "Fix me something? You? I kinda had a little more in mind than instant coffee and microwave popcorn."

I had to smile, too. One of the reasons Dolores had stayed on after I had recovered from my injuries was my total inability to function in the kitchen. Rob, who did all of the cooking when we lived in Charleston, had attempted to teach me over the years of our marriage, but I just couldn't seem to get the knack of it. Though I called Dolores my housekeeper, there really wasn't that much to do for a widow-woman who was tidy and organized by nature. Her most important contributions to my well being were her cooking and her friendship.

"What am I going to do?"

I didn't realize I had spoken out loud until Red responded. "About what? Evenin', Jim." He nodded to the night-duty security guard who waved us through the gate into Port Royal Plantation.

"Everything," I mumbled, suddenly so tired I wasn't sure I could stay awake long enough to drag myself into the house.

"Come on." Red pulled up behind my Z3 in the driveway and hurried around to open the door for me. "That's not like you. Things'll look better after we get some food into you."

"Really, Red, I'd just rather fall into bed and—"

"Here, give me that." He took the key from my fumbling fingers and led the way into the darkened house. "You can't just run away from this one, Bay," he said, resuming his interrupted monologue as he wandered through the great room turning on lamps. "Someone attacked Dolores in *this* house less than eight hours ago. You can't go pull the covers up over your head and pretend it didn't happen."

"That's a load of crap, and you know it," I growled, kicking off my shoes and tossing my bag into one of the Queen Anne wing chairs flanking the fireplace. "I'm not trying to duck what went on here. And besides, you're usually bitching at me about sticking my nose into things when I shouldn't. Now I'm getting lectured about *not* getting involved? Let's try for some semblance of consistency here, Tanner, whadda ya say?"

Red ignored me, trotted up the three steps into the kitchen, and yanked open the refrigerator door. "Hey, there's a tuna fillet in here marinating in something. Dolores must have left it for you. Won't take ten minutes on the grill. And some kinda pasta in white sauce. We'll warm that up. See if there's any rolls in the breadbox." He turned to grin impishly at me over his shoulder. "It's that white wooden thing on the counter. Next to the toaster."

"Smart-ass," I muttered and joined him in the kitchen, resigning myself to his company for at least as long as it took to get him fed.

We worked without talking for the next few minutes. Red quickly assembled the impromptu meal while I threw placemats and dishes on the glass-topped table in the alcove near the window. I poured him a beer from the stock I kept for his infrequent visits and iced tea for myself. When he slid the sizzling fish and creamy pasta onto my plate, I had to admit it smelled wonderful.

"Eat," Red commanded as he flopped himself into the chair opposite me and dived into his food.

"Fettuccini Alfredo at eleven o'clock at night. This is crazy," I said around a forkful of the rich noodles. "I won't bother to eat it—I'll just apply it directly to my hips."

"So run an extra mile tomorrow."

We finished the meal in silence, stacked the dishwasher, and headed for the deck which surrounded the house on three sides. It was a cool night, probably somewhere in the fifties. A million stars glittered high over the ocean, whose soft murmurs drifted faintly to us over the sandy dune just through a thin belt of trees. Instinctively I had reached for the afghan to wrap around me before realizing I had last seen it crumpled in the hallway, soaked in Dolores's blood.

As had so often been the case with my husband, my brother-in-law seemed tuned in to my thoughts. "What happened here, Bay? You have any idea of who, or why?"

I leaned my elbows on the railing. "Hector blames me, I know, but I swear I'm completely baffled. I take it your guys didn't find any signs of a break-in?"

"Nope. The front door was open, and the security system was disengaged."

"Well that's not unusual. Dolores never left it on when she was here. She was always afraid of accidentally setting it off. But I did think she kept the doors locked."

"I would have thought so, too. Especially after all the trouble you've had in the past few months. Would she let a stranger in?"

I studied the low-hanging quarter moon and considered his question. "Ordinarily I'd say no, but I think under the right circumstances she might."

"Like what?"

"Oh, like if it was a kid, maybe someone who said they knew Angie or the boys. Or if someone were in trouble. Despite all the things she's seen lately, she's still a trusting person. She would never turn away a fellow human being in need."

Red tilted his glass and drained the last of his beer. "I suppose there's no point in speculating. We might as well wait until she can tell us herself what happened."

"What if she can't remember?"

Red shrugged and avoided any clichéd references to crossing bridges when we came to them. "You sure nothing's been going on with you or the Judge I should know about?" he asked, using his index finger to turn my head around to face him. "Both of you have done a damn good job of keeping me in the dark lately about some of your more questionable activities."

I tried to be angry at his implication that I wasn't leveling with him, but he had only spoken the truth. My father and I *had* been less than forthcoming about a number of things in recent months. But it had mostly been for Red's own protection, of the what-you-don't-know-you-won't-have-to-lie-about variety.

"The only unusual thing that's happened in the last few weeks is the appearance of a long-lost relative. Well, not exactly 'lost,' I guess, since we never even knew she existed until yesterday."

I stretched out on the wooden chaise, devoid of its usual flowered cushion since the weather had turned cooler, and proceeded to fill Red in on the saga of Mercer Mary Prescott.

"You think it's connected?" he asked when I'd finished the sketchy story of my half fifth cousin's arrest and transport to Columbia that morning.

"I don't see how it could be, do you?"

"Maybe some of her radical friends came looking for her."

"But why would they come here? All anyone knew for certain was that she was at Presqu'isle last night. There's no reason for anyone to associate that with my house here on the island. And why would they hurt Dolores?"

"You're probably right. Even so, I think I'll see what I can find out about this group your cousin was involved with." A huge yawn escaped, nearly swallowing the end of his sentence. "I guess I'd better be going, let you get some sleep."

"You, too," I said, reaching up to allow Red to pull me out of the chaise. "Thanks for hanging around tonight. I hope it didn't mess up your plans."

Red followed me into the great room and out into the front hallway. "Like I have a social life," he said ruefully, and his eyes suddenly fastened on mine.

We'd been down this road before, his interest in expanding our relationship from filial affection into something more intimate apparent in so many of his looks and gestures. His divorce and Rob's death, coming almost on the heels of each other, had left him lonely and angry at the world, and it broke my heart to see him so unhappy.

I'd often thought how easy it would be to meet that searching gaze of his, to step into arms that couldn't help but feel comforting and familiar. But would that be enough? For either of us? How could I ever get past thinking of him as a brother, a trusted friend and confidant? Could he live with knowing that Rob's ghost would always hover somewhere between us? Could *I*?

And besides, there was Darnay, whose deathly pale face in the dim light of a storm-battered cottage still haunted my dreams . . .

"Go home," I said, gently pushing Red toward the door. "And let me know when they say Dolores can have regular visitors, okay?"

"You aren't going to try and see her tomorrow?"

"I think it's better if I just stay out of Hector's way for a while."

"Well, you know he's being unreasonable, don't you? I mean, no one seriously entertains the idea that any of this is your fault."

"I hear you. Now get out of here, okay? And Red?" I called so that he turned at the bottom step to look back up at me. "Thank you."

He nodded, touched a finger to his forehead in a mock salute, then strode off toward the driveway.

As I moved to push the thick oak door closed, I heard the familiar scrabbling of claws on wood, and Mr. Bones bounded up onto the porch. With a yowl of welcome, he shot through the gap I held open for him and rubbed his night-damp fur against my bare ankles.

"It's been quite a day, hasn't it, old friend?" I murmured, leaning down to stroke his battle-scarred ears. I stood up and reached for the keypad of the security system, punching in the series of numbers designed to keep the bad guys out. It had certainly failed miserably in protecting Dolores.

Saturday morning rose bright and fair on a gentle wind blowing out of the Caribbean. I'd spent most of the night curled up in a chair in my bedroom, alternating between trying to read and watching the night pass from black to steel gray to the soft violets and mauves of impending sunrise. By the time I'd given up on sleep and showered and dressed, the temperature was already in the sixties—warm even for us at this time of year. I carried my carefully constructed bowl of Cheerios topped with sliced bananas over to the breakfast alcove. Mr. Bones jumped immediately onto the table and dipped a tabby paw into the milk. I didn't have the stomach for a battle, so I retired from the field and left him to it.

I checked in with the hospital and learned Dolores had been moved out of ICU and into a semi-private room early that morning, having "rested comfortably" through the night. That meant she could now have regular visitors. The Information Lady couldn't tell me whether or not she'd regained consciousness, so I decided to try Angie. I had the portable phone in my hand, ready to dial, when the doorbell rang.

Averting my eyes from the bloodstained carpet in the hallway, I clutched the phone unit tightly as I made my way to the front door. Whether I intended to use it as a weapon or to call for help if I needed it, I wasn't at all sure. I just knew I felt better with something solid in my hand.

The two boys appeared to be about ten or eleven, their sharply pressed Boy Scout uniforms making them look like miniature soldiers. They were collecting canned goods for Deep Well, the local food bank, always in particular need as the holidays approached. Since Dolores didn't believe in cans—buying everything fresh on her daily trip to the market—I wrote them a check and sent them on their way.

I walked back across the great room and stepped through the French doors onto the deck. The sun was just topping the tall pines and live oaks, and little flickers of dappled light danced along the weathered boards. I perched in a pool of warmth on the top step leading down to the beach path.

"Hell and damnation!" I muttered to a pair of jays squabbling over spilled birdseed on the crisp layer of dead leaves littering the yard.

The Boy Scouts had made me realize that the next Thursday was Thanksgiving. That meant a command performance at Presqu'isle, the heavy mahogany table in the cold dining room sagging under a ton of food we'd never make a dent in. Red would probably join us, if he wasn't on duty, since his ex-wife Sarah usually took the kids to her parents' in Hampton. It would be so much easier just to skip the whole, dismal exercise, or even to go out to a nice restaurant. I felt confident the Judge would be much more amenable than in years past to venturing out of the house. I was sure I could coax him into it.

But Lavinia Smalls would have none of that nonsense. *You can take that to the bank,* I thought, leaning back into the widening circle of sunlight. Lavinia was a great one for tradition, despite the debacle my mother used to make of almost every holiday. I tried to conjure up some way to wiggle out of the whole damned miserable thing, but I knew I'd never get away with it. And then there was Christmas . . .

I shook off that equally depressing thought and punched in the Santiago's number. I let it ring six times before giving up. *Probably all at the hospital,* I thought. *Where* you *should be,* the small voice inside my head chided me.

I told it to shut up and dialed my shrink.

CHAPTER SIX

"Hey, Tanner, what's up?"

The disembodied voice with its strange accent brought an immediate lightening of my somber mood. Dr. Nedra Halloran, my former college roommate at Northwestern and the Lowcountry's premier child psychologist, had a nasal Boston twang softened by the slow drawl of her adopted Georgia.

"Hey, Neddie," I replied, suddenly reluctant, uncertain of why my fingers had automatically selected her office number on a Saturday morning. The expansive suite of rooms on the ground floor of a turreted Victorian mansion on one of Savannah's historic squares should have been empty except for the clutter of toys and books normally strewn across her waiting room floor.

Neddie believes clutter makes kids feel more at home.

"You're lucky you caught me. Saw your number flash on the Caller ID, or I wouldn't have picked up. I just came in to drop off a couple of files. Believe it or not, I've got an actual date tonight, so tell me your troubles in fifty words or less. I need to get home and make myself gorgeous."

I smiled, picturing the tall redhead whose creamy Irish complexion and voluptuous figure struck terror into the hearts of every woman forced to compete with her for male attention.

"So who's the target of your unbridled lust?" I asked, stretching my legs out and resettling myself on the steps of the deck. "That guy you met at the Halloween party last month?"

"Yeah, him. Tyler . . . something. He's some high mucky-muck in the arts council. We're going to the symphony."

"Oooo, I'm impressed! You have anything to wear that's conservative enough for the symphony?" Neddie's clothes tend toward the flamboyant—usually brilliant greens and flowing reds, often in combination.

"Thank you, Miss-Khaki-Slacks-and-Blue-Oxford-Shirt, for the fashion critique. Tyler happens to *adore* my sense of style."

I could hear the muted sounds of file drawers closing and metal locks being pushed into place, could envision my friend consulting the functional old Timex strapped to her wrist by frayed, brown leather. It had been a gift from her younger brother just a few months before his death from a drug overdose had sent her off on her career path to help other lost, confused children.

"Bay? You still there?"

"I'm sorry. I just . . . Look, I know you're in a hurry, so why don't I . . ."

I heard the creak as Neddie settled into her antique desk chair. "Okay, kid, spill it. And let's have the whole story. Just because I give you the former-roommate-almost-lifelong-friend discount doesn't mean you don't get the full treatment. Talk."

And so I did, the tears I'd been swallowing for nearly twenty-four hours finally spilling over to dampen the patchy sunlight pooling on the wooden deck.

"Of course you're blaming yourself," Neddie said matter-of-factly when I'd finally hiccupped my way into silence.

"How could it be my fault?" I demanded, denial rearing its ugly head. "We don't have any idea what happened. Red didn't see any sign of a break-in."

"The fact that it makes no sense has no bearing whatsoever on whether or not you've convinced yourself you're at fault. You'd take the hit for avalanches and tornadoes if there was the slightest chance you could justify it. It's one of your more endearing qualities."

"That's bullshit, Halloran. It's you Irish Catholics who're awash in guilt, not us staunch Episcopalians. You're projecting."

Her snort of derision crackled down the phone line. "Projecting? What have you been doing, actually paying attention during therapy? I'm impressed."

Despite my bluster, I had to admit—at least to myself—that much of what she said was true. And I was grateful for all the help she'd given me in the past few months when it seemed as if death and destruction had stalked me like an evil shadow.

"Feel better now that you've vented at your poor shrink?" she asked when I failed to rise to the bait.

"Sorry," I mumbled into the phone.

"No problem. Comes with the territory. Anything I can do to

help? With Dolores, I mean?"

"No, but thanks." I smothered a yawn and realized that talking to Neddie really *had* helped. Maybe I could manage to sleep now. "You'd better get a move on," I said, rising to dust off the seat of my pants. "You wouldn't want to disappoint Tyler, and getting gorgeous could take you at least the rest of the day, considering what you have to work with."

"Go to hell," Neddie replied cheerfully and hung up in my ear.

Laughing, I carried the phone back into the house. I contemplated a nap, then decided it would be a shame to waste this beautiful weather, so I pulled on my running things and trotted down the path to the beach. A slight onshore breeze kicked up the loose sand of the dunes into whirling eddies that danced along ahead of me. I concentrated on my form and endurance, banishing all thoughts of bloodstained carpet and mangled legs to the waiting room of my conscious mind. Gulls wheeled overhead, and sandpipers skittered away on spindly legs as I pounded down the beach, punishing myself for unspecified, though acknowledged crimes.

When I finally pushed myself up the last two steps onto the deck, my clothes were plastered to my skin and my venerable old Nikes soaked through. I pulled them off, along with my socks, and carried the dripping mess gingerly across the white carpet. My mind was so totally focused on the blessed relief of a shower, it took a couple of minutes for the ringing to register.

"Shit!" I muttered, dropping my soggy footwear onto the chair next to the built-in kitchen desk and snatching up the phone. "Yes?" I growled into the receiver.

"Bay, your father wants to see you." Lavinia's voice carried a tone I remembered well from my childhood, the one that meant someone—usually me—was in big trouble.

"Now?" I spluttered.

"Yes, now. He needs you here as soon as you can make it."

"Why? What's happened?"

I could sense her indignation all the way from St. Helena. "It seems your no-good cousin, Miss Mercer Mary Whatever, has run away from the police again. The Judge wants you to help track her down before they do."

"How the hell am I supposed to know where she'd hide?" I

demanded from across the kitchen table as my father forked a dripping mass of gray-green collards into his mouth, forcing me to wait for an answer I knew he didn't have.

Lavinia had gone all out in preparing him an authentic Lowcountry feast, complete with pulled pork in her famous simmered-all-day barbecue sauce along with warm, crumbly cornbread and an assortment of the revolting greens.

"How can you eat that stuff?" I buttered another square of cornbread, my third or fourth since I'd politely refused Lavinia's invitation to join them for dinner. "It actually makes spinach look appetizing."

" '*De gustibus non disputandum*' my child," he replied, wiping a dribble of collard juice from his chin and fixing me with an expectant grin.

"Hey, no fair! The quotations aren't supposed to be in a foreign language." Although he'd invented the game in the far reaches of my childhood, we had agreed over the years on a pretty strict set of rules.

"Quit whining, daughter. It's Latin. You studied it in high school, did you not? Figure it out."

"I have no idea what it *means*, let alone who said it. Although, the first part does sound sort of like 'disgusting' which is probably why you thought of it in connection with that stuff you're eating." I washed the last of the cornbread down with my second glass of cold milk. "I haven't checked the score recently, but you must be pretty desperate for points."

"It means, 'There is no accounting for tastes.' And it's an old proverb, so I don't think it can be attributed to anyone in particular." Lavinia's voice held no trace of uncertainty as her eyes met the Judge's in unspoken challenge.

"Bravo, Vinnie! Exactly right on both counts! What do think of that, Bay?"

"I think it proves Lavinia is every bit as smart as I always thought she was," I said, giving her shoulder a squeeze as I carried my empty glass to the sink. "Not to mention a paragon of virtue for putting up with *your* nonsense all these years. But none of this is getting us any closer to figuring out what to do about Mercer Mary Prescott."

"Let's go have a smoke and ponder on it." My father toggled the controls on his wheelchair, and I followed him down the long hall into his study, then up the ramp onto the back verandah.

The apparatus for his after-dinner indulgence was already laid out on the table next to my designated rocker. I clipped the cigar for him as he maneuvered his chair into position next to me. When he'd gotten the illegal Havana going, I touched the crystal lighter to a cigarette and joined him in contemplation of the moon rising slowly out of the Sound. The mild night air was alive with the squeaks and whirrings of the inhabitants of the thin strip of marsh which separated Presqu'isle from the water, and we sat for awhile listening in companionable silence.

"So how on earth did they let Mercer bamboozle them like that?" I finally asked when it became apparent my father was not going to be the first to broach the subject. "What idiot decided to let a male officer escort her to Columbia? Didn't they think she'd have to pee sooner or later?"

His snort held derision, but I wasn't quite sure for whom. "She can be quite convincing, in case you hadn't noticed."

"You mean playing the poor little orphan girl? The abandoned waif? You'd think the cops had at least *some* experience with seeing through that kind of smoke screen."

You'd think you *would, too,* hung unspoken in the air between us.

"Apparently the man they sent along was not entirely experienced in delivering prisoners," my father added.

I squinted at him through the gathering dusk, certain I had detected a hint of laughter in his voice. I spared a moment to hope the unfortunate bungler had been Tommy Daggett, my uniformed nemesis. The thought of his being busted down to rousting drunks and vagrants out of urine-soaked public rest-rooms brought a smile to my face, as well.

"So how did she convince the other girl to change clothes with her?" I asked.

Again I could hear grudging approval, even admiration, in my father's tone. "Told her she was playing a trick on her parents, sneaking off to meet with her boyfriend of whom they dis-approved. Plus she promised to pay her a hundred dollars."

According to the expurgated version the Judge had received from one of his courthouse informants, Mercer had emerged from the ladies' room at the crowded truck stop just off I-26 wearing a twin set complete with a single strand of fake pearls, sharply pressed slacks, and shiny Bass penny loafers. With her hair held neatly back by two gold barrettes and her face nearly covered by oversized sunglasses, she had sashayed right past the unsuspecting officer and disappeared into the bustle. You had to give the girl credit for audacity.

"Why are you so determined to find Mercer?" I asked.

"She's family," he mumbled around the corona clamped between his teeth.

"She's *mother's* family. You've never given two damns about them, and you know it. I haven't even talked to Aunt Eliza since Uncle Rupert's funeral, and that was what? Twenty years ago?"

"Your mother was never close to her sister-in-law. After her brother died, she didn't see any point in maintaining the connection."

"She didn't *approve* of Aunt Eliza, is what you mean. The daughter of a minister. Not nearly good enough for the almighty Tattnall/Baynard clan." I worked my arms into the sleeves of the sweater I had draped around my shoulders. The night was cooling rapidly. "What made you drop your teacup that night you first saw Mercer?"

The sudden change of subject took him enough by surprise that he answered without thinking. "She looked just like your mother at that age."

"You've got to be kidding!" I spluttered. "Mother may have been an unrepentant snob, but she was beautiful! Mercer is—"

"Undernourished? Uncared for? You mark my words, Bay. With a little fattening up and some attention paid to her clothes and grooming, your cousin Mercer could well surpass all the Baynard women."

I bit back a snort of disbelief in case my father should think I felt threatened by his prediction of Mercer Mary Prescott's unrealized potential. "So what are we going to do about finding her? We don't know a damned thing about her past except the generalities she shared with us that first night. We don't even know for sure where her grandparents are, or even if they're still alive. I don't have a clue where to start."

"How about that disreputable bag Vinnie said she was carrying when she was arrested? Didn't the officers make her leave it behind? I'm sure she won't mind our invading her privacy if it will enable us to offer her assistance."

I thanked the deepness of the shadows on the wide porch for

concealing the guilty rush of blood to my cheeks. Now didn't seem a good time to admit I had already pawed through my cousin's paltry possessions. I remembered the pages of computer-generated genealogy I'd glanced over briefly before stuffing them back into the envelope postmarked in . . . *Honea Path*.

I drew in a quick breath. "Where did Aunt Eliza and Uncle Rupert live?" I asked my father, although I was fairly certain I knew the answer already.

"Eliza is still there, so far as I know, in that mausoleum of a house Rupert bought for her when your grandmother died and your mother inherited Presqu'isle. Let's see, it's a little town, nothing much more than a crossroads last time I was there. Two words, I think. Maybe something *Trail*? No, that doesn't sound right."

I let him work on dragging the name up from the depths of his considerable memory while I concentrated on wondering if the spidery handwriting on the brown mailing envelope did indeed belong to my Aunt Eliza, and what exactly dear, sweet Cousin Mercer had really been up to before she dropped so unexpectedly into our lives.

It was time to find out.

CHAPTER SEVEN

Since his acceptance of our offer to join the loose confederation we had tentatively named Simpson & Tanner, Inquiry Agents, Erik Whiteside and I had gotten into the habit of touching base over the weekend. Normally we communicated by modem, using AOL's Instant Message function to carry on a real-time, electronic conversation. But tonight, as I set the brass screen in front of the modest fire in the great room and settled onto the white sofa facing the hearth, I felt the need for old-fashioned human contact. Though Erik, who managed a high-end computer store in Charlotte, spent most of his non-working moments on the Internet, he had had the good sense to install an alternate line. The only question was whether or not he could tear himself away from his keyboard long enough to pick up.

I knew from past experience I needed to let the phone ring a long time, so I pulled back the drapes and stood for a moment staring through the night out toward the ocean. Even through the heavy doors I could hear the soughing of the wind in the tops of the loblolly pines. I hoped we weren't in for another storm. I'd had my fill of cold and rain, and we weren't even into December yet.

As I reached for the pull to close the curtains against the gloomy darkness, I heard a muffled voice and realized I had been clutching the portable phone against my chest. "Erik," I said quickly before he got disgusted and hung up, "it's me, Bay."

"Well, hey, partner, what's goin' on down there? Got computer problems?"

Erik Whiteside and I had met under distressing circumstances several months before when murder had touched his quiet, middle-class family, leading him to construct an ingenious Web site which I had accidentally stumbled onto. His sensitivity, rare in one who had not yet reached thirty, coupled with an uncanny knack for penetrating supposedly secure databases, had convinced my father and me to invite him into our fledgling venture.

"No, nothing like that," I replied, "I just sort of wanted to talk to you for real. You know, like regular people. I've got a job for you."

"A job? You mean, like, for the business? *Our* business?"

"Yes."

"Cool! Who's the client?"

I reached across the purring cat tucked into the curve of my left hip and removed the much-handled brown envelope from my cousin's duffel bag. I had retrieved it from my old room before leaving my father's house earlier in the evening. Without really knowing what I was looking for, I'd checked out the labels in Mercer's clothes and riffled through the pages of the romance novels and guidebooks she carried, but none of it was any help at all. I even examined the silver-backed hairbrush. If any of the intricate design was supposed to reveal the initials or identity of its original owner, the pattern completely escaped me. The genealogy, and the envelope it had been mailed in, would have to provide whatever scanty information I would be giving to Erik as a starting place.

"We are. The Judge and I. We're the client."

Briefly I sketched out our encounter with Mercer Mary Prescott and our need to locate her. "The Judge thinks we need to convince her to turn herself in before something worse happens to her. If her name and picture go out as a federal fugitive, my father is afraid she could get hurt, regardless of how minor her offense is. Some back-road, local lawman could get carried away. It's happened before."

"What have we got to go on?" Erik asked without editorial comment on the validity of the Judge's fears. "I'm going to put you on the speaker so I can type and listen at the same time."

"Well, she talked some about herself that first night, but I've come to realize, in thinking back over the conversation, it was all generalities. This genealogy thing is about the best we have, I think. Her mother's name is Catherine Marie Prescott, born 1962."

"What's your cousin's birth date?"

"All I have is the year—1978." I realized I would have to stop thinking of my cousin as a child. She was, in fact, a woman grown.

"Father?"

"Unknown. Or at least, unnamed. There was no marriage. And get this—Catherine disappeared when Mercer was six. Went out to work one day and never came back. So that would be—what? Sometime in '84 maybe?"

"Any idea what kind of work she did?" Erik asked. I could hear the soft patter of the keyboard as he entered the data onto his computer.

"None. She finished high school, but never made it to college. It could have been anything."

"Where did this all take place?"

"Somewhere in northern Georgia. There's no place of birth listed on any of the documents I have here. Mercer did mention going to the lake in the summers with her grandparents, but she never said which one. The grandparents are William and Mary Ellen Prescott. Mary Ellen's maiden name was Glover." I leaned closer to the lamp trying to decipher the badly faded chart and its tiny print. "I think I can make out the great-grandmother's name. Will that help at all?"

"I don't think so, but let me have it anyway."

"Rebecca Mercer Cooper, born 1901."

"Any of these people still alive?"

"Who knows? Mercer Mary did tell us her grandfather fell ill and required her grandmother's full-time care. They had to place her in a foster home."

"That's a great clue! Got to be official records of that somewhere."

"You can't get into that kind of stuff, can you? Isn't it illegal?" A long, pregnant silence greeted my question. "Right," I answered myself, "I'd rather not know."

"Anything else you can think of?"

"I don't . . . No, wait! This envelope—the one with all the genealogical stuff in it? It was mailed to Mercer from a little town called Honea Path. It could have come from my Aunt Eliza. She lives there. I'll check that part of it out myself."

"Where was it sent *to?*"

I hesitated, reluctant somehow to betray the last of Mercer's secrets, even to someone I trusted as much as I did Erik

Whiteside. But the point of this exercise was to locate my cousin before she got herself into more trouble than she'd already managed to do. We needed to find out who she'd go to if she were seeking a safe place to hide. It wasn't fair to send Erik gunning for her without providing him with all the ammunition we had.

Oops, bad metaphor.

"Bay?" Erik's voice over the speakerphone sounded tinny and far away.

"It was sent to Mercer in care of the Herbert-Hanson Clinic in Columbia."

"Why did I have to drag that out of you, partner? What is it, a funny farm or something?"

"Or something," I answered softly.

"I'll be discreet. Count on it. I'll be back to you tomorrow with preliminaries."

"That soon?"

"Hey, you're dealin' with the fastest modem south of the Mason-Dixon Line. Say 'hey' to everyone down there for me, okay?"

"Will do. G'night, Erik"

"We'll find her. Don't worry," I heard him say as I pushed the OFF button and set the phone back on the side table.

In a silence underlain by the rhythmic purring of the cat curled at my side, I heard the first, faint patter of rain against the windows. I wondered if Mercer Mary Prescott was somewhere warm and dry, or if she had once again been reduced to sleeping on benches and foraging for food in restaurant garbage cans.

I snuggled down into the cushions as the wind-driven rain now battered the French doors and beat against the roof. I wondered if I should get up and put another log on the fire. I wondered how the Santiagos were faring without the heart of their family to hold them together. I wondered if Dolores lay awake in her hospital bed, listening to the rain and wondering why I hadn't been to see her. I wondered . . .

By Monday morning, my gloomy mood and its matching weather had both been blown out to sea. Buoyed by Angie's report of her mother's improving condition, I sat in the patch of welcome sunlight streaming through the kitchen window and planned my strategy for the day.

Erik had gleaned a remarkable amount of information in his less than twenty-four hours of cyber-snooping. Sipping Earl Grey and munching on a slightly scorched bagel, I studied the yellow legal pad on which I'd scribbled the highlights, while Mr. Bones bathed himself at my feet.

Cousin Mercer had been born in Tucker, a hamlet I finally located on the map in Georgia's Chattahoochee National Forest, not far from the Tennessee border in the foothills of the Blue Ridge Mountains. Her grandfather's illness and subsequent death had apparently drained what meager finances the family had managed to accumulate, so that when her Nana Mary died, just over a year ago, there had been barely enough to cover the remaining debts. Mercer would have left Tucker with little more than the clothes on her back.

Or the meager contents of her duffel bag, I thought.

Pushing aside the uneaten, blackened edges of the bagel, I tried to put myself in Mercer's shoes. Erik reported she had spent ten apparently uneventful years with the same foster family in nearby Toccoa. At least there was no record of her having passed back into the system during that time. I tried to recall how she had spoken of her surrogate family during the Judge's interrogation of her in his study at Presqu'isle. It seemed to me her tone had been one of mild affection, displaying no strong feelings of love or devotion which might have bound her to them.

Or led her to believe they might now offer her sanctuary from the law.

I nudged the cat off my feet and carried my mug to the dishwasher, wrapping the bagel remains in a paper towel and tossing them into the trashcan beneath the sink. I didn't think even the birds could have made any use of the scraps.

Edible food—and my own inability to provide it for myself— had been much on my mind. With Dolores likely to be out of commission for weeks, if not months, I had to find a viable solution which didn't require surviving on pizza delivery and cold cereal.

"So, okay, how difficult can it be?" I said aloud. Mr. Bones, his striped tail wrapped around his feet as if he posed for a cat sculptor, cocked his head to one side and regarded me quizzically.

"You get a cookbook, you read the recipe, you follow the directions, right? I mean, I have two master's degrees. I should be able to figure this out. And it's all about numbers. One of this, a quarter of that. Bake for so many minutes. We can do numbers, can't we, Bones?"

The cat yawned and stretched and bounded into the great room. Over one shoulder, his slanted eye regarded me with impatience.

"Okay, I'll let you out, since you asked so nicely."

I reached through the partially drawn drapes, unlocked the French door, and slid open the screen.

The muzzle of the gun shoved straight into my chest sent me stumbling back into the room. I clipped the end of the coffee table and fell hard on my left elbow.

The figure looming over me could have been black or white, bald or covered with masses of hair. All my eyes could focus on was the gaping hole in the end of the pistol. Later I would recall the pungent smell of oil on his stained fatigues and the strange symbols tattooed across the middle knuckle on each of his fingers.

But at that exact moment, as he stood framed in the soft light of the late autumn morning, all that existed for me was the gun and his deep, guttural snarl.

"Okay, bitch, I'm tired of screwin' with you people. Where the hell is my wife?"

Chapter
Eight

"Who are you?"

It was the inane question of every inane heroine who peopled those gothic novels of my youth, but it was the best I could manage, sprawled across the carpet with my left arm gone totally numb and imminent death waving at me from a few feet away.

Who are you. God! As if he'd be stupid enough to tell me his name.

"Buddy. Buddy Slade," he said. "Now get up. Real slow. Sit on the couch."

He punctuated his instructions with careless flicks of the handgun, and I scrambled to comply. In nothing but Rob's old College of Charleston T-shirt, I was certain my one-armed awkwardness was giving him quite a show, but *Buddy* seemed indifferent to the unintentional display of my physical charms. I tugged the shirt down as far as it would go, then perched primly on the edge of the white sofa, my knees locked together.

Buddy Slade moved away from the window, out of the backlight, and I got my first real look at him. Medium-tall and stocky, he wore rumpled, camouflage-green military fatigues tucked into scuffed, lace-up boots. The hand gripping the gun was clean, but stained, as if grime had worked its way into his pores and refused to be eradicated by even the most persistent scrubbing. The ten tattoos, I now realized on closer inspection, were numbers, upside down to me, but no doubt perfectly legible to Buddy.

I kept waiting for him to speak again, to reiterate his strange demand about his wife, but he seemed content to stand, legs slightly apart, staring at something only he could see. The gun, however, never wavered from its direct line to my heart. I had to break the terrifying silence before I cracked and began screaming like a hysterical child.

"I don't believe I know your wife," I offered tentatively. "Perhaps you have the wrong—"

"Cut the shit, lady. I know who you are," he snapped, his attention once more riveted on me. "And you know my wife. I ain't got the wrong place. I ain't stupid."

As he spoke, I allowed myself to look squarely into his face for the first time and didn't know whether to gasp or laugh out loud. I forced myself to do neither, but the effort cost me every ounce of self-control I had.

Buddy Slade was Elvis, reincarnated or replicated I wasn't sure, but the King, nonetheless, from the carelessly handsome face to the sleek, black ducktail haircut. The sexy curl of his upper lip as he insisted he wasn't "stupid" could have come straight from any of Elvis's forgettable B-movies of the fifties and sixties. Even the voice, heavy with southern Tennessee or maybe northern Georgia, had that quivering timbre so exaggerated by Presley impersonators as they mocked, "Thank you, thank you *vurra* much."

Half-naked and facing the business end of a very nasty looking firearm, I decided I had nothing to lose by being honest. "Look, Buddy," I said, giving him my most earnest expression, "I really don't know who you are or anything about your wife. Believe me, I'd tell you if I did."

"Bullshit! She was at your house! Well, maybe not *your* house," he amended, moving to position himself in front of the cold, empty fireplace, "but your old man's anyway."

It still didn't register with me who he could be talking about. I didn't know anyone named Slade, certainly no one who'd been at the Judge's. I opened my mouth to reiterate my denial when it hit me, but Buddy was there before me.

"Come on, *Lydia*, or Bay or whatever your real name is. You're the la-di-dah cousin that Merce is always yappin' about, the one with all the bucks. So quit playin' cute with me, okay? Just don't piss me off no more than I already am!"

His deep, Elvis-voice rose in pitch on the tide of his anger, and I threw up my hands reflexively to ward off—what? A blow? A bullet? I sat back, lowering my arms, knowing instinctively it would do me no good to challenge him.

"You're talking about Mercer. Mercer Mary Prescott, right?

I'm sorry, I wasn't lying to you. It's just that she never said anything about being married, never—"

"That's because she's a slut, that's why," Buddy spat between clenched teeth. The numbers on his knuckles blurred as his hand tightened around the grip of his weapon. "But she's my ol' lady, make no mistake. I mighta been outta circulation for a while, but that don't change nothin'. And when I find her," he added, his upper lip curling into a caricature of that famous sneer, "she's gonna wish she never spread 'em—"

At that exact moment, a great blue heron, disturbed no doubt by a foraging Mr. Bones, let loose a blood-curdling screech and took flight almost directly over Slade's shoulder. Buddy whipped his head around toward the source of possible attack, crouched in the approved defensive stance, and brought his gun to bear on the deck.

Before he could blink, I was off the couch and sprinting for the hallway.

I stumbled on the naked square of plywood, exposed when I'd cut out the carpet which had soaked up Dolores's blood. I heard Buddy Slade's roar of anger as I skidded into the guest bath and rammed home the bolt. I snatched the portable phone off the granite vanity top and leaped into the tub.

After my near miss the past summer, I had had metal doors with sturdy bolts installed on every room in the house. Never again would I be trapped behind a flimsy, hollow wood door with only a handle lock between me and a possible assailant. And every room, even the pantry and bathrooms, now contained a telephone as well.

I hit speed dial and got the 911 operator on the first ring.

"Intruder," I said, more calmly than I felt, knowing she would have my address flashing on her screen as I spoke.

"In the house?" she asked, wasting no words.

The metal door shuddered under the assault of Buddy Slade's army boots.

"Yes, ma'am," I said over the din of Buddy's shouted frustration. "He sure as hell is."

"On the way," the operator said, then asked if I thought I was in imminent danger.

"I don't think so, but he has a gun."

"I'll pass that along. Stay on the line with me now, the deputies are only a minute or two out."

Even Buddy wasn't stupid enough to fire point-blank at a metal door, but he kept up his attacks, both verbal and physical, calling me names I hadn't heard since junior high school.

Which is probably the point at which his mental capacities reached their high-water mark, I thought, feeling smugly secure behind my steel barricade.

He gave one last, vicious kick, then ran through a brief litany of what he intended to do to me when next we met. Through the sudden stillness I heard the faint wail of sirens and the receding thud of combat boots as Buddy Slade retreated along the wooden planks of my deck.

Deputy Tommy Daggett had apparently been instructed to adjust his attitude since last we'd met. He and Charity Bell smothered me in *yes, ma'am*s and softball questions, and wandered through my house as if they were frequent guests instead of uniformed intruders. Neither seemed able to understand why I wasn't the same quivering mess they'd encountered just a few days before.

Frankly, neither could I. I had no doubt Buddy Slade would have hurt me in exactly the manner he described, had it not been for the metal shield between us. And in the few moments between his escape and the welcome pounding of the deputies on my front door, I had concluded that the ex-con was probably responsible for the attack on Dolores as well. I didn't share this theory with my rescuers, although Deputy Bell looked smart enough to work out the connection for herself.

I answered their questions perfunctorily, anxious for them to be gone now that the immediate threat had voluntarily taken himself off. I insisted there was no need for fingerprinting or lengthy descriptions of my would-be assailant. Daggett, however, seemed determined to stick to procedure. Apparently he had *not* been the victim of Mercer Mary Prescott's ingenious escape from custody.

"For God's sake, the moron told me his name!" I said for the third time in the half hour they'd been prowling around my living room. "He talked about being married to my cousin and being out of circulation for a while. He can't have been out of prison too long. Surely you can check that out with a phone call!"

"Mrs. Tanner, we need to handle this by the book. He could have been lying, you know. Not many perps volunteer their names like that. And what makes you so sure he's been in prison?"

Exasperated, I ticked the points off on my fingers. "One. He's looking for his wife. Two, he talked about being out of circulation for a long time. And he was waving a gun in my face. It seems an obvious conclusion."

"*Hmmm.* Well, we'll certainly check that out. Now, did he have any distinguishing characteristics? Scars, tattoos?"

I almost preferred the snarling, surly Tommy Daggett of a few days ago. This polite, condescending version was fast getting on my nerves. There's not much in this world I hate more than being *humored.*

"Numbers," I replied, remembering the stained fingers clutching the grip of the automatic. "He had numbers tattooed on his knuckles."

"Strange," Daggett said, glancing over at Deputy Bell. "Any idea what they were? I mean, what they mighta stood for?"

"How the hell should I know?" I yelled, giving up pacing the carpet in front of the French doors and flopping myself down on the sofa. "Maybe it was his lottery picks or the password to his Swiss bank account. Maybe he has trouble remembering his phone number. If it were his IQ, he would only have needed two fingers!"

Daggett flipped his notebook closed and slid it into the breast pocket of his sharply creased khaki shirt. Behind him, Charity Bell raised a pudgy brown hand to conceal the smile twitching at the corners of her mouth.

"I think that'll about do it, Mrs. Tanner," Daggett said. "If you think of anything else, you give us a call, okay?" He nodded curtly and headed for the door.

"You gonna be all right, ma'am?" Deputy Bell asked, one large, brown hand momentarily resting against my upper arm. "You had more 'n your share of troubles lately. Want me to call anyone for ya?"

"No, thanks, Charity," I said, touched by the concern in her deep-set eyes. "I'll be fine. You guys just nail this jerk. He's ready to explode, and the fallout could hurt a lot of innocent people."

"Bell! Let's hit it!" Tommy Daggett hollered from the porch.

"How'd you get stuck with him?" I asked as the deputy gave my arm a maternal pat and turned toward the door.

"Luck o' the draw," she said with a twinkle. "But I got me five brothers, all older. Ain't nothin' here I ain't been through before. You take care now."

"Thanks. You, too."

I closed and locked the heavy oak door behind them and engaged the alarm. The icy-hot fist of anger lodged just under my breastbone kept my hands steady and my heart rate slow and even. I paused in the hallway to stare down at the bare spot in the carpet, then made my way into my bedroom.

I'd pulled on a pair of sweatpants while the deputies were searching the exterior of the house, and now they seemed to be stuck to my skin. I peeled off my sweat-soaked clothes and let the needle-spray of a steaming shower sluice away the contamination I felt from having shared breathing space with Buddy Slade.

Dressed again in jeans and a Carolina Panthers sweatshirt, I dropped Indian fashion onto the floor of my walk-in closet and pulled up the panel concealing the safe. The black nylon case lay on top, the last deposit I'd made to what had once been Rob's repository of secret files and computer discs.

The Glock felt different this time, more at home in my hand than when Red Tanner first tried to teach me how to shoot it some months before. As my index finger settled comfortably around the trigger, the knot in my chest eased a little.

After I'd been forced to kill a man, I'd sworn never to touch a firearm again. But that was before I met Buddy Slade, before he'd battered an innocent Dolores into unconsciousness, then shattered her leg just for the hell of it.

I checked the clip, slipped the automatic back into its case, and shoved the carry permit into the back pocket of my jeans. I closed the safe, then pulled on my scruffy running shoes. The Glock went into the big denim bag which replaced my canvas tote as my sole fashion concession to the change of seasons.

When I stepped out of the closet, the bag weighing heavily on my shoulder, I felt as if some watershed had been reached, some dividing line in my life had been crossed. If this had been a movie, the music, heavy with horns, would have soared on a rising crescendo.

I was tired of being afraid. I was tired of *reacting* to the blows that had been raining down on me, beginning with the day the burning metal from Rob's shattered plane had marked me forever as a victim of violence. Buddy Slade had picked the wrong time and the wrong woman.

And he would live to regret it.

It took Erik Whiteside less than an hour to come up with the particulars on Walter Jerome "Buddy" Slade, product of the north Georgia mountains, and recent guest at the state penitentiary just up the road. Armed robbery was apparently the young man's chosen career, with a decided preference for liquor stores.

I'd assumed Buddy had escaped, even though I'd seen no mention of it in the local papers, but Erik informed me my would-be attacker had actually been released. Obviously another well-reasoned judgment on the part of a parole board somewhere. At any rate, he'd been out less than two months before he came threatening me with a gun, so it looked as if his chances of a lengthy stay on the outside were right up there along with the Mets winning another World Series and hell freezing over.

Erik hadn't been able to locate any record of a marriage between Walter Slade and Mercer Mary Prescott, at least not in Georgia, but he promised to keep trying. "Oh, and I got some more info on your cousin since we last talked," Erik added as I was about to terminate the call. "She wasn't a patient in that clinic in Columbia, so you can put your mind to rest about that."

The fact that Mercer hadn't required psychiatric treatment should have come as something of a relief, but I had a hard time believing that anyone who had voluntarily gotten themselves tangled up with the likes of Buddy Slade could be entirely of sound mind. "What was she then, an employee?" I asked.

"You got it. Worked there for about eight months, up until this past summer, then just took off. No notice, no explanation, just didn't show up for her shift one day."

"Was she a nurse?"

"No, more like an aide, from what I can gather. Helped out with the recreational therapy, crafts and games, things like that. Covered some when they were shorthanded. They thought very highly of her, apparently felt she had real potential, a flair for working with disturbed people. I think they were sorry to see your cousin go."

"How do you find out all this stuff?" I asked, eyeing the clock over the kitchen sink. It was almost two, and I wanted to get up to the hospital before the kids got out of school and came visiting Dolores. What I had to discuss with her probably wasn't for the ears of her children. "Is that kind of information just hanging around on the Internet?"

Erik laughed, and I envisioned the open smile lighting up his suntanned face. Tall and broad-shouldered, he had the fresh good looks of the boy next door, with clear brown eyes and hair so blonde it was almost white. "A lot of it is, if you know where to look. And how to access it once you get there. But what I just gave you on your cousin didn't come from a database. I got all that with a simple phone call."

"You conned all that out of the personnel department at the clinic?"

Again his laugh brought an answering smile to my face. "Not exactly. I had to wait quite a while for the supervisor of personnel to come on the line, so I just chatted some with the receptionist. I find most people will tell you just about anything if you seem interested and ask them nicely enough."

"Amazing! I'll have to remember to be wary of charming young men trying to worm my innermost secrets out of me over the phone."

"One other thing. Kind of odd, I thought."

"What's that?"

"Well, I sort of hesitate to mention it, because it wasn't anything specific, just an impression really, but I think there might have been some problem surrounding your cousin's leaving the clinic."

"What kind of problem?" *Thievery* was the first thought that popped into my mind, although I couldn't have said why.

"I don't know. It's just that, when I finally got put through to the supervisor, I gave her my spiel about Mercer's having applied for a job and that I was doing a background check. She seemed real reluctant to talk about your cousin."

"Maybe they have a confidentiality policy or something."

"Could be. But this woman ended up pumping *me* for information before it was all over. Wanted to know where I was calling from, and if I had Mercer's current address or knew her whereabouts. It sounded as if they'd like to have a chat with her, and I don't think it's about her walking out with a few paperclips or rifling the petty cash drawer. Like I said, though, it could just be my imagination."

"You're right, it's strange. You'll keep at it, won't you?" I asked, sobering as another thought struck me. "It's even more important now that we find Mercer soon. Before Buddy does."

"I understand. I'll try the direct approach with her foster family in Toccoa when I get home from work. I think I'd have a better chance of catching both parents in the evening."

"Good. Just be sure to keep track of your time. I don't want you doing this for nothing. And I also don't want you to jeopardize your regular job, hear?"

"Okay, I hear you." He paused a moment. "Bay?"

"Yes?" I replied absently. With the phone tucked between my left ear and shoulder, I was gathering up my things and searching around the kitchen for my reading glasses.

"Well, please don't take this the wrong way, but I don't think you should get messed up in this thing with your cousin. I mean, you've already been through enough stuff lately. And this guy Slade sounds like he doesn't have all his oars in the water, you know? Maybe this would be a good one to leave to your brother-in-law and the cops."

I smiled, touched by his concern. "I'll be careful," I said, my glance straying to the denim bag wherein nestled the innocent-looking black case. "Thanks for worrying about me, though. Keep me posted, okay?"

"Sure," Erik replied, the reluctance plain in his voice. "I'll probably talk to you tomorrow. Take care."

"You, too."

I clicked off the phone, hefted the bag, and scooped my keys off the counter. It felt good to be on the offensive. I needed to find Mercer Mary Prescott, not only to prevent her from being picked up by the feds, but to reach her before the moronic, Elvis-clone she'd married did. There were people and problems to be dealt with, and the weight of the gun banging against my thigh as I jogged down the steps gave me confidence that this time I would be able to handle them.

CHAPTER NINE

Dolores Santiago's blue-black hair and deep olive complexion stood out in stark contrast to the crisp, white pillowcase. Thankfully, only one oblong plastic bag hung suspended from the chrome pole next to her bed, a single IV line snaking into the needle taped to the back of her left hand. I figured that was a good sign. She didn't notice me peering cautiously around the heavy door to the semiprivate room, her attention engaged by Oprah and her wildly screaming audience somewhere above and to the right.

Either she's giving something away or she's interviewing Mel Gibson, I thought as I slipped inside and approached the bed, cranked up to about three-quarters to make TV-viewing more comfortable.

"Hi," I said tentatively. "Okay if I come in?"

Dolores turned her head, and the beatific smile I'd come to rely on so much in the past year lit her tired face. "Of course, *Señora,*" she replied, holding out her unencumbered hand to me. "You are always much welcome."

I had sworn to myself I wouldn't get weepy, but it was a near thing as I scooted the visitor's chair closer to the bed and took the proffered hand in mine. I made a production out of sitting down and settling my bag on the floor to give myself time to get my face under control. "How are you feeling? Are you in much pain?"

"*Un poco.*" With typical Dolores understatement she gestured toward her left leg, encased in plaster and suspended by a series of ropes and pulleys attached to a contraption which looked as if it might have been used on an oil rig.

"How about your head?" The ugly gash I had watched seeping blood onto her still face as we waited in my hallway for the paramedics to arrive was covered now by a clean white bandage, a much smaller one than I would have thought necessary to contain that gaping wound.

Dolores's shrug dismissed what might have been a fatal injury. *"Esta bien.* No hurt like before."

I had worked on my speech on the short drive from Port Royal Plantation to the hospital, but now I didn't know how to begin. This sweet woman's care of me had probably saved my sanity in the months following my husband's death. How could I convey to her what she meant to me? And how sorry I was that her willingness to stay on, long after I had supposedly recovered, had put her in harm's way? And how guilty I felt about that?

I should have known it would be unnecessary. In the relatively short time we'd been together, Dolores had learned to read me far better than my own mother ever had in the twenty-some years we'd occupied the same house.

"Is no your fault, *Señora.* You no worry, *por favor."* She squeezed my hand gently to punctuate her reassurance.

"What happened? Do you remember?"

The usually sparkling black eyes clouded over as Dolores nodded twice.

"You do? Have you talked to Red? Or any of the other deputies?"

"They come soon."

"Can you tell me?" I could feel my heart pounding in anticipation. All I needed was confirmation that Walter Jerome "Buddy" Slade had beaten my friend, and the floating piece of pond scum would be toast.

Dolores drew a quick little breath. In halting English, liberally scattered with Spanish substitutions for words she was unable to dredge up or had never encountered before, she told me her story.

I lowered myself gratefully onto the wooden bench just outside the automatic doors of the hospital entrance and lit a cigarette with visibly quaking fingers. The weak sunlight of waning afternoon filtered down through high, thin clouds. I shivered in a light breeze, wishing I had thought to toss Rob's weathered bomber jacket into the car. November is always such a changeable month in the Lowcountry.

My shakes, however, were not entirely due to the northeast wind and the rapid approach of nightfall. Dolores's account of the assault had been sketchy in places, but of one thing she was absolutely certain: her attacker was *not* Buddy Slade.

"How can you be so sure?" I'd asked when she began shaking her head almost before I finished describing my cousin's ex-con husband.

"*Niñas*," she said, the improbability of it apparent in her voice. "*Dos niñas.*"

Two girls? I was still stunned by the revelation as I watched the smoke from the end of my cigarette swirling away into the deepening twilight.

Dolores had answered the doorbell sometime in the middle of the afternoon, perhaps around two-thirty, she couldn't be sure. The girls—one dark, one fair—were young, about Angie's age, she guessed, and her first thought was that something had happened to her daughter. They were quick to reassure her, claiming to have had car trouble on their way to visit a friend in the plantation. Could they please use the phone?

Although dressed roughly—*como l'ejécito*, which I thought roughly translated probably meant in army-type fatigues—they were no scruffier than many of Angie's high school contemporaries. She had unlatched the door and led them into the kitchen.

Once inside, though, they ignored the telephone and began to prowl the great room, peering out the tall windows onto the deck as if verifying that no one else was around. When the blonde pulled the drapes closed, then moved toward the hallway, Dolores knew she had been duped. It took only a few moments for them to check out the rest of the rooms.

A cold knot tightened its grip on the bottom of my stomach as I imagined tiny Dolores quivering in fear while strangers stomped through my house. I blew on my hands, then stuffed them into the pockets of my jeans. The temperature had dropped several degrees along with the sun.

The interrogation of my housekeeper was short and to the point, and its object had shattered all my preconceived ideas of what had happened. The girls were looking for Mercer!

Who was this scruffy child-woman, claiming to be my cousin, who made so many people ready to commit violence in order to find her?

Of course Dolores had no answers for them. She had never *heard* of Mercer Mary Prescott, never laid eyes on her. And of course they didn't believe her. At first she'd pretended not to understand their shouted questions, but the dark one proved fluent in Spanish, and continued to insist that Dolores was lying.

The blow to her head came out of nowhere, her only clear recollection of it being the swift downswing of the blonde's right arm. Through the haze of semiconsciousness, she heard them yelling, this time at each other, and could recall only a few of the words. Her impression was that they were arguing about what to do next.

The soft blue of sodium-vapor light spread over the sidewalk in front of me as the lamps around the parking lot glowed into life. Darkness had fallen as I'd sat there chain-smoking, oblivious to the visitors and outpatients who hurried or shuffled or limped by in front of me.

I was trying to recreate in my own mind the horror my friend must have felt. I needed to make her fear and her pain as real as if they had been my own, as they should rightfully have been. Dolores was an innocent player in this vicious drama, thrown into the path of danger only because of me. The guilt of that was already eating away at my soul.

I closed my eyes as a shudder which had little to do with the cold washed over me. Dolores had feigned unconsciousness, hoping the girls would give up and go away. When they moved their argument into the foyer, my friend seized her opportunity. Unable to stand, she dragged herself toward the guest bath and the safety of its reinforced metal door.

In the dark corners of my imagination I watched her crawl cautiously down the hallway. But some small grunt of pain must have alerted her attackers, for they were on her in seconds. The blonde raised one heavily booted foot and brought it smashing down. I cringed at the sharp snap of bone, felt the searing pain and the blessed relief of oblivion as she fainted. The assault must have continued for some time after Dolores lost consciousness. Only a thorough beating could account for the extensive nerve and tissue damage surrounding the mangled bones of her leg.

With hands numb from shock and cold, I wiped the tears from the corners of my eyes and pulled my bag onto my lap. The package of tissues had settled onto the bottom. In groping for them, my fingers brushed the smooth nylon of the gun case. I stroked the metal outline of the Glock through the thin fabric, remembering how hard I had resisted my father's single-minded determination that I learn how to use it. Had he been able to view the black fantasies of retribution now boiling in my mind, he would have paid more heed to my reticence.

"What are you doing out here in the cold?" Red's voice shattered the nighttime stillness.

"Thinking," I said, jerking my hand guiltily out of my bag as my brother-in-law seated himself, uninvited, beside me.

"Not about me, I hope." He laid an arm tentatively across the back of the bench, carefully avoiding my shoulder. "You looked like you were plotting to kill somebody."

If you only knew, I thought, and rearranged my face into a less murderous expression.

Over steaming helpings of chicken pot pie, its rich gravy bubbling up out of slits in the golden pastry, Red and I exchanged information. That I was not entirely as forthcoming as he was, passed—I hoped—unnoticed. Jump and Phil's, our favorite neighborhood watering hole on the south end of the island, was relatively quiet. We sat beneath the massive head of Waldo the Moose at our usual table near the fireplace, its gas logs flickering brightly on the chilly November night. Only a few other tables were occupied, and the bar was lined with regulars getting settled in to watch Monday Night Football on the big-screen TVs.

"I suppose you're feeling like some kind of disaster magnet, right?" Red asked, using his maroon linen napkin to swipe at the errant dribble of gravy sliding down his chin.

His observation bore a distinct similarity to the one Neddie Halloran had made a couple of days before. Everyone, it seemed, felt it incumbent upon themselves to offer an opinion as to the guilt-ridden state of my psyche.

"I won't even dignify that with a reply." I pushed a few peas off to the side of my bowl and stabbed a huge chunk of white meat. I chewed, swallowed, then used the empty fork to punctuate my next words. "I know what you're trying to do. You can make light of this all you want, but it isn't going to make me feel any less responsible for what happened to Dolores."

"I'm not making light of it, Bay. I'm trying to get you to step back and view it with a little more objectivity than you've been demonstrating lately. Some bad things have happened to people you care about, but they weren't your fault. None of them. Try laying the blame for this where it belongs—on the two Rambo-ettes who actually beat up Dolores."

That did bring a reluctant smile to my face. "*Rambo-ettes?* God, Tanner, we're getting old. I actually understood that. Those kids probably never even heard of Sylvester Stallone."

The waitress appeared and whisked away our bowls, Red's as empty as if he had licked it clean, and mine with its tidy pile of uneaten peas nestled in the bottom. We ordered coffee and tea, and I lit a cigarette.

"I thought you were giving those up," Red remarked as I blew smoke in Waldo's face.

"I was doing pretty good, until this whole mess happened," I replied ruefully. "I've got that nicotine replacement gum stuff in my purse, but it tastes really nasty. I'll get back on track as soon as I—" The arrival of our hot drinks saved me from revealing more to my deputy-sheriff brother-in-law than I had meant to. I performed my own little tea ritual, hoping Red hadn't noticed.

"If you're planning on getting involved in tracking down these people, forget it." Red blew across the top of the cup of steaming coffee and fixed me with his most intimidating stare. "Your half-whatever cousin is obviously poison. You stay as far away from her as it's possible to get. I mean it, Bay. I know you and the Judge and that kid you got mixed up with think you can play detective, but this is police business. Leave it to the professionals."

"Oh, right! And you *professionals* have done such damned fine work! Let's see," I said, counting off their recent failures on my fingers. "First Mercer walks away from a court appearance. Then, your local confederates let her out before discovering belatedly that she's wanted by the feds. So they take her back to Columbia, let her use the restroom at some truck stop off the interstate, and she disappears into thin air."

All the anger I had tried so determinedly to hide from Red bubbled to the surface. He sipped coffee and let me vent it.

"Then your moronic judicial system lets a piece of garbage like Buddy Slade out on parole so he can force his way into my house and terrorize me. *He* gets away clean. Two more teenaged degenerates nearly beat my housekeeper to death, and they escape without a trace!" I squashed out the butt of my cigarette in the clear glass ashtray and folded my arms across my chest. "Oh, yeah, you *pros* have done a hell of a great job!"

"And your solution would be what? Strap on that Glock you've been trying to pretend you're not carrying and go play *Gunfight at the OK Corral?*"

The snort of derision which followed this attack completely overrode my embarrassment at being nailed about the gun. "You think I *can't?*" I demanded, my voice rising above the muffled groans from the bar as one of the white-clad television warriors let a punt dribble through his fingers.

"I *know* you can't. I've seen you shoot, remember? You couldn't hit the broad side of an LRTA bus if it was standing still."

I swallowed the clever retort I'd been about to fire back, and Red's smile faltered as we both remembered the only time I had ever fired in a real-life situation. That I was still here to trade banter with my brother-in-law was a testament to the benevolence of the gods rather than anything remotely to do with my skill.

"I'm not stupid," I finally said, more quietly this time. It was important I made him believe me. "Erik and I are only going to work in the background, see if we can get a line on where Mercer might be hiding out. The Judge is concerned about her. If we find her first, we'll see that she turns herself in. Judging by the past couple of days, the safest place for her right now is probably in jail."

"I'm glad to hear it."

The waitress poured Red more coffee and set our check face down in front of him. I wasn't sure whose turn it was, but I let him get it this time. Nothing is more certain to bolster a male ego than letting him pick up the tab.

"Besides," he said, dropping some bills on top of the check and pushing back his chair, "those jailhouse jumpsuits are definitely not your style. You look crappy in orange."

"Bullshit. I look stunning in orange," I replied as he followed me out to where we had parked our cars side by side. The equilibrium of our relationship had been restored. "Thanks for dinner."

"My pleasure. What are you going to do about food while Dolores is laid up?"

"I thought I might adopt the pizza delivery boy. Or I can always learn to cook. Maybe I can take a class somewhere."

"Seriously. Eating out all the time can get to be a drag, not to mention expensive. Ask me about it."

"I am serious! Millions of people all over the world know how to cook. Even you. There's no reason I can't learn." I fished out my keys and leaned against the door of the Z3. The wind had died, and the air had that crisp clarity to it I always associated with autumn at Northwestern. The sky from the beach would be spectacular tonight. "How likely do you think it is you'll catch Buddy Slade or those two degenerates who beat up Dolores?" I asked, all trace of joking gone. "Did she give you anything at all to go on?"

"Not much, I'm afraid. We didn't lift any useful prints from your house. The descriptions are pretty vague. I'm going to have someone take some mug books up to the hospital, but I don't have a lot of confidence these girls will be in there. According to Dolores, they were pretty young. Even if they've been in trouble as juveniles, there won't be any record of it we can access."

"Keep me posted, okay? Like it or not, I'm involved in this. Mercer Mary Prescott may have been the catalyst, but I seem to be the one attracting all the attention. If Erik and I manage to track her down, you'll be the first to know. I don't want her hurt."

"Fair enough. I think we might have a better shot at Slade. Anyone stupid enough to identify himself to the person he's attacking probably isn't clever enough to stay under wraps for long." Red swung the door open for me. "Hey, am I still invited for Thanksgiving? I've got the day off."

"Ask Lavinia," I said, sliding behind the wheel. "She's in charge. Maybe she'll let me help her stuff the turkey this year. Might be a good way to get my feet wet, so to speak."

"I'll alert the hospitals," Red called as I backed out and accelerated toward Greenwood Drive.

I congratulated myself as I roared around the Sea Pines Circle and onto William Hilton Parkway. Red's suspicions had been allayed, at least temporarily. With the influx of visitors which always accompanied a holiday, he would be kept busy for the rest of the weekend. Time for me to plan a road trip of my own.

CHAPTER
TEN

Having been born in the South, I've never had a problem understanding the concept of a "groaning" table. As I rearranged the serving dishes one last time to accommodate the creamed onions we'd nearly forgotten, I could almost hear the huge Duncan Phyfe sideboard creak in protest. Though we had acquired some unexpected mouths to feed, my assessment of a few days before had been accurate: it would have taken ten times our number to do justice to this incredible feast.

Lavinia had shunned my offers of help in the preparation of our annual Thanksgiving tribute to overindulgence and conspicuous consumption. The dressing, I had been informed, was an old Tattnall family recipe, held in almost religious awe, and involved oysters, freshly shelled pecans, and a combination of herbs and spices whose exact proportions she carried around in her head from November to November. Although I was technically the daughter of the house, I had never been privy to the *Secret*.

I was, however, held to be fully capable of handling the grunt work. I cleaned snap beans, shelled peas, washed collards and spinach leaves. I even managed to peel about a hundred pounds of potatoes, both white and sweet, without losing more than a few layers of skin off my knuckles.

Law and Amelia Merriweather had been welcome, last-minute additions to what was normally a strictly family gathering. When Lavinia learned they would be unexpectedly alone, she had urged the Judge to extend an invitation. Surprisingly, it had been accepted. Miss Melie, who had become nearly as much of a recluse as my father, seemed genuinely pleased to be with us.

When I heard that the no-outsiders ban was being lifted, I immediately made plans to rescue Adelaide Boyce Hammond, my mother's old friend, from what I imagined to be a dismal community celebration in the dining room of the retirement home. The alacrity with which she accepted confirmed my suspicions. Though we had not seen each other in some time, Miss Addie had been largely responsible for yanking me back into the world after Rob's death with her plea for help the past summer. She and Amelia Merriweather greeted each other like long-lost sisters, and I beamed on both of them, proud I had been the catalyst which had enabled them to renew their friendship.

Lawton presided over the turkey, my father having been forced to relinquish his carving duties after his last stroke. Seeing him wield the bone-handled carving set as he stood tall at the head of the massive table brought uncomfortable memories and an unexpected lump to my throat.

That's what I hate about holidays. Somehow you always expect them to turn out better than they do. The reality never seems to measure up to the anticipation. Maybe it comes from watching too many reruns of *Leave It to Beaver* and *It's a Wonderful Life*.

What saved me from turning into a blubbering fool were the children, Elinor and Scotty. Red's ex-wife, Sarah, had suddenly decided to let him have his kids for the day, even though this was his year for Christmas. While their divorce had been relatively amicable, Sarah had so far been a stickler for adhering to the visitation schedule. Lavinia seated them across from me, whether as a reward or a punishment I hadn't yet figured out.

She set the last dish on the table and slid into the chair next to the Judge, folding her strong, brown hands on the snowy damask cloth. She had removed the voluminous apron protecting her soft rose-colored dress, and the glow from the candles in their leaded crystal holders softened the normally sharp planes of her face.

She looks beautiful, I thought, then flushed that it should come as such a surprise to me.

For as long as I could remember, Lavinia Smalls had inhabited my life. She was the one constant in a household battered by the shifting tides of my mother's erratic mood swings. Lavinia had dispensed advice, discipline, food, and comfort and protected me as best she could. If I had turned out with any of the character and social graces my mother tried so hard to browbeat into me, it was due far more to Lavinia's influence than to her own.

The meal began with my father's traditional prayer, offering thanks for the many blessings already bestowed, and imploring the Almighty to continue to look with favor upon those here assembled. He spoke in his deep, courtroom baritone with the calm assurance that a reasonable God had no choice but to acquiesce. I glanced sideways beneath lowered lashes and caught Red, seated on my left, grinning along with me at the Judge's temerity.

At the last murmured *amen*, the room erupted into general chatter as the many serving bowls were passed along the vast expanse of the table. It seemed to take forever before everyone had gotten their dollop or slice or spoonful of the wonderful array of Lowcountry dishes Lavinia had spent the entire week preparing. The lavish praise as each was tasted was not mere politeness. Here was the person I should get to teach me how to cook.

"Thanks again for letting me bring the kids." Red addressed the Judge around a mouthful of thinly sliced ham, dripping in honey and brown sugar. "If it hadn't been for you and Lavinia, we'd have been at McDonald's or Pizza Hut today."

"You're more than welcome, I'm sure," my father replied. "After all, 'Wealth and children are the adornment of this present life . . .' "

" '. . . but good works, which are lasting, are better in the sight of thy Lord . . .' " I finished for him. "The Koran, if I'm not mistaken."

"How do you two do that?" Red helped himself to another serving of candied sweet potatoes and dropped a generous pat of butter on top. "I have a hard time remembering what I read in the paper this morning."

"Years of practice and a solitary childhood spent with my nose stuck in a book," I replied without thinking. I ignored the guilty flush on my father's face and lapsed into silence, concentrating once more on my heaping plate.

At last I sat back, unable even to contemplate lifting another morsel of food to my mouth, and watched the interplay among this diverse collection of ages, interests, and backgrounds. Law Merriweather unobtrusively cut the slice of breast meat on Miss Melie's plate, watching solicitously in case her arthritic hands were unable to manage the heavy silver fork, while she and Miss Addie murmured softly of days gone by and friends departed. Red kept a sharp eye on his children, nodding proudly to himself when they exhibited the proper table manners he and his wife had so determinedly drummed into them. Lavinia, unselfconsciously the hostess, surveyed the company, offering seconds to those who had managed to clear their plates, retreating occasionally to the kitchen to replenish a serving dish or refill a water glass.

It surprised me that, in spite of everything, I suddenly missed my mother.

When the phone rang, I excused myself, waving Lavinia back into her chair, and slipped into the Judge's room to answer it. Erik Whiteside's voice jerked me out of my nostalgia.

"Sorry if I'm taking you away from your dinner," he said over a background hum of voices and clattering dishes that told me he, too, was in the midst of the holiday meal, "but I think I've found her."

It took me a minute to realize who he was talking about. "Mercer?"

"Right. I finally talked to her foster parents today, and they were very upset that I'd called. They claimed to know nothing about your cousin's whereabouts, even when I gave them my spiel about being a relative looking to track her down."

"So why do you think they know where she is?"

"Because they didn't ask any questions."

"I don't get it."

"Well, think about it. If someone called you out of the blue, looking for someone you hadn't seen in a couple of years, wouldn't you be a little curious? All I got was a basic 'haven't seen her, don't know where she is, don't call here again' routine. I think they're hiding something—probably Mercer herself."

"I don't know," I said. "It sounds pretty flimsy to me."

"Want me to run over there and do some digging around in person?" Erik sounded just a little too eager.

"No, thanks. You've got a business to run. I was planning to head up in that direction myself this weekend. I'll take it from here. Got an address for me?"

Reluctantly Erik parted with the information. I promised to keep him posted and sent him back to his dinner. I rummaged in the Judge's desk and finally located my mother's old address book, her bible of social and family resources.

I wondered what the protocol was for just dropping in unannounced on my Aunt Eliza after twenty years of silence.

Lavinia served coffee and dessert in the main sitting room, an area of the house off-limits to me as a child and virtually unused since my mother's death. Here were the most precious pieces of her collection, the family heirlooms handed down through generations of Baynards and Tattnalls.

Red refilled his cup from the massive coffee service set out on the oak butler's tray in the center of the blue and gold patterned carpet. I knew he was probably itching to catch one of the many football games being broadcast, but some traditions die hard. Polite conversation, not blitzing linebackers, was the accepted denouement to holiday dinners at Presqu'isle. He carried his cup back across the room, then seated himself in the wing chair next to mine and followed my gaze to the deep blue settee drawn up in front of the fireplace.

Adelaide Boyce Hammond and Amelia Merriweather sat as straight as age allowed, neither slightly curved spine resting against the tufted back of the loveseat, each set of narrow ankles crossed primly in front of them. Miss Addie held a fragile saucer in her left hand, her right occasionally lifting the translucent teacup to her wrinkled, narrow lips. Miss Melie's gnarled, arthritic hands rested in her lap. They spoke softly, their heads inclined slightly toward each other.

The tableau would have made a wonderful painting. *"Southern Charm"* or maybe *"Gentlewomen at Tea,"* I thought.

I glanced down the long, narrow room to where the Judge and Lawton sat huddled together in the far corner, no doubt gossiping about local politics and commiserating with each other over being unable to light up their after-dinner cigars. I was getting a little itchy myself and had sought temporary relief for my cravings by working on a piece of nicotine-replacement gum.

"That stuff work?" Red asked with just a trace of amusement, breaking the spell.

"Sort of. At least it takes the edge off until I can get access to the real thing." I picked at an imaginary thread on my black trousers, not for the first time wondering what people who didn't smoke did with their hands.

"Well, your restraint is admirable. I know how difficult it must be for you, and the kids and I appreciate it."

"Setting a good example seems to me to be a giant pain in the butt. However do parents stand it on a day-to-day basis?"

Red laughed. "I use a tried and true maxim: 'Do as I say, not as I do.' I suppose now you're going to tell me who said it."

"Isn't that funny? It's a common enough saying, and I have no clue. I'll have to look it up." I reached for my teacup on the octagonal drum table next to my chair, then turned to my brother-in-law, lowering my voice. "Red, what's the deal with Sarah? It's so unlike her to relinquish the kids on a holiday. How come they didn't go to her parents' house in Hampton?"

He shifted uncomfortably in his chair and ran his hands through his close-cropped hair. "I'm damned if I know. It came right out of nowhere. She called last night and asked if I could take them. It seems her folks are off on a cruise this week, celebrating their anniversary. I guess all the kids chipped in to get it for them."

"But surely that's been planned for months. Why would she suddenly need you to take them? She could have gone to her sister's or any number of friends if she didn't want to cook dinner."

"I know. That's what I asked her when she called. All she'd say is that something had come up and could I bring them here with me. Thank God Lavinia said it was okay, or I don't know what I would have done with them."

"Let's take a walk," I said, the overpowering need for a cigarette finally breaking through my defenses.

We stopped to retrieve our coats and my bag from the guest closet. In the kitchen we could hear the clatter of pans and low conversation as Lavinia directed the temporary girl she'd hired to help with the massive cleanup of the dozens of dirty dishes and vast quantities of leftovers. I stuck my head in the door to tell her where we were going.

"Fresh air, my foot," she muttered after me. "You need to be givin' up those nasty things, Lydia Baynard Simpson, you hear me?"

We trotted down the narrow front stairway. A stiff wind off the Sound struck us full in the face as we turned the corner of the house, so we retraced our steps and headed off down the rutted, muddy avenue of oaks. I exhaled gratefully as I got the cigarette alight. "So tell me what's really bothering you about Sarah."

Next to me, hands stuffed in the pockets of his brown leather jacket, Red's long stride halted momentarily, then resumed. "I don't know what you mean," he said.

"Cut the crap, Tanner. There's more to this than your ex-wife just taking it into her head to have a day off from mothering. Look, you've gotten stuck lately bailing me out of trouble of one kind or another on a fairly regular basis." I glanced quickly over at his dear, familiar face, partially concealed by the upturned collar of his jacket. "Let me help you, for a change, okay?"

He was a long time answering. "You're right," he said finally, stopping in the middle of the road to face me. "There's something going on I don't like, and I don't know what the hell I can do about it."

"Tell me."

"It's a guy. A man Sarah's been seeing."

I could almost have guessed it. "And what? You don't approve? I know this divorce wasn't exactly your idea, Red, but Sarah's single now and—"

"Don't lecture me about my ex-wife's right to a social life, okay? It's not that. It's the guy himself. She won't tell me anything about him, not even his name, and neither will the kids. She's sworn them to silence. I can't force them to break a promise to their mother, but I don't like the idea she's enlisting them in whatever game she's playing. If there's nothing wrong with the guy, why is she being so secretive?"

Such actions seemed so unlike the sweet, devoted Sarah I remembered that I had a hard time reconciling Red's account with my own experience of her, and said so.

"Imagine how I feel," he countered as we reached the end of the road and turned back toward Presqu'isle. We walked a long way in silence before he spoke again. "You know what I really think? I think this guy's got a record, and she's afraid that if she tells me his name, I'll check him out. Officially, I mean."

The same thought had crossed my mind, but I hadn't wanted to burden him with it. "Maybe he's someone you know, and Sarah's afraid it would be awkward."

"It's more than that. But one thing's for certain."

"What's that?"

"She took off somewhere with him today without giving a damn about where her own children were going to have Thanksgiving dinner." We paused at the foot of the steps, and I looked up into the concerned face of my brother-in-law. "And anyone who can have that kind of effect on a person as level-headed as Sarah, scares the hell out of me."

CHAPTER
ELEVEN

The party broke up shortly after our return. I dropped Miss Addie off at The Cedars, escorting her personally up to her apartment where I helped her stow the "meals" Lavinia had prepared for the older folks to take home with them. At a little before nine o'clock I lumbered up my own front steps laden with enough leftovers to last me well into December.

On the porch, Mr. Bones greeted me with a yowl of protest at having been left outside to fend for himself since early that morning. On this annual tribute to excess and gluttony, he had been reduced to scavenging among the local rodent population, and he let me know he wasn't happy about it. He was somewhat mollified when I emptied the container of chopped turkey gizzards and gravy into his bowl.

It took me less than five minutes to free myself from my holiday clothes and pull on my favorite gray sweats. The house seemed chilly, so I built a fire and added a thick pair of socks to my at-home ensemble. I put the kettle on, then rooted in the deep side drawer of the built-in desk until I found the road maps. I noticed they were all outdated as I unfolded the South Carolina one and spread it out on the counter, but I didn't think the roads I wanted to use had probably changed much in the last ten years. Or maybe even the last fifty. I carried the steaming mug, the maps, and the phone back into the great room where I settled into a corner of the sofa with a light cotton blanket tucked around my legs.

I located Toccoa, just inside the Georgia border, then ran my finger back into my home state, moving southeast along thin, gray lines until I came to Honea Path, halfway between Anderson and Greenwood. I'd head there first, I decided, see what I could discover from my Aunt Eliza about Mercer Mary Prescott. The postmark on the genealogy my cousin had been carrying seemed to link the two of them, though just how I hadn't yet figured out. Regardless, it wouldn't hurt to have as much ammunition as possible in case Erik Whiteside's deduction proved accurate, and our little fugitive was in fact holed up with her old foster family.

As I refolded the map, a blob of pale orange just below Augusta caught my eye. It was labeled *Department of Energy . . . Savannah River Site*. This had to be where Mercer was first arrested with her nuclear protest friends, I thought. On closer inspection, it looked as if Route 125 passed through the heart of the facility. I found it hard to believe they let ordinary citizens drive in an area once involved in the production of atomic bombs, but that's certainly what it looked like. I could check that out, then head toward Aiken and on to my aunt's house without even going out of my way. Perhaps I could . . .

I didn't even realize I was drowsing until the telephone jangled next to my ear, and the cat leaped up from where he had draped himself across my feet. My mumbled "Hello?" was swallowed in a barely stifled yawn.

"*Allô? C'est toi?*" His voice, though soft, sounded strong, almost back to normal.

Darnay!

A million questions whirled through my head: *Where are you? How are you? Why haven't you called? How could you just leave me hanging like this for weeks, not knowing if you were alive or dead?*

I asked none of them. I simply replied, "Of course it's me. Who were you expecting?"

That stopped him, but just for a moment. "Perhaps that infernal machine of yours that tantalizes with your voice, then rewards with only silence."

"You've called before? Why didn't you leave a message?"

I tried to keep it from sounding like an accusation, but my joy at hearing his voice was fast being replaced with anger. He had been whisked away from me, only to disappear into the shadowy world of his masters. One brief phone call, my only confirmation that he had survived, and then—nothing. I had pushed his face, his devastating smile, the feel of his hands on my skin, to a deep recess of my mind where the agonizing uncertainty of it wouldn't gnaw at me constantly. The effort had been only marginally successful.

My question hung unanswered for a long moment, so I tried another. "How are you feeling?"

Safer ground. "I am much improved. The result, no doubt, of what I believe you Americans call the 'home cooking', *non*?"

It took a moment to register, and I felt the hard knot of my anger dissolve "You're home? From the hospital? Oh, Alain, that's wonderful! When? Where? I mean, I don't even know—"

"Easy now," he said, laughing. "All will be revealed in due time, *ma petite*."

I loved it when he called me his "little one," especially since I was nearly as tall as he. I pictured him that night aboard ship, tanned and fit, his steel-blue eyes softening as he bent his face to mine. It was such a relief to be able to release my last memory of him in the cottage: pale, limp . . .

I opened my mouth to tell him I was coming, that I could be there in twenty-four hours. A dozen jumbled thoughts, the most prominent of which was that I hadn't yet been asked, raced through my mind. "Can you at least tell me where you are?"

His hesitation gave me the answer before he did. "Not yet, Bay." He sensed more questions and moved to forestall them. "You must understand. It is the nature of my business."

"I realize that, but—"

"Listen to me now. For years I worked undercover."

"I know all that, you told—"

"Quit interrupting, my darling, and let me finish. We have only a little time."

"I'm sorry. Go ahead."

"*Bien*. I am retiring. Officially, this time."

"When?"

"A few weeks, perhaps less." I heard mumbled voices in the background and wondered who was with him. And if it was because of these people that he seemed so hesitant to speak openly of his plans. "I must go now," he said.

"Wait! This retirement . . . it's for good? They'll really let you go?"

Alain Darnay heard all the unasked questions and answered them with one of his own. "Do you have any warm clothes, *ma petite*?"

"Warm clothes? Of course, but I don't—"

"Paris at Christmas can be quite chilly. *Au revoir*," he whispered, as the connection was broken.

I built up the fire then, more for comfort than for warmth. Mesmerized by the flames, I let my thoughts float through time: back, to the night Rob and I had made love on the sand inside the shell of this house, with a slice of moon just visible through the open beams; to the present and Red, to the need and anger that flashed in his eyes whenever they fastened on mine; and ahead, to a little girl in black patent shoes, with my eyes and Darnay's chin.

I flipped the cigarette I didn't remember lighting into the fire as Mr. Bones arched and stretched and trotted off to the kitchen. Nothing would be resolved so long as the Atlantic Ocean and the paranoia of Darnay's employers separated us. Speculation was useless.

I rose and poked the fire down to scattered, glowing embers, then carried my tea things to the sink. In the bedroom, I packed a small case with what I thought I might need for a few days. It was bound to be colder in the upstate, so I went heavy on the slacks and sweaters. If I needed anything fancier, I could always pick something up. It had been a while since I'd treated myself to a genuine shopping spree, and Atlanta wasn't that far from anywhere I planned to be.

I set my alarm for six. If I timed it right, I could arrive on my aunt's doorstep just as she was about to sit down to lunch. No self-respecting Southern gentlewoman would even contemplate not inviting her husband's niece to join her.

I fell asleep wondering if my long, camel's hair coat would be warm enough for Paris at Christmastime.

Early morning rush-hour traffic crawled by on the opposite side of the divided highway as I sped along, unimpeded, over the bridges and off Hilton Head Island. Every time I traveled U.S. 278, I marveled at the explosion of development which had occurred over the past few years. Where once pristine stands of pines and hardwoods had stretched uninterrupted for mile after mile, now sprawling auto dealerships, giant home improvement centers, and superstores vied for attention with banks, office buildings, and assisted living compounds. In many areas, the only green came from glimpses of the lush fairways of the newest Arnold Palmer- or Jack Nicklaus-designed golf courses, most surrounded by enclaves of huge, ridiculously expensive homes.

As I bypassed the entrance to I-95 and turned instead toward Hardeeville, I wondered how the natives of the Lowcountry—the Gullah and their descendants—viewed all this expansion. I couldn't help but believe that most of them, despite the increase in jobs and prosperity, harbored at least a tiny bit of nostalgia for the days when they towed cows behind their boats as they rowed over to Hilton Head to tend their fields of tomatoes and melons.

I stopped at a little diner in Estill just as the sun broke through the thin overcast which had followed me since I'd set out shortly after six-thirty. Over fried eggs and grits I studied the map. I'd passed the turnoff to the federal detention facility just before entering the town proper. An involuntary shudder rippled over my shoulders as the image of Buddy Slade popped unbidden into my head. Though Red had assured me there was a warrant out for his arrest for parole violation and menacing, I could almost guarantee that his apprehension wasn't at the top of any law enforcement agency's list of priorities.

I smiled at the chubby waitress who set another pot of hot water on the table and cleared away my empty plate. I hadn't really given much thought to *why* Buddy Slade was willing to risk being sent back to prison on the off-chance I might know the whereabouts of his wife. I leaned back against the cracked red leatherette of the booth and contemplated the possibilities. It could simply be an ex-con's natural desire to reunite with his family, though somehow I couldn't see the not too bright Buddy as a sentimental kind of guy. No, I decided as I dropped a few bills on the check, it was more likely that Mercer had crossed her charming husband in some way, and he was looking for revenge.

After a quick stop at the ladies' room, I got back on the road. A few miles north I slowed gratefully so the tractor-trailer I'd been stuck behind could take the turnoff for Hampton. The name brought Red's ex-wife to mind.

What is she up to? I wondered as I approached Allendale and the junction of the road to the Savannah River Site.

Despite our relative proximity and the closeness the brothers had always shared, the four of us had never socialized much except for family gatherings at holidays and the occasional dinner at each other's homes. I knew it sounded snooty, but we hadn't moved in the same circles. After all, I told myself, they were busy producing and raising Elinor and Scotty, and their friends tended to be Red's fellow police officers and ex-Marine buddies, most with young families. Sarah's somewhat eclectic group of acquaintances included those she met through the wide variety of causes she supported. Anyone seeking a diligent worker for a worthy endeavor, especially one involved with children's or conservation issues, had to look no farther than Sarah Jane Tanner.

Which is what makes her uncharacteristic behavior of yesterday doubly perturbing, I thought, easing through the stoplight next to the railroad tracks and onto Route 125. *And none of your business*, I concluded, finally able to give my high-powered sports car her head as we left the town behind, and the speed limit jumped back up to fifty-five.

The two-lane road wound through open, hilly countryside with small farms and fields and an occasional orchard providing the scenery. Traffic was nearly nonexistent on this second day of the long, holiday weekend. Passing stretches of dense woodlands, I noticed a faint blush of gold and red fading across the tops of the deciduous trees. Our autumn foliage bears no resemblance whatsoever to the spectacular display which erupts in the foothills of the Smokies a couple of hundred miles to the north, but we do manage a little color to remind us of the change of seasons. It is a great part of the charm and lure of the Lowcountry that fall arrives late, spring bursts forth well ahead of schedule, and winter is only a rumor.

With both windows rolled down, the pungent scents of pine, manure, and newly turned earth were carried to me on a warm, soft breeze. I had just about decided to pull over and put the top down when I rounded a long, sweeping bend, and the stark white gates and guardhouses of the Savannah River Site suddenly barred my path.

I braked, expecting a young, crew-cut soldier with an M-16 slung across his shoulder to step out and challenge me. It took a few seconds for me to realize that the arms of the gates were permanently raised and the checkpoint unmanned. Amid a flurry of signs I couldn't possibly have read unless I came to a complete stop, I rolled through the entrance.

The two-lane blacktop road was well maintained. The woodlands I passed through looked not much different from those outside the facility, except for the lack of any sign of human habitation. At a sedate forty-five miles an hour I would have had plenty of opportunity to study the landscape if there had been anything to see. Every mile or so a sign announced that stopping was strictly prohibited, though why anyone would want to escaped me.

About ten minutes in I noticed a flash of blue interrupting the unbroken green of the forest. It proved to be a large billboard with faded yellow lettering: DON'T BE LAX! REPORT SUSPICIOUS ACTS! That had to be a holdover from the nuclear weapons days, I thought. Surely there was nothing going on here now to warrant this loose-lips-sink-ships admonition.

When I came upon the set of overhead pipes, I gave some thought to revising that conclusion. Large in diameter and dazzlingly white against the clear sweep of the sky, they erupted from a cut on either side of the road, crossed over, and disappeared again into the trees. It was the kind of swath cleared for power lines and seemed to follow the path of a sluggish stream choked with algae.

I'm ashamed to admit that my heart rate doubled as I approached this probably innocuous piece of the facility's infrastructure. I blame it on Rob and his fascination with old, early fifties horror movies. He'd collected dozens of the B-grade, black-and-white videos over the years, and we'd spent many a stormy weekend at the beach curled up with popcorn watching the good guys wipe out every irradiated mutation the mind of Hollywood could conceive of. I can hardly be blamed, then, for conjuring up images of huge scaly creatures slithering from the depths of that slimy stream or of an army of crazed, elephant-sized ants suddenly exploding from the tree line.

I closed my eyes as I passed beneath the pipes.

A second later I was still motoring down a quiet country road on the way to my aunt's house for lunch. I had heard no ominous hum, smelled no noxious fumes, and hair had not begun to grow on the backs of my knuckles. I laughed out loud at my own absurdity.

Twice I obeyed large orange signs, slowing to thirty-five as I approached an intersection. A quick glance revealed a wide roadway leading to a checkpoint—manned by uniformed men in both instances—and protected by chain-link fence topped with barbed wire. At one, a huge flatbed truck, its cargo concealed beneath a heavy tarp, awaited admittance. I had a brief impression of sprawling buildings beyond the gates, but not enough time to discern any details before trees once again surrounded me.

I estimated I had been inside the Savannah River Site for about twenty minutes and should be nearing the northern perimeter, when I suddenly saw brake lights flash in front of me. Until then I had encountered only a few other vehicles, all going in the opposite direction. I slowed behind a massive Ford Expedition with Mississippi license plates and a bumper sticker which read PROUD PARENTS OF AN HONOR STUDENT AT JACKSON MIDDLE. I wondered if it was this little paragon who was making obscene gestures at me through the back window.

I moved out a little into the left lane to see if I could spot what the holdup was. Ahead on the opposite shoulder a paramedic unit, its back doors standing open, was pulled up in front of a police cruiser. The pulsing blue of the light bar cast eerie flashes across the face of the trooper who held southbound traffic at bay with his left hand while motioning for the rest of us to keep moving. As we crawled by I could see no signs of an accident, only a brief glimpse of two uniformed men struggling to lift something from the tall grass bordering the tree line.

The honor student waved his middle finger at me as he and his proud parents roared off, but my mind was too filled with what I had just seen to take much notice. It didn't take a rocket scientist—or a nuclear physicist—to figure out that these guys wouldn't be out here to dispose of a dead deer. I was almost certain the black, shiny burden which had bowed the backs of the paramedics was a body bag.

I made my way through several small towns, around Aiken with its wonderful horse farms and numerous golf course complexes reminiscent of Hilton Head, and finally decided on a pit stop in Edgefield. I couldn't remember the last time I had been in this jewel of the old South, but I could detect no coarsening of its serene, antebellum facade except for the new McDonald's hunkered down right across the highway from the Hardee's on the way into the village.

I pulled up in one of the parking spaces surrounding the green in the town center dominated by the architectural splendor of the white-columned, brick courthouse. Beside the requisite memorial to the brave lads of the Confederacy, there was another one, obviously newer. I slung my bag over my shoulder and went to investigate. The life-sized statue memorialized Strom Thurmond, a native son whose tenure in the United States Senate had continued until he was nearly a hundred years old. He was also a former governor of South Carolina, a distinction he shared with nine other men who had either been born or had lived at one time in Edgefield.

I crossed the square to a small, narrow drugstore squeezed in between two deserted storefronts, their dirty windows revealing cracked wooden floors and the abandoned litter of their former occupants. I wound my way through tightly packed shelves crammed with cold remedies, hair coloring, and all the other necessities of modern life. I bought a Snickers bar and asked the obviously bored cashier where I might find a pay phone.

"Around the corner," she said, pointing to her left, "about a block, in front of Miss Dora's. If it's working."

I accepted my change and let her get back to the new issue of *Soap Opera Digest* spread out on the counter.

Few people were out and about on what had turned into a delightful, late fall morning. I supposed anyone interested in participating in what is always billed as the busiest shopping day of the year would be found at whatever giant mall serviced Edgefield and the surrounding towns. Besides, almost every other building I passed sat forlorn and empty. I spotted the booth ahead and dug my calling card out of my bag. If the number of public telephones continued to dwindle, I supposed I'd be forced to acquire a mobile one, much as I hated the idea.

Miss Dora's proved to be an old-fashioned tea shop complete with tins of Earl Grey and Darjeeling, along with some luscious looking pastries, displayed in the gingham-decked front window. I calculated it had been a couple of hours since breakfast, more than enough time ago to warrant a little midmorning snack. I dropped the phone card in the pocket of my tan gabardine slacks and pulled open the wooden door. A collection of tiny bells fastened to the top jingled as it closed behind me.

The yellow-checked window theme was carried inside, and the walls were hung with framed samplers of the kind young girls of centuries gone by were expected to produce as evidence of their embroidery skills. "God helps those who help themselves," the one closest to me announced in ornate letters surrounded by bunches of rose-shaded tulips worked in tiny, perfect stitches.

Amen, sister, I thought, smiling.

As I pulled out the wooden ice cream chair, a voice from the back called, "With you in a tic!"

The woman who appeared a few moments later couldn't have been less like the Miss-Jane-Marple-type I had conjured up in my mind as the probable proprietress of this dainty enterprise. Tall and rail-thin, she wore a baggy red sweater which hung almost to her knees, over black leggings and scuffed clogs. Her nearly white hair was cropped close to her head in a gamin-cut, and her face, devoid of makeup, wore its laugh lines and crow's-feet with unadorned pride.

"Oops, sorry," she said with just a trace of an accent I couldn't immediately identify, "you're not one of my locals. Regulars usually just help themselves. What can I get you?"

"May I see a menu?"

"Oh, Lord, dear, we don't have menus. Name a tea, and I probably have it. Or I can surprise you. Only thing is, it'll take some time. I have to brew it properly, and that can't be rushed. But then, nothing worthwhile can, eh? As for goodies, the scavengers haven't left us much. A couple of croissants, some beignets, and a cherry-cheese Danish I wouldn't recommend. Ed is always a little heavy-handed when it comes to his Danish. Just can't seem to restrain himself, but then men so seldom can, don't you find?" She cocked her head to one side, birdlike, awaiting my response.

"What's a beignet?" I asked, avoiding involvement in the social commentary.

"French fritter," came the prompt reply, "famous in New Orleans. Sometimes filled, today not. Just a little powdered sugar—for presentation, as they say. And English Breakfast, I think. Makes a nice contrast. I'll get the pot warming."

I shook my head. If I'd decided on a croissant, I was apparently out of luck. "I'm going outside to use the phone," I called over the sound of running water. "Be right back."

"Take your time."

I retrieved my card and the slip of paper on which I'd copied down Aunt Eliza's number from my pocket. I'd decided it was pretty rude to drop in *totally* unexpectedly, especially given my aunt's advanced years. Although I remembered her as one of those storied women of the South—all honey and magnolias on the outside, tough as old leather underneath—I'd still feel better giving her a little advance warning.

After four rings, the machine clicked on. I left the lie I'd been practicing, the one about being in the area and deciding on the spur of the moment to stop by, adding that it would be somewhere around twelve-thirty by the time I got to Honea Path.

I glanced into the tea shop at my still-empty table and decided I had time for a quick check with the hospital. I dialed the room directly and waited through more than a dozen rings before hanging up. Maybe they had taken her out for therapy or some more tests. Again I punched in my string of access codes, then the switchboard number. The nurse at the floor station was no one I knew, so she refused to answer my questions. All I got was the standard "resting comfortably" crap they routinely handed out to nosy non-relatives.

I smoked half a cigarette, pacing up and down in front of the phone booth before I saw Miss Dora beckon to me through the window. Inside on my table I found a delicate, bone china cup and saucer, decorated with violets, and a matching teapot covered loosely with a lavender knitted cozy. The beignets were warm and yeasty and seemed to dissolve in my mouth. I added a thin slice of lemon to the steaming tea and sipped cautiously.

"Mind if I join you?"

Her voice at my elbow startled me into sloshing a little English Breakfast onto the saucer. "Please," I said, and she pulled out the chair opposite me.

She'd brought her own cup, actually a rather ugly green mug with *G.R.I.T.S.* enameled in yellow, and the unmistakable deep aroma of coffee drifting from it. I made no comment, but she answered the question she apparently read on my face. "I can't stand tea. My mum made me drink gallons of it as a kid. And the mug was a gag gift. Know what it stands for?"

"Girls Raised In The South," I said. "I am one."

"Well, I'm not. Toronto. Still be there if my great-aunt hadn't left me her house and this shop in her will."

"So you're not Miss Dora?"

Her deep laugh seemed way too robust for her skinny frame.

"Lord, no! Louise Cameron."

"Bay Tanner." We shook hands awkwardly across the tiny table.

"You're here about our local mystery, I suppose. What paper are you with?" She added more cream to her coffee and regarded me with an intense curiosity which made me slightly uncomfortable.

"Sorry," I said, "I have no idea what you're talking about. I'm just passing through. What's your local mystery?"

"Oh, dear, I feel the fool! I suppose it's terribly provincial of us to expect that our little problems merit worldwide attention. Although there have been several journalists in our fair hamlet lately. From Columbia and Raleigh and one, I think, from Atlanta. I guess it's because it's connected to the old bomb plant."

That got my attention. I refilled my teacup and said in what I hoped was an offhand manner, "That would be the Savannah River Site? Does it involve theft or something?"

Louise Cameron shook her head. "No, it's one of their security people. Local chap gone missing. Couple of weeks now. Right after that lot created the ruckus down there. Some folks think he might have run off with them."

Sudden images of Mercer Mary Prescott, Buddy Slade, and a shiny black body bag turned the yeasty beignets to a glutinous lump in the bottom of my stomach.

CHAPTER TWELVE

If I had been dropped down into the center of Honea Path, South Carolina, with no prior knowledge of where I was supposed to be, I never would have recognized the place. My childhood memories, sketchy as they had become, were of a quaint village not much changed since its Civil War days, except for the necessary concessions to electricity and automobiles.

Approaching from the southeast, I passed a sprawling Bi-Lo supermarket on the left, just across the two-lane highway from a series of shops and stores, none of them recent additions, but all new since my last visit. I bumped across the railroad tracks—the town's original reason for existence—and pulled up at the stoplight, completely disoriented. The block-long main street stretched off to my right, and I could tell even at a cursory glance that many of the stores stood empty. Only a few cars occupied the parking places, and I saw not a single person on the sidewalks.

When the light changed, I eased down the hill, looking for the florist shop. It was the only landmark I truly recalled with any clarity. Thankfully it was still there—though completely rebuilt and modernized—just past an outdated drive-thru bank. I turned right and followed the narrow lane around a sharp bend.

It had to be Uncle Rupert and Aunt Eliza's place, this huge Victorian monstrosity which stood directly in my path, towering over its neighbors, and yet nothing about it seemed familiar. My child's eye pictured a rolling lawn, croquet wickets set up on one end, a tiny gazebo crouched amid a riot of flowers at the other. And where were the trees? I remembered one in particular, a venerable live oak whose snaking limbs nearly brushed the ground. It had provided the ideal place for a solitary child to conceal herself behind a swaying curtain of Spanish moss and eavesdrop on her elders.

I didn't see a driveway, just a pattern of wear on the flattened grass, leading to what appeared to be the side of the house. I pulled up behind a battered Ford station wagon, its once yellow finish faded almost to white against the peeling, fake wood paneling along its doors. I uncoiled myself from the Z3, stretching as I surveyed the devastation time had wrought on the picture of grace and beauty I had stored away in my memory more than twenty years before.

The town seemed to have grown up around the house. It stood now on a treeless lot surrounded by concrete and asphalt, a discount store and its sparsely tenanted parking area almost abutting what I remembered as a thick hedge of holly running along the front of the property. The single vestige of green still remaining was a tangled mass of some thick-stemmed shrubbery covering the foundation and threatening to engulf the first-floor windows, the only ones in the house not boarded up. Apparently my aunt had abandoned the upper floors.

I stood at the bottom of uneven concrete block steps and rapped loudly on the warped screen door.

Elizabeth Baynard peered out cautiously, then her thin, wrinkled face broke into a welcoming smile. "Lydia! Oh, my dear, how wonderful! I thought at first your message must be some kind of cruel hoax, but here you are at last! Come in, come in." She waved clawlike fingers in my direction as she pulled open the heavy inside door.

I stepped directly into a kitchen that obviously hadn't been updated for thirty years. But the faded linoleum shone with recent waxing, and the avocado-green appliances sparkled. A single light in the hood over the range did little to dispel the interior gloom, compounded by the encroachment of the shiny-leafed shrubs against the only window. It took a moment for me to realize that the rhythmic tap-tap-tap was the sound of my aunt's cane as she disappeared through the doorway ahead of me.

I followed her into another dim room which suddenly sprang to life as she touched a light switch, leaving me to gasp at the perfect jewel of a parlor in which not a piece of bric-a-brac seemed to have been moved since my last visit. I turned at my aunt's childlike giggle and tried not to show my dismay.

I found her face several inches below where I had auto-matically sought it, tilted up at an impossible angle so that she could gauge my reaction. The dowager's hump of osteoporosis had bowed her head until her chin nearly rested on her bony chest. I had remembered her as a woman of probably moderate height, thin even then, but with an erect posture which made her seem tall to my childish eyes. It was a shock to recognize the countenance of that calm, poised matron in this bent and shriveled body. Still, the dance remained in her bright blue eyes, magnified behind rimless glasses.

"Sit down, my dear," she said, lowering herself painfully into a bentwood rocker, "there, on the loveseat. It was your favorite place to curl up, do you recall? And there's Ulysses, just where he was the last time you were here."

The crystal unicorn, which I had named on a rainy afternoon during one of my mother's infrequent "duty" visits, still caught the light of the shaded lamps and reflected it back in a kaleidoscope of ever-changing colors.

I hesitated, and again my aunt's girlish laugh made me smile in response. "It's all right, Lydia. I think you're grown up enough now to be allowed to pick him up."

I held the tiny treasure, suddenly awash with memory and guilt. "Aunt Eliza, I'm sorry it's been so long. I have no excuse, none whatsoever. Our neglect of you—the Judge's and mine— has been . . . unforgivable." I felt hot tears dropping onto the hands which cradled the fragile creature.

"Oh, nonsense, child! After Rupert died, I never expected your mother to keep up the connection. She never really approved of me, you know." I started to protest, but she raised her knobby hand to forestall me. "It's all right. Truth of the matter is, I never quite approved of her either. Not very Christian of me, but there it is."

"I can understand that," I replied, digging a tissue out of my bag and trying to blow my leaking nose in a ladylike a manner. I felt like a great oaf in this little room crammed with glass and china ornaments. "I don't think I ever made it to the top of her hit parade myself."

"On the contrary, she was very proud of you, Lydia. As were we all. It's a shame she didn't live to see all you've accomplished. You're the image of her, did you know? Especially around the eyes, although your face is softer. There's a gentleness there I never saw in Emmaline. Despite the tragedy of your husband's death, I believe you have come to terms with your life much better than your mother ever did."

I was surprised she knew about Rob's murder and unsure how to reply, but a sharp rapping saved me the necessity.

"That will be Thomas with our lunch. Would you mind letting him in?"

I retraced my steps back into the kitchen just as a small, white-haired gentleman stuck his head around the door. "Oh, hello. You must be the niece. I'm Tom Wentworth, from Meals on Wheels."

"Hi! I'm Lydia Tanner." My aunt was never going to get used to calling me *Bay*, and there was no sense confusing everyone.

"Nice to meet you. Eliza called us earlier and asked if we could bring enough for two. I'm afraid it's only meatloaf today. With some more warning, I'm sure the ladies at the church could have whipped up something a little more festive."

"Meatloaf is my favorite," I lied.

Tom Wentworth moved around the kitchen with the ease of long familiarity, opening the foil-wrapped packages of food and distributing them onto blue-flowered plates he took from the cupboard. "There'll be iced tea in the fridge. Glasses to the right of the sink. I'll just take this into the dining room, get you ladies all set up."

"Fine." I wrestled ice cubes from an antiquated, metal tray and carried the filled glasses through the parlor and into a space which apparently served several functions for my physically disabled aunt. Another rocker sat in one corner in front of a nearly new television set with a floor lamp nearby. The dining area contained a round oak table where Tom had spread a cloth and arranged silver, napkins, and the serving dishes of food. He pulled out one of two matching chairs and assisted my aunt to her seat.

"No cheating now, Miss Eliza," he said from the doorway. "That's Ruth Travis's pecan pie, but you have to save it until after lunch. She told me to get your promise."

"You tell Ruth I thank her kindly, but remind her that I'm seventy-eight years old. If I want to eat dessert first, I will." The smile transformed my aunt's face, making it almost possible to forget her twisted spine and hunched neck. "Thank you, Thomas."

"You're welcome. I'll be back around three to clean up."

"No, need," I said quickly, "I'll be glad to take care of that."

"Great. Nice to have met you, Lydia."

"You, too."

I picked up the platter of meatloaf, one of the few foods in the world I truly loathe, and served myself a generous slab.

I thought I would have to work up to the subject of Mercer Mary Prescott. During the long drive, I had mentally written a brief, one-act play, with Aunt Eliza and me as the dramatis personae, in which I gently urged her toward revealing her connection to my fugitive, half fifth cousin. I had forgotten about the pace of life in quiet Southern towns, and the loneliness of old widow ladies.

"I must say, it's been quite an interesting year for me," my aunt remarked as she maneuvered the last flakes of piecrust onto her fork. She'd taken only meager portions of meat, mashed potatoes, and green beans, but had demolished the pie in record time.

"How so?" I gathered up the dishes and carried them out to the sink. "More tea?" I called from the kitchen.

"No, thank you, dear."

I helped my aunt from her chair and guided her back into the parlor to her bentwood rocker. With her feet settled onto a needlepoint-covered stool and her cane resting within easy reach, she answered my question. "Well, I don't get many visitors, as you can imagine. Oh, Tom, of course, and the ladies from the church. They keep me fed and looked after. I'm something of a project for them," she said with a twinkle. "My father was pastor here—at First Methodist, you know—for nearly fifty years, so they feel an obligation."

I had settled myself once more onto the faded loveseat. I resisted the urge, no doubt fueled by childhood memory, to kick off my shoes and tuck my feet up under me.

"Where was I? Oh, yes, visitors," my aunt continued. "Well, a few months ago I got a call from another young woman, a cousin or some such. She was researching the Tattnalls and the Baynards, she said, and wondered if I had any old papers. Well, of course I told her your mother had inherited Presqu'isle, and that she probably had whatever family records survived."

Her words recalled the image of twine-bound pages slipping from the Judge's lap the night we'd sprung Mercer from jail.

Hadn't he said Lavinia retrieved them for him from the attic? I was aware that the entire upper floor of the house on St. Helena was taken up with storage. Why had I never explored it? I didn't remember ever having the slightest curiosity, even as a child, about what lurked up there in the dust.

I knew without asking that Aunt Eliza would not approve of my smoking, especially in the airless parlor, so I slipped a piece of gum from my bag, careful not to disrupt the flow of her reminiscences. Hopefully she would be getting to the good part soon.

"But I did tell her that your Uncle Rupert had done some dabbling in genealogical research. While he was still teaching, we used to spend our weekends traveling around the countryside trying to pinpoint the location of some of the old family homesteads. Most of your ancestors came from this area, did you know that? The Chases, the Perrys, and the Tattnalls all had holdings in this part of the state. Houses like Presqu'isle were only used when the ladies wanted to get away from the plantation for a while or when the men needed to consult with their cotton factors in Beaufort or Savannah." She sighed gently. "Rupert did love history. I don't know how many times I told him he should have been teaching that instead of mathematics. He spent hours poring over the few documents and mementos his mother left him. By the time he passed away, he had compiled a fairly extensive family tree, along with some quite good maps."

I sneaked a look at my watch. I figured I had at least another two hours of driving to reach Toccoa, and I'd still have to find someplace to stay once I got there. I'd hoped to make it before dark, but it was already well after two o'clock. Still, I'd come to find out about Mercer Mary Prescott, about what it was she wanted from my family and me. I just hadn't planned on its taking the entire afternoon. "So you invited her to come and look at his papers?" I prodded.

"Of course I did no such thing! I may be elderly, Lydia, but I'm not totally lacking in common sense. Why, she could have been a thief, or one of those despicable people who charm their way into the houses of doddering old fools and cheat them out of all their money."

I blushed, properly chastised.

"No, I asked her some questions about her own family, wrote

it all down, then took her address. I did think it strange she used her workplace, some clinic in Columbia, but then perhaps she was only being cautious as well. At any rate, I checked out her information against the papers in Rupert's old desk, and satisfied myself that she was who she said she was. Then I had Tom make copies of the documents for me, and I mailed them to her."

"Very wise of you, Aunt Eliza," I said, again checking my watch.

This time she noticed. "You're not thinking of leaving, are you Lydia? Not so soon!"

The disappointment I heard in her voice was not the polite regret of a hostess. My aunt seemed genuinely stricken at the thought of my going.

"Oh, not just yet," I lied, "although I do have to be somewhere by later this evening. Go ahead with your story." I smiled brightly, hoping to banish both my guilt and her fear.

"Well, there's not much more to tell," she replied, much of the enthusiasm gone from her face. "She wrote back, thanking me. Such a sweet letter, really. I invited her to tea."

I tried to picture Mercer Mary Prescott, in her army fatigues and adhesive-taped glasses, perched stiffly on the edge of this loveseat, a fragile teacup balanced on the ripped-out knee of her jeans. "And how did that go?"

"We had a delightful afternoon. Mercer is very shy, and quite unlike most of the young people I've come in contact with recently. She had on the prettiest little yellow dress. I didn't think girls these days even knew what proper attire was."

Ah, I thought, *good call, Merce.* I should have guessed from my recent experience with my cousin that she had more sense than to show up for tea looking like a militia reject. The girl was proving to have a few more layers than I had originally given her credit for.

"Ruth and the ladies provided a quite respectable table, complete with finger sandwiches and petits fours. We talked at length about Rupert and your mother and Presqu'isle. She was particularly interested in the stories about Perdition."

"Perdition? What's that?"

The old woman brought a lace-edged handkerchief to her mouth and covered a dainty sneeze. The unexpected jolt to her damaged spine and neck contorted her sagging face in a paroxysm of pain.

"Aunt Eliza? What is it? Can I get you something?" I knelt in front of her and tried to take her thin hand, but it was locked onto the arm of the rocker. I could feel the effort it was costing her not to cry out. "Please! Tell me what to do. Should I call someone?"

I heard the slow exhalation of her breath and felt her fingers relax. Apparently the spasm had passed.

"I'm sorry, Lydia," she finally said, using the twisted handkerchief to dab at the beads of sweat which had popped out along her upper lip. "Usually I manage quite well. But sometimes a cough—or even a sneeze—can just tie me up into knots. I'm fine now, really."

"Let me get you a glass of water. Do you have medication for the pain?"

"No, dear, don't trouble yourself. I just need to lie down for a little while. It relieves the pressure. Will you help me?"

In the room where we'd had our lunch, I pulled the flowered throw from the daybed tucked into the far corner, and rearranged the pillows. I bent and slipped off my aunt's shoes, then stood back as she settled herself onto her side, her knees drawn up as much as age and arthritis would allow. Her thin body formed a wizened letter **C** in the center of the soft yellow sheet. Gently I draped the coverlet over her.

"You'll stay a while, won't you, Lydia? I'll just have a quick nap, and I'll be right as rain again."

What could I say? *No, sorry, Aunt Eliza, now that I've completely exhausted you with my thoughtless, selfish visit . . . now that I've found out how Mercer Mary Prescott insinuated herself into your house and convinced you to provide her with information about our family . . . I think I'll just leave you here alone and trot on off to stick my nose into someone else's business for a while. Thanks for lunch. See you in another twenty years or so.*

"Of course," I said, garnering myself an undeserved smile as my aunt murmured, "Good . . ." and drifted off to sleep.

I washed and dried the dishes and returned the uneaten food to one of the Styrofoam containers it had been delivered in. The refrigerator held little beyond milk, orange juice, and half a loaf of whole wheat bread. I refilled the ice cube trays, smiling to myself as I replaced them in the freezer alongside one container of Rocky Road and another of Chocolate Almond Fudge.

A woman after my own heart.

I stepped out the kitchen door, shivering a little in the brisk breeze which had sprung up while I'd been indoors. The sun had disappeared behind a bank of gray clouds. I lit a cigarette and perched myself on the massive fender of the ancient Ford station wagon. Across the way, business had picked up at the Dollar Store, two cars and a rusty pickup now sitting with their noses practically in my aunt's rutted front yard.

What are you doing here, Tanner? I asked myself, rubbing the sleeves of my black cashmere sweater against the chill. I'd come for information and gotten emotionally tangled up—again. Lavinia. Miss Addie. Even Dolores, though she was not much older than I was. And now Aunt Elizabeth Baynard. I seemed to draw these surrogate mother figures to me like iron filings to a magnet. Hadn't I had enough trouble with the genuine article? Or was that the point? A good question for Neddie, when next we met.

I flipped the cigarette butt into the parking lot next door, not the least contrite for my littering. The whole town was littering my aunt's once magnificent home, and no one seemed to give a damn about *that*. A pile of dead, brown sycamore leaves skittered across the cracked asphalt as I turned back into the silent house to find a telephone.

CHAPTER
THIRTEEN

I spent the rest of the afternoon trying to extricate myself from Aunt Eliza. The telephone attached to the answering machine rested on a table right next to where she napped, so I wandered down the long hallway searching for another. I found it in what must once have been the library—an ancient black rotary squatting on the corner of Uncle Rupert's desk. The floor-to-ceiling shelves lay bare except for a thin coating of dust, and the heart pine floor creaked under my feet as I crossed to the cracked leather chair.

The desk itself was massive, its once golden oak patina worn dull from decades of use. I walked all the way around it, trailing my fingertips across the smooth finish, admiring the incredible workmanship now lost to an age of mass production. On the side farthest from the door I was surprised to find the surface cracked and blistered, almost as if someone had attempted to set the wonderful old piece on fire. I dropped into the creaking swivel chair and surveyed the raised credenza. Pigeonholes and tiny drawers with intricately wrought designs invited exploration for secret panels and hidden compartments. It didn't feel exactly like snooping as I leafed through my uncle's meticulously labeled files, arranged with a mathematician's eye for order and logical progression. I wished I could remember him. A pale re-creation of his domineering older sister, he seemed always to be hovering in the background of my sketchy recollections of our rare visits to Honea Path. I wondered if he ever resented the fact that, in spite of being the only son, he had failed to inherit Presqu'isle and the wealth and position which went with it.

I opened a folder, slightly out of line with the others as if it might have been carelessly replaced, and pulled out the originals of the family tree documents I'd found in Mercer Mary Prescott's duffel bag. Overhead I caught the muted squeak of old boards settling in the cooling night air, followed by the unmistakable skittering of small claws on wood. I wondered if the upper stories, closed off for God knew how long, had been taken over completely by mice and rats or other equally disgusting rodents. I shivered and returned to the papers spread out in front of me.

Maybe *because* of my mother's obsession with all this sort of thing, I'd never had much interest in my ancestors. But sitting there, in the heart of a strange house whose walls had sheltered generations of families, witnessed dozens of births—and deaths—I felt the first stirrings of curiosity about how *I* fit into this neatly arranged cascade of interconnected lines and boxes that delineated my history.

I don't know how long I sat there studying the charts of the descendants of Charles Morgan Robichoux, one of my French Huguenot progenitors. His marriage to Lucy Mercer apparently began the line which resulted in one of my half fifth cousin's given names. I don't remember switching on the gooseneck lamp. Its feeble light became immediately swallowed up in the vastness of the empty library, and I had to direct its beam directly onto the papers I was studying. I had just begun on the maps—faded, miniaturized reproductions from the huge plat books usually found in the musty storerooms of county courthouses—when the *tap, tap, tap* of my aunt's cane was followed by her high, thin voice.

"Lydia? Lydia, dear, where have you gotten to?"

"In here, Aunt Eliza," I called, hastily returning the scattered pages to the folder, and the folder to the drawer. "In the library." I stood, embarrassed at being caught going through my uncle's things, and moved quickly around to the far side of the desk. "I was just going to use the phone."

"Oh, gracious, that one hasn't worked in years," she laughed, shuffling into the room. "I just left it there because Rupert thought it looked more in keeping with the ambiance than one of those modern things with all the buttons." She tapped her way to the chair. "Come over here, Lydia. I want to show you some-thing."

The drawer she pulled open had completely escaped my notice, its seams so entwined with the intricacy of the carved pattern I hadn't seen it. "This old desk has lots of secrets," she said with a twinkle. "Your mother wanted it desperately, of course, but it's one of the few things his mother left specifically to Rupert. The men of the family had used it for generations, and your grandmother felt it should pass on through the male line." The gentle sigh reminded me that Aunt Eliza had outlived not only her husband, but both her children as well. Their death dates had been penciled in beneath their names on the family tree I'd just been studying. It was strange to think that I had had cousins, dead before I ever had an opportunity to know them in any meaningful way.

The bundle Aunt Eliza pulled from the narrow compartment smelled faintly of lavender and mildew and was held together by a frayed blue ribbon.

"What is it?" I asked.

"Letters. Rupert and I found them, shortly before he died, in this hidden drawer."

"Who wrote them?"

"Most of them are to Isabelle Chase, Isabelle Robichoux as she was, and a few are from her son and her husband. They both died in the Late Unpleasantness, you know. So sad. She and her twin daughters were the last ones to occupy Perdition House before they lost everything."

I smiled at her genteel euphemism for the Civil War. *The Late Unpleasantness* seemed so much more palatable than the reality of death and dismemberment which had destroyed the South and all the wealth and grace of its aristocracy. I remembered then that my aunt had mentioned how interested Mercer Mary Prescott had been in the stories surrounding Perdition. So it had been a house—a plantation, probably. Why would that have intrigued my cousin?

"Would you like to see them?" My aunt held out the letters, and I accepted them gingerly.

"You needn't be afraid. They've held up remarkably well. Even so, Mercer insisted on wearing her white cotton gloves when she handled them. I never thought I'd see a young woman in white gloves again. I swear, it quite took me back to my girlhood."

Mercer Mary Prescott in a dress and gloves? It was an image I couldn't square with my own brief experience with the child. This didn't sound like someone so bereft of resources she was forced to rummage for restaurant leavings in back alley garbage cans. Nor someone with the audacity and cunning to elude her police escort with such apparent ease. Nor again someone who had ever shared a bed with the oily Buddy Slade and his tattooed fingers. I renewed my hope that I was just a short span of time and distance from sitting my cousin down and dragging some straight answers out of her.

I perched on the corner of Uncle Rupert's desk and carefully unfolded the first sheet. The formal, slanted script and smooth flow of lines penned with ink dipped from an actual inkwell, hurtled me back a hundred and fifty years. The letter, obviously written in some haste, was signed *Dora*. The author urged "Belle" to take the greatest care, and to be on her guard against "ruffians, miscreants, and foragers" sent out in advance of the Union Army to secure provisions and generally lay waste to whatever stood in their path. She and her children were fleeing inland to Columbia and urged Belle to do the same before "Sherman's hordes descend like a plague of locusts to plunder and pillage our sacred homeland."

"Who were these women?" I asked my aunt who sat gazing up into the dark recesses of the twelve-foot high ceiling.

"Belle is Isabelle Chase and Dora is her older sister, Theodora Rutledge. It's all there in Rupert's papers."

"I take it she's referring to General William Tecumseh Sherman of the 'March to the Sea' fame. He ended up capturing Savannah, if I remember correctly, but spared it from destruction as a Christmas gift for Lincoln."

"So they say. The wildest tales flew around during the last months of the War. 'Sherman the Butcher' they called him. Some claimed that he roasted children alive on spits over his campfires. Nonsense, of course, but real news was impossible to come by, so every rumor became embellished and repeated as fact."

I opened another letter, this one dated "21 January 1865." "Dearest Mama," it began. I hadn't realized Aunt Eliza had risen from the chair until she spoke next to my shoulder. "That's the saddest one of all. Isabelle's last letter to her mother. She wrote it apparently not realizing the old lady had passed away some months before. Or perhaps the pressure of the War had unhinged her mind. Her husband was already dead, and her son dying in a prisoner of war camp in Ohio. At any rate, it was never posted."

I scanned the page, my eyes bright with unexpected tears.

21 January 1865

Dearest Mama,

This will be my last letter to you, though I know you shall not read it. Still, the need to share all with you remains as strong as in those first, frightening days of my marriage to Bennet.

We buried the last of Tattie's silver this morning. Mercer and Morgan helped Jubal dig the hole while I ripped up the last of my lawn petticoats to wrap the shrimp forks. Thank goodness the twins are still too young to regard this horrible War as anything other than an adventure, though it has been a part of their lives for almost as long as they can remember. If I close my eyes, I can see them now, fidgeting on the verandah while I said my last farewells to Bennet, their golden curls shining in the morning sun. The lacy ruffles on their pantaloons peeked out from under their hoop skirts as they pranced from foot to foot, anxious to be done with all the grownup folderol and be about their play. They were only four then, do you remember, Mama? How they have had to grow up!

We had such hopes that bright spring day, it fair breaks my heart to think on it. My dear Bennet kissed me once, then swung up into the saddle. "Home by Christmas," he said, with that calm assurance which always made you believe every word. Do you remember, Mama? Then he and Henry wheeled their horses and rode off down the drive. So like each other they looked that day, tall and proud and confident. Now both are gone, like so many others. Oh, yes, I've all but given up hope for Henry, too, my poor boy, shut up in that filthy Yankee prison in Ohio. I have not heard officially, you understand, but my letters have gone unanswered for months now.

But I must not dwell on sadness. Bennet would want me to be brave, for the girls as well as for our people, though only Jubal and Maudie have remained faithful. I expect they will abandon us, too, once the Yankees actually arrive, which should be sometime tomorrow or the next day, according to the Duprés negroes who passed by here last night on their way to join up with that butcher, Sherman. At least they had the decency to spare us the last of the turnips and corn, all we have left now from the fall harvest.

Oh, Mama, how could this have happened to us? Bennet was never the cruel slave master those horrid Northern newspapers depicted in their vile broadsides. He loved our people, cared for them as he did our own children. But there, enough. This is the last of the ink, and I must not waste it on self-pity and maundering. We have saved what we could, and the rest must be left to the murdering Yankee blue coats. I have cut down some of Henry's old things to fit the girls so none may guess their true gender. All of us, even Jubal, shed such tears as we chopped off their lovely, golden hair! But I must keep them safe, and one has heard such stories of the depravity of Sherman's foragers.

If we should not be spared, I pray that we shall meet our fate with the same proud spirit which burned so brightly in my brave husband and son. If that be so, I will be with you soon, dearest Mama, in that Land where dwell all who have loved God and served His wishes. Unto Him I commend myself and my children, and unto you I entrust the guardianship of our family's future.

Yr loving dtr,
Belle

That sounded to me as if Isabelle Chase were well aware of her mother's death, but I kept those thoughts to myself. Perhaps I needed to have read more of the documents in order to get a full appreciation and understanding of the situation.

But what women these had been! They had gone from pampered paragons of Southern femininity to slave masters, overseers, and farmers in a matter of months. That the defeated Confederates had anything at all to return to was a testament to their strength of will and iron determination. It seemed I came from pretty good stock after all.

A glance at my watch had sent me into a panic. *Nearly four-thirty!* No way could I make it to Toccoa before dark, which the fading light through the tall windows told me wasn't very far off. Aunt Eliza's invitation to stay was half-hearted at best, and I could tell without any further exploration of the echoing house that she had nowhere to put me. I would have to set out and find a motel not too far down the road. I was certain Honea Path had nothing to offer in the way of Holiday Inns or Best Westerns.

I offered to get her something for dinner, but she assured me she'd just pick at the lunch leftovers as she usually did. I also figured she'd probably have a little nibble from one or both of the ice cream cartons I'd seen in the freezer.

With sincere assurances that I'd see her again soon, I finally managed to ease my way out to the car and back it around into the narrow alleyway. I tooted the horn at the fading image of the frail, hunched woman waving dispiritedly at me from the concrete stoop and wished I'd made sure she locked up behind me.

Taking the back roads to Toccoa next morning had seemed a fine idea back at the coffee shop adjoining the Hampton Inn just outside of Anderson where I'd been lucky to find a bed only half an hour or so after leaving Aunt Eliza's. Damn lucky, according to the garrulous desk clerk who chattered away while I filled out the registration card. When Clemson played football at home, he'd informed me, hotel rooms within a hundred-mile radius of the sprawling campus were as scarce as tickets to the game.

Studying my map over breakfast that morning, I'd decided to do whatever it took to avoid the interstates and give myself an opportunity to enjoy the glorious fall weather. According to my best estimates, the trip shouldn't take more than a couple of hours or so, provided I didn't get lost. I'd sipped scalding tea, offered in a dented metal pot with a generic tea bag dangling inside, and smiled at the contrast with Louise Cameron's elegant presentation. Then, fortified with over-easy eggs and crisp bacon, I'd set out on the last leg of my journey.

The two-lane road wound northwest, crossing and then skirting the upper reaches of Lake Hartwell. The fall foliage was well past its peak here, the once vivid yellows and golds faded to a uniform rusty brown as the land rose gently toward the foothills. Most of the vehicles I encountered were pickup trucks, many with men in red plaid jackets behind the wheel and spotted hounds balanced precariously in the back.

Hunting season, I thought as I eased through Westminster and turned south toward Georgia. It brought back memories of chilly November dawns, shivering at my bedroom window at Presqu'isle. Below, the Judge and his cronies, shotguns lying broken in the crooks of their arms, shushed the baying dogs.

I reached the outskirts of Toccoa just before eleven and followed a small sign into the driveway of the welcome center, a squat brick building whose resources proved to be extensive. The unlikely attendant—a teenaged girl in black leather pants and a nearly incomprehensible drawl—provided me with a detailed map of the town and pointed out the best route to the address Erik Whiteside had given me on Thanksgiving afternoon.

I stopped at a nearby McDonald's. Leaning against the side of my car in the warmth of the midday sun, I sipped a Diet Coke and suddenly realized I was procrastinating. I forced myself back into the Z3. I practiced a dozen opening lines as I crawled through the Saturday traffic. The rutted street I finally pulled onto was little more than an alley, one narrow lane between old, but well-kept houses perched along a steep hill.

The house numbers seemed to be in no logical order, and I might have missed it altogether except for the children. While its neighbors' yards stood browning and empty, the one in front of the rambling white three-story with the slightly weary look teemed with the bright yellows, reds, and blues of plastic trucks and playhouses and echoed with the delighted squeals of several kids of all sizes and colors. This had to be the home of Toccoa's preeminent foster parents, Bill and Vesta Scoggins.

I eased the car onto a worn patch of dirt next to a driveway already crowded with a dusty Ford van and a gleaming red monster of a pickup truck with yards of chrome and a dealer tag. As I tossed the map into my bag, I suddenly felt that prickle along the back of the neck which tells you someone is watching. I glanced up to find five pairs of eyes regarding me solemnly through the windows of my low-slung car.

I was surrounded.

My experience with young children has so far been limited to brief encounters with my niece and nephew and with the four belonging to Bitsy Elliott, my best friend since grade school, so I am generally clueless about how to deal with them. I pasted my best Aunt-Bay smile on my face and eased open the driver's door. The two little girls guarding my left flank stepped back

"Hi!" I said brightly, unwinding myself from the bucket seat. "Is this where Mr. and Mrs. Scoggins live?"

Two very direct gazes—one blue, the other the limpid brown of a startled doe—studied me with interest as the others crowded around to trap me against the side of my car. Three girls, two boys. Three white, two black. All appeared healthy and well cared for, their clothes obviously not new, but clean, as were the children themselves. Still, there was something in their faces, a mingled look of fear and hope I couldn't quite put a name to, a vulnerability that stabbed at my heart. I shook off the feeling and tried again.

"Do I have the right house? I'm looking for Mr. and Mrs. Scoggins."

The owner of the blue eyes nodded, sending her twin blond ponytails swishing on either side of her head.

Progress, I thought. I pushed the door closed and squatted down on my haunches, thinking perhaps my nearly five-foot, ten-inch height was intimidating them. "Are they home?"

Again the little blond girl nodded, and I suddenly got the message. "You're not supposed to talk to strangers, are you?" A vigorous shake of her head which traveled down to her denimed knees. "Good! That's a good rule." I thought for a moment, then held out my hand. They all stepped back, skittish as newborn colts. "It's okay." I tried to keep my voice low, nonthreatening. "I'm looking for my cousin. She used to live here, so that sort of makes us cousins, too, doesn't it? My name's Bay. What's yours?"

The group exchanged looks, a couple of them glancing over their shoulders toward the house. As if some silent agreement had been reached, they suddenly crowded around me, and I gathered as many of them as I could into my arms. Miss Ponytails appeared to be the designated spokeswoman. One thin arm snaked its way around my neck as I settled onto my knees, and I felt the warmth of the sun on the soft cheek she laid against mine.

"My name's Carly. I'm six." She had a slight lisp which only added to her charm. "Are you going to adopt me? I can play the piano and I clean up my room and I always eat my veg'ables. E'cept for greens. But I would, if you really wanted me to."

"Children! Come away from there! Let the poor lady stand up."

They scattered toward the porch where a pretty, slightly plump woman stood drying her hands on a dish towel tucked into the waistband of her rumpled khakis. I could feel the reluctance with which Carly disengaged her arm from around my neck, but she went without a word. I rose and followed them.

"Help you?" Vesta Scoggins had a pleasant face, devoid of makeup and slightly flushed as if she had just come from stirring a bubbling pot on the stove. I watched her assess my Hilton Head sweatshirt, sharply creased jeans, and tasseled loafers as I approached the wide porch.

"Mrs. Scoggins? My name is Bay Tanner, and I'm trying to locate a cousin of mine who used to stay with you."

I saw suspicion creep into her hazel eyes. "We've had dozens of kids over the years, Ms. Tanner. It's difficult to remember them all."

I stopped on the cracked sidewalk and shifted my bag from one shoulder to the other. Erik had been certain Mercer's former foster parents were either harboring her or knew where she was. Two people inquiring after long-lost relatives in the space of a couple of days had sent alarm bells clanging. I could almost feel the drawbridge being cranked up, troops rushing to man the battlements.

"Look, Mrs. Scoggins," I began, deciding honesty was the best weapon I had, "Mercer is in a lot of trouble. My father and I only want to help her. Is she here?"

"Vesta? Honey, the sandwiches are ready. Where's the kids? It's Robert's turn to fill the glasses." Bill Scoggins, rail thin and lanky, followed his deep voice out onto the porch, then stopped short. "Who's this?"

The look he and his wife exchanged told me everything I needed to know.

"Ms. Tanner. She's looking for some of her kin. I told her we don't remember every kid who stayed here for a couple of weeks ten years ago. I have to feed these children."

Casting a fearful look at her husband and completely ignoring me, she turned and herded them ahead of her into the house. "Now everyone wash up. And Robert, you get the water pitcher and fill those glasses, hear?" Her voice receded down the hall.

"Mr. Scoggins—" I began, but he cut me off with an upraised palm and a glance over his shoulder toward the front door.

"Bill," he said, extending his hand.

I walked up the four steps onto the porch. "Bay Tanner."

His grip was dry and firm, his long, slender fingers smooth. Definitely not a man who worked with his hands. I wondered if he was the one who taught piano to the kids. He motioned me to the wooden swing suspended on chains from the ceiling, then settled himself into a weathered Adirondack chair.

"You're looking for Mercer Mary Prescott." It wasn't a question.

"Yes, I am. She needs help."

"What makes you think so?" He reached in his shirt pocket and extracted a pack of Dorals. "Mind?" he asked.

I smiled, shook my head, and got a Marlboro going. "She's a fugitive. She's run away from the law twice now, and they'll be looking hard for her this time." I tapped ash into the cracked saucer my host held out to me. "My father's a retired judge down in Beaufort County, South Carolina, but he's got connections all over the state. Maybe we can keep things from going too hard for her. But first, she has to turn herself in. I came to convince her of that."

Bill Scoggins nodded, then stared off into the rising column of smoke from his cigarette. "Other folks lookin' for her," he said, studying my face for a reaction.

I assumed he meant Erik Whiteside. "The man who called works with me. He means her no harm."

"I figured that."

He rose from his chair and leaned across the railing. When he turned back, his eyes held a look of expectancy I couldn't quite decipher, almost as if he were waiting for me to ask another question. Other *folks*, he had said. Plural. My mind flashed to Buddy Slade and his armed determination to locate his missing wife. Had he been here before me? Had he somehow intimidated or coerced Bill Scoggins into giving up his foster daughter's whereabouts, then threatened him into silence? Or was it possible the two girls who had battered Dolores had come sniffing around here? I was damned if I could figure out what made my cousin of such intense interest to so many people.

"Who is Mercer running from, other than the police?" I asked.

Apparently that wasn't the question he'd been expecting. "She's not here," he said, ignoring it, "not any more."

"Where—?" I began, but he anticipated me this time.

"I don't know. But Vesta does. She's the only one Mercer would confide in. You're gonna have to convince Vesta you're okay."

I sighed, remembering the fear on his wife's face as she ushered the children inside. This wasn't going to be easy.

"Guess you'd better stay for lunch." Bill Scoggins forced a smile and held the screen door open for me.

The long kitchen table accommodated all of us with ease. Carly managed to commandeer the chair next to mine, although she had to kneel on the blue corduroy seat pad in order to reach her plate. She laid her tiny hand in mine for the murmured grace, and the smile she bestowed on me nearly stopped my heart. The quick *amens* were followed by noisy slurping as the children dived into homemade turkey noodle soup and sliced turkey sandwiches which testified to the quantity of leftovers from what must have been a bountiful Thanksgiving feast.

After a whispered consultation over the stove, both Bill and Vesta Scoggins treated me as an unexpected, but not entirely unwelcome, guest. I was introduced to each of the children in turn, with Carly adding helpful insights such as, "Keisha lets me play with her Barbies," and "Tony cheats at Candyland!" as each name was called. By the time they had been excused and scampered back outside to resume whatever game I had interrupted, I felt as if I wanted to pack them all into the nonexistent backseat of the Z3 and whisk them off to the beach with me.

Vesta made no demur when I began clearing the table. While she stored the remaining soup in freezer containers, Bill loaded the dishwasher, then washed up the cooking pots while I dried. We made small talk as we worked, carefully skirting the subject of Mercer Mary Prescott until the kitchen was once again put to rights and we had carried glasses of iced tea out onto the porch. Bill settled into his chair, while Vesta and I sat stiffly side by side on the swing.

"Tell me something about my cousin's growing up here," I finally said when it had become apparent no one else wanted to initiate the unavoidable discussion of the purpose of my visit. "She told us so little about herself in the few hours she spent with my father and me."

"That doesn't surprise me," Vesta replied, the relaxation in her tone reflected in the easing of her rigid posture. I could hear the warmth in her voice. "She was about nine when she came to us, isn't that right, Bill?" Her husband nodded. "Cutest little thing you ever saw, with those big brown eyes. But quiet, almost too quiet, if you know what I mean. Solemn, like a little old lady who's seen too many troubles. And I guess she had."

"Her momma was a little on the wild side, or so we hear." Bill Scoggins picked up the narrative. "But she came from good folks, and that's what told, in the end. And we don't hold with visitin' the sins of the parents on the children. The Prescotts did the best they could after her momma ran off, but then he got sick, and they just couldn't handle a youngster that age. We only had two others stayin' with us at the time, so we were glad to be able to help out. And she was never any trouble, was she, honey?"

Vesta Scoggins surprised me by flinching a little as her husband reached over to pat her arm. She held my eyes as she picked up what sounded almost like a rehearsed recitation of my cousin's virtues.

"Not at all. In fact, she pitched in and helped with chores right from the get-go. Didn't ever need to be reminded. Come from good folks, like Bill said. And smart! Why she took to that computer like she was born to it. Same with the piano. Bill tries to teach all the kids a little music, even the ones with no real talent for it. But Mercer just lapped it up. Couldn't seem to learn things fast enough. Always wanted more." Vesta sighed and again fixed me with a pointed stare. "She's the last one of our kids I ever figured to run afoul of the law. Can't believe it, unless she was pushed or tricked—"

It might have been my imagination that the imperceptible tightening of her husband's hand on her wrist cut Vesta Scoggins off in midsentence. Regardless, she fell silent, slumping back against the swing. There were undercurrents here I couldn't quite figure out.

"There may be extenuating circumstances," I offered, rising to lean against the railing. "Her trouble seems to stem from this wacko group of protesters she's involved with. Do you know anything about them?"

Again husband and wife exchanged looks. When Bill finally answered, the warmth of his north Georgia drawl had dropped several degrees. "I can tell you it's a legitimate movement. Antinuclear. They're fighting the government's plan to transport nuclear waste across the country to this underground storage facility the Energy Department's buildin' at Yucca Mountain. I mean, think about it. Railroad cars and big semis full of radioactive material traveling through every little town from here clear to Nevada. The potential for disaster is incredible. But this group is peaceful, strictly opposed to violence."

"What interest would they have in the Savannah River Site?" I asked, surprised at the vehemence with which he spoke.

"That's where they plan to store a good chunk of this waste

first. Fools are plannin' to cart it into South Carolina, then ship it back out again. They talk about *reprocessing*, but we aren't all idiots, fallin' for that government propaganda."

Through the haze from his cigarette I studied this new Bill Scoggins. I judged him to be in his late forties, maybe fifty. Just about the right age to have participated in the antinuke movement of the early seventies, I decided. Was this where Mercer Mary Prescott had been taught adherence to the *Cause* along with her scales and arpeggios? The light of the true believer burned brightly in Bill's eyes. It shocked me to realize this soft-spoken man, who'd told me he ran the service department at the local Ford dealer and taught Sunday school in the Methodist Church, had been a zealot. I wondered if he himself still participated in sit-ins and picketing, or if he left that to the needy, receptive young ones he managed to brainwash. Including my cousin.

Or maybe I was being unfair. Just because Bill Scoggins still believed passionately in a cause fallen generally out of fashion didn't make him evil. Many of his fellow protestors in the early days of the movement had abandoned their active participation and gone on to lead button-down lives in which their checkbooks replaced their placards. Perhaps he should be applauded for trying to instill a sense of social responsibility into a generation of kids whose primary concerns seemed to be acquiring the latest rap CD and dying their hair pink. Still . . .

"Do you know where Mercer is, Mrs. Scoggins? My father and I want to help her. After all, she is a member of our family, no matter how distantly related."

I had hoped to gain Vesta's trust by appealing to her sense of family, but I could tell immediately it wasn't going to be enough. She was shaking her head before I'd even finished.

"I'm sorry. I believe you have her best interests at heart, I really do." She studied her hands clasped tightly in her lap and avoided looking at her husband. "She's safe, I can promise you that. You needn't worry about her."

"Vesta, maybe you should reconsider. After all, they are her kin—"

"No!" The vehemence of that one word startled us all. "I mean, I gave her my word. I can't go back on that. I'm sure you understand." It was almost a plea.

I tried another tack. "I trust you realize you could be in trouble yourselves. Harboring a federal fugitive is a pretty serious offense." When this elicited no response, I added, "You know, the cops and I aren't the only ones trying to find her."

I waited, but Bill Scoggins refused to rise to the bait, so I played my last card.

"Two girls came to my house a few days ago and beat up my housekeeper. They put her in the hospital." I paused dramatically. "They were looking for Mercer."

I heard Vesta's sharp intake of breath, but Bill forestalled any response she might have been about to make by rising and holding out his hand.

"I'm sorry, but that has nothing to do with us." Dismissal was hard in his voice. "If she calls, we'll tell Mercer about your concern for her. If she wants to get in touch, she has your number."

I admitted defeat and reached down to retrieve my bag from the floor of the porch. "May I say goodbye to the children?" I asked.

"Of course. They're around back." Vesta seemed almost relieved to have an excuse to move off the porch and out from under Bill's gaze.

I shook hands with Bill Scoggins and followed his wife around to the side of the house where a raucous game of tag seemed to be in progress. Carly broke away from the group as soon as she spotted me and flung herself against my legs, wrapping my knees in a bear hug.

"Miss Bay, Miss Bay! Can you come play wif us? I'm *it*."

I disentangled her arms and knelt down to eye level. "No, honey, I have to go. But I just wanted to say how much I enjoyed meeting you. And all your friends."

"And I'm staying here?" Her impossibly tender lower lip quivered, and her huge blue eyes filled with tears.

Stricken, I looked to Vesta Scoggins. "Miss Bay just came to find her cousin, sweetheart. She has to go home now."

"But I want to go, too! Please?"

Her foster mother swept the weeping child into her arms and shrugged at me in sympathy. "Don't take it to heart, Ms. Tanner. This happens all the time. I'm afraid they think every adult who comes to the house wants to adopt them. She'll be fine as soon as you've gone."

I reached out a hand to stroke the silky blonde hair, then drew back. Tears welled unexpectedly in my own eyes, and I ducked my head to hide my embarrassment. "I'm sorry," I said. "Thank you for lunch. Please tell Mercer to call if she needs anything, anything at all."

Vesta seemed about to speak, then changed her mind and merely nodded.

I wiped my eyes on the sleeve of my sweatshirt as I backed the car around. The image of Carly's tiny hand waving disconsolately stayed in my head long after it had disappeared from the rectangle of my rearview mirror.

CHAPTER
FOURTEEN

I rarely attend church, for reasons I refuse to examine, but the events of the past two weeks somehow urged me into a black jersey dress with a long, matching cape and black leather heels whose pinch reminded me my feet hadn't been confined in dress shoes for far too long. I even managed to find a pair of usable pantyhose stuffed into the far reaches of my lingerie drawer.

I chose the anonymity of the huge First Presbyterian Church just outside the entrance to Port Royal Plantation and eased into a back pew just as the organ prelude thundered to a close. For the next hour I let the liturgy and the music wash over me, a soothing, comforting backdrop to the chaos of my thoughts. If I prayed, I don't remember it, but the message awaiting me when I returned home gave evidence that any inadvertent pleas in That Direction had gone unheard.

Angelina Santiago's voice cracked around the tears she was obviously trying desperately to control. "Mrs. Tanner, it's Angie. They've . . . they've moved my mother. To Memorial Medical Center. In Savannah? The . . . the doctor said it's a staph infection."

My knees refused to support the implication of this news, and I folded onto the chair next to the telephone.

Angie's voice stumbled on. "They think, they think she might lose her leg." My own gasp echoed the teenager's sharp intake of breath. "I have to go now, we're leaving right away. I'll let you know what happens." She finished on a strangled sob and hung up.

The call had come in only twenty minutes before, so I snatched up the phone and dialed the Santiagos' number. When the answering machine finally clicked on, I heard Dolores's voice inviting me—in both English and Spanish—to leave a message. I don't remember how long I sat there, listening to the tape whirring in my ear, before I slammed the receiver back into its cradle and bolted for my room.

A moment later I was pulling the black jersey dress over my head and kicking off the narrow pumps. Outside the French doors of my bedroom, the sky had darkened. A rising breeze rattled the palmetto fronds and whispered through the high branches of the loblolly pines as I dragged on sweats and my battered running shoes. I shoved a baseball cap on my head and trotted down the back deck stairs toward the beach. At the end of the boardwalk over the barren dune, I turned left, into the teeth of the northeast wind.

And I ran.

Away from the house where every room carried a reminder of Dolores. And of Rob. Away from hospitals and weeping children and hard, black, accusing eyes. Away from pain and loss.

Away from guilt.

The rain came suddenly, in stinging sheets, squall-driven off the ocean, and still I ran. My sodden clothes weighed me down, and my cold-numbed feet squished inside saturated Nikes. I could feel myself slowing, my breath coming then in ragged gasps. With a final burst which drained me of my last ounce of strength, I flung myself onto the meager protection of the dune, barely a yard ahead of the inrushing tide.

And in the misery of the cold and the rain and the wind, I finally wept. For my wounded friend. And for myself.

I have no clear memory of returning home.

I awoke to total darkness and the soft purring of Mr. Bones on the pillow next to my head. Beneath the weight of the light blanket and downy comforter, I lay naked. The bedside clock read *10:37*; and, though I knew it must be night, the dreamless sleep of total exhaustion had left me disoriented. I flipped on the light and tried to run a hand through my hair, only to encounter a salt-encrusted helmet.

Twenty minutes later I emerged from the steaming shower, wrapped my old chenille robe tightly around me, and slid my feet into warm slippers. I gathered up the soaked, filthy clothes I had dropped in the middle of the bedroom floor and carried them out to the laundry room. I fed the cat, made tea, scrambled three eggs and piled them on top of two slices of whole wheat bread. I ate standing at the counter with Mr. Bones draped around my ankles, his contentment reverberating in his throat as he meticulously cleaned his paws.

I disengaged myself and went to build a fire in the great room, then settled onto the sofa with a fresh cup of Earl Grey. In seconds the cat curled himself into a tabby ball against my hip.

Which is where Red found us. "Bay? You all right?"

So lost was I in the mesmerizing dance of the flames, his voice barely registered until he came around to kneel in front of me.

"Hey! Anybody home in there?"

"Hi." I dragged my gaze away from the fire. "What are you doing here?"

Red stood, slid off his jacket, and tossed it on a chair. "I rang the bell. Knocked, too. I guess you didn't hear me. The door was unlocked. You really shouldn't leave—"

"Don't start on me, Red, okay? I've had about all I can take for one day."

"Got any beer? Never mind," he said, ignoring me and moving toward the kitchen, "I'll check." He came back carrying a bottle. "Gettin' cold again out there. Wish to hell this damned weather would make up its mind."

"What are you doing here?" I repeated, eyeing the clock on the mantel through the curling haze of my smoke. "It's after midnight."

He settled on the far end of the sofa and pulled my slippered feet into his lap. As I leaned over to stub out my cigarette in the overflowing ashtray on the coffee table, I saw his gaze flick to the curve of my left breast, exposed in the gap of the robe. I jerked the lapels tightly together and swung my feet onto the floor.

"I'll be right back," I said, moving quickly toward the hallway.

"Good idea," I heard him mumble as I slid my bedroom door closed.

When I returned, covered from throat to ankles in clean, dry sweats, Red had the fire rekindled and blazing. He'd pulled several throw pillows from the couch and now lay stretched out on the floor, his shoes tucked neatly under one of the wing chairs, a fresh bottle of beer in his hand.

"You need to keep your wood in the garage or under a tarp or something. A lot of it's wet. I had to dig down to the bottom of the pile to find some that would burn."

"I'll remember that," I called over my shoulder as I climbed the three steps up to the kitchen and poured myself fresh tea. "The thing is, I don't build fires that often." I settled again into my favorite corner of the sofa.

"Why not? I'd love to have a fireplace again."

"Because . . ." I began, then stopped, tears suddenly choking me. I bit down hard, but despite my efforts a tiny sob escaped from my throat.

Red rolled over to face me. "What is it?"

I shook my head, swallowed against the pain, and managed a wavering smile. "Because Dolores always insists on cleaning out the ashes every time I have a fire. I can't convince her just to let them be for a while."

"So you've heard," he said softly. "I'm sorry."

"How did you . . . ?"

"The hospital kept us informed as a matter of courtesy. In case we needed to reinterview her." He sat up, wrapping his arms around his long legs. "You know, it isn't a done deal that she'll lose the leg. Memorial has a great reputation."

"People *die* of staph infections, Red."

"And you have a terrible habit of expecting the worst."

"And I'm so often right."

He didn't have an answer for that. "Anything I can do to help?" he finally asked.

I crushed out my cigarette and immediately lit another. "You can catch the harpies who did this to her. If she dies, they'll be murderers."

"Dolores is not going to die. And even if she did, they can still only be charged with assault."

"That's bullshit!" I shouted, startling the cat, who leaped over the back of the sofa and streaked off down the hallway. "If they hadn't beaten her up, she wouldn't have been in the hospital to catch an infection in the first place."

"You're not thinking this through clearly, Bay. What you say has no legal basis, and you know it."

A shower of sparks flew up the chimney as a log settled onto the grate. In the silence, I heard the splatter of rain against the narrow windows beside the French door.

"You're right. It's why I got out of pre-law when I was in college." I had my voice—and my emotions—under control again. "I remember all that stuff about proximate cause and intervening cause, and I know that legally you're right. But the law shouldn't just be about rules and procedures. It should be about *justice.*"

"You won't get any argument out of me. Hell, I see it every single day. Forget to dot an *i* or cross a *t* on a search warrant or a Miranda warning, and some scumbag who everyone—including the judge—knows is guilty as sin gets a walk." Red swung his legs around and settled back against the pillows. "But it's the only system we've got. I guess it's probably better that a few bad guys skate than that innocent people get railroaded, don't you think?"

It was a rhetorical question, and I didn't bother to answer. I stifled a yawn, covering my mouth with the back of my hand. "Sorry," I murmured. In spite of my extended afternoon nap, I was suddenly weary.

"I'd better go." Red stretched and set his empty bottle onto the raised stone hearth.

"No, wait. What did you really come over for? It wasn't just to hold my hand about Dolores, was it?"

"It'll keep. You look pretty done in. I'm sure it's been a tough day for you."

"I'm fine. It must have been important, or you wouldn't have driven all the way over here after your shift. What's the problem?" I watched the blush slide up from beneath his collar and took a stab. "Is it Sarah?"

When he pulled the beer bottle onto his lap and began picking at the paper label, I knew I'd hit the mark. "Come on," I said, "talk to me."

"You sure you want to get into this now? It could take a while."

"I'm yours for as long as the cigarettes and tea hold out," I replied and earned a tentative smile for my efforts.

It turned out to be one of those nights when I was glad I had no near neighbors. I didn't like to think how the local gossips would have responded to a sheriff's cruiser easing out of my driveway at four in the morning. I'd already provided so much ammunition for them over the past few months, this might just have been the final straw which got me drummed out of the plantation.

But it would have been worth it. For the first time I felt as if I had been as much of a comfort to Red as he had always been to me. For the most part I'd let him talk, interrupting him with questions only when I felt it was absolutely necessary, despite the rambling incoherence of much of what he had to say. Absorbed in my own life before Rob's murder—and in my grief and loss after his death—I truly *listened* to Red for the first time in years, understanding at last the depth of his suffering in losing both his marriage and his brother in the space of a few short weeks.

But his present concerns were more urgent. When I'd nestled again into the curve of the sofa, he began immediately, in mid-sentence, almost as if he'd suddenly decided to give voice to an ongoing, interior monologue.

". . . but the trouble is, you were right when you said it isn't really any of my business who Sarah sees. Unless it affects my kids. Then I have every right to draw the line, don't I?"

"Of course," I answered, sipping from a fresh, steaming mug of tea. "Has something changed since Thanksgiving?"

It didn't seem possible our last conversation on this subject had taken place only a few days before.

"Just that I had the kids almost the entire weekend. Sarah called Thursday night and told me not to bring them back until yesterday, that she'd been delayed, wouldn't be able to get home before then. She wouldn't say where she was calling from, but she wasn't alone."

"How do you know that?"

"There was an undercurrent in the background, conversation and some strange kind of music or chanting or something like that. I swear to God, it was spooky."

"Maybe she was calling from a pay phone in a bar or a restaurant."

"No, she was on her cell. I insisted she get one in case she ran into any trouble with the car or the kids."

"Well, I'll grant you it wasn't very considerate of her to leave the kids with you with no warning, but you obviously managed and—"

"I think she's involved with a cult."

I could only gape in astonishment at my brother-in-law. "A cult? Sarah?" I completed the ritual and exhaled smoke around a skeptical snort. "That's crazy! I've never met a more down-to-earth, sensible person in my life than Sarah. Besides, those things went out with the sixties, didn't they? No one takes the idea seriously any more."

"Oh, really? What about David Koresh and the Branch Davidians at Waco? What about that bunch of kooks in California who killed themselves so they could hitch a ride to Heaven on that comet thing? Scoff if you want to, but those people are still seriously dead."

I opened my mouth to remind Red of his penchant for seeing conspiracies behind everything from the Kennedy assassination to the latest airline disaster, then stopped, noticing for the first time the lines of worry and sleeplessness etched into his usually boyish face. Regardless of my doubts, *he* believed what he was saying. We had to deal with that.

"What other evidence do you have besides a bad feeling and some weird music? You're a cop, Red. Let's hear something concrete, something besides your natural concern that the mother of your children is acting out of character. It can't be easy for her, holding down a job and being a full-time, single parent, you know. She's probably entitled to go a little bonkers once in awhile."

My brother-in-law stood, stretching out muscles cramped from sitting cross-legged on the floor for so long. "Maybe. But Sarah quit her job, right after the divorce. She only works a couple of days a week now, at the school. In the office. And she still has her 'causes,' so it's not as if she's tied to the house twenty-four hours a day."

Red ran his hand through his hair, leaving several strands standing straight up, and I had to smile. "Have you thought about just *asking* her what's going on? Wouldn't that be the simplest thing to do?"

"I finally got Scotty to give me the guy's name." Red paced in front of the last of the fire and ignored my question. "I turned it into a guessing game so he wouldn't feel as if he was breaking his mother's trust. John Wilson, can you believe it? They call him 'Jack.' I ran the name through the computers and came up with about a million hits, of course. What I really need are his prints.

Maybe one of the kids can get hold of a glass, or maybe . . ."

"Red! For God's sake, listen to yourself! You're seriously considering enlisting your children to *spy* for you? I'm beginning to think maybe *you're* the one that's gone over the edge."

His smile told me I had made my point. "Okay, you're probably right. Listen, Bay, I hate to ask this of you, considering everything you've already been through in the past few days, but would you talk to her? To Sarah? Kind of feel her out and see if you think there's anything to worry about? I swear I'll abide by what you say. If you tell me to back off, I will. It's just . . . this thing's driving me crazy. I'm scared for my kids."

"Of course," I promised without thinking, "if it'll help you put your mind at ease. I'll invite Sarah to lunch. It's been too long since I've seen her anyway."

"Thanks." Red picked up his jacket and pulled it on while I uncurled myself from the couch. "You'll do it this week, right?"

"Go home," I said, following him into the foyer. "I'll let you know what happens. And quit worrying."

Physician, heal thyself, I thought as watched him pull out of the driveway. I had punched the code into the alarm system and padded wearily down the hall, certain I would be too exhausted to sleep. I was out in thirty seconds.

CHAPTER
FIFTEEN

I motioned from the back of the Fig Tree and watched as Sarah Tanner wove her way among the closely packed tables. Like my childhood friend, Bitsy Elliott, she had that all-American blond freshness that made people smile just to look at her. Petite and only a little heavier through the hips than when I'd first met her more than a decade and two children ago, Sarah still appeared as fit as when she'd led the USC gymnastics team to glory. Her trophies and pictures had adorned their mantel alongside Red's numerous track cups and ribbons.

"Bay," she said as I stood to receive her offered hug, "I'm so delighted you called. I'm thoroughly ashamed of myself that it's been so long." Sarah dropped her bag onto an empty chair, then settled in across from me. "I heard about your housekeeper. I'm so sorry. You must be devastated. Is there any news?"

"It's good to see you, too," I replied, ignoring her remarks and question about Dolores. Already that morning I had rebuffed several attempts to open the subject. It was painful and private and no one else's business. Besides, until I heard something from Angie or one of the other Santiagos, I had no more information on Dolores's condition than I'd had the day before. "So how are the kids? Back in school, I suppose? I can't get over how much they've grown. Elinor looks amazingly like you, and Scotty is the picture of Rob at his age."

Gilly Falconer, no doubt eager to enlarge her store of gossip, moved out from behind the bar and approached our table, thankfully saving me from the necessity of any more inane chatter. "Well, if ain't the Tanner ladies. Haven't seen you two together in dogs' years."

"Hey, Gilly, how you been keepin'?" Sarah turned her quizzical gaze from me and smiled up at the café-au-lait face of the Fig Tree's proprietress.

"Tol'rable. And you?"

I smiled at Gilly's stock answer. If she hit the lottery for a million dollars, she'd still just be *tol'rable.*

"Oh, I'm fine," Sarah answered. "Startin' to get a little frazzled with thinking about Christmas. I swear it just sneaks up on me every year."

Gilly nodded and turned to me. "Bay. Sorry for your trouble." Her acknowledgment was brusque, and her failure to use the hated *Lydia* told me more than if she'd poured out volumes of sympathetic platitudes.

We all turned as the door onto the back porch opened, admitting a swirl of cold air and a few cracked, brown leaves along with two hard-hatted workmen in heavy parkas. The weather forecast had called for a warm-up into the mid-sixties, but the lowering skies over the Beaufort River made that seem like an empty promise.

"Corn chowder," Gilly said, scribbling on her pad, "that's what's needed on a day like this. Henry just made it up fresh this mornin'. I'll get y'all some whilst you think on anything else you might like." A few steps from the table, she turned back and called to Sarah. "And don't be doin' no talking 'bout that new man of your'n 'til I get back, hear?"

Well, Gilly, I owe you one, I thought, watching the blush spread from the top of Sarah's white turtleneck sweater up to the roots of her sleek, blond pageboy. I couldn't have asked for a better way to introduce the subject of my interrogation if I'd planned it myself.

It's been my experience that silence frequently elicits more information than a barrage of questions, so I smiled across the table at Red's ex-wife and waited for her to fill the void. She inspected the silverware, used her heavy paper napkin to polish a water spot from the knife, and rearranged the packets of sugar and sweetener in their plastic holder before finally looking up at me.

"I swear you can't belch in this town before word of it has spread from one end to the other," she said with an attempt at nonchalance that fell just short of believable.

"And?" I prompted in an eager, *tell-me-all-girlfriend* manner that reminded me of what I disliked most about my newfound career as Bay Tanner, Girl Detective. Prying is definitely not my natural style.

"Oh, it's nothing serious," Sarah said as the young waitress set the earthenware bowls of bubbling chowder down in front of us and dropped a basket of warm rolls onto the table. "We haven't even had what you could call a real date." She lifted a spoon of soup to her mouth and blew across it.

"Anybody I'd know?" I asked, buttering a roll.

"No, he's not from around here. North or South Dakota, I think. Or maybe Montana. Anyway, out West somewhere. His name's Jack."

So Scotty had been right about that part. Strange, though, that Sarah didn't seem sure about his background. "Where'd you meet him?"

"Oh, at one of my groups. My *causes*, as Red used to call them. Jack was the main speaker, actually."

The introduction of my brother-in-law's name into the conversation made me squirm a little. I hadn't told Sarah the real purpose of my invitation, chattering instead about how long it had been since we'd gotten together and how much I'd missed seeing her. I let her think having Thanksgiving dinner with her kids had prompted me to call.

"Is that what he does? Speak, I mean? Is he a professor or something?"

Sarah used a few spoonfuls of chowder to delay answering. After that initial blush, she had displayed a detachment I couldn't quite read. Either she really didn't care all that much about this Jack person, or she was trying her damnedest to make me think so.

"He's done a lot of things, mostly involved with environmental issues."

"So he works for the government?"

"Not exactly."

"Then what, exactly?"

Sarah nodded to the waitress hovering with a coffeepot and lifted her cup to accept the refill. Across the room I caught a glimpse of Gilly Falconer, trapped behind the bar by an influx of customers, no doubt fuming that she had missed the gossip that was life and breath to her. Sarah's next question snapped my head around.

"Did Red send you here to pump me for information about Jack?"

I hesitated only a moment. "Yes," I said, with more relief than guilt, "yes, he did. I'm sorry, Sarah. I should have been straight with you right from the jump. I told Red just to ask you, but he's so paranoid about this guy, he was sure you wouldn't talk to either one of us about him if you knew the real reason."

"And what is the real reason?"

"He's worried about you. And the kids."

"Bullshit." The vulgarity sounded even cruder coming from the mouth of the usually straitlaced Sarah Jane Tanner. "He didn't want me, but he's going to make damned sure no one else ever has me either."

"Wait a minute. You divorced him, if I remember correctly."

"He didn't fight too hard, did he?"

"Is that what you wanted, a fight? Was he supposed to duke it out with whoever it was you were leaving him for? That's a little 'high school' for people in their thirties, don't you think?"

Sarah's face flushed, and she reached out to yank her purse off the chair next to her. When she began dropping bills onto the table, I knew I'd blown my assignment big-time.

"You don't understand the first thing about it," she said, pushing back her chair. "Not that I'm the least bit surprised you're sticking up for *him*. I always knew he had a thing going for you, even when we were still married. He thought you and Rob were just so damned *perfect*. Now that his brother's out of the way, I suppose he's following you around like some eager lap dog."

"Sarah!" I was astounded by her accusations, by the venom in her voice. All around us, conversation stopped, and heads swiveled in our direction. "Knock it off!" I said between clenched teeth, my own frayed nerves ready to snap in anger. Then I saw the tears pooling in her eyes, and all the fight went out of me. "That's nonsense, and you know it. Red will always love you and the kids. It's who he is." I laid a hand on her arm, felt the tension in her muscles. "But you're right about one thing. I *don't* know exactly what happened between you and Red, and I don't want to. It's none of my business."

"That's for damned sure." Her eyes still blazed, but she did settle back down in her seat. "Look," she said, drawing a calming breath, "I'm sorry. That was totally out of line. It's just that you and Rob *were* the perfect couple. I envied you that, I'll admit it. But you weren't around much toward the end. You didn't see how bad things had gotten by the time I filed for divorce."

It was a charge I couldn't defend myself against, so I simply said, "I know."

"There wasn't anyone else. I didn't divorce Red for another man. We just didn't share anything anymore, other than the kids. And, believe me, I've never for a moment doubted Red loves his children. But in every other way, we'd become nothing more than bickering roommates. He mocked me and everything I believe in, and I hated his job and everything it stands for." She sighed and managed a rueful smile. "Didn't seem to me to be a basis for a lasting relationship."

I nodded and silently accepted her assessment of the reasons for the end of her marriage. Although her eyes held a trace of remembered pain, she seemed to have made the transition to single parenthood with grace and determination. *Steady*, that was our Sarah Jane. So why the uncharacteristic behavior last weekend? I still didn't have an answer to that.

"So, this Jack person, this environmentalist. Was that who you were with for Thanksgiving?"

"Ah," Sarah said with a knowing smile, "that's what this is all about. My ex-husband got his nose out of joint at having to deal with his two little rug rats for a few days, and sent you out to beat me up about it."

"Not exactly beat you up, but it did seem a little out of character," I replied. "He's concerned."

"Well, let me put both your minds at ease. At the last minute, Jack had an opportunity to speak at a rally in Charlotte and then participate in a series of seminars over the weekend, and he asked me to go with him. Red said he'd be off work until Monday, so I said yes."

"Why didn't you just tell him that?" I asked.

"Because he doesn't explain to me where *he* is every time he misses a visitation or shows up hours late. He's always messing up *my* plans, so I didn't have one single twinge of guilt about letting him see how it feels for once."

It sounded lame and petty, but I supposed she had a point. This kind of ex-marital sparring was totally outside my experience, so I probably had no right to judge. Sarah accepted another coffee refill, her fingers tensing around the cup when I asked, "So this is just a business sort of thing with Jack?"

"That's none of your concern, and certainly none of Red's. Right now *I* don't know where it's going, although I wouldn't say the thought hasn't crossed my mind that it could turn into something. You just tell Red that Jack is a highly educated, caring man who believes passionately about making sure there's a safe, stable world for Scotty and Elinor to grow up in. He's not afraid to challenge authority if he thinks it's harming the people, and he doesn't think of me as some liberal wacko who wastes her time with lost causes." This time when she stood she shrugged into her bright red jacket. "I really have to go. The kids will be home from school in a little while."

"Give them a hug for me. I'm sorry we got off on the wrong foot, Sarah. Red is just worried about you and the kids. I really don't think he's trying to interfere in your personal life."

"Sure he is," Sarah laughed, "it's what he does. He probably can't help himself anymore, after being a cop for so long. Tell him we're fine, Bay. For right now Jack is a colleague, someone I admire tremendously. He would never do anything to hurt me. And the kids adore him. Tell Red to butt out."

"I'll do that," I said, not entirely convinced myself.

Sarah slipped the strap of her bag onto her shoulder. "Let's do this again soon, okay? And next time I promise not to be so unbelievably bitchy. Deal?"

"Deal," I replied, waving as she strode purposefully toward the door and stopped to exchange a few words with Gilly as she passed.

I poured the last of the green tea from the metal pot and lit a cigarette. I made a mental note to contact Erik Whiteside and sic him on the elusive Jack Wilson. I also had to get him back on the trail of Mercer Mary Prescott since my trip to Toccoa had turned out to be such a bust. While he was at it, maybe he could check out the Internet for any stories about the body I'd watched them pull from the woods on the Savannah River Site. It would be interesting to know if those remains and the missing security guard Leslie Cameron at the tea shop had mentioned turned out to be one and the same. Why it mattered, I wasn't certain, just a nagging feeling that all these jumbled facts and characters were somehow connected to each other.

And finally I had to pay a long overdue visit to my father and see if I could con Lavinia into teaching me how to cook.

CHAPTER
SIXTEEN

I found the two of them in the main drawing room, seated companionably in front of a fire, with half-emptied boxes of Christmas decorations spread out around them on the royal blue and gold patterned carpet. This largest of the downstairs rooms, rarely used except on the most formal occasions, had always been the focal point of the holiday in our house. Each treasured crystal or porcelain figurine, carefully stored away in humidity-resistant crates for eleven months out of the year, was unpacked, washed and dried by hand, and placed in the exact same spot it had occupied the previous year. And the year before that, and the year before that, and so on, back to the time of whichever Baynard/Tattnall ancestress had first penned the diary my mother considered her bible of design for the interior of Presqu'isle. In fact, Lavinia had that same red, leather-bound journal open on the top of the three nested mahogany tables stacked next to her elbow. She looked up from her place on the gold silk Queen Anne chair and smiled as I picked my way around the open boxes and into the room.

"Hello, sweetheart," my father boomed from his wheelchair as he placed a delicate Lalique angel with outstretched wings on the claw-footed table centered beneath the massive chandelier. "You're just in time to help Vinnie with all this folderol. She's got it into her head we need to decorate for Christmas. Can't think why she wants to go to all this trouble. Won't be but the three of us here to see it."

A vision of gray-blue eyes and a slightly cleft chin flashed briefly across my mind's eye, and I heard Darnay's strengthening voice say, *Paris at Christmas can be quite chilly.* The issue would have to be addressed, but I sensed this wasn't the time to broach the subject of my possible defection from the family gathering.

"Traditions are important," Lavinia said, eyeing me warily, almost as if she might have read my thoughts. "Your mother always brought out the holiday things right after Thanksgiving. It took us nearly two weeks just to get everything cleaned and arranged."

"I remember," I said, shrugging out of my trench coat and draping it over the back of the settee whose upholstery matched her chair. Ignoring Lavinia's pointed look of disapproval, I knelt beside one of the open crates and lifted out a green velvet box.

"Be careful with that," she said, leaning slightly forward in the chair, her hands cupped as if to provide a safety net in case I dropped the treasure. "That's—"

"I know what it is, Lavinia. Boy, 'This is like déja vu all over again.'" I looked to the Judge to see if he was in the game.

"Yogi Berra," he announced without hesitation. "A lot of people think Casey Stengel, but it was Yogi."

I smiled as Lavinia shook her head in exasperation and gently relieved me of the chest containing the jade-and-ivory crèche. "I suppose you mean I sounded like your mother just then," she said.

"Exactly, but I won't hold it against you. Besides, I came to ask a favor."

I watched in the same wonder I'd felt as a child as Lavinia removed the tiny, hand-carved pieces of luminescent stone and tusk. It seemed impossible that clumsy human fingers could have fashioned anything so exquisitely detailed, from the tails of the camels carrying the three wise men to the gentle smile of satisfaction on the face of the new mother bending over the manger. I'd never asked about its provenance, preferring my own imaginary tales of a fierce ancestral sea captain fighting off hordes of bearded pirates or enraged Chinese mandarins in order to deliver the treasure safely into Beaufort harbor and the delighted hands of wife or daughter or sweetheart.

"Would you like some tea? I have carrot cake, too, if you're hungry."

"That's what smells so heavenly," I said, pushing myself up off the floor. "Sit still, I'll get it."

The Judge rolled himself back into the center of the room. "We'll all go," he said, glancing out one of the narrow, eight-foot tall windows draped in gold silk and crowned with deep blue velvet cascades. "I believe the sun is officially over the yardarm, and I could use a drink." As if to punctuate his words, the gilt clock on the Italian marble mantel chimed four clear notes.

I gripped the handles of the wheelchair and guided my father around the boxes, down the hallway, and into the kitchen where the soft light of the waning winter afternoon fell in dancing patterns across the heart pine floor. I mixed the Judge's bourbon and lemon while Lavinia set out our tea and thin slices of the redolent, cream-cheese-laden cake.

As I raised the thin china teacup to my lips, I saw the two of them exchange a pointed glance across the table before their eyes dropped again to their plates.

"What?" I asked, fear rising like bile in my throat. "Have you heard something about Dolores?"

My father shook his head. "Nothing official, just information from a couple of the boys I asked to keep their ears open and their lines out."

"What kind of information?"

"It doesn't look good, Bay," Lavinia answered for him. "It's looking more and more as if the leg may have to come off. They can't seem to get the infection under control. I'm sorry."

"Sweetheart, you have to quit blamin'—" the Judge began, but I cut him off.

"I don't want to talk about Dolores any more. I've said everything there is to say on the subject, and nothing you can add will change the reality of it one bit. I know what my culpability is in this whole thing, and you're not going to be able to persuade me otherwise, so just save your breath."

I was surprised to see Lavinia nod, almost imperceptibly, in what I took to be at least tacit approval of my little speech.

My father shook his head, but for once restrained his natural inclination to butt into my life. Instead he ignored me. "Wonderful cake, Vinnie," he said, extending his empty plate with his good right hand. "How about another slice?"

"I don't think so." I snatched the plate from his outstretched fingers and carried it, along with my own, to the sink. "Any more of this and you'll turn into one of those sloppy old men who can't see over their bellies."

My father patted his still trim waistline, then maneuvered his chair away from the table. Mumbling something about meddlesome women, he headed off toward his study and his postponed afternoon nap. Lavinia hurried after him, ready as always to assist in getting him into his recliner and tucked up with an afghan to ward off the evening chill. I hoped he had some idea of how fortunate he was to have her.

By the time she returned to the kitchen, I had the few dishes washed and dried and replaced in the glass-fronted china cupboard which held the everyday dinnerware. "You didn't have to do that," Lavinia said as she opened the door of the refrigerator and began pulling things from its deep recesses.

"I know. I'm trying to get on your good side."

"Oh, yes, I remember now. You wanted a favor. Here, take these."

She loaded my outstretched arms with icy plastic bags which I dumped onto the counter while she followed with a large slab of some orange-colored fish which she laid out on the deeply scored surface of the old cutting board.

"Well?" Lavinia pulled a knife from the block on the counter and tested its edge against her thumb.

"What's that?" I asked, suddenly hesitant.

"What? This?" She eyed me quizzically. "It's a fish."

"I know *that*. What kind of fish is it?"

"Salmon. You like it. There's more than enough if you want to stay to dinner."

"What are you going to do with it?"

"For heaven's sake, Bay, I'm going to cook it. What's gotten into you?" She sliced the raw, slimy carcass into half a dozen pieces, then washed her hands. "Might as well make yourself useful," she said, handing me a pair of shears from the drawer in front of her. "Go out on the sun porch and cut me some basil. And a few sprigs of dill, while you're at it."

I stood gazing at the red-handled scissors, unsure how much of my ignorance to display, finally deciding I had nothing to lose. "I don't know what they look like," I said, "except that they're herbs and they're green. I think."

It had been a long time since I'd heard Lavinia laugh, and her whoop of delight took me completely by surprise. "Lord, girl, you are a pitiful specimen, aren't you?" she finally managed to gasp out. "You want to learn how to cook. That's the favor."

I watched as the reason for my sudden need to fend for myself in the kitchen dawned on her, and she sobered quickly. "We'll start tonight, with grilled salmon and pesto," she said, gently taking the shears from my hand. "It's one of the Judge's favorites."

"Couldn't we start with something simple, like toasted cheese sandwiches or oatmeal?" I asked as I followed her onto the enclosed section of the back porch where she kept her herb garden.

"Honey," Lavinia said over her shoulder, "cookin's like anything else in this life. Once you figure out the big stuff, the little things just naturally take care of themselves."

I smiled, and one of the dark closets in my soul opened just a crack. Dolores might be gone—*temporarily*, I insisted to myself— but I still had Lavinia.

Hallelujah and amen.

I staggered under the weight of no fewer than six cookbooks as I negotiated my way up the steps from the interior of the garage to the foyer. Ever since the attacks and Red's walking unannounced into my unlocked house, I'd given up leaving the car in the driveway and using the front entrance. I remained firmly seated, locks engaged on my car, until the heavy overhead door came to rest with a comforting *thunk*. The house felt chilly, so I set the accumulated culinary knowledge of the centuries on the floor in the great room and kicked the thermostat up a notch.

The light on the answering machine flashed furiously, but I ignored it, crossed the room, and stuck my head out the French door to the deck. Mr. Bones didn't respond to my repeated invitations to come in out of the cold, so I reset the alarm and wished him good hunting. I stowed the leftovers Lavinia had forced on me in the empty refrigerator and placed the suggested shopping list she'd prepared on the desk by the phone. Tomorrow I would have to face the wild, uncharted territory of the local Publix. Finally, fortified with tea and a cigarette, I pushed PLAY.

It was the usual suspects. Bitsy Elliott and Adelaide Boyce Hammond, along with some other friends and acquaintances, tendered sweet offers of whatever help or commiseration I might need in dealing with Dolores's injury. Dr. Neddie Halloran's nononsense approach was simple: if I didn't call her within twenty-four hours I risked her appearing unannounced on my doorstep for an unheard-of shrink house call. Red wanted to know if I'd had a chance to talk to Sarah yet. Erik Whiteside said he had news and that he'd also left me a couple of e-mails which I should check out as soon as possible.

While the computer booted up, I changed into flannel pajamas and washed my face. The lines were jammed, as they usually are in the evenings, so the machine did its magic of canceling the call and retrying automatically. As I watched the numbers flashing across the screen and listened to the rhythmic series of beeps as it redialed, I felt an overwhelming need to talk to Alain Darnay.

It seemed impossible we had known each other such a short while, had actually spent no more than a few days in each other's company. Perhaps it had been the intensity of that time, rather than its length, which had forged this bond, this . . . I couldn't put a name to the feeling I had for him. It certainly wasn't love. At least I didn't think it could be, and yet the ache I felt at his absence had a depth and breadth beyond all reasonable ex-planation. A *coup de foudre*, Darnay had called it. A thunderbolt. Yes, that was as good a description as any.

I jumped as the pleasant male voice said, "Welcome! You've got mail!"

It had been more than a week since I'd been online, and I had twenty-seven messages. Most of them were *spam*, offers ranging from special deals on software to registering my name as a website domain. I scanned through several personal messages, saving them to my filing cabinet for later perusal and reply. I was about to open the first message from Erik when the sound of an electronic door opening issued from the speakers, and his name popped up on the Instant Messenger screen. I slipped on the headphones and waited for him to contact me.

"Bay. Good, you're home," I heard him say after I'd accepted his request for a cyberspace parley. "How are you doing?"

"I'm okay, considering."

"Considering what?"

It occurred to me then that Erik knew nothing of Dolores's injury and subsequent complications. Such a nice little euphemism for maybe having your leg amputated or dying of a staph infection: *complications*. Although at the time I knew I had a good reason for keeping this from him, I couldn't remember what it was, so I just gave him the expurgated version.

"Good God, the poor woman! And this has got something to do with your cousin and that Buddy creep and all that?"

"I'm certain it's all connected, though I'm damned if I know how." I took a deep breath and chased the images out of my head.

"Gosh, things sure happen to you."

I couldn't argue with that. "So, what's up?" I asked.

"Did you get a chance to read my e-mails?"

"No. I was just ready to open them when you came on-line."

"Well, you can check them out later. I'll fill you in, plus I have some more info since I sent them earlier today. Are you sure you're up to this?"

I still marveled at the ease with which we were carrying on a conversation in real time without benefit of a telephone, although I realized we were connected to the Internet over a phone line. Still, it seemed strange to be hearing him like this, his voice emanating from the two speakers on either side of the monitor. Next he'd be wanting me to get one of those little floating eyeball camera things so we could see each other while we talked.

"I'm fine. Fire when ready. Do I need to take notes?" I asked into the tiny microphone that protruded in front of my face from the side of the headset. It made me feel like a switchboard operator in one of those black-and-white movies from the forties.

"Probably, although you can print out my e-mails after we're done."

"So what's the scoop?"

"Well, first off, I know where your cousin is hiding out."

"What? How did you manage that? And how did you even know she wasn't still in Toccoa?" Erik and I had had no contact since my abortive trip into Georgia.

There was enough of a pause that I thought the system might have disconnected us before he finally said, "Well, when I didn't hear from you, I figured you'd struck out, so I did a little un-authorized detecting on my own. I hope you aren't going to be pissed off. I drove down there on Saturday night. Well, actually, Sunday morning, I guess."

"You drove from Charlotte to Toccoa, Georgia?"

"Sure. It was no big deal. Took less than four hours. I'm actually a lot closer to there than you are. I went home after I closed up the store and slept until about three, then headed down 85. I had time enough once I got there to have a really good breakfast, clean up a little, and still be on their doorstep to intercept them on their way to church."

"What on earth did you say? Who did you tell them you were?"

I could hear the smile in his voice when he said, "I don't think I want to go into that on an open line like this. Let's just say they were convinced I had official standing."

"Erik, that's crazy! You can't go around impersonating a police officer. You could go to jail for pulling a stunt like that!"

"Hey, take it easy. I never *said* I was anything. I can't help what they chose to assume." His tone softened. "Believe me, Bay, I would never do anything to jeopardize what we're trying to build here. I would never put you in harm's way, legally or otherwise. Okay?"

I forced myself to speak reasonably. "I appreciate what you're saying, Erik, but it was still a dangerous thing to do." When he didn't answer, I lit a cigarette and exhaled slowly. "Okay, lecture over. So what did you find out?"

"You're not going to like it."

"Try me."

"She's staying with a relative."

I propped my feet up on the desk. "I don't get it. I thought both her grandparents were dead, and her mother's been gone for years."

"Think more distant than that."

"You mean in miles or in relationship?"

"Relationship. Bay, maybe I should just tell—"

"Son of a bitch!" I exploded, my feet crashing to the floor. "Aunt Eliza!"

"Bingo."

"Did Vesta actually tell you that?"

"Well, not exactly. But she said Mercer was with 'family,' and we shouldn't worry about her. As you said, everyone in her immediate family is gone, so who else could it be?"

"But wait a minute, that doesn't make any sense!" I struggled to put the timeline together even as a deeper, more intuitive part of my brain shouted the answer at me. "If Mercer had just been with her foster parents, and she was already gone when I got there on Saturday, then . . ."

Erik supplied the incredible, but obvious solution for me. "Then she was probably hiding out at your aunt's house on Friday. While you were there."

CHAPTER
SEVENTEEN

My foray into Publix next morning proved only slightly less onerous than I'd expected.

As I wheeled the massive cart up and down the wide aisles, Lavinia's list clutched in my sweaty hand, I found myself being pretty much ignored by my fellow shoppers. My brief attempts at striking up conversation as I contemplated the vast array of cereal choices or studied the various packages of dead cow carcasses were smilingly rebuffed. I was surrounded by women who located exactly what they wanted in a swift glance, pitched it into the cart and moved on. My plodding perusal of brands and labels certainly marked me out as a novice.

I tried to console myself with the fact that most of them couldn't tell a 5500C/R from a Subchapter S return, but it didn't help much. My lack of knowledge in the hunter/gatherer skills was an affront to my womanhood. Society decreed that since I had breasts and ovaries, I should have sprung from the womb knowing how to shop. And cook.

Back home, with the groceries successfully stowed away, I no longer had any excuse to postpone thinking about Erik Whiteside's revelations of the night before. I microwaved a cup of hot water, dropped in a teabag, and settled onto the top step of the back deck. The weather had finally shaped up, bringing a return of cloudless blue sky and warm sun. In a light sweater and jeans, I felt just right.

The image of Aunt Eliza Baynard suddenly popped into my head. She had seemed to be a woman without guile, a proper preacher's daughter who would no more lie than she would cheat or steal. Could I seriously imagine her concealing something as serious as a federal fugitive's crouching somewhere in the upper stories of her house while she sipped tea and reminisced with me in the downstairs parlor? Her pain and loneliness had been real, of that I was certain. And, if she really hadn't wanted me there, she could have refused to come to the door. Hadn't I already berated myself by that time for assuming she'd be home just because I wanted to see her? Another couple of minutes of silence, and I would have gotten in my car and driven away, sad at not having made connections with my aunt after all those years, but at least none the wiser about the houseguest she was already harboring. So why was she so eager to invite me in, insist I stay for lunch, try to hold me there longer with the letters and stories about my Baynard ancestors? It made no sense, unless . . .

Suddenly I remembered the creaks and moans of the boards over my head as I sat in my uncle's library and rifled his desk. I had put it all down to rats and the usual protests of a centuries-old house settling in for the night. Had it been more than that? Was Mercer Mary Prescott even then lurking somewhere on the upper floors, biding her time until I finally got out of there and left the field open for her? Honea Path was a small town. Probably no one worried much about locking doors. How difficult would it have been for my cousin to sneak into a house she was already familiar with and conceal herself in one of the abandoned rooms?

Did Aunt Eliza appear so innocent simply because she *was*?

I hauled myself up and trotted back into the house. I heard a sharp *miaow* as Mr. Bones voiced his protest at nearly getting caught in the closing door. I scooped him up and carried him with me into the kitchen. I looked up my aunt's number, dialed, and stuck the portable phone between my left cheek and shoulder while I tore open a foil pouch of cat food and poured it into the blue china bowl on the rug in front of the sink.

I dropped onto the floor and began picking little bits of twig and fluff out of the old tabby's matted fur while the measured ringing continued unanswered in my ear. I couldn't remember how many tries it had taken before the machine picked up when I called last week from Edgefield, but I was sure it hadn't been this many. Annoyance and fear vied for dominance as I punched the OFF button with more force than was strictly required and swore softly to myself.

What should I do? There could be a perfectly reasonable explanation of why my aunt's answering machine hadn't picked up. Maybe the tape was full. Maybe she had accidentally turned it off or disconnected it in some way. But even if she were napping, I'd given her plenty of rings to get to the phone, despite how slowly her infirmity forced her to move. So she probably wasn't home.

Did she drive? I remembered the beat-up Ford station wagon in the side yard, but there was something . . . I closed my eyes and conjured up a picture of the huge old relic, it's faded paint and peeling, wood-grain paneling, and— No plates! That's what I had been trying to remember, what had struck me as strange about the car. It had no license plates.

So where was Aunt Eliza? I pushed away all the awful images my brain was trying to force me to look at and reached again for the phone. I'd call information for the number of the church and get them to check on her. Failing that, I'd have Red contact the local cops and ask them to stop in and make sure she was all right. No mention of Mercer Mary Prescott or federal warrants or missing security guards. Just an overly concerned relative wanting reassurance. And if that didn't work, I'd get in the car myself and—

The loud banging on my side door sent the cat scurrying under the table and all thoughts of Aunt Eliza fleeing from my mind.

I wasn't expecting anyone, and no one had called from the security gate for authorization to issue a pass. I had been beyond paranoid recently about making certain the doors were locked and the alarm set at all times, but even so, I reached into my bag and wrapped my fingers around the Glock.

In the foyer I approached the door and stuck my eye to the peephole. The face was bloated and distorted by the tiny lens, but even so I was certain this was no one I knew. I switched the gun to my left hand and fumbled with the button on the intercom unit next to the keypad.

"Yes?" I spoke into the white plastic grille.

"Mrs. Tanner? Bay Tanner?" The voice, deep and broad, with a hint of some sort of twang, boomed over the speaker.

"What can I do for you?" I hadn't confirmed his identification of me, but I hadn't denied it, either. In truth he probably wouldn't have asked the question if he didn't already know the answer.

"I'd like to talk to you. It's important."

I risked a quick peek out the sidelight window. He seemed to be standing quite at ease, one hand in the pocket of his faded, but neatly pressed jeans. He also wore a khaki blazer hanging loose over an open-collared, white dress shirt. It was hard to tell for sure, but I thought he held some kind of hat in his other hand. He didn't look like a serial rapist, or one of Buddy Slade's henchmen, but then neither had Ted Bundy. Still . . .

"This is a gated community," I said in the stern tone I'd used with clients who dared to suggest I cheat, just a little, on their income tax returns. "How did you get in here without a pass?"

"Look, Mrs. Tanner, we have mutual friends. If you want to check me out first, call your sister-in-law. Sarah's the one sent me here to see you."

Jack Wilson! The environmentalist from Montana or South Dakota Sarah had spent Thanksgiving with. It had to be. That would account for the accent. And it was probably a cowboy hat he was slapping lightly against his thigh as he shifted from one foot to the other, waiting for my response.

"That still doesn't explain how you got in here, Mr. Wilson. Or why she didn't call me for a pass."

I could hear the smile in his reply. "Ah, Sarah was right about you. You are quick. She was afraid you'd refuse, so she called one of her other friends in the plantation. They cleared it with the gate."

That didn't sound like Sarah. I'd never thought of her as devious. But then, at least according to my brother-in-law, she'd been acting strangely in a lot of ways lately. And that outburst in the Fig Tree had been just as uncharacteristic. Perhaps this would be a chance to find out what was really going on with Red's ex-wife. Curiosity won out over paranoia, but not over caution.

"Hold on."

I retreated into the great room to stuff the Glock behind a cushion on the sofa before returning to the foyer to disarm the security system. When I pulled open the door, Jack Wilson met my eyes with a level gaze and a crooked grin beneath a neatly trimmed, black mustache which gave him a slightly disreputable look.

"Thank you, ma'am," he said, exaggerating the Western drawl, "much obliged." He was my height, maybe a little taller, and my first impression was of a man who, whether by good fortune or design, could have easily passed for the actor Sam Elliott. His straight, black hair was drawn back in a ponytail held in place by a knotted leather thong. "Guess there's no need to introduce myself, except to say that I appreciate you seeing me like this, with no notice or anything." I closed the door behind him and led the way into the great room.

I settled myself on the sofa, my right arm draped across the cushion where I'd stashed the gun. Jack Wilson took a chair by the fireplace, his long legs stretched out in front of him. To my disappointment, he was wearing scuffed loafers instead of snakeskin boots, but the weathered hat he tossed onto the floor beside him was at least of the five-gallon variety.

"So. How can I help you?" I asked, watching my guest survey the room with the practiced eye of a real estate appraiser. "You said Sarah sent you to see me?"

"Yes, she did." He leaned forward, elbows on knees, and fixed me with a look of studied sincerity that would have done credit to an infomercial pitchman. "Sarah told me about your lunch the other day. About her ex-husband's concerns, and I think she just wanted me to stop by and let us get acquainted so you could reassure him."

"About what?"

He grinned, and I could feel the charm rolling off him in waves. It was hard to tell if it was intentional, or if he was just one of those men who couldn't help coming on, even innocently, to any female who happened to be in range.

"Oh, I guess that I'm relatively harmless. That I have no 'designs' on Sarah, even though I find her incredibly attractive, not to mention bright and dedicated. That I think his kids are great, but I'm not lookin' to take his place."

"Don't think for a minute you could," I snapped back, a little more forcefully than I'd intended. "Red is crazy about Scotty and Elinor, and they feel the same about him." I eased back a little onto the pillows and made myself relax. No sense getting him riled up before I had a chance to pump him dry. "Excuse me a moment," I added, rising and crossing to where my bag sat on the chair in front of the built-in desk in the kitchen. I returned with my cigarettes and lighter and set them beside me on the end table.

"Mind if I join you?" Jack asked, pulling his own crumpled

pack of Marlboros from his jacket pocket.

I would have been so disappointed if it had been any other brand. "Be my guest. There's another ashtray on the mantel."

In this day and age of virulent antismoking sentiment everywhere you looked, it was refreshing to be able to light up, even in my own house, without having to apologize for it. Nonetheless, I found it pretty strange that this man Sarah Tanner had described as committed to making the world a safer place for her children would be so cavalier about his own contribution to polluting their atmosphere.

"So what exactly is it that you do?" I asked when we had both exhaled plumes of smoke into the air above each other's heads. "Sarah was a little vague."

Again I was struck by the grace of the man, the smooth economy of movement as he crossed his legs at the ankles and settled back into the chair. "I'm an advocate for environmental issues," he said without preamble. "I help organize protests— letter-writing campaigns, petition drives, and so on—against companies and organizations that threaten to harm the environment. I also lecture on ecological preservation and land use management."

"Does that pay well?"

This time his laugh held just a little less good humor. "Leave it to an accountant to cut right to the money questions."

So he had been checking me out, too. Old information, though, since I hadn't been practicing my profession for more than a year. Which probably meant it wasn't Sarah who had given him the lowdown on me. *Interesting.* Unfortunately, Erik Whiteside hadn't had time to get back to me with any background on Jack Wilson, and Red's attempts to trace him through the criminal justice system had met with zero success.

I sized him up through a haze of smoke as I crushed out my cigarette and found his hazel eyes studying me just as intently.

"Sarah should have warned you about me," I said, squaring around on the sofa to face him directly. "Due to some bizarre circumstances over the past few months, I've come to the conclusion that life's too short to waste it on tap dancing. What is it you want from me, Mr. Wilson?"

"Your stamp of approval, I suppose. Your assurance to Sergeant Tanner that I'm not Charlie Manson or Svengali. Look,

Sarah is very important to me. To my work. She's afraid her ex-
husband will cause trouble for me if he thinks I'm not on the up-
and-up. I just want you to convince him that I am."

Again he cranked up the charm machine, with a diffident
shrug and a self-deprecating smile intended to demonstrate to me
his complete candor.

I had to admit he was good. The problem was, in the course of
my dealings with some of the high fliers and pampered playboy
sons of my wealthier clients, I'd been flimflammed by the best of
them. With a couple of notable exceptions, my bullshit meter is
generally right on the mark.

"I'm not sure I can do that without a lot more information.
What kind of trouble do you think my brother-in-law could make
for you? Does what you do put you into conflict with the law?"

"Not as a rule," he replied, lighting another Marlboro with a
slim, silver lighter studded with flecks of turquoise stone. "But I'd
be lying if I said we *never* stepped over the line when it comes to
the authorities. We have a lot of folks who believe passionately in
what we're doing." Jack Wilson fixed me with an earnest stare.
"When a cause is this vital, this *compelling,* sometimes the
frustration spills over into actions we later regret."

"I think you're tap dancing again, Mr. Wilson. Just what is this
organization you keep referring to, the one you've apparently
gotten Sarah Tanner involved in? I think that's what's concerning
Red, more than anything to do with whether the two of you are
romantically involved or not."

"Our name isn't important, *Mrs.* Tanner." He sounded
frustrated that I had refused to be enticed into putting our
exchanges on a more intimate, first-name basis. "But our work is.
We're not about saving whales or protecting the habitat of the
spotted owl." He crushed out his cigarette and leaned over to
retrieve his well-worn cowboy hat from the floor. "Our mission is
much more encompassing than that. More global. We're fighting
for the survival of the planet."

I wondered if he realized how pompous he sounded, even as I
recognized the same convert's zeal I'd seen gleaming in the eyes
of Bill Scoggins a few days before. "I seem to remember Carl
Sagan's saying something like we shouldn't worry too much about
the Earth's survival. *People* might not be around to enjoy it, but
the planet did pretty well before we showed up, and it will

probably get along just fine even if we do manage, through war or pestilence, to wipe ourselves off the face of it."

"Are you a religious woman, Mrs. Tanner?"

The question took me completely off guard, and I stumbled a little over my answer. "No, not particularly. Why do you ask?"

"Perhaps if you studied my people's spiritual beliefs concerning the interrelationships of all the creatures and forms of life we share the earth with, you might not be so quick to dismiss us." Abruptly he stood up. "Thanks for seeing me."

He strode toward the foyer, his anger evident in the stiff set of his wide shoulders beneath the casual jacket.

"Mr. Wilson! Jack! Hold on a minute." He turned at the door and waited for me to catch up to him. "I didn't mean . . . that is, I'm sorry if I offended you." I paused, surprised by the raw power the man exuded in the confined space of the entryway. "I had no idea this was a religious movement." When he didn't reply, I added, "But in fairness, you did barge in on *me*."

"You're right, and I apologize for that. Just let your brother-in-law know I'm not the leader of some crazed cult and that his ex-wife and kids are in no danger. At least not from me."

With a nod he settled his hat onto his thick hair and trotted down the steps.

I closed the door and reset the alarm, then retrieved the Glock from behind the sofa cushion and returned it to my bag. I poured myself a glass of iced tea and carried it into the office where I fired up the computer. Hopefully, Erik had had an opportunity to garner some information on this mysterious man who had captured Sarah Tanner's devotion—to his cause, if not yet to himself. The reference to his *people,* as well as his appearance, made it pretty obvious he was at least part Indian. I know *Native American* is more politically correct these days, but old habits die hard.

The flag was up on my cyberspace mailbox, and I eagerly clicked through to the messages. There were three from Erik Whiteside, two from the day before which, in the shock of his revelations about the probable whereabouts of Mercer Mary Prescott, I'd completely forgotten about. A fourth displayed no subject and an unfamiliar sender ID. When I clicked it open, I found myself staring down the barrel of a gun. Before I could react, an animated finger closed around the trigger and the screen exploded with a *crack!*

The whine of the bullet sounded so real I threw myself out of the chair as if it might actually tear through the monitor and into my chest. As I lay quivering on the floor amid spilled tea and scattered ice cubes, I heard a harsh, computer-generated voice say, "Stay the hell out of our business, bitch. First and last warning."

CHAPTER
EIGHTEEN

I changed out of my iced-tea-spattered sweater and jeans and smoked two cigarettes before I felt steady enough to confront the computer again. What I found was a completely blank e-mail screen innocently awaiting my instructions. Whoever had sent me the animated death threat knew his—or her—way around. The header containing the sender's address had disappeared as well. I tried clicking on my "Old Mail" file as well as on my Personal Filing Cabinet, but it was as if the message had never been sent or received.

Mr. Bones watched from a safe distance as I mopped up the mess from the carpet and tackled the stain. As I worked, I ran down a mental list of possible suspects. Whose territory had I invaded, whose person or livelihood had I threatened enough to warrant such a chilling and graphic response?

During Rob's tenure as head of Special Investigations for the State Attorney General's office, he had made some powerful enemies. They had blown his plane out of the sky, killing innocent people, in order to silence him. I had made my own enemies over the past few months, but none of them had any reason to threaten me now. That left the current crop of bad guys. I conjured up the image of Buddy Slade, the Elvis clone with the weirdly tattooed fingers, and Dolores's description of his female cohorts. This bunch had certainly proved itself more than capable of violence, although none of them seemed to possess the subtlety or sophistication for a cyberspace attack. They had clearly demonstrated their preference for the direct approach.

As I carried my cleaning supplies out to the kitchen, I forcibly shut out the picture of Dolores as I had found her, curled in her own blood in the middle of the hallway.

Jack Wilson? Despite Red's misgivings, I couldn't see him as the e-mail sender. Besides, he had just left my house after trying to enlist my support in keeping the authorities off his back. What reason would he have for resorting to threat when he hadn't yet determined that his considerable charm had failed?

Mercer Mary Prescott, my half fifth cousin, had somehow set everything in motion with her phone call to the Judge when she'd first been arrested for vagrancy. In the intervening weeks, my father and I had chased after her, but only in an effort to keep her out of jail. What could we have done to cause her to turn on us in such a drastic fashion?

Nothing. Not a damned thing, I told myself, slamming the cabinet door in frustration. So what in the name of sanity was all this about?

Some day, when I felt more emotionally detached, I'd have to sit down and figure out why I kept attracting these kinds of people and situations into my life. In the meantime, I desperately needed something to force all this pointless conjecture out of my brain. I pulled the blood-soaked chuck roast I'd purchased at Publix out of the refrigerator, wiped off my hands, and opened the oldest, most food-stained cookbook to the page Lavinia had marked with a yellow sticky-note. As I studied the ingredients and surprisingly simple instructions, I decided I would not allow the day to end before I had reduced my own muddled thinking to a similar order.

I thought of Rob and smiled.

I would make a list.

The kitchen looked as if a tactical nuclear weapon had been detonated somewhere in the vicinity of the stove, but I couldn't help grinning as I sat back from the glass-topped table and touched the napkin to my lips.

Why had I always thought this was so difficult?

I carried my plate and silverware to the counter and set the stopper into one half of the divided sink. The meat had been tender and delicious, the vegetables browned to perfection. True, I had scraped a couple of knuckles before I got the hang of Dolores's new-fangled potato peeler and had carefully retrieved the end of a fingernail from the pile of sliced onions, but all in all my first culinary attempt had been a resounding success.

What next? I wondered to myself, squirting dish soap under the running stream of hot water. I conjured up memories of all the fabulous meals Lavinia had provided over her years at Presqu'isle, from the Judge's Lowcountry favorites like Frogmore stew and dirty rice to my mother's more genteel preferences. Perhaps something with shrimp, I thought, as I poured myself a cup of tea, and carried it, along with the tattered cookbook, back to the kitchen table. I leafed idly through the seafood section, suddenly realizing some of the pages in the three-ring binder were handwritten. Apparently my mother had copied some old family "receipts" and added them to the publisher's collection. Suddenly one name leaped out, startling me with its familiarity, and destroying the sweet contentment which had surrounded me for the past few minutes.

At the top of a page headed *Catfish Soup*, someone had written "Isabelle Robichoux Chase, from her Mama," and my eyes flew immediately across the room to the yellow legal pad I'd abandoned on the kitchen desktop. My list. Reality beckoned. With a sigh, I closed the cookbook, refreshed my tea, and headed for the computer.

When I finally took a break at a little after ten, I'd already covered three sheets of paper with lists of names, dates and places, and diagrams of relationships, many of them connected to each other by sweeping arrows or squiggly lines, but I was really no farther ahead than when I'd begun. Erik's e-mails, neglected after my encounter with the cyber-pistol, had provided additional information which I'd duly noted, without having any concrete idea about exactly where it fit into the total picture.

Basically, he'd unearthed some old newspaper articles about the disappearance of Mercer Mary Prescott's mother some fourteen years before. The dates on the stories gave me a momentary jolt. At almost the exact moment that Robert James Tanner and I had been making eye contact across the ballroom at the Charleston Chamber of Commerce gala, Mercer's Nana Mary would have been pacing the worn linoleum floor of her outdated kitchen, wondering why her daughter Catherine hadn't come home from work.

Tucker and Toccoa had been even smaller towns then with

only a weekly newspaper. The Prescotts had been reluctant to involve the authorities, convinced their daughter would return on her own, but friends and coworkers seemed certain Catherine would never have gone off voluntarily, with no word of goodbye to her parents or to her daughter. She had left no note, and the tiny closet in the bedroom she shared with her little girl remained crammed with the bright yellows and reds of the flashy clothes she favored.

In the end, with no evidence of foul play, the town apparently came to accept the fact that Will and Mary Prescott's only child had suddenly found the burden of single parenthood too much to bear and had simply walked away.

And within a few short years of that wrenching abandonment, Mercer had once again been torn apart from her family, I thought as I carried the dregs of my tea out to the kitchen and dumped them into the sink. And even though I had observed first hand what a stable and caring environment the Scogginses had provided for her, it must still have felt to the little girl as if she had been discarded. I turned on the tap and let the water run hot, then swung the faucet over to the other side where the roasting pan sat floating beneath a layer of carrot and potato bits and congealing fat. I rummaged beneath the sink and located a pair of faded yellow rubber gloves.

As I scrubbed away at the encrusted gunk on the bottom of the pan, I wondered what kind of psychological damage such upheaval might have done, how much it had influenced my cousin's choice of lifestyle, work, friends. *Husband.* There would certainly have been anger, along with the sadness and loss. I knew something about those feelings. The hardest part of trying to come to terms with Rob's murder had been the guilt. Not guilt that I had survived or had in any way contributed to his death, but rather for being so incredibly *furious* with him for dying. For leaving me alone.

How much worse it must have been for a little girl to cope with it all. And Mercer hadn't even had the solace of knowing that those who had abandoned her hadn't had any choice. In both cases, a conscious decision had been made to separate from the child, first by a selfish mother and then by an overburdened grandmother. As I returned the now spotless roasting pan to the cupboard and dried my hands on the dishtowel, I realized I had talked myself into sympathizing with Mercer Mary Prescott. It was a much more comfortable emotion than the barely suppressed hatred I had been feeling, blaming her indirectly for my friend's injuries.

I fed the cat and turned out the lights, pausing on the second step to survey this room which Dolores had designed just a few short months ago, remembering the pride and delight she'd felt when it was completed. For a moment the idea of selling the house flashed briefly across my mind, but I quickly suppressed it. True, there was way too much death and mayhem in my life lately, way too many ghosts trailing after Mr. Bones and me as we padded down the hall to the bedroom. But I refused to let them chase me out of my home, to allow them to dictate how or where I lived.

Tomorrow is another day. In the past, like Scarlett, I had used her mantra as an excuse to postpone dealing with my problems. That night as I pulled a soft flannel nightgown over my head and slid beneath the cool sheets on the king-size bed, I turned it instead into resolve: I would find Mercer Mary Prescott. I would wring from her the truth about Buddy Slade and his Manson-like followers and their attack on Dolores.

I would begin to exorcise the ghosts.

CHAPTER NINETEEN

It's amazing what a sound night's sleep and a good breakfast can do to restore your soul.

I got on the road just as the sun had begun to spread its soft glow over the cold gray of the winter ocean, the vibrant oranges and reds promising warmth and hope for the new day. Sometime in the night my subconscious must have sorted through all the jumble of the last few days, because I awoke in the predawn stillness with a plan fully formed in my mind.

Fortified with perfect eggs and the best redskin home fries on the planet, I sped west from Frank's Diner and onto the mainland. Even this early, traffic toward the island was heavy with the hundreds of workers needed to keep the hotels, retail stores, and restaurants humming. The lack of tourist hordes only meant that activity on Hilton Head had slowed to a manageable flurry compared to the frenetic pace of the summer. Except for the coldest weeks in late December and early January, conventions and golf packages now kept everyone busy year-round.

I had to take the long way around to avoid the Savannah River bridge, my inexplicable fear of the span and its towering super-structure making all my forays into the city more complicated than for most other people. Even so, I managed to pull into the parking lot of Neddie Halloran's office just as she was unwinding her long legs from the cramped front seat of her pearl gray Mercedes. As I whipped my car in beside her, I had to smile at the look of total confusion which wrinkled her brow.

"I know I'm getting old, but I'd bet my incredibly naturally curly hair against a shaved head that you don't have an appointment," Neddie said when I'd managed to extricate my own nearly six-foot frame from the tortuous bucket seat of the Zeemer.

"Much as I'd like to see the noble shape of your headshrinker's skull, you are correct."

"So to what do I owe the pleasure? Everything okay?" she added, her smile fading a little.

"Coping," I said by way of forestalling any discussion of Dolores or the aftermath of the attack on her.

Neddie must have read the resolution on my face as we walked up the wide porch steps. She unlocked the solid oak door of the restored Victorian mansion and, without further comment, led the way into her office.

"Where's Carolann?" I asked while Neddie fumbled with the coffeemaker, ripping the first filter she tried to pry from the stack on the counter.

"Sick. Some kind of flu she picked up, either here or from her own two. Want a job for a couple of days?"

"No, ma'am!" The thought of dealing with a steady parade of messed-up kids and their anguished parents made my problems seem somehow a little less daunting. "Unless you're desperate," I added as the renowned child psychologist finally managed to get her morning coffee brewing, having spilled only about a cup of granules and half a gallon of water in the process.

"Thanks, but I've got a temp coming. I've used her before, so it shouldn't be too much of a disaster. All I really need is a warm body, preferably taller than my patients, to keep the little monsters from destroying the waiting room." She paused before adding, "So?"

"So, what the hell do I want and how much is it going to screw up your day, that kind of *so*?"

"Exactly."

"I only need a few minutes. I promise I'll be on my way before ten."

Neddie poured coffee into a huge blue mug, grimaced at her first taste, then dumped in milk and about a pound of sugar. "Okay," she said, sliding behind her desk, "shoot."

I dropped into the only other grown-up-sized chair in the office and crossed my black trousered legs. "You haven't heard the saga of my cousin, Mercer Mary Prescott yet, have you." I ached for a cigarette, but my determination on that front had stiffened, too. I plucked a pencil out of the bouquet sprouting from a small glass vase on the desk and twirled it to occupy my idle hands.

"Cousin? No."

Briefly I sketched it all out, from that first phone call, through the attacks on both Dolores and me, and everything I'd learned from the Scogginses and Erik Whiteside's Internet snooping, throwing Sarah Tanner and Jack Wilson in at the last moment, though why I couldn't have said.

"Where do you find these people?" was Neddie's first comment, followed immediately by, "Wait, never mind that. How can I help?"

"Given everything I've told you about Mercer—her birth, her mother's bailing out, her grandparents' handing her over to foster care—what's the likelihood that she'd go bad? I mean, could she be something more than the innocent little victim of circumstances she portrays? Could she be capable of violence?"

"Ah, Tanner," Neddie sighed, setting aside the coffee and slipping on her glasses, "I suppose I should be flattered by your boundless faith in my abilities. I know 'psychologist' and 'psychic' sound a lot alike, but personally I find it very difficult to diagnose a patient I've never seen or spoken with."

"I'm not asking for a clinical diagnosis, Neddie. I'm working on a theory, and I want to know if some of my assumptions are valid, or if I'm just whistling up a stump."

" 'Whistling up a stump'? Is that one of those charming Southern colloquialisms, like 'might could' and 'a whoop and a holler'?"

"I've never said 'might could' in my life. And quit stalling. I need an answer. Even a semi-educated guess would help at this point."

"Okay, okay." Neddie leaned back in her antique oak desk chair and steepled her fingers under chin. "Let me think about this a minute."

I dropped the pencil back on her desk and began fidgeting with the items within my reach, arranging the letter opener, stapler, and a few loose pens into perfect alignment with each other. I'd just begun to untangle the mass of paperclips when Neddie reached out and slapped my knuckles.

"Stop that! God, you are so obsessive it's scaring me!"

I sat back in my chair and folded my hands in my lap.

"Okay, look at it like this. Let's say you have an abused child, battered around either physically or emotionally, who manages to survive to adulthood in relatively good shape. Mentally, I mean."

"But Mercer wasn't abused, at least . . ."

"This is hypothetical, okay? What I'm saying is, this person can go one of two totally disparate ways. Either they adopt the lifestyle of the parents and become abusive themselves, which is the most common outcome, or they could go completely in the opposite direction and seek out people who will abuse them in the same manner they were used to as children."

I found the nest of paperclips back in my hand, my fingers working frantically at rescuing each individual piece of metal from the twisted mass.

"Bay! Will you stop that?" Neddie thundered just as the office door slid open a crack, then banged shut on a squeak of alarm from the other side. "Oh, damn!" Neddie said, her voice now at half its previous decibel level. "Come in," she called sweetly.

"Dr. Halloran? It's me, Shelley Hixon. From the agency? I'm sorry, I didn't realize you already had a patient."

The face which peeked timorously around the doorway was young and tan and topped by an impossibly huge halo of white-blond curls.

"It's all right, Shelley. I'll just be another few minutes. Keep them occupied out there 'til I'm done, okay?"

"Yes, ma'am. I mean, yes, Dr. Halloran," she almost whispered as the door clicked shut.

"Nice hair," I said to break the tension, and Neddie laughed.

"Yeah, a little far out, but Shelley's a good kid." I saw her eyes slide pointedly toward my hands. I took the hint and dropped the paperclips back into their holder.

"Can I have a cigarette?" I asked, leaning over to rest my elbows on her desk.

"No. In a few minutes I'll have a twelve-year-old in here who's tried every legal drug known to man, including nicotine, alcohol, glue, and anything else that can be chewed, swallowed, or inhaled. I don't want him getting a whiff of your stale smoke."

"Tyrant. So how does all this apply to Mercer?"

"Same principle. She could either use her perceived rejection as a reason to seek out loving relationships to compensate, or she could turn into a hard-hearted sociopath who trusts no one and so operates to satisfy only her own needs. No empathy at all for how her actions affect others. Most kids would fall somewhere in between. Without more to go on, I can't really give you any definitive answer."

"I guess that makes sense, but it isn't a whole hell of a lot of help."

"Sorry, honey, but this isn't accounting, you know. I can't just tote up the ducats and credits and give you a perfect, unassailable answer."

"*Debits*," I laughed, "*debits* and credits. Ducats are gold pieces or something like that."

"Whatever. You know what I mean."

I rose and slipped the strap of my bag over my shoulder. Neddie stepped from behind her desk and hugged me warmly. We walked arm in arm toward the side door which would allow me to leave without encountering the patients waiting in reception. "But think about this." she added as we paused in the doorway. "Whichever way Mercer has decided to jump, one thing is pretty certain. Two things, actually. First, she'll have a rich fantasy life, imagining either warm, loving relationships with everyone she meets, or dreaming of revenge for all her hurts, real and perceived."

I fished my car keys out of my bag. "And the second?"

"That she'll be a master of manipulation. I wouldn't put a lot of stock in any story she spins you without checking it out pretty thoroughly. Remember, she's managed to survive for twenty-some years with all the pain and anger these abandonments have caused her. Trust me, she's learned to be a good little liar."

"Not bad for someone who said she couldn't give me a diagnosis. You should stop underestimating yourself, Halloran."

"As I've said before, that's why I get the big bucks. Now get out of here," she said nudging me through the doorway, "and let me earn some."

"Thanks, I owe you," I called as I crossed the side porch to the street.

"I'm putting it on your tab." I heard her short bark of laughter as the door eased shut.

I made myself wait until I was out into the stream of mid-morning Savannah traffic before I lit a cigarette. The earlier mist hovering over the river had dissipated, burned away by the strengthening sun. I flipped on the local FM oldies station just in time to hear the tail-end of the weather forecast. Seventy-five today, possibly close to eighty by tomorrow, and zero per cent chance of rain.

About time, I thought as I took the ramp onto I-95 north. Such temperatures are not normal this late in the fall season, but it was my firm opinion that the damp ugliness of November had entitled us to a break.

As I let down the windows and breathed deeply of the moist, warm air, I took stock of what I had just learned from Neddie. Her assessment of Mercer's psyche had raised almost as many questions as it had answered. Nonetheless, I had confirmed that violence could not be ruled out as a potential reaction by Mercer to the trauma of her childhood. It was this possibility which had led to my predawn phone call to Aunt Eliza in Honea Path . . .

Thankfully, like many older folks, she was an early riser. Her Southern-bred manners had kept her from displaying annoyance at my guarded questions, but it also kept her from grasping the urgency of the situation. We had fenced for several minutes, exchanging pleasantries and oblique references, until frustration finally edged me into bluntness.

"Is Mercer Mary Prescott there with you?" I asked, noting the extended pause before the answer.

"Why no, honey, she's not. Why do you ask?"

"Has she been? Before?"

"Well, of course, Lydia, don't you remember?" An unfamiliar asperity had crept into my aunt's usually sweet tone. "I told you she came to tea. To discuss the genealogy I sent her."

"I mean since then. Aunt Eliza, this is very important. Has Mercer been staying with you? Has she been hiding out there?"

"Hiding out? Dear, I'm afraid I don't understand."

"Mercer is wanted by the authorities for trespassing and destroying government property. She's run away from them twice, and there's a federal warrant out for her arrest. If you're letting her stay there, it could be considered harboring a fugitive. You could be in serious trouble."

"Lydia Baynard Simpson, I swear I don't know what's gotten into you. Of all the outlandish things! Are you accusing me of being a criminal?"

I opened my mouth to deny it, but my feisty aunt gave me no opportunity.

"I believe you must have taken leave of your senses, girl. It comes from your father's side of the family, no doubt. Your mother and my Rupert may have had their little idiosyncrasies, but the Baynards have never been given to delusions, which must surely be what's overcome *you*."

I almost laughed, despite the seriousness of the situation. I had been well and properly put in my place, and with such grace I nearly thanked her for it. "I'm sorry, but I needed to know. Is there any chance she could have sneaked in without your being aware of it? Could she be hiding in some of the upstairs rooms?"

"Of course not! Why, I know every creak and flutter of this old place. I may be old, but my hearing is fine. I'd know in a heartbeat if anyone were moving around up there. Besides, I don't believe Mercer would be too happy about sharing the space with the bats."

"Bats?" I gulped, recalling again the scrabbling noises I'd noticed in the ceiling above my uncle's library.

"Bats. Taken over, lock, stock, and barrel. Too much trouble and too expensive to get them out, so I just left it to them. Believe me, my dear, no one could last very long upstairs . . ."

And now, despite my newfound resolve to be more tolerant of my half fifth cousin, I couldn't quite suppress a smile at the memory of my aunt's description. The image of Mercer, trapped in the nether regions of Eliza's decaying mansion with a few dozen flying rodents for company, gave a perverse lift to my spirits. As I roared around a slow-moving UPS truck, I cranked up the volume on the radio and joined the Beach Boys in a pounding rendition of "Surfin' USA."

I eased through the curve where Boundary Street becomes Carteret and came to a sudden halt behind a line of traffic that stretched ahead of me for blocks. The bridge from downtown Beaufort across to Lady's Island had to be open, allowing some tall-masted sailing ship to pass through from the little waterfront dock. Depending upon how many boats were in line to make the passage, we could be stuck for half an hour or more. I gave a brief thought to reversing around and trying the fixed-structure bridge closer to Parris Island. Instead I used the opportunity to unlock the hinges, then lower the top of the Z3. The sun held none of the blazing heat of July, but its almost spring-like warmth felt good against the skin of my upturned face, the cloudless sky an unexpected but welcome gift on this first day of December.

Hard to believe Christmas would be upon us in just a few short weeks. I had made absolutely no preparations. No wreath hung upon my door, no crinkly plastic bags stuffed with presents to be wrapped littered my tables, no boxes of cards decked with unfamiliar snow scenes waited to be addressed. This would be my second holiday season without Rob. I had made it through the first by pretending it didn't exist, sending Dolores off to spend Christmas with her family and ordering her not to return until after the New Year. Mr. Bones and I had slept, watched old black-and-white movies on TV, and subsisted on tuna fish and baloney and peanut butter. At the first hint of carols or a commercial remotely resembling any sappy *I'll-be-home-for-Christmas* sentiments, I had stabbed at the remote control, preferring anything—even wrestling or the Three Stooges—to the slightest reminder of what I had lost and would never regain.

This year, the Judge and Lavinia seemed determined to rope me into their own festivities which, to gauge by the load of boxes they'd been unpacking the last time I visited, would approximate the elaborate celebrations of my mother's era. I knew it was partly on my behalf that they labored, their efforts a thinly disguised attempt to help me make it through a season which, by its very nature, made loss and loneliness seem more deeply felt, more unbearable than at any other time of the year. I loved them for it, and I thought I might actually be ready to shed my pain and join in the spirit of the holidays again. But then there was Darnay . . . and Paris . . .

I jumped as a light tap of the horn from the big Lincoln filling my rearview mirror jarred me back to the moment. Traffic had begun to inch forward. I cranked the Z3 to roaring life and waved my thanks to the gray-haired gentleman in the black Town Car. Ten minutes later I was through the light at the foot of Bay Street, my eyes squinting against the glare of an unimpeded sun reflected off the placid surface of the Beaufort River as I rose slowly to the crest of the bridge.

I must not have been the only one lulled into a feeling of goodwill and serenity by the soft, warm wind. Although we all had to sit through the traffic light at the intersection on Lady's Island several times, there was none of the usual honking or grumbling or solitary fingers raised in obscene salute. The procession dwindled, drivers turning off into cross streets and businesses as we made our way across the narrow causeway to St. Helena. The marsh grass, dry and golden in its winter beauty, waved lazily on either side of the road.

As I bumped down the moss-draped drive to Presqu'isle, I spared a moment to order my thoughts. My plan was to head out tomorrow to retrace my itinerary of a week ago, stopping again in Edgefield to pursue the story of the local man whose disappearance I was convinced had been explained by the black body bag I'd seen lifted from the side of the road in the heart of the Savannah River Site. Surely the corpse had been positively identified by now. If my theory held water, his death would prove not to have been from natural causes, rather laid at the feet of the group of protesters of which my cousin had been a part. The timing fit, as did Mercer's twice running away from the law. It never made sense to me that she would have gone to such lengths to escape a simple trespassing charge. Maybe it was an accident, a confrontation gone horribly wrong. Perhaps she had been an unwitting accomplice or a witness. Or her fear of the law could stem from something in her past, something entirely unrelated to her present trouble. I hadn't worked that part out yet.

But that was exactly the reason it was imperative for me to find her, and fast. If the charges had been altered to include any connection with the unfortunate guard's death, or she had seen something or knew something that could compromise or implicate others in a murder . . . I knew my speculation was pointless. Mercer Mary Prescott knew the answers, and I intended to spend however long it took to track her down and shake the truth out of her scrawny frame. I'd start at Aunt Eliza's, search the place myself until I was satisfied she wasn't hiding in some unused, bat-infested room, then drive over to Columbia and the mental hospital where she'd last worked. If that didn't pan out, I'd head back up to Toccoa and camp on the doorstep of Bill and Vesta Scoggins until one of them gave her up. Either way, I did not plan to return to Hilton Head without my elusive cousin firmly in my grasp. As for the legal entanglements, we'd worry about that once I had her safely stashed away.

I slammed the door of the car and paused for a moment to

admire the way the winter sun bathed the stately old mansion in its pale yellow glow before bounding up the steps onto the front porch. As I turned the polished brass handle and eased into the dimness of the entry hall, I felt the familiar tightening of my shoulders. So many times I had walked through this heavy door, not to the welcome and safety of a refuge, but to anger, resentment, and raised voices. I had learned not to look for approval in this house, and I didn't expect it now. My mission was simply to *inform* my father of the decisions I had made, not to ask his blessing on them.

And in case anything went wrong, I wanted someone to know where to find me.

The clink of silver on china and a muted voice led me past the curving stairway. I peeked into the empty dining room, then followed the tantalizing smell of hot apples and cinnamon toward the kitchen. Lavinia stood at the stove, her back to me as I paused, stunned, in the doorway.

"Better cut another slice of pie, Vinnie," my father said matter-of-factly, "we've got company for dessert."

"Hi, Bay," my cousin Mercer Mary Prescott said, her muddy brown eyes regarding me solemnly from her seat at *my* place at the worn oak table.

CHAPTER
TWENTY

Of course the Judge did the bulk of the interrogating, his ability to badger, entice, and cajole being the stuff of local criminal justice lore. But in Mercer he had met his match. Neither of us could persuade her to part with any of her story.

But on that mild December afternoon, with both of us "girls" tucked into identical rocking chairs on the back verandah and the Judge contemplating the glowing end of his illegal Cuban cigar, we agreed I should drive Mercer "home," a destination whose location she also refused to divulge but where she obviously felt safe. Once there, she promised to explain everything. I believed her, though I had the feeling she hadn't anticipated my being at Presqu'isle, that my barging unannounced into the kitchen had forced her to change her plans in midstream. She was quick on her feet, you had to give her that. Once again she had sought us out, and I hoped we had made it clear this time that full disclosure would be the price of our help. It apparently never occurred to the single-mindedly selfish Mercer Mary Prescott that *we* were now the ones harboring a federal fugitive.

"I want you checking in with me hourly," my father said, lifting his nearly empty glass of bourbon and lemon and tossing off the last swallow. "Damn it, daughter, you should have one of those cell phones."

"We don't have time for that now." I watched Mercer twist a lank strand of her dull blond hair around one bony finger while she stared, unblinking, out toward the Sound. "Can you be ready to leave soon?" I asked, and she swiveled her head slightly to glance up at me.

"Just give me time to take a piss, and I'll be ready to roll." She continued to hold my gaze, almost as if she were gauging my reaction to her unnecessary crudeness.

"Then go take it, and let's get on the road," I said, refusing to flinch away from her unnerving stare. "I don't like driving on unfamiliar roads after dark."

"I need my duffel."

Her statement took me by surprise, and I broke eye contact. I felt somehow as if I had lost a contest by flinching first. Was that the *real* purpose of this unannounced visit? "I have it. It's home, on Hilton Head."

The Judge raised a quizzical eyebrow at me, but refrained from comment.

"Find anything interesting?" The question was delivered with a snide, accusing tone that translated immediately to her face. The open, innocent look of a few moments before had coarsened into something sly, almost sinister.

Remembering the tattered romance novels stuffed in the bottom of her bag, I said, "Yeah, your taste in literature sucks," as I rose and pulled open the screen door.

Her snort of laughter held only a trace of humor.

"Go do your business and let's get saddled up," I said, staring pointedly toward the ramp into the house. "I'll be right behind you. I need to speak to the Judge."

"So none of us are sharing our secrets today," Mercer quipped, sidling past me and inside.

"I'm having second thoughts," my father said as soon the sound of my cousin's booted footsteps faded into the depths of the old house. "I thought I had the child figured out, but she's like a chameleon. There's a dark side there."

"Too late to worry about it now." I, too, had begun to question the wisdom of spending several hours alone in my tiny car with a girl/woman who may or may not have been an accomplice to murder. "I talked with Neddie about her this morning, and I think I have a handle on where she's coming from," I added. "At least I know enough to be on my guard with her. Don't worry."

"Pah!" It was a sound I hadn't heard him make since the days of my childhood when I held the power to exasperate him beyond all measure. "Why do women always say inane things like, 'Don't worry'? What else will I have to do but sit trapped in this goddamned chair and worry?"

"I'll check in, Daddy, I promise." I bent to plant a kiss on the

top of his full head of snowy hair. The tenderness of it surprised us both, and I stepped back awkwardly. "Not hourly, but regularly."

"I'm ready, Cousin Bay," Mercer called sweetly from the doorway of the Judge's room.

"Right there," I hollered back. "Listen," I said, kneeling by my father's wheelchair, "call Erik Whiteside and bring him up to speed. See if he's managed to get hold of any information on the security guard who disappeared from the Savannah River Site. Remind him the guy lived in Edgefield, so the local papers should be a good source. And anything he's dug up on this bunch Mercer got arrested with. He can relay the information to you, and I'll pick it up when I call in."

"I don't like this, daughter," the Judge began, but I cut him off.

"We have to follow this through. You said it yourself: she's family. We owe her the benefit of the doubt now, no matter how it turns out in the end."

"Just be careful. And remember—if I don't hear from you within a reasonable amount of time, I'm going to have Redmond breathing down your neck, along with every damned law enforcement officer in the state, hear?"

"I hear you. Don't—" I caught his glare and stopped myself from saying *worry*. "Don't forget to call Erik," I amended.

As the screen door banged shut, I could still hear him muttering to himself about damned fool stubborn women.

By the time I'd thrown a few things into an overnight bag and retrieved Mercer's duffel from the back of my closet, it was after three. Besides khakis, sweatshirts, and a couple of changes of underwear, I'd also tucked in the spare box of ammunition Red had left me when he first brought me the gun. When we finally headed out, I set my tote bag, heavy with the weight of the Glock, just behind my seat where I could get to it in a hurry if the need arose. I tried not to analyze too closely why its presence gave me such a feeling of comfort and assurance.

I'd also taken the time to check in with the Santiagos, and I was grateful it had been Angie who answered the phone. I don't think I could have dealt with Hector's accusations and anger.

Unfortunately, the news was not good. The infection continued to rage, proving resistant to any of the usually effective drugs. I cringed at the fear that crept into Angie's voice despite her efforts to appear calm and upbeat. Time was running out for Dolores.

I shook off my own anxiety and gave my concentration over to the problem I thought I had a hope of resolving.

The air had begun its inevitable late-day cooling, but Mercer pleaded for me to leave the top down. We stopped briefly at a fast-food place at the intersection of I-95 so I could quiet the insistent rumblings of my stomach, then passed quickly through Hardeeville and turned north onto the same narrow, two-lane road down which I had traveled just a week before. Then I had been on an adventure, a quest whose goal had been simple and straightforward: find my cousin and convince her to turn herself in to the authorities. As I'd admired the last of the fall color not yet leached from the vast stands of trees stretching away toward the rising Piedmont, I had no inkling what pain the next few days would bring.

I pushed back the wave of guilt which rose through my chest at the thought of Dolores by shaking a cigarette out of the pack on the console and stabbing in the lighter. I jumped as Mercer spoke for the first time since we'd left the Hilton Head bridges behind.

"I can't believe a smart, educated woman like you still smokes." Her voice carried the familiar smugness of the unaddicted. "I mean, there must be like nine zillion studies proving it causes cancer. Not to mention endangering everyone around you."

I exhaled, watching as the wind rushing by us ripped the smoke into oblivion, and spared a glance at my cousin. She lay sprawled in the contoured seat, her head thrown back, face raised to the dwindling sun. She seemed oblivious to the long strands of mousy hair which had been pulled loose from their restraining band and now whipped against her cheeks as we sped along toward dusk.

"Living is hazardous to your health," I said, stung by the rebuke from this little troublemaker whose entry into my life had so far proved nothing but disastrous. "I suppose eating out of trash cans is considered politically correct in your environmentally sensitive crowd. What is it, some New Age brand of recycling? I can see the placards now: 'SAVE OUR LANDFILLS! EAT YOUR GARBAGE!' "

Her shout of laughter made me look her way again, and for a moment I caught a glimpse of what the Judge must have seen that first night at Presqu'isle when Mercer's sudden entrance into the room had caused him to drop his teacup. There *was* something there, a vague look of my mother as she had been in the gilt-framed wedding photo that adorned the mantel in her sitting room. Something about the curve of the lips, the strong line of the nose. Even her eyes, alight now with amusement, carried a reminder of Emmaline Baynard as she must have been, before age and bitterness had hardened not only her face, but her heart as well.

"Touché," I thought she said before her voice was drowned in the roar of the approaching lumber truck. I gripped the wheel tightly in both hands as the behemoth thundered past, rocking my little sports car like a canoe being tossed about on a raging sea. The stripped, naked trunks of once magnificent pines bounced crazily off the back of the open trailer, and we were suddenly engulfed in a swirling cloud of needles, chips, and dust.

Through the film of dirt now streaking my windshield I spied a speed warning sign and realized we must be approaching one of the many small clusters of civilization which seemed to have sprung up wherever an east-west access road crossed the north-south artery. This one featured only a tiny gas station and an old church with an historical marker out front. From the corner of my eye I watched Mercer pick dry, brown pine needles from the legs of her ripped jeans, then touch a finger tentatively to her left cheek where a small ribbon of blood trickled toward her chin.

I pulled into the gas station, away from the pumps, and cut the engine.

"You're bleeding," I said, pulling my bag out from behind the seat and handing her a tissue. "One of those chips must have nicked you. Let's go find a restroom and get that cleaned up."

My cousin rubbed the sleeve of her army fatigue jacket across the small cut and graced me with a genuine smile. "I think what we need is a hose," she said, sending herself off into peals of laughter.

I checked out my reflection in the rearview mirror and joined her.

Mercer insisted I use the cramped, musty restroom first. I did what I could with cold water and gummy pink soap scooped out of a broken plastic dispenser. I carried wet paper towels out to clean the worst of the mess from the windshield, then wandered into the dim interior of the little station. From the meager selection displayed on racks next to a huge, antiquated cash register, I retrieved a couple of candy bars and a bag of red licorice. I handed over a ten and accepted my change from the bored teenager behind the counter, then stepped back out into the deepening twilight.

Across the road, the freshly painted, white clapboard church seemed to beckon to me from where it lay nestled under the arms of a mammoth live oak. I strolled onto the front lawn, grass sparse in the sandy soil, and admired the modest, almost New England-style simplicity of the Robertville Baptist Church. A few mockingbirds called to each other from the pines behind the small cemetery as I approached the weathered historical marker close to the deserted road. Time and neglect had nearly worn away the silver patina, making it difficult to read the inscription. I squinted in the last rays of the sun as it descended in the west behind the narrow belfry and threw an orangish tint over the short history of the town:

Robertville. Named for descendants of Huguenot minister Pierre Robert, it was the birthplace of Henry Martin Robert, author of Robert's Rules of Order, and of Alexander Robert Lawton, Confederate Quartermaster General. The town was burned by Sherman's Army in 1865. The present church was built in Gillisonville in 1848 as an Episcopal Church, moved here by Black Swamp Baptists in 1871.

"Sherman," I said aloud, shaking my head. Amazing how often his hated name appeared in the history of the Lowcountry, in fact of the whole South. While we can now look kindly upon the revered Abraham Lincoln, it is still acceptable to revile General Sherman as the personification of all the evil of the War of Northern Aggression. Computers may shrink to the size of a pea, and men may one day step onto the red dust of Mars, but true Southerners will still be spitting at the mention of William

Tecumseh Sherman.

"Bay! You want a soda?"

I turned at Mercer's shout from across the road to see her standing by the car with two bottles raised in the air. "Sure," I hollered back.

"Diet okay?"

I waited while an ancient pickup truck, its faded red fenders rattling in the wind, zoomed past, then trotted back to the gas station. "Diet's fine. You need money?" The familiar scowl creased my cousin's forehead as she dug in the pocket of her shabby jeans and stomped inside. "Sorry, just asking," I mumbled to myself, sliding behind the wheel. I raised the top and had just clicked the latches closed when Mercer climbed in beside me.

"Do you have to do that?" she asked, passing over the plastic bottle of Coke. "The breeze felt so good."

"We're gonna be freezin' our butts off here in a minute," I replied as I checked for traffic and wheeled back onto the highway. "Try to keep in mind that it's December." I glanced sideways to find that Mercer had resumed her slouch, but had neglected to buckle up. I'd had to remind her on our way out of Hilton Head, too. She'd grumbled, but complied.

"Seat belt," I said, flipping on the headlights against the gathering gloom. The vast stands of pine and hardwoods bordering the narrow road seemed to close in around us. Here and there the dying sunlight glinted off the many ponds and lagoons visible in the gaps left by the loggers after they systematically stripped the land of its trees.

"Mercer?" For all the response I'd gotten, she might have been asleep. "Did you hear me?"

"What was on the sign you were reading by the church? Was that one of the towns Sherman burned on his way to Columbia?"

"How'd you know that?" I don't know why I should be surprised my cousin knew this stuff. I had no reason to assume she was ignorant, just because she'd made some stupid choices. "Are you interested in history?"

"Can you live in the South and not be?" she countered. Still beltless, she shifted herself around in the seat to face me. "Old William Tecumseh sure has taken his knocks, hasn't he? To hear our folks tell it, you'd think he destroyed the Confederacy single-handed."

"He made a pretty good dent in it, didn't he?"

"Sure, but he was just doing what he felt he had to do to end the war."

"Wait, let me be certain I'm hearing this right. A *Georgia* girl is sitting here defending General Sherman?"

Mercer pulled the bag of candy up off the floor and extracted a Baby Ruth bar. "Saving this one for yourself?" she asked.

"No, go ahead. You can unwrap the Snickers for me."

We chewed on delicious chocolate-and-caramel fat grams while around us night fell completely. Roaring down the deserted road with only the feeble stab of the headlights to pierce the rolling blackness felt almost surreal, like the opening scene in a *Twilight Zone* episode. I almost expected to hear the clipped voice of Rod Serling begin, "Submitted for your approval . . ."

"So tell me more about the virtues of General Sherman," I said, motivated more by a desire to break the eerie spell settling over me than by any real interest in the subject. "You realize, of course, that any attempt to excuse him is considered blasphemous."

"That's bull."

No one could accuse my cousin of being wishy-washy on the subject. "So go ahead. Convince me."

"Sherman believed the only way to end the war was to take it to the civilian population in the Deep South: Georgia, the Carolinas. Up until 1864, most of the fighting had been done in the northern part of the Confederacy, in Virginia mostly, and Tennessee. Some in Kentucky and Maryland, too." In the dim glow of the dashboard lights I could see the enthusiasm sparkling in Mercer's eyes. "The General thought if he could prove to Jeff Davis and Robert E. Lee and the others that their homeland was vulnerable, they'd be more inclined to look favorably on a peaceful solution. And he was right. The burning of Atlanta, the March to the Sea, and the surrender of Savannah pretty well broke the spirit of the South. It drove home the point that the whole underbelly of the Confederacy was indefensible."

"But what about his reputation for butchery and cruelty? Was it really necessary for him to burn, rape, and loot his way from the coast to Columbia?" I couldn't help but be impressed with my cousin's knowledge. I wondered what had engendered this passion in her for local history, when and where she had acquired all these facts. "And why Columbia? You'd think he would have headed straight for Charleston, the cradle of the rebellion."

"Exactly why he didn't! Whatever else they may say about him, Sherman was a superb tactician."

I glanced up to the rearview mirror at the reflection of lights far behind us. For many miles we had been almost the only vehicle on the road, and the sight of another sojourner was comforting.

"As for the burning and all," Mercer continued, "I suppose it was understandable, in a way. I mean, the General never *ordered* his men to destroy everything, but in truth he did very little to stop it, either. Remember, these men had been fighting for years, watching brothers and cousins and neighbors blown to bits right beside them, or dying of untended wounds and disease in ill-equipped field hospitals. Y'all started the war, you South Carolinians, and I guess it was too much to expect the foragers and bummers riding out ahead of the main troops to tip their hats politely to the ladies and negroes left at home to guard the towns and plantations in their path. Sherman needed food and horses for his men, and he took them."

I nodded, struck by how well she had articulated her arguments. *Foragers.* The word, strange and anachronistic, struck me as one I had heard or seen not too long ago. I tried to remember where.

"We're running right along the path they took on their way from Savannah to Columbia," Mercer said, unscrewing the top of the soda bottle and handing it to me.

I took a quick sip and passed it back. "Thanks."

"Back there, at Robertville? That's right by where the left flank came across the Savannah River and met up with the troops Sherman himself was leading up from Beaufort. Everything from here on up pretty much got torched. Slow down a little," she added, turning back around in her seat to stare out the windshield. "The turn is coming up in just a minute."

I clicked off the cruise control and let the Zeemer's speed drop. The headlights which had been keeping a steady distance behind us suddenly loomed larger as Mercer peered out into the night. By the time she finally said, "There!" I was almost past it and had to whip the little sports car into a tight, skidding right turn which made the tires squeal in protest. I hadn't even had time to flip on my signal, and I mentally apologized to the big vehicle that roared by just inches from my tailpipe.

"Sorry," she said, releasing her death-grip on the dashboard. "It's kind of hard to locate in the dark."

"I don't know why you couldn't just tell me where we're going to begin with," I said, relief sending my held breath out in an audible *whoosh*. "It's not as if I've been blindfolded or something. I really think I'll be able to find my way back."

My cousin's smile froze on her lips as a blaze of lights suddenly exploded behind us. I threw my hand up to block the glare from the mirror just as I felt the first tap against the bumper, heard the first screech of protesting metal. The little car bucked in my hands, and I fought hard to steady her while tromping on the accelerator.

"You moron!" I screamed. "What the hell's the matter with you!"

I managed to put some distance between us, but the advantage was short-lived. Out of the corner of my eye I saw Mercer fumbling with her seat belt. The next push sent us rocketing off the road. I aimed for what looked to be a narrow gap in the trees, but we hit the outside edge of the ditch, and the car went airborne, crashing through low-hanging branches that ripped at the convertible roof and splintered the windshield.

In the crazily bouncing beam of the one still operable headlamp, I thought I saw a shimmer of silver just seconds before we plunged, nose first, into the water.

CHAPTER
TWENTY-ONE

"You stupid cow, you weren't supposed to kill 'em! The bitch is no good to us dead!"

The shouted string of obscenities could barely be heard above the roaring in my ears. The tiny portion of my brain still functioning recognized the voice as familiar, but could dredge up neither face nor name to go with it. I tried to lift my head, but the barely perceptible movement sent a wave of dizziness washing over me.

Fragments of memory, tangled in flashes of panic, lapped at the edges of my consciousness . . .

A jolt, breath expelled sharply . . . Can't move! Get out, get out . . . Blood pounding, head pounding, cold, cold, can't breathe . . . Hands fumbling, tugging, release! Floating, rising, cold, can't breathe . . . Air! Gasping, rasping breath . . . Mine! Black . . . Cold . . . Hand . . .

Off to the left I heard grunting and thrashing, the snap of limbs and swishing of branches as if a herd of crazed animals were stampeding through a woods. The darkness surrounding me was so complete I couldn't tell if my eyes were open or closed. Something hard and pointed jabbed at the skin just below my left breast. I was trying to shift my position away from it when a trembling, slimy hand clapped itself over my mouth, and an unbearable weight pressed down on my back, driving the object into my flesh.

"*Ssshhh!* They're close!"

The words, hissed directly into my ear, failed to penetrate the fog which blanketed my mind, but I stilled, my body pinned to the ground by some wet, dripping mass. I had no answers to the questions of *who, where, why* that danced just out of reach of my awareness. I felt the sharp sting of something sweet and pungent being pulled over my head.

The hand clamped across my cheeks relaxed a little, and I struggled to speak, to understand . . .

"Lie still!" the disembodied voice whispered again, and the grip tightened.

The crashing noises sounded nearer. Again I heard words shouted in anger, and again I could find no meaning in them, no sense, only a flicker of remembrance which brought an instinctive rush of fear.

"They went in the goddamned water! You drownded them, Nilla! I never shoulda let you drive! Now what? Now what?"

I could feel the weight on my back tense, and without thinking I held my breath. The animals were right beside me.

Girlish giggles, then, *Did you see 'em take off, Buddy? Shut up! It was so cool, wasn't it, Mags? Like that guy that used t' jump his motorcycle over them buses. Ever see 'im do that, Buddy? I said shut up! Hey, there's the car! Where? See? Over there, with its ass end up in the air. Ah, shit! They're drownded for sure. Maybe we can still find the stuff. How? You gonna jump in there and dive down to the bottom? You're dumber 'n dirt, Nilla. You got no call to talk to me like that, Buddy. I just done what you said. I never tol' you to kill 'em, you . . .*

Noise then. Feet moving. Away. More crackle of underbrush, more whining, nasal voices. Fading . . .

Quit callin' me names! It ain't my fault, is it, Mags. Well, is it? Like I knew there was a freakin' lake here . . . Aw, come on, Buddy, we can still find it . . . Buddy?

I exhaled slowly, quietly, and felt the weight shift and roll off me. Far in the distance I heard the roar of a powerful engine, screech of tires, then silence, full and complete. I brushed the pine boughs away from my head, grateful I had regained enough of my senses to identify them and to appreciate that they had probably saved me from discovery. No, not the branches, the weight. The body . . .

"Mercer?" It came out a croak, a raspy hack, but she heard me.

"Right here, Bay. God. God!"

The vertigo was manageable this time as I rolled onto my side, then tentatively eased myself into a half-sitting position. Next to me, my cousin hunched over her drawn-up knees, water streaming from hair tangled with soggy bits of weed and tufts of pine needles. In the thin light of a rising quarter moon, I noticed she was wearing only one boot.

A low gurgling sound pulled my attention toward the water. The rear wheels of the Zeemer inched closer to the cloudy surface of the pond as the front end settled deeper into the muddy bottom.

Mercer heard it, too. "I have to get my bag," she said, scattering me with cold drops of water as she shook out her hair and levered herself to her feet.

"Wait!" I hissed, clutching at her sodden pants leg in fear and disbelief. "You're not going back in there? For God's sake, Mercer, are you crazy? Whatever's in that bag can't be worth your life! Let it go!"

My cousin shook off my feeble grasp and limped toward the water. "Get a grip on yourself, Bay. It's not that deep, barely over our heads. Thank God Buddy Slade is such a complete moron, or he would have figured that out and looked a little harder for us."

"How did we—?" I began when Mercer's "Aha!" cut me off.

I watched her bend down to retrieve something from the mud at the edge of the pond, comprehension dawning as she pulled on her missing boot and stooped to lace it up.

"How did we get out?" she parroted my question back to me. "With the windshield gone, it wasn't too tough. The worst part was getting you unhooked before you swallowed too much of this disgusting water." She turned and began wading toward my half-submerged car. "Probably a good idea not to rag on me anymore about wearing the damn seat belt, you know?"

I listened to her splash her way out to the wreck, surprised that only for the last few feet did she actually have to dog-paddle a little. The screech of a barn owl sent me scrambling to my feet, and I suddenly realized that, miraculously, I appeared to be okay. I took a couple of tottering steps, then crumpled as pain buckled my right knee. Gingerly I probed at it through my soaking slacks and tried flexing it slowly. It seemed to be functioning fine, just not able to bear any weight.

Probably a sprain. I felt around for the boughs Mercer had used to conceal us from her murderous husband and his cohorts. Two women, I remembered then, to judge by the voices. *What had they called each other?* My hand fastened around a stout limb, and I pulled it toward me. *Nilla* I'd thought he'd said, but what kind of a name was that? Perhaps my muddled brain had gotten it wrong. And Mags. That one I was sure about. Two women. Young. One dark, one fair? In my house. Beating Dolores, demanding to know where Mercer Mary Prescott was hiding? It had to be.

I stripped away some of the smaller branches, then used my improvised cane to haul myself upright again just as my cousin emerged from the pond, like some slimy creature in a bad horror movie, to drop her burdens at my feet. Two bags. Her battered duffel and my own soggy, but relatively unscathed denim tote.

"Good thing we stashed them behind the seat and not in the trunk," Mercer gasped, flinging herself down on the ground and hugging her knees to her chest. "If they'd been in the trunk, we'd be screwed. I don't think I could have gotten to them."

I hobbled over to stare down at her heaving shoulders, water again cascading off the soaked jacket. "Are you okay?" My hand hovered just over her streaming, matted hair, but I checked the impulse to stroke her bowed head as she nodded briefly. "Sure?" I asked more briskly, and she looked up.

"They tried to kill me," she said, more in surprise than in fear at the memory.

"I don't think so." I shifted my weight onto my good leg and used the branch for balance. "From everything I heard them say, they don't give a damn about either one of us. You have something he wants, Mercer." I needed every ounce of self-control I had left not to scream the accusation at her: *And to get it, they were willing to threaten me, beat my friend into a coma, and run us off the road in the middle of goddamned nowhere on the off chance you had it with you.* Instead I said calmly, "You saved me in there, Mercer, and I owe you. I'll never forget that. But it's time for you to come clean with me, to stop this childish game you've been playing and let me help you. The next time we might not be so lucky."

Her head was already shaking in denial as she clambered to her feet and glared up at me. In the pale moonlight I could see the determination in her eyes. "No! I'm sick of everyone telling me what I have to do!"

"How many other people have to be hurt or killed before you grow up? I don't give a damn about this big *secret* of yours. Whatever it is, it's not worth the price everyone else has been paying for it. So you're going to spill it—all of it—right now, or I'm going to take this stick and beat it out of you!"

Her head snapped up just as I caught it, too: the faint whine of a racing engine far off in the distance, growing louder with each passing second. "He's coming back!" Mercer whirled and grabbed up the duffel, flinging it onto her shoulder as she sprinted toward the woods.

"Wait!" My hoarse whisper failed to check her flight, so I shuffled to where my bag lay, hefted it, and hobbled after her. I exhaled deeply as I spotted her hovering just inside the cover of the swaying pines.

Without a word Mercer snatched away my bag, then draped my right arm across her back. I leaned heavily against my cousin, dragging one useless leg behind me, as we moved off into the thick woodland. We both turned back at the sound of the muted splash as the taillights of my beloved little sports car disappeared beneath the murky surface of the shallow pond.

"He's not getting it," Mercer said, forcing me to move in the direction she had chosen. Lights flickered in the tops of the murmuring trees as we stumbled farther away from the road. Above the slamming of doors and raised, angry voices, I thought I heard her say, "It's mine."

CHAPTER
TWENTY-TWO

The squeal and *whoosh* of the air brakes jerked me awake as the big rig bounced along the uneven grass shoulder and heaved to a stop. Next to me I could feel Mercer hauling up our bags from the gritty floor under my feet.

"You gon' be okay, missus?"

The low, soft drawl came from just above my left ear. In the second or so it took for me to force my eyes open and turn my face in the direction of the voice, I remembered where I was.

"Yes, thank you. Thank you, Jimmy Luke."

The old black man, his few remaining teeth visible in a tentative smile, eased his shoulder out from under my head and helped me straighten myself in the wide seat. "I don' know," he said, hitching himself around to face us. Mercer's hand rested on the pitted handle, her body already leaning into the door. "Don' feel right somehow leavin' you ladies out here by yo'selves. No sir, it don'."

"We'll be fine. Thanks again for the ride, sir. My cousin and I are very grateful for your kindness." Mercer moved out onto the high step, then hopped to the ground. She reached a hand back up to me. "Come on, I'll help you down."

When Mercer finally felt comfortable that we had put enough distance between ourselves and the Buddy Slade gang, she'd moved confidently into the narrow road and flagged down the first vehicle to approach. To my surprise, the huge truck had ground to a stop. James Luke Matthew Carver waited patiently while Mercer dragged me into the steamy safety of his spacious cab. He accepted without question her story of a blown-out tire, no spare, and a fall into an overflowing drainage ditch as explanation for our battered, bedraggled appearance.

Once settled between them, I found myself fading in and out

of a half-sleeping state that felt like losing consciousness, but couldn't have been, for I was still aware of the conversation going on between my suddenly garrulous cousin and this kindly stranger. The names she offered were pure fiction, culled from an imagination Mercer had kept carefully hidden during our few brief, but intense past conversations. Our rescuer, however, proudly announced that his mama, "a God-fearin', Bible-readin' woman," had called him after every Apostle's name she could squeeze onto the single line of his birth certificate.

I turned now to our benefactor and smiled. Jimmy Luke patted my hand and nodded, then ground the big rig into first gear as I climbed slowly and painfully from the truck. We stepped back and waved at the retreating taillights which flickered briefly off, then on again in coded farewell.

"Now what?" I asked, testing my knee and finding it a little less inclined to buckle under me when I put weight on it.

"Now we walk," Mercer replied. She shouldered both bags and offered me her arm.

"I think I can do better on my own, thanks." I limped ahead a few steps, trying to force the soreness out of my leg. Not that everything else didn't ache as well. I smiled, ruefully, thinking how many times I had described myself at the end of a grueling day at the office as feeling as if I had been hit by a truck. I'd had no idea what that truly meant.

"Suit yourself." Mercer set off down the right-hand lane of the narrow blacktop road, and I shuffled faster to catch up.

"Where are we going?" I asked when I'd managed to reach her side.

"My place."

"How far?"

"About a mile, I'd guess. Maybe a little more."

"Why didn't you have Jimmy Luke drop us a little closer?" I asked, stumbling on a patch of loose gravel some inconsiderate motorist had flung up onto the roadway.

Off to our right, the first hint of sunrise etched a faint line at the edge of a barren expanse of farmland, left fallow for these few weeks between fall harvest and winter sowing. Mercer ignored my question, then with a curt, "Come on," veered away down the grassy culvert and up into the open field.

"Wait!" I called, as her camouflage-jacketed back faded into the predawn darkness.

I heard her return, the crunch of her boots loud against the dry stubble, then once again she draped my arm across her shoulder and set off. I tried to voice my thanks, but found I needed all my available breath to maintain the pace my cousin seemed determined on setting. I spared a brief smile for the picture we must have made, two damp, muddy figures, limping our way into the rising sun.

Hopefully we would reach Mercer's sanctuary before our pursuers discovered we had not gone down with the car to its watery grave at the bottom of the pond. A sudden thought struck me, and I stopped dead, sending my cousin into a headlong stumble. She barely managed to check her fall.

"Does your husband know where to find you?" I asked, shifting onto my left leg to give my wounded knee a rest. "I mean, could he figure out—"

"First of all, the stupid bastard is *not* my husband. Never has been, never will be. And no, I didn't have any connection to this place when I knew him, so there's no way he—" She broke off abruptly, swiveling her head to watch a car roll by on the road we had just left behind. "But then I never thought he'd get this far, so . . . Let's go." She turned and strode off again, her pace quickening so that I had to break into a shambling trot to keep up.

As we neared the tree line she slowed, and I spotted the faint outline of what looked to be farm buildings: a barn, sheds, chicken coop. And a house, low and rambling, with a sagging porch hanging off the front. I could feel some of the tension ease out of Mercer. We crossed a dirt yard, devoid of even a single blade of grass. Inside the house a dog barked once, then fell strangely silent. The steps creaked under our weight, and somewhere off to the left I heard the muffled clucking of hens disturbed too early from their nests.

A light snapped on, startling me so that I tripped, cracking my already throbbing knee against an old metal chair, half-concealed in the dark recesses of the porch.

"Son of a bitch!" I spluttered, hopping on one leg to collapse into the offending chair.

"Honey? Is that you?"

"Yes, it's me," Mercer replied softly to the low voice which floated out into the dawn. "Don't worry. I've brought a friend."

I heard a click as the metal hook of the screen door was flipped from its eye, and a figure glided out onto the splintered boards. I saw my cousin reach for the hand, long-fingered and pale against the filth of the pond and the forest that still clung to both of us.

"Bay," Mercer said, and I rose without conscious thought to face the thin woman, shivering in a white cotton nightdress, standing before me. "Bay, I'd like you to meet Cat. Catherine Prescott. My mother."

What the house lacked in curb appeal, it more than made up for in plumbing.

Gallons of heavenly hot water sluiced away the encrusted sludge of our night's adventures, and not once did the temperature dip below scalding. When the last pine needle and chunk of dried pond mud finally swirled away down the drain of the spacious shower stall, I stepped out into a steamy cloud and wrapped myself in a thick, soft robe someone had left draped across the closed lid of the toilet.

I used my sleeve to wipe away the mist dripping down the mirror and surveyed my wavering reflection. The purpling knot on my forehead, just below the hairline, explained the fuzziness I'd been experiencing since coming to, facedown, by the edge of the pond. Tender to the touch, it had probably resulted from Mercer's efforts to drag me out of the car through the shattered windshield. I could tell by the stiffness in my bad shoulder as well as a slight bruising between my breasts that the harness had done its job. How ironic that I had been spared serious injury by having been buckled up, while my life had been saved because my cousin had refused to fasten her own seat belt.

I groped inside my tote bag for a comb, then ran it through my blessedly clean hair, carefully avoiding the bump. I took another swipe at the steamy mirror and decided I really looked quite presentable, all things considered. Hopefully, a few hours of uninterrupted sleep would bleach the dark smudges from beneath my bloodshot eyes.

I eased open the old painted door and nearly fainted with delight at the smells wafting up the steep, narrow staircase.

Someone was frying bacon. Mingled with the yeasty aroma of freshly baked bread, it was enough to send me flying down the steps half-naked. Instead, I turned toward the small guestroom under the eaves and pulled on the sweats laid out on the coverlet of the iron bedstead. Both the sleeves and the legs were a good six inches too short for me, but being in clean, dry clothes again was far more important than worrying about whether or not I looked like a gangly child who had outgrown last year's things. I stuffed my feet into thick socks and eased my way down the steps into the sun-filled kitchen.

Catherine Prescott—*Cat*, Mercer had called her—glanced over one shoulder at me, then turned back to the stove. In faded jeans and baggy T-shirt, she looked much more substantial, less ethereal than she had in the shadowy, predawn light of the porch. About medium height—somewhere between Mercer's and my own—and with dark blond hair hanging loosely down her back, Cat seemed little more than a teenager herself. At least from behind.

"Good morning," I said, pulling out a chair from the scarred wooden table set with yellow and green Fiesta ware. "Everything smells wonderful."

"Good morning," Catherine replied, turning at last to face me. Her deep brown eyes, sad and oddly unfocused, passed briefly over mine, then slid away as she set the plate of eggs on the table. "I hope over-easy is okay."

"Perfect," I said, eyeing the battered tin teapot resting on a trivet. "May I?"

For a moment she paused, seemingly confused by the question.

"It is tea, isn't it?" I said.

"Oh, yes, of course. Mercer said you don't drink coffee. Help yourself. Please."

I poured, then added sugar as Catherine moved to the bottom of the steps. "Mercer! Breakfast's ready!"

"Coming!" The call was followed almost immediately by the sound of my cousin bounding down the stairs. The beautiful little Sheltie, whose single bark had raised goose bumps on my arms the night before, trotted close behind her. "God, I'm starving!" She dropped into the chair opposite me and immediately reached for the eggs. The dog sat to attention at her feet, its long, delicate nose raised in anticipation.

"We have a guest," Catherine chided, joining us after setting the rack of drained bacon strips in front of her. "And please put Raphie out while we eat."

Mercer relinquished the plate to me, then held the screen door open for the black and tan miniature collie to wander slowly and reluctantly onto the porch.

She had just resumed her seat when Catherine said, "For what we are about to receive, make us truly grateful. Amen."

The brief prayer, uttered softly and without preamble, took me by surprise. The simple sincerity of Catherine's grace held me motionless until Mercer's exaggerated

"A-men" broke the spell.

Food occupied us for the next several minutes. While my cousin and I had to restrain ourselves from shoveling in the perfectly prepared eggs and crisp bacon, Catherine Prescott merely toyed with her plate, pushing things around in a parody of eating, while never actually bringing the fork to her mouth. A couple of times I noticed Mercer watching her anxiously, seeming almost to be willing her mother to take some food. If the woman performed like this at every meal, it was not surprising she looked so frail and thin. In fact, as I refilled my cup with tea from the tin pot, I wondered if she were ill. Her skin had that pale, translucent quality often seen on the faces of the dying.

I pushed that morbid thought away and reached for another piece of the fragrant, homemade bread. What I desperately needed—would *kill* for, actually—was a cigarette. When I'd first gained the sanctuary of the sprawling bathroom, I'd scrabbled like a woman possessed for the pack of Marlboros in the bottom of my denim bag. What I'd found was a soggy mass of wilted paper and mushy tobacco. The cellophane wrapper had proved worthless, and the pond had done its worst. I laid a few of them out on the windowsill where I still hoped the strengthening sun would dry them out enough to be usable, but I didn't have a lot of hope in that plan succeeding. *Maybe this is The Big Guy's way of telling me it's time to quit,* I thought, although He could have used a less life-threatening way to deliver the message.

The dog whined from the porch and raised one dainty paw to bat ineffectually at the screen. I drew a deep, shuddering breath and tried to take my mind off my body's insistent demand for nicotine.

"That was a wonderful breakfast, Catherine."

"Thank you," she replied, getting up from her chair to carry both of our plates to the worn linoleum-covered counter. "I'm glad you enjoyed it."

Her smile never reached her eyes as she bent to scrape the bulk of her uneaten food into a red plastic bowl on the floor. From a bottom cupboard she pulled out a nearly empty bag of dog food and mixed a handful in with the egg and crumbled bacon. Outside, the dog began to leap and prance.

"Be still, Raphie," she said with a mixture of pride and annoyance. "Mommy has your dinner all ready." She crossed to the door and set the bowl on the splintered boards of the porch.

I caught Mercer's look—startlingly similar to the one her mother had just given the dog—and wondered again about how this woman who had supposedly disappeared nearly twenty years before had ended up in this run-down farmhouse in the middle of nowhere and how she had come to be reunited with her abandoned daughter. But, judging by my recent experience with Mercer, direct questions were going to get me nowhere. I decided to ease my way into it.

"He's a beautiful dog," I said, reaching for another slice of bread. If I didn't get a cigarette soon, I could be pushing four hundred pounds by lunch time.

"Raphie is a *girl*," Catherine snapped, showing the first sign of anything resembling an emotion I'd seen from her. "Her name is Raphaela. All my animals are *girls*."

"Sorry." I wondered why the idea of a male occupant of her house bothered her so much, and how the hens produced eggs with no rooster around.

"You'll have to excuse me. I have chores."

I watched Mercer's mother move onto the porch where she stooped to pull on a mud-spattered pair of rubber boots. Raphie, apparently finished with her morning meal, trotted obediently behind her as the two made their way across the barren yard toward the barn.

I opened my mouth to give voice to one of the thousand questions rattling around in my brain when my cousin said, "I'll finish clearing up the table. You'd better call the Judge."

The Judge! God help me, I'd forgotten all about him. He'd be frantic!

I swiveled my head, searching for a telephone amid the clutter on all the countertops, when the distinctive sound of an engine badly in need of a tune-up broke the early morning stillness. Mercer and I exchanged looks of panic as the ancient truck rattled into the yard. I was just about to express my relief that this old clunker bore no resemblance to the shiny monster Buddy Slade had been using, when my cousin hissed, "Quick, upstairs!"

"What? It's not—"

She grabbed my arm and dragged me from my chair. My knee had stiffened up, and I nearly fell as Mercer pulled me toward the stairs.

"What?" I demanded again, hobbling ahead of her up the steep, narrow steps. Her hands on my back continued to urge speed. "What's the matter?"

"Ben can't know I'm . . . *we're* here." She guided me toward another door along the corridor, and I stumbled into a room nearly identical to the one in which I had changed after my shower.

"Why not?" I asked, collapsing on the bed and easing my throbbing knee onto the coverlet. "Who is he?"

"Ben Tyler. He runs the store in town. He comes out every other morning to pick up the eggs he buys from her and to deliver whatever stuff she's ordered from him." She crossed to the window which overlooked the yard and peeked out from a crack in the dingy curtains. "We don't have a car, and anyway Cat doesn't drive," she added, as if that explained everything.

"So what's the big secret? I'd think you'd want to shout to the world that you two have found each other again."

"It's not that simple." Mercer settled into a cane-backed rocking chair and propped her feet up on a worn plaid ottoman.

"So enlighten me." I bunched the pillows up under my head and stretched out on the bed. I hoped my relaxed posture would invite intimacy, a collapse of the barrier Mercer erected every time I tried to probe into her life and troubles.

"Everyone thinks she lives alone. And Cat doesn't use her real name here."

"Why not?"

"It's complicated."

I remembered Neddie's admonition then, about my cousin's probable ability to lie, fabricate, and deceive. And not only others, but herself as well. Still, as I watched the battle of her thoughts reflected in the changing expressions which flickered across her face, I had an almost ironclad certainty that she desperately wanted to tell me the truth. *Needed* to.

I waited, motionless, fearing that even the slightest movement might break the spell. I knew I should be on the phone to my father, who was no doubt in a panic at not having heard from me in so many hours. I sent him a silent plea for forgiveness and prayed that he had not yet called out the National Guard. Morning sun filtered through the threadbare curtains, and tiny dust motes, disturbed by the rhythmic motion of the rocking chair, danced in the light.

When Mercer finally spoke, her voice held resignation, and an odd note of relief as well. "I found Cat last summer."

"Here?"

"No. We've only been here since . . . a couple of months. I found her in Columbia. Where I worked."

My cousin looked at me expectantly, inviting me to make the connection for myself. I strained to recall what it was I knew about her job. Then I had it. The address on the envelope containing the genealogy papers.

"The Herbert-Hanson Clinic," I said softly.

"Yes." Mercer nodded, the sadness pooling in her shining brown eyes. "My mother has been confined to a mental institution for the last fifteen years."

"But surely there's no stigma attached to that. After all, if she weren't cured, they wouldn't have . . ."

The full implication of Mercer's revelations finally hit me, and I gasped at the audacity and bravery of this child/woman rocking quietly before me. "She wasn't released, was she?"

My cousin shook her head. "No."

I turned toward the window as the old truck squeaked and wheezed its way out of the yard onto the rutted dirt road into town. "And Ben Tyler? He's not just the local grocer, I take it?"

Mercer shrugged and gave me a watery smile. "Nope. He's also the local police."

CHAPTER
TWENTY-THREE

Mercer and I both ran out of gas at the same time, just a few moments after her revelations about her mother. In unspoken agreement, I rose from her bed as she crawled gratefully into it, then hobbled off to my own next door, collapsing onto the lumpy mattress and falling immediately into a deep, untroubled sleep.

I awakened, only four hours later, completely refreshed, my mind clear, determined to wrest the whole story from my cousin. As I washed my face at the cracked pedestal sink and scrubbed ineffectually at my teeth with a toothpaste-laden finger, I planned my strategy.

First, I needed a car. And clothes. My neatly packed overnight case, tucked securely into the trunk, had gone down with the car. *Thank God Mercer had the foresight to bring my tote bag up when she went back for her duffel,* I thought, easing my way down the hall to peek into her room. She lay just as I had left her, sprawled on top of the faded quilt, almost as if her body had been too tired even to roll over and settle itself more comfortably on the bed. I pulled the door closed then and made my way cautiously down the steps to the empty kitchen, the telephone, and my father's wrath.

The Judge railed and ranted for a full five minutes before I was able to get in a word of explanation. He finally shut up long enough for me to give him an extremely sanitized version of the previous night's events, downplaying the accident and failing to mention at all the injury to my leg or the fact that I was calling him from Catherine Prescott's kitchen.

After giving him the number and assuring him that I would call at least twice a day from now on, I hung up and went exploring. Besides the kitchen, the downstairs of the old farmhouse contained three other rooms. The dining room stood empty, a cheap, imitation crystal chandelier lending very little illumination to the dark, windowless space. Rectangular patches of bright blue gave mute evidence to the presence, at one time, of massive sideboards and tables set in place on the otherwise faded, threadbare carpet. A parlor, crammed with shabby forties-era sofas and overstuffed chairs, lay just across the hall. It looked completely abandoned, a thin layer of dust overlying the cluttered tables and what-not shelves. Next to it, I finally discovered signs of recent habitation. In what might once have been an office or a morning room, I found two fairly new reclining chairs, separated by a side table littered with books, magazines, odd coasters, and an old lamp. The cozy arrangement sat in front of what appeared to be at least a twenty-seven-inch color television on a rolling stand.

The sound of the screen door banging shut sent me scurrying guiltily back to the kitchen, but I found the room still empty. Perhaps Mercer had come downstairs looking for me, I thought. I stepped out onto the porch and surveyed the farmyard for the first time in full daylight. I was surprised at how small everything appeared. Earlier, in the smoky haze of the waning night and the cloud of my own fear and exhaustion, the spaces had seemed vast and menacing. In the pearly light of the mild December afternoon, I could see that Mercer's hideout was nothing more than a run-down old homestead, probably abandoned through death or discouragement. My cousin and her mother no doubt rented it for a song.

I turned back into the house and crossed again to the telephone. The Judge had said he'd had no response from Erik Whiteside in answer to the questions we'd put to him, so I again punched in the seemingly endless series of numbers required to access my prepaid phone account and waited while the receptionist at his electronics store went to track him down. A running loop of canned "hold" music, bland and unidentifiable, was interrupted every thirty seconds by a chirpy, female voice telling me how important my call was and thanking me for my patience. After the third go-around I began talking back to her and was in the middle of telling her what she could do with her insipid assurances, when Erik came on the line.

"Erik Whiteside."

"Erik, it's Bay."

"God, woman, where are you?" he demanded in much the same tone of voice my father had used. "I just talked to the Judge, and he told me about the accident. Are you and your cousin okay?"

"We'll live," I said, dismissing his concern. "Were you calling Presqu'isle to report? Did you find anything on the death of that security guard?"

I glanced over my shoulder at the sound of voices in the yard. Cat and Mercer called to Raphie, whose yips and yelps were accompanied by four-legged leaps of anticipation. I stretched the phone cord as far as it would reach and watched as the three of them turned toward the woods and set off on what was probably a ritual daily walk.

"Bay? You still there?"

"Yes. Sorry. What did you say?"

"I said, the guard's death was big news in Edgefield and over at that end of the state. Guy named Jerry Singleton. The local papers were full of it. Even a mention in the local Charlotte papers."

"So? Was he murdered?"

"Absolutely. Strangled. *Garroted* is probably a more accurate description, since they seem to think wire was used. Nearly took his head off."

I swallowed the bile which rose immediately from my rumbling stomach. "Any clue as to who might have done it?"

"Well, that's the strange thing about it. There wasn't one bit of speculation about that, or about a possible motive, after the first stories came out. SLED has been called in, and I heard that the feds are involved now, too. You know how those guys are. They apparently clamped a lid on any information leaks and must have put the fear of God into the media, because the story disappeared almost the next day. Not a peep since."

The State Law Enforcement Division was an organization I had had many dealings with in the past, due mostly to Rob's antidrug work for the State Attorney General's office. They worked closely with the FBI and other federal agencies as well. This was obviously something more than just a domestic quarrel or a robbery attempt gone bad.

"I need to get up there and check it out myself." I thought of Louise Cameron and her quaint little tea shop. She would know the local scuttlebutt, what was being bandied around in the grocery stores and on the streets of Edgefield. Rob always said you could learn more about what was happening in a small town from fifteen minutes in the barber's chair than from fifteen hours in an interrogation room.

"I'm going to need a car," I said half to myself, my mind already leaping ahead to how all this might fit into last night's attack on Mercer and me. Could Buddy Slade and his murderous groupies have been involved somehow in the death of Jerry Singleton? What possible connection could this ex-con, who claimed to be Mercer's husband, have with a security man at the old bomb plant? And what was it he thought my cousin had that made it worth twice attacking *me* in order to get it?

"Yours isn't drivable?"

"What?" So deep was my concentration on the tangle of conflicting motives and players, I had momentarily lost the thread of our conversation. "Oh, the car. No. It's at the bottom of a lake."

"A lake? I thought you just had a little fender-bender."

"That's what I told the Judge. He's worried enough already. Actually, somebody ran us off the road last night. Luckily, we missed most of the big trees and landed in fairly shallow water."

"Who? Why?" I heard the incredulity in his voice. Despite our recent joint experiences with the less desirable elements of society, Erik still had trouble believing in the bad guys. His naiveté was one of his more endearing qualities.

"Buddy Slade," I answered his first question, "and his two sidekicks."

"The ones you think hurt Dolores?"

"The ones I know *battered* Dolores," I snapped back, then swallowed hard and softened my tone. "As to why, I'm not sure. There's something of Mercer's he wants, something she has that he's willing to do just about anything to get his hands on. So far I haven't been able to drag it out of her. But that's next on my agenda." I sighed, and some of the turmoil eased out of my gut. "Did I tell you we're staying with her mother?"

"Catherine Prescott? She's alive? God, Bay, what the hell *else* has been going on that you haven't told me about yet? Talk about Mercer not being willing to volunteer information."

"I haven't been holding out on you, Erik, honestly. All this has gone down in the last twenty-four hours." A cacophony of squawking, followed by the delighted barking of the sheltie as she scattered the chickens pecking in the yard, announced the imminent return of my cousins. "Look, I have to get off the phone. Here's the number where I'm staying."

"Already got it. Caller ID, remember?"

"Right. The thing is, I don't even know where the hell I am. Check it out and get back to me, okay? And find out where the nearest town is that might have a Hertz or an Avis or anywhere I can rent a car. I'll need someone who can pick me up early tomorrow morning. When you call back, ask for Ms. Tanner and pretend you're with the rental company. I don't want to spook Cat and Mercer. I need to have their confidence if I expect to pry any information out of them."

"No way. I'll come get you myself."

"Erik, that isn't—"

"Yes, it is. You invited me in on this enterprise, and I'm not going to sit up here on my butt in Charlotte while you set yourself up as a target. I won't do it, Bay. Don't ask me to."

"How will you even find this place? It's out in the middle of nowhere, at the end of a dirt road." My excuses were beginning to sound lame, even to me. Still, I had enlisted Erik into our venture primarily because of his computer expertise. I had never anticipated his becoming involved in anything more dangerous than illegal hacking.

"I'm a detective, remember?" he answered. "Same as you." His voice rang with the assurance of one who has never stared into the barrel of a semiautomatic handgun or been sent hurtling through the air into a pond. "Don't worry, I'll find it."

I heard footsteps on the porch, then the screen door creaking open. "I don't have time to argue with you, Erik," I hissed, my hand cupped around the mouthpiece. Then, more loudly, "That would be fine. Have the car here by eight tomorrow morning."

"I'll be there, don't worry. And thanks for choosing Whiteside Auto Rental."

I could almost see the grin on his boyish face as I gently replaced the receiver.

I soon discovered why Catherine and Mercer Mary Prescott kept chickens: apparently eggs, in various guises and combinations, comprised the only dish Cat could cook, aside from homemade bread. I was hardly in a position to cast aspersions, my own burgeoning culinary skills barely developed yet, so I wolfed down the ham-and-cheese omelet which constituted our dinner that night and held myself to only two slices of the wonderful bread. Afterwards, Mercer cleared and her mother firmly rejected my offer to help with the washing up, so I bundled myself into the buffalo-plaid jacket I found hanging on a peg near the door and wandered out onto the porch.

It felt good to be back in my own clothes. While Mercer and I slept, Catherine had laundered them as best she could, hanging them outside to dry, to judge by their stiffness and that sweet, distinctive smell which no amount of fabric softener can quite achieve.

I settled on the top step and surveyed the clear sweep of sky stretching away to the horizon. The absence of city lights allowed each star in the vast darkness to gleam in solitary splendor. It reminded me of the night sky over the ocean, except that the accompanying, rhythmic *shush* of the Atlantic rollers was missing, replaced by a stillness so complete not even the squeak of a bird disturbed it.

The screen door opened and closed quietly as Mercer crossed the splintered boards and sat down beside me. I jumped at Raphie's cold, wet nose brushing against my cheek and smiled when she insinuated herself between us, her long muzzle resting on what must have been a familiar spot across my cousin's knee. We both reached for the silky, black-and-tan ruff around the dog's neck. Mercer started as our hands touched, then drew her own back to allow me to stroke the sheltie. I found the repetitive action strangely soothing.

"I bet you wish you'd never answered the phone that night I called you from the jail." Mercer's eyes cut briefly toward me, then slid back to her contemplation of the rising moon. "Every time you see me, something awful happens."

I swallowed the anger which rose like a tide of nausea in my throat whenever I thought about what my involvement in all this had cost Dolores and her family. True, Mercer had had no direct hand in that, but I had been blaming her, nonetheless. I tried to remember she was just a kid, really, and that a lot of terrible things had happened to her, too.

"You do sort of keep turning up like a bad penny," I said, gratified at the brief flicker of a smile which crossed her face.

I reached a hand up to the pocket of the warm, wool jacket in a gesture so automatic it took me a moment to remember that I had no pack of cigarettes and lighter tucked in there. I had tried to light one of those I'd left on the windowsill to dry, but only succeeded in filling the tiny bedroom with an acrid smoke which tasted just as nasty as it smelled. I sighed and clasped my hands in front of me. I was completely surprised by how little I minded. Perhaps the spell of my addiction had finally been broken.

"The Judge told me about your friend," Mercer said, somehow homing in on my thoughts. She stared straight ahead as if she were afraid to witness my reaction. "I'm really sorry. Did Buddy . . . I mean, was it because of him that she's so sick?"

"No, not directly." As soon as I said it, some of the pain of my own guilt lifted from the place deep in my chest where it had weighed on my heart for the past week and more. "It's an infection she picked up in the hospital."

"I'm sorry," she said again.

Behind us in the kitchen, I heard the clatter of china as Cat stacked the dried dishes into the tall cupboards. I drew a long breath of cold, crisp air into my lungs and turned to face my cousin. "We had a deal, remember? I've kept my end of the bargain, and now it's time for you to keep yours. Finish what you started this morning. I need to hear all of it, Mercer, and I need to hear it now."

"Let's walk," she said, rising from the step and tucking her hands into the pockets of her baggy jeans. The dog jumped immediately to her side.

My loafers, still damp despite their many hours of drying in the sun, squeaked in the heavy silence as we rounded the side of the house. A light snapped on as we passed a back window, and I envisioned Cat settling herself into one of the reclining chairs. The muted voices of what sounded like game show contestants followed us out into the dark.

"*Jeopardy*," Mercer said, heading down a narrow path barely discernible in the blackness behind the old farmhouse. I could just make out the clink of Raphie's metal collar as she trotted ahead of us. "Cat loves that show. She's better than anyone I've ever seen on it. She almost never misses a question."

She stopped so abruptly I almost ran into her. She turned sharply left, then stepped up into the rotted remains of what must once have been a delightful little gazebo set back nearly to the tree line at the edge of a small pond. Only the glitter of the risen moon across the once-white flooring made it visible at all. Mercer dropped onto one of the seats, bringing her legs up and resting her back against a splintered upright. I groped my way to the one opposite it, tucked my hands under my armpits to warm them, and waited.

"I was six when my mother disappeared," Mercer began, "too young to understand anything except that she was gone. Nana Mary tried to make it up to me, in all kinds of ways, but she never could. You know how kids always think everything that happens is their fault? Like the whole universe revolves around them?"

I was pretty sure she couldn't see my nod of agreement, so I simply said, "Yes." Thoughts of my own mother, long buried, flooded into my consciousness, and I shivered. "Yes" I repeated, "I do."

"Well, I always thought she left because of me. Because she didn't want to be tied down to a kid and a job and all that. She was so young, younger than I am now, almost. As I got older, I could kinda understand that, you know?" She paused, and I could just make out the movement of her thumb to her mouth. For a moment she worked at peeling away the small fragment of fingernail left there. "Nana always tried to convince me something bad must have happened to her, that she would never have left us like that on her own. But they never found anything, no body, no sign of a struggle, nothing. So I became convinced that *my* version was the truth. She'd just gone away."

I tried to suppress another shiver which had only partly to do with the damp night air, afraid that any sudden noise or movement would break the spell of Mercer's reminiscences. I felt certain she was finally ready to tell her story, but that she would do it in her own way and in her own time. Though she had come to the Judge for help, she had been adamant in her refusal to explain either her involvement in the protest rally or her subsequent arrests and escapes until I had brought her back here. Wherever "here" was. None of us had mentioned her mother, primarily because all but one of us were convinced she was dead. I sighed softly and pulled a piece of rotted wood from the planks of the seat, picking at it as my cousin resumed.

"So I sort of spent my childhood looking for her. Oh, not a

search, nothing like that," she added quickly, "I just mean that, like, whenever I was in a crowd of people, or if I went somewhere new, I'd kind of scan women's faces. To see if I recognized her." Her sigh held more resignation than remembered pain. "But, of course, I never did."

I shifted a little on the hard boards and saw Raphie sit up, suddenly alert. Whatever sound had caught her attention had escaped our human ears. In a moment, she settled back down at Mercer's feet.

"When my grandfather got sick and I went to live with the Scogginses, I decided I had to put it away, stop hoping she'd come back. And I did, sort of. I got involved with the other kids, and learning to play piano and run the computer. Bill and Vesta were wonderful—*are* wonderful, as I guess you found out. I couldn't have asked for better foster parents."

"How do you know I've met them?" I asked, breaking my silence for the first time in many long minutes.

"I talked to Vesta right after you left."

"Where were you hiding out? At Aunt Eliza's?"

I could feel Mercer's smile, although her face was still only a white blur in the darkness of the ruined gazebo. "That's what we wanted you and that guy that works for you to think. No, I was here. I haven't seen Aunt Eliza since that day she invited me for tea. What an old darling she is, don't you think?"

"So why all the subterfuge? If you didn't trust me—and the Judge—why did you come to us in the first place?"

"To find out what you knew. To pick your brains." Again she worked at her thumbnail. "I thought getting myself arrested would win me your sympathy, that you might be less suspicious if you thought I was just your poor, white-trash cousin who couldn't get along without the help of the almighty Judge Talbot Simpson and his famous daughter."

I wondered if Mercer realized the level of contempt in her voice when she spoke about my father and me. I wondered if we were really so arrogant that we deserved it.

"So you deliberately let yourself get arrested for vagrancy?"

I sensed her shrug as she shifted herself into a more comfortable position on the seat. "It's happened to me before. For real, I mean. I knew you could probably just pay my fine, and they'd let me go. I never counted on them finding out about the other thing."

"You should watch more TV," I said, remembering Rob's fondness for *Law and Order* reruns. He'd sat through each episode so many times, I often caught him mouthing the dialogue right along with the actors. And on *Law and Order*, they always did a check for wants and warrants on everyone they picked up, even the vagrants. "But back up a minute. What do you mean you needed to pick our brains? About what?"

I had a feeling we were about to get to the heart of things, the core of the mystery surrounding all the strange happenings of the past few weeks. In spite of the cool December night and the chill wind blowing out of the north, my palms had begun to sweat.

"Perdition."

I could feel her leaning forward in anticipation. It seemed as if something vastly important—at least to Mercer—rested on my reply.

"Perdition," I repeated, certain I had heard the name before, but unable to dredge up where or when . . . And then suddenly the musty odor of the old paper, the looping, formal handwriting appeared magically in my mind's eye, and I knew why Mercer's use of the word *foragers* yesterday had seemed so familiar. It, too, appeared in those pitiful, fearful letters from Isabelle Robichoux Chase and her sister, Theodora Rutledge, as they awaited the arrival of the hated Yankee troops. I flashed back to my Uncle Rupert's library, dim and musty in the fading afternoon light. "Perdition House. The old family plantation," I said out loud.

"So you *do* know!" Mercer's exclamation—part relief, part accusation—burst from her as she jumped to her feet.

"Know what? I never heard the name before Aunt Eliza showed me some old letters in Rupert's desk."

"I don't believe you." She crossed the creaky flooring and stood looming over me, her shredded fingers clenched in fists at her sides. "The old woman said your mother had all the papers, all the records, going back centuries. You had to have known." Her breathing had quickened along with her agitation. "That's why you went there, isn't it? You thought you could find the missing pieces and take it all for yourself!"

The dog, sensing the changed atmosphere, growled low in her throat and stationed herself stiffly at my cousin's side.

"I have no idea what you're talking about," I repeated. I was beginning to wonder if perhaps Mercer had inherited the family madness. No one had yet enlightened me about Cat's specific mental problems, but they didn't keep you in the Herbert-Hanson for fifteen years for mild depression.

"I can't believe you could be so selfish, so . . . so greedy! My God, you already have everything! Houses, money, status. *Everything!* It's not fair!" Mercer was shouting, totally out of control, her words ripping the silent fabric of the night like a slashing blade. "Well, let me tell you something, Miss High-and-Mighty Lydia Baynard Tanner of Hilton Head, South Carolina. You can claim that you're entitled to a share, and you can probably afford to hire all kinds of fancy lawyers, and you'll probably win. But it won't do you a damn bit of good." The storm subsided as quickly as it had arisen. Smugness replaced the anger in her voice, and the dog settled once again onto the floor between us. "You need me more than I need you, because *I* know where it is. And without me, you'll never find it."

I resisted the urge to slap her resoundingly. Instead, I forced myself to speak calmly. "Mercer, what in God's name are you talking about? A share of what? Find what?"

"The treasure, of course. Isabelle's treasure." She rose then and started down the crumbling steps of the gazebo, pausing at the bottom to look back up at me. "And I've got the map." She whirled and disappeared into the dark.

The dog trotted after her, and I let them go. As long as the light still gleamed in Cat's window, I could find my way back. My hands shook, and I shoved them into the pockets of my slacks. I knew the trembling did not come entirely from the aftermath of this bizarre conversation with my cousin. So much for being cured of my addiction. The overwhelming desire for a cigarette washed over me in waves of need and longing.

So that's it, I thought. Simple, really, when you had all the pieces. A child's game. *X* marks the spot. And Mercer held the key.

For this Dolores had been bludgeoned, for this the security guard had probably died. And somewhere out there, Buddy Slade and his twisted accomplices prowled the night, desperate to get it at any cost. Was Mercer stupid or just naive? I turned and dragged my stiffening leg down the steps, determined to find out.

And then I heard the screams.

CHAPTER
TWENTY-FOUR

I fell twice in the dew-damp grass, my bruised and swollen knee refusing to obey my brain's commands to run. The screams grew louder as I rounded the corner of the house, and then Mercer's voice, strong and soothing, mingled with Cat's shrieks. For a moment I thought they were fighting, my cousin trying to pin her mother's arms to her sides as they struggled in the bright rectangle of light which spilled from the open kitchen door onto the porch.

"What's the matter? What happened?"

I rushed to help, until Mercer growled, "Stay back!" and I stopped dead at the bottom of the steps.

"Mama, Mama, it's all right. Shush now, shush. I'm here. Your baby's here. I won't leave you again, Mama, I promise."

She repeated the words, over and over, until gradually her mother quieted, the fragile hands no longer beating against Mercer's back and sides, the screams subsiding into a sad, pathetic mewling, and then silence.

"Didn't you take your medicine, Mama?" My cousin held her mother close, stroking her hair much as I had earlier stroked the dog's.

Catherine's voice when she answered carried a whining, spoiled-little-girl note. "I forgot. You're supposed to remind me."

"I know, Mama, I'm sorry. Let's go take it now, shall we? And I'll help you get ready for bed." Mercer used her thumbs to wipe the remnants of Cat's streaming tears from her face. "I'll brush your hair, too. Would you like that?"

I watched in numbed silence as Mercer supported her mother across the porch. Just before she stepped through the doorway, Cat paused to throw a glance back over her shoulder at me, and I gasped. Her eyes, completely aware and lucid, held triumph, and the smug satisfaction of a sly child who has just bested a rival.

Then the screen banged shut behind them.

I made myself a mug of tea and sat slumped at the worn kitchen table until I heard them move from the bathroom into the large bedroom at the back of the house. I dragged myself up the steps and retrieved the crusty brown cigarettes from the windowsill in my own tiny quarters. Back downstairs I rummaged through drawers until I finally located a box of wooden matches, then walked outside and settled myself onto the squeaky metal chair I'd banged my injured knee against the night before.

By the time Mercer found me there with my feet propped up on the porch railing, I'd gagged my way through three of the vile, pond-soaked Marlboros and had just lit a fourth.

"I'm sorry," she said, hitching herself onto the railing next to my ruined loafers.

I exhaled and watched her begin chewing at her fingers again. "I'm really sick of hearing that, you know? It doesn't mean a damn thing to you, except it's what you think you're expected to say. And stop gnawing on your skin like that!"

She jumped at my sudden attack, then righted herself on her precarious perch. She glared at me across the narrow stretch of darkness that separated us, but she dropped her hands back into her lap. "What do you want me to say?"

"Nothing, for the moment. I want you to shut up and listen for a change." I flipped the cigarette expertly past her, and it fell in a flickering arc onto the dirt of the front yard. "The Judge and I have done nothing but try to help you out of this mess you've gotten yourself into, right from that first lying phone call from the jail. We told you that back at Presqu'isle, and I think we've demonstrated our concern every damn time you've shown up on our doorstep. As for this so-called treasure you keep going on about, we have no knowledge of it, nor do we have any designs on it. If the damn thing actually does exist and if you find it, it's all yours. Will you at least believe that much?"

The angry set of her chin before she finally nodded her acceptance again reminded me of old photographs of my mother. At least she hadn't been lying about our relationship, tenuous though it might be. About everything else? Well, we'd see.

I'd had plenty of time to think about all the bizarre happenings of the past few weeks. I'd made lists and plans, had puzzled over every aspect of the enigma that was Mercer Mary Prescott and her sudden, disastrous entry into my life. I knew the questions that needed to be asked, and I knew, for the first time since I'd faced her through the bulletproof glass in the Beaufort County Jail, that she was finally going to tell me the truth, or I was going to strangle her with my bare hands. I'd had enough.

"Talk," I said, leaning toward her in the heavy darkness.

And so she did . . .

The moon reached its apex, then slid slowly down across the night sky, fading from sight behind the pines. The first shimmer of dawn edged the clouds hovering along the horizon. And in the end, as the rooster crowed his welcome and his harem of hens clucked their good mornings, I had it all. Or at least as much of it as my cousin knew.

I called my father then, while Mercer sat bleary-eyed at the kitchen table, her chin resting in the cup of her hands. I spared him the details, except for the fact that I believed my cousin when she claimed to have no knowledge about the death of the security guard at the Savannah River Site. I'd pumped her pretty hard, but she'd remained adamant that she had simply carried a sign, shouting antinuke slogans along with about thirty others, until the police had come in force to round them all up. In true seventies protest style, they had all collapsed on the ground, making themselves dead weights, but not resisting. A few people got rapped with nightsticks anyway, which accounted for the bruises I'd noticed on Mercer's chin that first night, but in general they were merely manhandled into waiting vans and hauled off to appear before the local magistrate. By morning, everyone was released on bond, the money provided by the New Earth Defense Network, sponsors of the illegal incursion onto federal property.

When I told the Judge about my next destination, Mercer's head snapped up, anger replacing weariness in her dull brown eyes, but I ignored her. For the first time since this whole mess had begun, I finally felt in control of the situation. I knew what had to be done, whether my cousin liked it or not.

By the time I hung up with assurances that I'd keep him fully informed of my whereabouts, I felt ready to drop into a heap on the floor and stay there. Instead I dragged myself up the narrow stairs into the bathroom, stripped off my blouse and bra, and dashed cold water over my face and neck. It was certainly no substitute for a good night's sleep, but it would have to do.

My face in the mirror looked puffy and wan, so I repaired it as best I could and ran a brush through my tangle of curls. It was starting to grow out now, no longer the tight cap I'd been forced into when my masses of dark brown hair had been hacked off in the emergency room the past summer. Before I knew it, it would be hanging on my shoulders again, just the way Darnay had said he'd like to see it.

The smell of bacon once again drifted up the stairs, giving me a strange feeling of déja vu as I descended to the kitchen. Cat stood at the stove, her back to me, exactly as she had the day before. This time the eggs were scrambled, and her bright response to my muttered "Good morning" held no trace of embarrassment or guilt over the previous night's performance. Perhaps she didn't even remember it, although I knew I had not been mistaken about that gleam of malice in her eyes as Mercer led her inside.

When my cousin joined us, the two Prescott women carried on as if nothing had disturbed the tranquility of our previous evening, as if Mercer and I had never talked and plotted through the long night. They chattered of farm matters, feed for the chickens, groceries to be ordered. I shrugged and attacked my breakfast, leaving them to it. I had just shoveled the last, fluffy forkful into my mouth when Raphie leaped against the door and set up a furious barking, and a massive SUV wheeled to a stop in front of the house.

The cavalry had arrived.

Having your luggage sitting at the bottom of a lake has its advantages. It took me only a minute to wipe my mouth, sling my bag over my shoulder, and pronounce myself ready to roll. Since Mercer had decided to come clean with me, I felt I owed her the same courtesy, so I introduced Erik as my partner instead of trying to maintain the charade that he was from a rental car company. Cat smiled and offered breakfast, which he politely declined, while my cousin seemed totally captivated, despite the seriousness of the situation. I'm not certain if his blond good looks and easy charm are what made her suddenly decide she wanted to go with us, but I put a stop to any such notion almost before the request was out of her mouth.

"No, absolutely not," I said in a voice I hoped indicated I would tolerate no opposition. The three of us had moved out onto the porch, while Cat had returned to the table. "How can you even think of it, after what happened last night?"

"That was a . . . oh, what do you call it? Something that's out of the ordinary, that doesn't happen very often?"

"An aberration?" Erik offered, and earned himself a beaming smile in return.

"Exactly! An aberration. She's only done that once before in all the time we've been here. She's fine as long as she takes her meds."

I wondered what threat—real or perceived—had sent Catherine Prescott off into the kind of hysterics I'd witnessed the night before. Was she truly mentally unstable, or simply a selfish, manipulative woman, intent on keeping her daughter strictly to herself now they'd finally been reunited? Either way, I had no time to worry about it. Circumstances dictated that we get moving.

I climbed into Erik's black beast of a vehicle, and Mercer jumped up onto the running board, preventing me from closing the door. "Bay, it's not fair if you're going to look for Perdition on your own. Besides, you'll—"

"—never find it without you," I finished for her, "I know. We have no intention of going anywhere near there, I swear to you. Our business is in Edgefield, and we need to get up there as soon as possible."

"But you promised you'd help me."

"And I will. *We* will. It's just going to have to wait." I pulled on the door, forcing her to jump down as Erik fired up the Expedition. I retrieved my wallet from the bottom of my bag, extracted all the slightly damp cash, and handed it to my cousin. "Here, take this. Just in case you and Cat need to get out of here in a hurry. If that happens, head straight for Presqu'isle. The Judge will know what to do."

"But why? I mean, Buddy has no idea . . ."

"Buddy isn't as stupid as you seem to think he his. He found me—twice—and there's no point in taking any chances. Are you sure you want to keep the map with you? I can put it somewhere safe, somewhere he'll never get to it."

I watched that stubborn look which reminded me so much of Emmaline creep into her eyes. I shrugged and slammed the door shut. Despite our mutual soul-baring of the night before, she still didn't entirely trust me. So be it. I didn't have time to argue with her. "Just make sure you have it hidden well. And if somehow you should run across him, give it up. No matter what treasure you think you're going to find at the end of this mythical rainbow, it's not worth your life. Or Cat's."

"You'll call? When you hear something?"

Despite her previous show of bravado, I heard fear in the question. Last night, for the first time, I'd forced her to look at the very real possibility she could be facing serious jail time. She had shown remarkable ingenuity and resourcefulness, not only in stealing her mother from the mental hospital in Columbia, but in finding this place, concealing their identities, and in doing everything she knew how to make a new life for both of them. But in other things, she had been unbelievably stupid and gullible, and there was a real chance that even the Judge wouldn't be able to save her now. And if Mercer went to jail, what would happen to Cat?

"I'll keep you posted," I promised, trying to put more reassurance into my voice than I truly felt.

She stepped back then as Erik reversed and headed us out. I glanced in the big, rectangular side mirror as we pulled onto the dirt road which fronted the farm. I watched Mercer, her hand stuffed full of limp fifty-dollar bills, wave dispiritedly, until her image disappeared in a haze of dust.

CHAPTER
TWENTY-FIVE

"So where are we?"

Erik paused to check for traffic at the intersection, then turned left onto another narrow road, this one, thankfully, paved. The marker identified it as Route 61, but that meant nothing to me.

"About halfway between Orangeburg and Walterboro, near as I can figure." He glanced at me briefly as the mammoth vehicle gathered speed.

"How did you find it? I have to admit, when you said you'd figure it out, I sort of had my doubts."

"The area code and prefix from the caller ID narrowed it down. I studied some maps, did a little checking around on the 'net, then stopped this morning at a couple of gas stations. Aren't too many old farms with only a couple of females in residence, especially ones who haven't lived around here for most of their natural lives."

A couple of females. I wondered if Mercer realized that her carefully planned charade that Cat lived alone was a complete bust. Coming from a small town herself, she should have known better.

"Pretty clever," I said.

Erik smiled in acknowledgment of my approval, then pointed to a small device about the size of a cellular telephone clipped to the dashboard. "I was kind of hoping to get a chance to try out my new toy, but no such luck. Too far out in the boonies to be of much use."

"What is it?"

"A GPS unit."

"Oh, well, that explains everything," I said with a smile.

"Global Positioning Satellite. A lot of rental cars come equipped with them now, to help tourists find their way around strange cities. We sell them at the store."

"And?" I rummaged in my bag, my fingers closing finally around the last of my sun-dried cigarettes. I fondled it, wondering if I could hold out until we encountered any place civilized enough to sport a vending machine.

"And that's it. It's sort of like an electronic map. Actually, you can load it with lots of different maps, and you tell it where you want to go and it tells you how to get there. If you have the coordinates—latitude and longitude—you can do it that way, too."

"Fascinating." I drew a deep breath and dropped my bag back onto the floor.

"You know, for a woman who's just about as smart as anyone I've ever met, you sure are technologically challenged."

I laughed. "What can I say? Just about the time I figure out the latest thing, like instant messaging on the computer, it becomes old hat, and something newer and more sophisticated has been invented. This world of electronic gadgetry moves too damn fast for me. I guess I'm just an old-fashioned kinda girl at heart."

We drove on in silence, the clear December sky a brilliant background to the endless miles of woodland streaming by outside.

"You can smoke if you want to," Erik said after several minutes. "Just crack the window a little."

"Thanks, but I can wait. I need to find an ATM and someplace to pick up some clothes, too. I lost everything except my tote bag in the crash." I slipped off my loafers, scrunched down in the soft leather seat, and propped my bare feet up on the dash. I could feel myself drifting off and forced my brain back to consciousness by trying to count the number of hours I'd been without sleep. Near as I could figure, I'd been awake for about forty-four out of the past forty-eight, not taking into account however long I'd dozed against the bony shoulder of James Luke Matthew Carver.

"You gonna tell me about it?" Erik checked the rearview mirror, then accelerated around an ancient John Deere tractor hauling some giant, mysterious piece of farm equipment behind it.

I straightened myself in the seat and drew a deep breath to clear my head. "Where would you like me to start?"

"I don't know. The beginning always seems like a good place."

"Well, that could be anywhere from yesterday to last summer

to twenty years ago. Actually, it could be as far back as a hundred and forty years ago, if you want the complete, unabridged version."

I turned to judge Erik's reaction and caught his eyes fixed on the purpling lump on my forehead.

"I'm not suffering from brain damage, if that's what you're thinking," I said lightly, hoping I was speaking the truth. "Hey, there's a gas station. Pull over."

Erik wheeled up to the ramshackle building with two ancient pumps out in front, stopped, then pulled a wad of bills from the front pocket of his well-worn jeans. "I assume you gave all your cash to Mercer," he said, peeling off a twenty and extending it to me.

"Yes, I did. Thanks. Want anything?"

"A Pepsi, if they have it."

"Be right back."

When I climbed back into the truck, I carried a brown paper sack bulging with goodies. "Road food," I said, handing Erik his soda and dumping the candy bars out onto the seat between us. I set my own Diet Coke in the cup holder and forced myself to remove the cellophane slowly from the pack of Marlboros. I hesitated, stroking the bright red package, then dropped it into my bag and peeled the wrapper from a Snickers.

"You quitting?" Erik asked as we bounced back onto the highway.

"For at least the next ten minutes." I kicked off my shoes again, tucked my uninjured leg up under me, and tried to order my thoughts. "Okay, let's start with Perdition House, since I'm pretty certain that's what precipitated Mercer's involvement in all of this. Well, that and the fact that she finally located her mother."

"Where? And what's Perdition? Aside from the obvious."

"Hold on, I'll get there." I licked the chocolate from my fingers and stuffed the candy wrapper into the empty bag. "Mercer and I are shirttail cousins, as you already know. Our common ancestor, Charles Morgan Robichoux, had two wives. The one I'm descended from died during the Civil War, and he remarried. Mercer's family comes down from the second."

"Okay, got it."

"Here's where it gets tricky. The first wife, Lucy, had two daughters, Isabelle and Theodora. Isabelle married Bennett Chase and they lived—"

"In Perdition House. It's a plantation."

"Hey, you're pretty good at this."

Erik grinned. "Go ahead."

"Okay. Bennett and Isabelle had three children—Henry, who supposedly died in a Union prison camp on Johnson's Island in Ohio—and twin daughters, Mercer and Morgan, who were much younger than Henry. Oh, and Bennet got killed in the war, too. We're talking the Civil War, now, 1860s."

"I figured that. So then what happened?"

"Well, Isabelle was left to try to hold on to the plantation, keep things running as best she could. I've read one of her letters—Aunt Eliza found them—and it appears that near the end of the war, she and her girls and a couple of slaves were the only ones left. There's another letter from Isabelle's sister, in which Theodora urges them to abandon the place and get themselves to Columbia because Sherman is on the way."

I noticed then that we were entering some small town. Huge moss-draped oaks shaded beautifully restored houses along both sides of the street, and I glimpsed wide porches hung with pots of fern, and here and there a Victorian turret topped with slate shingles. We pulled to a stop at the single traffic light.

"Keep going," Erik prodded me. "This is fascinating stuff."

"You think so?"

"Sure. Gosh, I have no idea about any of my relatives past the grandparents. I don't think anybody's ever bothered to try to find out about them."

"Don't knock it," I replied as Erik eased the big SUV through the light, and we picked up speed again. I couldn't help remembering all the time and devotion my mother had lavished on her ancestor obsession, and how little of either she had managed to spare for her only child.

Erik set the cruise control and tactfully didn't pursue my last remark.

"Anyway," I continued, "back to Sherman." I recalled then how, at this point in Mercer's recitation the night before, the reason for her voluminous knowledge about the hated Union general had suddenly made sense to me. "Remember, this is late in the war, January, February of 1865. Sherman has just accepted the surrender of Savannah, the culmination of his March to the

Sea, after having burned Atlanta and pretty much everything in between. Everyone is sure he's heading for Charleston, the place where the whole thing started, to do the same to them."

"But instead he turns north, toward Columbia." Erik grinned at my start of surprise. "Hey, I paid *some* attention back in school, you know. History was my favorite class, besides computer science."

"I never would have guessed."

"I'm sorry. Go ahead."

"So, you're right, Sherman sends half his troops up the Savannah River, feints toward Charleston, then heads north to meet up with the others and march on Columbia. Most everyone in his path is abandoning their plantations, carrying what they can salvage, and moving inland. But apparently Isabelle is determined to stay at Perdition. She cuts off the twins' hair, dresses them like boys, loads up the pistols, and prepares to defend her home."

"By herself?"

"That's not clear. As I said, there were a couple of slaves who'd stayed on, but they may have run off before the Yankees actually arrived."

"You know, I love this stuff, I really do, but I'm not getting what all this has to do with Mercer Mary Prescott and this Slade character and everything."

"It took me awhile, too, but hang in there. I'll try to get to the point. Isabelle wasn't successful in saving Perdition House. Sherman's advance scouts, *foragers* they were called because their job was to steal food and horses to keep the Union troops supplied, stripped the plantation of everything portable and set it afire. Isabelle and her girls were spared, but herded out and forced to join the hundreds of others walking to Columbia. It's not clear how far they got, probably to some other relatives near the capital, but Isabelle died there shortly before the war ended. The twins went to live with their aunt, then got shipped off to their grandfather Robichoux when he remarried. Perdition, although too damaged to be salvaged, hadn't burned to the ground. In the summer of 1865, after the war had officially ended, Theodora and the other surviving relatives managed to rescue what they could from the ruins, including the desk in which Uncle Rupert eventually found Isabelle's letters. There, I think that's it."

I could tell by the increase in traffic we must be nearing Aiken.

I took a long drink of Diet Coke just as I spied the sprawling parking lot, jammed with cars, and the familiar blue sign atop a tall pole.

"Erik! Pull in to that Wal-Mart, will you? I can pick up some jeans and things and get some cash."

He deftly maneuvered the Expedition into a narrow parking space and shut off the engine as I reached for the door handle. "Wait," he said, his hand firm but gentle on my elbow. "You can't just leave me hanging here. I need to know the end of this story. Not the whole thing, but at least what all this family history has to do with anything."

I turned back toward him and clutched my bag in my lap. "Okay, the abbreviated version. Family legend—on both Mercer's side as well as mine, apparently—has always held that Isabelle stashed the family treasure somewhere on the property before Sherman's troops arrived."

"What kind of treasure?"

"The usual, I guess. Silverware, jewelry, gold. Nobody knows for sure. The twins were only seven or eight at the time, and Isabelle died before she could tell anybody about it, but Mercer is convinced it exists somewhere on the site of Perdition House. That letter I read at Aunt Eliza's seems to confirm it. Isabelle talks about burying the last of the shrimp forks or something like that. Anyway, Theodora and the others never found it. So, if it does in fact exist, it must still be there. And Mercer is determined to be the one to claim it."

"I still don't get it. You said before, back there at the farmhouse, that she has a map. If she knows where it is, why doesn't she just go dig it up?"

I pushed open the heavy door and paused for effect. I knew the answer would blow Erik away just as it had done me. "Because the ruins of Perdition are sitting right smack in the middle of the Savannah River Site," I announced triumphantly, and slammed the door on his look of total astonishment.

CHAPTER TWENTY-SIX

I moved as fast as I could, dragging my bad leg up and down the aisles of the superstore. I gave a fleeting thought to a book I'd heard about—one of Oprah's picks, if I remembered correctly—in which a girl takes up permanent residence inside a Wal-Mart. Totally believable. I flung clothes, toiletries, elastic bandages, sneakers, and a bag to carry it all into the squeaky shopping cart, then hopped into the shortest line. I slapped down my debit card, added two hundred dollars to the total of my purchases, and headed for the ladies' room. Fifteen minutes later I emerged in my new jeans and University of South Carolina sweatshirt, my damaged knee firmly wrapped, sparkling white Reeboks cushioning my walk. I felt one hundred percent better.

I found Erik slumped in the seat, his head thrown back, eyes closed. He'd locked the doors, and I had to bang on a window to get his attention.

"Sorry," I saw him mouth as he flipped up the automatic locks.

"You okay?" I asked, puffing a little at the extra effort it took to climb up into the Expedition with one knee which wouldn't bend.

"Sure. I wasn't asleep, just thinking."

"About the case?"

"Yup."

"And?" I snapped on my shoulder harness and stretched out my bandaged leg in the spacious cab as we backed around and rejoined the highway. After a few moments, when Erik didn't respond, I said, "I haven't had a chance to ask what you found out about that bunch Mercer got arrested with. Anything interesting on the 'net about them?"

"Some. But we'll get to that. Go ahead and finish your story.

How did your cousin manage to locate her mother after all these years?"

I knew I was being sidetracked, but there wasn't much I could do except relax and enjoy the ride. "Okay. When her grandmother died, Mercer was the only relative they could find. The lawyers communicated with the Scogginses, who sort of forced her to go back to her hometown and settle things there. The house was mortgaged to the hilt so it was only personal stuff she inherited— furnishings, clothes, papers. Didn't amount to much at all. There was a small life insurance policy, enough to give her a start. She sold off or donated everything except the letters and documents, which she stuck in a box and pretty much forgot about."

I paused, fiddling with the handles on my tote bag and trying to convince myself I could get through this recitation without a cigarette. I exhaled deeply and sat back in the seat, empty-handed. "Long story short," I resumed, "Mercer found two things of value when she finally got around to sorting out her grandmother's papers."

"The map?"

"No, I think she stole that from Aunt Eliza—or copied it— though she won't admit it, even now. Eliza showed me some old maps of local holdings back in the 1800s which Uncle Rupert had collected. I don't think she'd realize it if one went missing."

"But Mercer had been to your aunt's *before* she came to Beaufort, right?"

"Right. See, what she'd found in her grandmother's stuff were some old letters and a smattering of genealogical research. Enough to whet her appetite, but not nearly enough to tell her the whole story. Once she'd managed to finagle the complete family tree thing out of Eliza and had conned her into showing her Isabelle's and Theodora's correspondence, Mercer decided to start in on the remaining descendants. Because she'd picked up the idea somewhere that the Judge is rich, she moved him to the top of the list. Her plan was to worm her way into his confidence in order to see if he still had any of my mother's old family records or papers."

"And maybe see if he'd like to make a donation to the cause while she was at it?"

"Could be."

Erik slowed as we entered another small town, then suddenly

whipped the wheel to the right, sending me rolling against the door.

"What?" I demanded.

"Sorry," he said, "but I'm starving. This okay with you?"

I righted myself to find we had pulled up next to a giant menu board in the parking lot of a brand-new Sonic drive-in. We both ordered burgers, fries, and sodas. When the incredibly skinny, teenaged carhop roller-skated her way up with the laden tray, she spent an inordinate amount of time counting out Erik's change and simpering up at him from beneath her fringe of blonde bangs. I might as well have been invisible.

"So," he said around a mouthful of lettuce, tomato, and onion, "that explains why Mercer attached herself to that particular group of protesters."

"Exactly. I drove through the Savannah River Site last week, and there are signs all over the place warning you not to stop except for an emergency. I know they don't make atomic bombs there any more, but there must be a lot of dangerous material still around. I think they reprocess spent nuclear fuel or something like that. In fact, there's been a big flap in the paper lately about the Department of Energy's wanting to haul in more plutonium."

"I heard about that. Didn't the governor threaten to lie down in the road and block the trucks at the state line? Maybe that's what the demonstrators were protesting."

"You could be right. At any rate, it gave Mercer the perfect excuse to be on the property. But she didn't find the ruins of Perdition House, which is why she came to Beaufort looking for the Judge."

"She probably still didn't have a good enough fix on the location and thought there might be something in your mother's old papers which could help her pinpoint it."

"So she said. But even if she'd managed to dig up enough information at Presqu'isle, I still couldn't get her to tell me how she expected to get back inside the restricted area." I paused to wash down the French fries with a large swallow of Diet Coke. "Surely this New Earth bunch isn't going to be trying something like that again, at least not any time soon."

"What did you call them?" Erik had paused, the last of the loaded cheeseburger inches from his mouth."

"Call who?"

"The protestors. The ones Mercer got arrested with." His intent stare made me nervous, though why I couldn't have said.

"The New Earth Defense . . . something. I'm not sure. Maybe fund? No, network, that was it," I replied with a nod. "The New Earth Defense Network. Why? Is it important?"

"It could be. But go ahead and finish telling me about Mercer. You said she found two things of value in her grandmother's stuff."

I had no idea what Erik was driving at, but I let it go. For the moment. "Right. The other was the bombshell, what really set all the rest of this in motion. She found commitment papers from the Herbert-Hanson Clinic in Columbia."

"The place where she worked?"

"Yes, but that wasn't until later, after she realized what the papers meant."

Even greasy junk food couldn't dull Erik Whiteside's quick intellect. "Wait a minute! Her mother was in the mental institution—had been for years—and the grandmother knew it. Damn! The poor kid must have been beside herself."

"She was pretty pissed, but who was she going to vent her anger on? Everyone involved was already dead. So she got herself a job, insinuated herself into the good graces of the staff, and bided her time."

"No one made the connection with the names?"

"Apparently not. After all, 'Prescott' isn't that unusual."

"So she just walked out with her one day? How'd she manage it? And why?"

I handed over the remains of my soggy wrappers, and Erik pushed the arm of the metal tray back out of the car. This time, the urge overcame all my best intentions. I hauled up my bag, shook out a Marlboro and lit up before I had a chance to think about it. The first hit made me a little dizzy, but I rolled down the window on my side and exhaled smoke into the mild afternoon air.

"As to why, she knew the payments for Cat's care would have ended with her grandmother's death. No wonder there was nothing left when the old lady passed away. It must have taken every last cent she could scrape together to pay the fees. The Herbert-Hanson is a private clinic, mostly for drug-related mental disorders, and they were preparing to transfer Cat to one of the state-run facilities. Mercer couldn't let that happen. As for how, she just gathered her mother up in the middle of one of the midnight-to-eight shifts, waited for the right opportunity, and they simply walked out the door."

"No wonder the woman I talked to at the clinic was so interested to find out if *I* knew where to find Mercer. Why didn't they notify the police?"

I shrugged. "I don't know. Maybe they didn't want the publicity. It wasn't as if Cat were dangerous or anything. Mercer says all her problems are related to the drugs she did as a teenager. So long as she takes her medication, she's pretty functional, although what I witnessed last night makes me wonder. Mercer thinks she'll improve away from the institution, maybe be able to get off the meds one day. She's convinced her grandparents just shut Cat away in another state to keep from dealing with the humiliation of having a junkie as well as a slut for a daughter."

"Pretty cold."

"Yeah. There's probably a lot we won't ever know because Mercer has already decided for herself who the villains of the piece are. She sees Cat as the victim, and I don't think anything's going to change that. Her views are pretty colored by her own particular prejudices."

"So after they walked out of the clinic, Mercer took her to that farmhouse. Did she steal enough drugs to keep her mother going?"

"Another topic which proved to be off-limits last night, although I don't see any other answer to how she could be getting them. She's surely not having a prescription filled at the local pharmacy."

Again I had to admire the ease with which Erik made these leaps of deduction. Without realizing it, I had chosen for my partner not only a near-genius with computers, but someone who seemed more qualified for the role of Holmes than for the one I had subconsciously assigned to him, that of the faithful but bumbling Watson.

I dropped my cigarette butt into the inch or so of Diet Coke remaining in the bottom of the plastic cup and handed it across to Erik who added it to the rest of our trash. I expected him to crank the engine then and get us back on the road, but instead he rested his hands on the steering wheel and gazed out through the windshield, his thoughts apparently far away. When he finally spoke, I could see the doubt reflected on his boyishly handsome face.

"This whole thing is beginning to sound like one of those made-for-TV movies, you know? Do you actually believe her story? And what about this Buddy Slade thing? What explanation did she have for that?"

I had to admit Erik had a point. Much of what had seemed reasonable when told in my cousin's halting, emotionally charged voice now appeared, in the cold light of day, somehow almost too pat, too . . . *exculpatory*. Nothing had been Mercer's fault; everything she'd done was a result of some outside force or circumstance conspiring against her and her mother. As for Buddy, that too had been waved away, dismissed with what had sounded like an incoherent, though plausible story. Again I heard the calm voice of Neddie Halloran, warning me that Mercer had no doubt become, over years of practice, an accomplished liar.

Erik started the car then, and we moved out into the sparse, midafternoon traffic as I related to him the tale of Walter Jerome "Buddy" Slade. When I'd finished, my partner nodded once, mumbled, "Right," then fell silent again. In a few minutes, he flipped on his right turn signal and eased the Expedition into a roadside rest area, its two weathered picnic tables looking somehow forlorn squatting on the brown winter grass. He pulled up next to the dented trash barrel and cut the engine. He unclipped the GPS unit from the dash, then punched in a series of numbers. The action was accompanied by a series of low-pitched beeps.

"What are you doing?" I asked.

"Programming the unit."

"But why? We can't be that far from Edgefield. I remember this area now. We're on the right road."

"You don't see the connection, because I haven't told you what *I* know. Let's take a break, and I'll fill you in. Then we can decide what our next move should be."

"Erik, I—"

"Look, we're only a few miles from Edgefield. Just give me ten minutes, okay? If you don't agree with my conclusions, we can just head on into town."

The sense of urgency I'd felt as we'd set off from the farmhouse that morning had not dissipated during our drive north. I couldn't have said exactly why, but some instinct told me things were coming to a head, that time was running out. I was certain the answers lay in the death of the SRS security guard, and I couldn't see what Erik might have found out which would change that. Still, ten minutes . . .

"Sure, okay," I said, and climbed down from the SUV.

We settled onto one of the tables. Dark clouds lumbered across the sky from the west, and the chill breeze which had kicked up made me glad for the bulky sweatshirt.

Erik Whiteside rested his well-muscled arms on his thighs and studied his hands for a moment, then drew a long, steadying breath and began.

CHAPTER
TWENTY-SEVEN

We stopped once for gas, and the storm hit us full-force just a few miles later. As we climbed higher into the Piedmont, the flat farmland gave way to rolling hills, and the rain turned to sleet. Locked in the warm cocoon of the Expedition, I stared intently into the deepening gloom, mesmerized by the rhythmic sweep of the massive wipers.

How could I have been so gullible? So blind? Granted, up until an hour ago, I had not had the benefit of what Erik Whiteside had learned over a period of nights spent scanning message boards and lurking in countless chat rooms populated by the fringes of the antinuke movement. And those fragmented pieces, culled from vague hints and obscure references, had made little sense to him either until he had matched it with Mercer's tale of her search for buried treasure in the ruins of Perdition House.

"Quit beating yourself up." Erik's voice sounded loud in the dim stillness of the darkened interior.

I looked up to find him smiling at me. "I can't help it. I feel like an idiot for not having seen some of this sooner."

"It just proves we have to keep in closer contact from now on. Both of us were operating in a vacuum. If we'd put our heads together right away . . . Still, I don't think either one of us could have made the connection without both halves of the story."

"Maybe not."

The final piece of the puzzle snapped into place for Erik when he'd heard about Mercer's involvement with Buddy Slade. The story she'd told me seemed innocent enough. They'd grown up together, had dated some in high school. One fall night in her sophomore year, mellowed by a few illicit beers under the bleachers after a football game, she had drunkenly agreed to marry him. They climbed into Buddy's old Chevy and roused an elderly justice-of-the-peace just across the state line. For the fifty dollars Buddy had stolen from a couple of school lockers, the old man performed the ceremony, knowing full well it had no validity since they had no license and it was obvious the bride couldn't be more than fifteen years old.

The next day, a badly hungover Mercer realized they'd done nothing more binding than get ripped off for fifty bucks, but Buddy insisted the marriage was valid. He continued to hound and harass his "wife" until the first of his numerous run-ins with the law sent him to the juvenile facility in Atlanta. Over the next years, Mercer told me, Buddy appeared on her doorstep every time he got out of jail. When he'd been sentenced to five-to-seven years for armed robbery, she thought herself rid of him for good.

She swore she had no idea how he came to learn of her quest for the treasure of Perdition House, or how he'd known about her involvement with me. As for his accomplices, the two women who attacked Dolores, my cousin pled total ignorance.

And, in spite of everything, I was inclined to believe her.

"How much farther?" I asked as Erik stretched and repositioned himself in his seat.

"I figure another hour, if this mess outside doesn't turn to snow first."

"You think it could? I haven't seen snow since I was at Northwestern."

Erik smiled. "You've gotten spoiled down on that tropical island of yours. We see it in Charlotte about once a year." He turned his attention back to the nearly deserted road. "You hungry?"

"A little. Want another candy bar?" I had replenished our supply of "road food" when we'd stopped for gas.

"No thanks. I can already feel the cavities forming from the last one."

We rode on in silence, my partner no doubt sharing my apprehension about what we would find when we finally reached our destination. I'd used Erik's cell phone to contact the Judge right after we'd made the decision to change course. Once he heard the story, he spluttered and fumed, demanding we turn around immediately and come back to Presqu'isle, although he knew full well we wouldn't. I did promise to call Red and bring him up to speed. Sarah was again out of town for the weekend, according to my father, and Red had his kids to entertain, so it was no surprise I'd been unsuccessful in tracking him down. I had to content myself with leaving messages for my brother-in-law at the sheriff's office as well as at his apartment.

"Why don't you try to catch a nap?" Erik asked, glancing at me across the wide expanse of seat. "You really looked whipped."

I smiled at him and shook my head. I couldn't begin to think about sleep. My mind was racing ninety miles an hour, imagining one scenario after another, not one of which ever resolved itself into the kind of outcome I was hoping for. No matter how much I might wish otherwise, my cousin was in this thing up to her neck. Erik and I had both beaten against the wall of trouble she had erected around herself, and neither of us could see a way out for her.

"We're here."

Despite my whirling thoughts, I must have dozed a little. I forced my eyes open just as we glided down the last hill into the little town. I squinted through the windshield at the squat buildings, remarking to myself as we passed the welcome center that the sleet which dogged us through the higher elevations had settled down once more into a steady, drizzling rain. Though night had closed in, and it seemed as if we had been traveling for weeks, the digital clock on the dashboard read only *6:10*. Erik guided the Expedition into the familiar driveway of the McDonald's, pulled into a space at the farthest edge of the parking lot, and cut the engine.

"You want to go in? Are you hungry?" Erik's voice betrayed the tension building in both of us now that we had finally arrived, and action could be postponed no longer.

"No, thanks. You?"

"I think if I got a whiff of the inside of that place I'd probably throw up." He tried to smile, but it showed up more like a grimace in the glow of the sodium vapor light hanging just above us. "Look, Bay, it's not that I'm a coward or anything, but—"

"I know. You think my stomach's not tied up in knots, too?"

"Yeah, but you've had some experience with this kind of thing."

"With what kind of thing?"

"You know." Erik squirmed in the seat and ran his hand across the pale stubble which had collected on his square chin since he'd shaved that morning in Charlotte. It must have seemed to him like a lifetime ago. "I think we should just drive straight to the police station."

The closer we'd gotten to our destination, the more Erik's enthusiasm had waned, until I was certain he was now wishing he had never made the suggestion to come here in the first place.

I glanced up into the lights and realized it had stopped raining. "And tell them what?" I asked, pushing open the door and easing myself down onto the gleaming blacktop. The wind had dropped, and the chill in the air felt almost refreshing. I propped my bad leg on the running board. "We have absolutely nothing in the way of evidence. *Nada.* Believe me," I added, when Erik seemed about to argue the point, "I've spent a lot of time around cops and lawyers. Oh, they'd be polite enough. Hear us out, promise to look into it, then laugh themselves silly as soon as we were out the door." I stretched, trying in vain to work out the knots of tension bunched around my neck and shoulders. "No, my friend, if anything is going to get resolved tonight, it's going to be up to us. And, trust me, this is totally outside of my meager experience, too."

"Okay."

I could hear the skepticism in his voice. True, I had seen my share of violence in the past few months, but that didn't make me an expert on dealing with criminals. In fact, I thought as I climbed back into the warmth of the SUV, it probably meant just the opposite. And I sure as hell wasn't planning on watching anyone else die, especially not Erik. Or myself either, for that matter.

"So what happens next?" he asked.

"Pull around to the drive-thru, and let's get something warm to drink. Then we'll head up there and just go knock on the door. All we want to do is talk, gather information. We make no accusations. Our line is that we're just trying to find a way to help Mercer out of her troubles. Surely no one could object to that."

While I spoke, Erik gave our order to the faceless voice behind the menu board, handed over a couple of bucks at the first window, and placed my steaming cardboard container of hot tea in the center cup holder next to his coffee.

"How much do we admit to knowing?" he asked, moving out into the sparse evening traffic.

"No more than we have to in order to get what we want. It's

best not to plan these things," I said, blowing across the top of the cup before sipping cautiously. "I learned that from dealing with IRS auditors. Volunteer nothing. Try to get them to put their cards on the table first, see what they think they've got, then react to it. Relax," I added, laying my free hand against the muscles bunched along his tensed-up shoulder, "and remember, we're not out to bust anybody. That's not our job."

Erik glanced down at my fingers resting on the sleeve of his light denim jacket. I jerked them away, gulping tea to cover my embarrassment, and spluttering as I scalded the inside of my mouth. There had been the merest hint of a question in that look, and I sure as hell didn't want him to get the wrong impression. Not that the thought hadn't flitted, however briefly, across my own mind in the past few hours . . .

He waited until I stopped coughing before he spoke. "You think either one of them is just going to tell us what we want to know?" He flipped on his turn signal, then slowed as we started up the hill on the narrow, poorly lighted street.

"We'll see," I said, responding to his business-like question as if the last minute or two had never taken place. "Just play it by ear."

I recognized the vehicle before I did the house, although a strange Jeep was pulled up in the yard just off the uneven pavement. Erik cut the lights as we eased in behind it. I lifted my bag from the floor, comforted by the heft of the Glock nestled just inside. I hadn't bothered to inform my partner that I was armed. No sense making him any more nervous than both of us already were.

I joined him at the front of the Expedition, and we slogged our way through piles of cold, wet leaves. Erik was a couple of steps in the lead when my sharp gasp made him whirl around to face me.

"What?" he demanded in a hoarse whisper. Then, when I didn't reply, "Bay! What's the matter?"

I stood, unable to speak, my eyes riveted on the sea-green paint imbedded in the scraped and dented front bumper of the big pickup truck parked in the driveway of Bill and Vesta Scoggins.

CHAPTER
TWENTY-EIGHT

I smelled him a second before I felt the cold steel against the back of my neck.

If I had been able to turn my head, I knew I would have seen the crude numbers tattooed across the knuckles of his greasy hand as it pressed the gun barrel into my flesh.

"Step back. Real slow. Hands out where I can see 'em."

I heard Erik's grunt of surprise, sensed his movement toward me.

"Hold it!" Buddy Slade growled as I raised my arms out from my sides. "Tell pretty boy to stop right where he is."

"He has a gun." I tried to keep my voice steady, to quell the fear clawing desperately at my throat.

Erik stopped, the confusion on his face almost comical. "Bay? What's going on? Who—?"

"Shut up! Turn around and move up the steps. Slow! You, too, you meddlin' bitch!" Buddy shoved me roughly away from the front of the truck, one hand gripping my upper arm while the other held the weapon tightly against my neck. When Erik failed to respond immediately, Buddy reached up to grab a handful of my damp hair and jerk me backward. "I'll blow her head off, man. I mean it. Now move!"

Without a word Erik turned, and we followed him up the driveway toward the old frame house. I shuffled along, limping on my injured leg, forcing Buddy Slade to half drag me. My denim bag, inexplicably still slung across my shoulder, banged against my thigh. Even though the antiquated street light was two houses down, I prayed some of its dim light might still reach far enough to illuminate the bizarre scene being played out in the middle of this quiet, residential neighborhood. Surely someone would drive by. Surely someone would twitch aside a curtain, adjust a blind, and realize what was happening.

But we reached the porch and then the front door with no shout of challenge, no swoop of headlights to distract our captor.

"Open it," Buddy ordered, "nice and easy."

He kept the two of us well back, out of range of any effort Erik might make to swing the storm door wide, perhaps knocking Slade far enough off stride to have a crack at overpowering him. The thought had crossed my mind, too, but apparently Buddy and I watched the same movies.

The interior door opened inward, and we stepped directly into the living room. For a moment the blaze of lights blinded me. There were people there, at least three, although I could make out only dim shapes in those first few seconds. A heated conversation had been cut off abruptly at our entrance. In the silence that followed, I worked at forcing my eyes to adjust from the blackness outside.

When they did, I could only stare in numb disbelief at the man seated comfortably in an overstuffed chair, the sheen of his black ponytail reflecting the glow of the old-fashioned floor lamp resting behind him.

"Ah, Mrs. Tanner. Bay. I'm really sorry it had to come to this." I watched him stub out his Marlboro in a dented metal ashtray and rise slowly to his feet. "Why don't you and your young friend have a seat in there while my colleagues and I conclude our discussion? Lend a hand, would you, Bill?" He smiled as Bill Scoggins rose obediently from the shabby sofa, and I felt my legs begin to quiver in fear. "Sarah will be devastated to have missed you," Jack Wilson added as Buddy Slade used his pistol to herd us through the dining room and into the kitchen.

They ran out of duct tape, so Bill Scoggins provided an extension cord to complete the process of tying us to stout wooden chairs placed at opposite ends of the kitchen table around which I had prayed with his wife and foster children barely two weeks before. Despite the ease with which he held the gun on us while Buddy Slade bound our hands and feet, I still couldn't reconcile him with the man who had spoken with such apparently sincere affection about Mercer Mary Prescott, the man who took in neglected, castoff kids and taught them how to play the piano.

With Erik already secured, Buddy forced my legs together and lashed my ankles to the rung of the ladder-backed chair. I cried out at the searing pain that shot through my sprained knee, and he reached up to backhand me across the face. The blow sent a shower of lights exploding behind my eyelids and a trickle of blood dribbling from my bruised mouth.

Bill Scoggins never flinched.

"You son of a bitch!" Erik strained against his bonds, and the muzzle of the handgun swung around in his direction.

"Erik! No!"

Buddy chuckled as Erik subsided, his awareness of the futility of any protest evident in the slumping of his shoulders. Without a word, Scoggins handed the pistol back to Buddy, turned, and left the room.

"Now, you two just sit tight until our fearless leader decides exactly what to do with you." Buddy tucked the gun into the back of the waistband of his skintight jeans. His resemblance to Elvis was emphasized by a dingy white shirt, collar turned up against his greasy ducktail haircut, and a scarred, black bomber jacket. He favored me with his caricature of the King's sexy smile. "If he lets me have my way, darlin', you might just wish you hadn't made it out of the lake."

I licked the dribble of blood from the corner of my mouth and ordered my brain to ignore the agony of my twisted knee. We had before us the weakest link in this chain of madness, and I desperately needed information. How I would use it, I had no real idea, but I knew Erik and I would have no chance unless we knew exactly where we stood.

"What did Wilson mean about Sarah?" I asked, forcing myself to speak slowly and without fear, since that seemed to be the one emotion Buddy got off on. "You don't expect us to believe *she's* involved in this."

"I don't expect you to believe jack-shit," Slade sneered. "But if you mean the big man's little girlfriend, don't be lookin' for no help from her. He's got her so hot for him she's practically pantin'. And besides, she ain't around anyway." He pulled a toothpick from the pocket of his jacket and began working it around under the fingernails on his left hand.

I took it as a bad sign that he was so eager to talk, but I pressed on. Erik looked at me strangely, but kept silent. For the moment, it was only Buddy and I and his need to prove his superiority.

"I know Sarah. There is no way she would condone any of this insanity."

Buddy tensed, and I knew immediately it had been a bad choice of words. "Who you callin' crazy, huh, bitch? You callin' me crazy?" His hand went to his waistband, to the gun he had shoved in there just moments before.

"No, not you," I rushed to assure him, "not you. It's just that this whole thing makes no sense to me. I can't figure it out. "

My admission of impotence must have hit just the right tone. His hand came back around, empty. He resumed digging at the grime under his nails. "I told them you weren't as smart as they all thought you were. I told 'em, just leave her to me." His eyes went dead for a moment, and a chilling smile flickered across his fleshy lips. "And after we're done with you, I'm goin' back and pay a little visit to my old lady. Think ol' Merce and her mama'll be glad to see me?"

I tried not to let him see the spark of fear his monologue had ignited. I glanced at Erik and knew he had caught the implication as well.

Buddy had not been surprised to find me in Bill and Vesta Scoggins's front yard! He hadn't gasped in shock to find one of the women he'd supposedly run off the road to their deaths wandering around alive and well. Did that mean he knew about the farm, the hideout Mercer was convinced he'd never find? My heart sank as I realized that, if he knew about Catherine, then he must know it all. But how?

I shifted slightly in the chair, trying to ease some of the pain in my arms drawn tightly behind my back, and the toe of my shoe brushed up against my bag. Apparently it had slid off my shoulder when Slade had flung me into the chair, and it suddenly dawned on me that no one had searched it. No one had even given it a second look. The Glock still rested securely in the top. For no logical reason whatsoever, it gave me hope.

I glanced at Erik, lashed in his chair at the far end of the table. Neither of us was totally immobilized. We could work the chairs around toward each other, use our fingers to work on each other's bonds. Once free, I had the gun. I'd seen no other weapons, only the pistol now stuck in Slade's jeans. If we could just get him out of the room, even for a few minutes . . .

I cast around, searching for some idea, some reason to get him to leave us alone. My eyes lighted on the sink, the remnants of some sort of meal congealing on the dirty plates and pots stacked haphazardly on the stove and countertops, and I remembered the spotless condition of the kitchen the last time I'd been here. Surely Vesta would never have left it in this state. Which meant she hadn't prepared the meal, hadn't been in the house for some time. And I realized with a jolt that something else was missing as well.

"Where's Vesta and the kids?" I asked, turning toward the passive face of our captor, his compact body still lounging against the door frame.

"What do you care?" He didn't look up, his concentration bent on the task of scraping under his nails.

"She can't possibly be involved in this. Any more than Sarah is." Horrible possibilities leapt into my mind, and I struggled to maintain control. "You haven't . . . done anything to them, have you?"

Buddy's smirk deepened as he flipped the wooden toothpick in the direction of the sink. "You got to quit watchin' them movies, girlie-girl. Miss Vesta and her pack o' little Indians went up to the big city to do some Christmas shoppin'. Go every year. Used to drag me along when I was a kid. Christ, I hated it! Used to make me wear a tie and a hand-me-down suit some little rich shit prob'ly threw out."

Buddy walked across the shining linoleum floor to the refrigerator and bent to pull a beer from the plastic rings which held the six-pack together. Behind his back, I mouthed to Erik, *Gun! In my bag!* and motioned frantically with both my eyes and head toward where it lay beneath the table at my feet. He nodded, barely perceptibly, just as Slade slammed the door shut.

Erik watched him pop the can open and drain a third of it in one long gulp. I could tell by the tensing of my partner's shoulders that he was planning some move, and I tried desperately to signal him to wait. We didn't need to try to overpower Buddy Slade. We just needed to get rid of him long enough to work ourselves free and get access to the Glock.

Buddy must have sensed the tension level rise, for he suddenly stared hard at Erik. Then, from out of nowhere, his fist shot out, catching Erik squarely in the temple. I watched in horror as his eyes rolled up in his head, and his whole body slumped forward, straining against the tape that bound him to the chair.

"What did you do that for?" I demanded, struggling myself against my sticky, silver bonds. "What's the matter with you?"

Buddy Slade shrugged, tilted the beer can against his lips, and gulped down the remainder. "Pretty boy there had somethin' on his mind." He crushed the can against the countertop and tossed the empty into the sink. "I spent a lot of time in prison, girlie-girl. You learn how to figure out what a guy's thinkin' almost before he knows hisself. Stay alive that way."

I watched Erik's head, hanging loosely on his neck, a thin stream of saliva running from the corner of his mouth. The pressure built inside me until I felt sure it would explode from my chest. I had not felt this sense of rage . . . of *impotence* since the day I'd realized the men who had murdered my husband would be allowed to get away with it. The level of my hatred frightened me. I knew with absolute clarity that if I had been able to lay hands on my weapon, I would have put a bullet into Buddy Slade's heart without a qualm.

"Readin' your mind, too, girlie-girl."

"Quit calling me that, you despicable little shit!"

"Oooo, now. Gettin' our dander up, are we? Well, you can call me names all you want, girlie-girl. It ain't gonna do you a god-damned bit o' good." He pulled out another chair and slid into it, his arms resting on the table. "You shoulda paid attention to that little e-mail we sent ya and stayed the hell outta this."

"That was you?"

"Bill programmed it out, but I'm the one sent it. What, you thought I was too stupid to run a computer? Hell, ain't much else to do in the slam 'cept let them fools try to teach us how to make it on the outside. Re-ha-bili-tated, that's me." He said the word with a sneer and shook his head at the absurdity of it. "Like I was gonna go get a freakin' job or something."

My eyes dropped, unable to stomach the triumph that glittered in his. There had to be a way out of this mess. Somehow I couldn't conceive of my life ending like this, trussed up like one of Catherine's chickens, helpless, vulnerable, out of control— *No!* I snapped my head back up and glared across the table at my captor.

"That's better," he said with a twisted smile. "You stay pissed. Won't be no fun if you quit on me. Hey, maybe you're thinkin' that little pal of yours, Miss Sweet-and-Sassy Sarah, or maybe Miss Vesta is gonna come ridin' in here to the rescue. That what's runnin' through that busy little mind of yours?" He grinned wider. "Nope, sorry, babe. They're gone for at least two days. By the time they get back, ain't gonna be nothin' left for them to worry about, if you get my drift."

Erik stirred, a low moan escaping from his dry lips.

Buddy Slade stood abruptly. "I gotta go take a leak while pretty boy here's still takin' his beauty rest. Now don't you run off 'til I get back, hear?" His thin laugh trailed after him out of the room.

The moment he disappeared through the door, Erik's head snapped up, and he began sliding the legs of his chair in my direction.

"But, I thought—" I began.

"*Sshh*! Work your way toward me. Back-to-back. Careful! Don't tip over."

It seemed hours, but could have been only a matter of seconds before I felt his hand against my wrists, his fingers working frantically at the edges of the duct tape which bound me.

"What about you?" I kept my voice to a hoarse whisper.

"Never mind me. You get loose and get the gun. I don't know how to use one anyway."

I felt the tape slackening. Then, with a final rip that pulled the hair from my arms and sent the sweetly excruciating pain of circulation returning to my dead hands, I was free. My numbed fingers refused to grasp the end of the tape holding my legs, and tears of frustration spilled over onto my cheeks.

"Don't worry about that!" Erik hissed. "Get the bag! Get the gun!"

I lunged from the chair, sprawling under the table, and snatched the strap of my tote. As I dragged it toward me, I heard voices erupt in anger in the living area just a room away. With trembling hands, I fumbled the Glock from my purse.

I was just pulling myself upright when I saw Buddy Slade's scuffed cowboy boots stop dead in the doorway. I brought the gun up, my elbows braced on the table, both hands wrapped around the stock just as Red had taught me. For the second time in my life I sighted down the barrel at another human being. This time, though, there was no fear. This time I felt steady, sure, powerful.

"Right there," I said calmly.

The smile told me he had no belief in my resolve, no faith in my willingness to kill him. I saw his hand slide imperceptibly toward his back, toward the pistol tucked into the waistband of his jeans.

"Please," I said softly, raising the barrel until it pointed directly at his left eye. For a brief instant the image of Dolores floated between us. Dolores smiling, urging me to eat. Dolores brushing out my hair in long, soothing strokes. Dolores curled in a pool of blood in the hallway. "Please make a move for it. I think I can kill you in cold blood, but it would be easier for me to sleep if you try for the gun."

Something in my voice, or in my eyes, convinced him, and his hands moved out away from his sides. "Got to hand it to you, girlie-girl," he began, but I cut him off.

"Shut up! Get over here."

He walked slowly into the kitchen, his eyes flickering toward the sounds of the argument taking place next door.

"Don't even think about it. Even if you yell, you'll be dead before they get in here. Or are you willing to die for the cause?" When he reached the edge of the table, I said, "Stop. On the floor. Face down, hands behind your head."

After he'd complied, I took my eyes off him long enough to work my legs free, then moved around behind Erik. It took only a few seconds to release his hands. While he unwound the extension cord from his legs, I moved to stand above Buddy Slade, the Glock trained on the back of his head.

Erik grinned at me over the prostrate body of our former captor. "Nice work, partner," he said. He reached down to yank Buddy's tattooed hands up behind him and bind them tightly with the cord. Then he grabbed a handful of the greasy black ducktail and jerked him into the chair. Apparently Buddy had enough experience with situations like this to keep from crying out, but the pain was etched plainly on his face.

"Get his gun," I said.

Erik had just jerked the pistol from Buddy's waistband and set it out of his reach on the table when the tenor of the noise in the living room suddenly changed, and I thought I heard the sound of the storm door bang shut. Erik and I exchanged a look of alarm. A woman screamed, then high-pitched shrieks preceded the children as they tumbled into the kitchen, little blonde Carly in the lead. She hesitated only long enough for recognition to dawn on her heart-shaped face.

"Miss Bay, Miss Bay, you comed back!" she cried a moment before flinging her tiny arms around my legs.

A moment later a white-faced Sarah Jane Tanner edged her way into the room. Jack Wilson's bronzed forearm encircled her neck, and the muzzle of a handgun was pressed against her temple.

"Miss Bay? Are you all wight?" Carly's clear blue eyes regarded me solemnly as I laid the Glock on the table.

"It's okay," I said, gently stroking her soft, straight hair, but I knew I lied.

It wasn't okay. It was over.

CHAPTER
TWENTY-NINE

We adults arranged ourselves on the floor while four of the five children draped themselves across both levels of the bunk beds attached to one wall. Carly had crawled up onto my lap, and I winced as she settled herself onto the thigh of my injured leg.

They'd stashed us in a combination bedroom/playroom on the third floor while the "brain trust" of the New Earth Defense Network decided our fate. Erik and I had already investigated the one octagonal window set high in the gable beneath the roof, but had soon proved to ourselves the validity of Vesta's whimpered insistence that it didn't open. For obvious reasons, the door didn't have a usable lock, but Jack Wilson had stationed Buddy Slade, his pistol once again gripped comfortably in his scarred fingers, right outside in the hallway. Erik would occasionally creep silently up to place his ear against the hollow-core panel, then return, shaking his head, when he caught the sound of movement which told us our jailer was still in place.

At least they'd done us the kindness of putting us someplace where we could keep the children occupied. Sarah had immediately selected a video from the stack arrayed on one of the bookshelves and popped it into the VCR. With all of them engrossed in the antics of *Bear in the Big Blue House* and his companions, the rest of us were able to converse in coarse whispers without, we hoped, frightening them any more than they already were.

Vesta sat hunched against the far wall, her legs drawn up, her head resting on her knees, in an attitude of utter dejection. She had been nearly hysterical in the kitchen, and her obvious terror had sent the kids off into a chorus of wailing and crying. As Jack Wilson released Sarah and shoved her roughly over toward the rest of us, Bill Scoggins gripped his wife's shoulders and shook her into silence. From that moment, even while they herded us all up the steep, narrow stairs and into captivity, she had not uttered a sound except to tell us that the window we'd been examining as a possible means of escape hadn't been opened in fifty years.

I felt Carly's blond head grow heavy against my chest and realized she'd fallen asleep. "Sarah," I whispered, and my former sister-in-law turned toward me. "Can you throw me a pillow off the bed?"

Despite the obvious shock of finding herself suddenly in the middle of what appeared to be a mass kidnapping, she seemed calm, under control. She pulled out a spare pillow with images of a perfectly groomed Barbie scattered across its case and helped me settle Carly onto the carpeted floor next to an overflowing toy chest. We draped a bedspread over her, and I watched as she curled up into a tight little ball, her left thumb finding its way unerringly into her tiny mouth.

I glanced at Vesta, her face still buried on her knees, and gestured for Erik to join Sarah and me in the far corner of the room.

"We have to get out of here," I said without preamble, my voice pitched so low the others had to strain toward me. "Any ideas?"

Sarah surprised me with a controlled, whispered burst of anger. "What the hell is going on here, Bay? Who are these people? What do they want with us? I swear, if one of them so much as looks cross-eyed at any of those kids, I'll kill him myself!"

Erik raised an eyebrow at me in mute question, and I nodded for him to go ahead. "Okay . . . Sarah, right? Here's the short version so you'll know what we're up against. It's pretty much circumstantial evidence, but Bay and I are convinced we've got most of it right." He glanced behind him at Vesta, then edged closer to us and lowered his voice still further. "Scoggins and Wilson go way back, into the protest movement of the seventies. Back then they were called 'Defend the Earth,' and they were known as one of the most radical and violent of the antinuke groups. Some of their members were prosecuted for some pretty heavy crimes, from manslaughter to armed robbery and worse. The top guys, of course, never got caught. There're probably still warrants out for their arrests, under their real names, but most of them went underground. The rest of the country, no matter how much they might agree with their aims, had started getting fed up with their guerilla tactics." He shifted his long legs into a more comfortable position and regarded Sarah intently. "Jack Wilson was the ringleader."

Sarah absorbed this news with an equanimity I found amazing, considering we were talking about the man she just might have been falling in love with. "What's his real name?"

"No one knows for sure. Back then he went by an Indian name, Wovoka. It's associated with a religious movement back in the 1880's called the Ghost Dance. It was supposed to unite the tribes, guarantee the disappearance of the white man from their lands, and herald a new age of abundance and prosperity for the Indians. But the massacre at Wounded Knee at the end of the last century pretty much discredited the prophecies."

"What does all that have to do with these . . . *people?*" Even in her fear and anger, Sarah couldn't bring herself to use the more colorful and descriptive epithets which raced through *my* mind.

Despite the rising wind, we heard the sound of a car door slamming, and Erik rushed to the window. "Looks like the party's breaking up," he said. "Two people just got into the Jeep, but I can't see them very clearly. They're pulling out now . . . They're down the road." Erik rejoined us on the floor. "How many were down there when you came in?" he asked Sarah.

"Four. Bill and . . . Jack or whatever his name is, and two more men. They both looked like Indians. Short, heavyset. One even had braids and a beaded headband."

"That seems to be the ones who just drove off. Okay, so that leaves Wilson and Scoggins."

"And Buddy," I added, shivering involuntarily.

"Right. So, four against three. That's better odds than we had before."

"You're forgetting the guns," I said. "And I wouldn't count on Vesta." I glanced again at the woman who had seemed so shy and reluctant on my first visit to her home, but who had made me welcome with food and kindness. It seemed as if she hadn't moved in hours. "And the kids," I added, knowing what a liability they were to any plan of attack we might be tempted to try.

"Bill would never harm the children." Vesta Scoggins spoke without raising her head, but the words carried a firm conviction.

I dragged myself over next to her. "How well do you really know your husband? Before you walked in the door tonight, can you honestly say you ever expected him to be holding other people at gunpoint while some ex-con tied them up in your kitchen?"

I could see the tears running down her face and onto her arms, but I couldn't let up. We needed Vesta on our side. "Did you think him capable of twisting the minds of the kids put in your care, turning them into killing machines for this crazy cause of his?"

"Buddy never killed anyone! That's a lie!" Her head snapped up, and she wiped her streaming eyes with the sleeve of her sweater.

Sarah moved to offer comfort, but I waved her back. Vesta angry was of much more use to us than the blubbering wreck she'd been just a moment before. "What happened to your truck?" I demanded in the same hoarse whisper we'd all been using to avoid attracting the attention of our guard in the hallway.

"I don't know what you mean," she replied.

"The front bumper. The big dent and the scratches."

"Bill had a little accident. Rear-ended someone out on the highway."

"Wrong. Buddy Slade was driving that truck night before last. He ran Mercer and me off the road with it."

"I don't believe you! Buddy's not like that! I know what everyone says, but he was a good child, never gave us a bit of trouble until he got in with that gang in high school. It was all their fault. They turned him wild, seduced him with money and drugs. He never would have gotten all those holes jabbed into his body or had those disgusting numbers tattooed on his fingers."

"What's that all about? The numbers?"

"They represent letters. You know, like one is *A* and so on. They spell out the name of the gang."

"Which is?"

Vesta swallowed hard, but met my gaze. "ALL MUST DIE," she said in a quiet voice that rose again before I could comment. "But you're wrong about Buddy, he would never do such a terrible thing. He would never have tried to hurt Mercer. I told her so, too." She stopped as the video tape abruptly came to an end, and silence descended on the cramped room.

Sarah rose and slipped in another, stopping by the bed to tuck a blanket around one of the little ones who had fallen asleep, in spite of the strain of the past couple of hours. I envied them their ability to escape the fear and anxiety in so simple a fashion. She walked around Vesta and me huddled close together on the floor and pulled herself up on her tiptoes to peer out the octagonal window. The wind continued to rise, and every now and then we could hear the scrape of bare tree branches against the glass. She seemed lost in thought, as if measuring some course of action in her mind, her head cocked to one side in concentration.

To the strains of the theme song from *Winnie the Pooh* now emanating from the television speakers, it suddenly occurred to me what Vesta had just said, and I whirled toward her. "What did you mean, you told Mercer that, too? Told her what? When?"

Erik sensed a change in the atmosphere and slid himself over closer to us. "What's the matter?"

Vesta stared at me, her face gone slack as if once again she might burst into tears.

"Did Mercer call you today? She did! You already knew about the attack on us, didn't you? Of course! You've always known about Catherine, about where they were staying. Both of you told me as much, at different times, but I never made the connection." I remembered then how Bill, seated in the old Adirondack chair on the porch three stories below us, had said to me that Vesta was the only one Mercer trusted, the only one who knew where she was. Had my cousin been suspicious of her foster father's involvement even then? But if so, why hadn't she told me? Even when I'd questioned her the night before in the chilly gazebo behind the old farmhouse, when I'd asked her if she had been hiding out at Aunt Eliza's during my frantic search for her, she'd said something like, ". . . that's what we wanted you to think." *We*. Mercer and Vesta. Had it been what they wanted Bill to think as well?

"You had to have some idea of what your husband was up to. You didn't trust him to know where Mercer was, and neither did she. Why?"

We waited, while Roo and Piglet giggled in the background, and Sarah continued to stare thoughtfully out the window. I watched as Vesta's love for the children finally overcame her loyalty to Bill Scoggins.

"He changed. As soon as Jack Wilson showed up, he began to act strange, secretive. They'd shut themselves up in the back room and talk for hours. They always made me stay away, but there were things I overheard, little bits and pieces, that made me afraid. I never knew about Bill's past, about his involvement in these protest things. By the time I met him, he'd put all that foolishness behind him. But when Jack began asking about Mercer, about this idea of hers that there was a fortune buried at the ruins of that plantation on the old bomb plant grounds, I knew it was trouble. Every time she came to visit, Bill pumped her about the details, things like how sure she was of the exact location and how much did she think was there." Vesta paused, pulled a rumpled tissue from the sleeve of her sweater, and daintily wiped her nose. "So I listened at the door, and I . . . I heard things. I had to get away, get the children out of here before . . . before something terrible happened."

Erik and I exchanged a look, not exactly of satisfaction, but more in acknowledgment that our guesses had been so close to the truth. All of this jibed perfectly with what Mercer had finally revealed to me and what Erik had found out from his hours of Internet sleuthing. In the home of his old lieutenant and most ardent supporter, Jack Wilson had stumbled into the perfect setup. He could carry out his own sinister objective and, in the process, acquire the funding to keep his group going for years to come. All they needed was to recruit the gullible Mercer Mary Prescott into their ranks. The night of the protest must have been a revelation to her. I wondered if Jack Wilson or Bill Scoggins had made a grab for the map or threatened her if she didn't give it up. Regardless, she had been running ever since, not only from the authorities, but from her foster father and his fanatical friends as well. And yet she had held back Bill's involvement, refused to implicate him even when it had become apparent he had joined forces with her pursuers.

"Why didn't you call the police? Why did you come back?" I tried, but failed to keep the accusation out of my voice.

"She didn't want to," Sarah answered from her station at the window. "It's my fault. Jack invited me to attend another rally with him, said we'd be staying with friends of his in Georgia." She sighed, unable to look at any of us as she told her story. "When we got here, apparently some crisis had arisen, and they needed to have a conference. Vesta had already decided to take the kids, supposedly on a Christmas shopping trip, so Jack suggested—insisted, actually—that I go with them. I was driving when we hit the snowstorm up in the higher elevations, and I refused to go on. Vesta didn't want to turn back, but I was afraid for the kids' safety." Again her sigh held both anger and guilt. "I'm sorry. If I hadn't been such a coward, we'd be miles away from here by now, and they'd be safe."

Vesta pushed herself to her feet and went to stand next to Sarah. "It's not your fault. It's mine. At first I wasn't sure. About you, I mean. You came with him, with Jack, and you seemed to . . . *like* him. I didn't know if I could trust you. If I had just told the truth, gone to the police, none of us would be in this situation. I'm the one to blame."

All this breast-beating was getting us nowhere, and I said so. "What we need," I continued, rising to join the other women, "is a plan to get us all out of here. From what you've both said, we can't expect any help from the outside, so it's going to be up to us."

Erik levered himself to his feet and again crept to place his ear against the door. He stood that way for a long time before crossing the room to where we all stood. "I thought for a minute Slade might have left, but he's still out there. Unfortunately, I can still hear him breathing."

"How did he get involved in all this?" I asked, of no one in particular, but it was Vesta who once again had the answer.

"When he got out of jail, he came here looking for money," she said wearily. "He always did that, came to us when he needed something. I guess I was blind, but I've always had a soft spot for the boy. I really believed I could turn him around." She shook her head in resignation. "Once Jack Wilson got ahold of him, I knew I didn't have a chance. I think they used him and those two girls he hangs around with to keep tabs on Mercer. I know Jack was yelling at him about 'losing her' one night when I came down-stairs unexpectedly."

So Mercer gave them the slip, I thought, probably when she skipped out on her court appearance and showed up in Beaufort. Jack must have been frantic. His potential meal ticket had flown the coop, so he sent the hounds in hot pursuit. Dolores and I had gotten in the way.

I pushed that ugly thought aside as something else popped into my head. "I don't understand why they took the chance of getting arrested in the first place. Did they stage that whole protest just to get Mercer onto the grounds of the Savannah River Site?"

"Not exactly."

We all whirled at the voice which spoke softly from the doorway. Bill Scoggins stood framed in the light spilling from the crowded bedroom out into the darkened hall. The image of Buddy Slade, gun in hand, was silhouetted just behind him. "I brought you something to eat." Bill pushed assorted stuffed animals and blocks from the low table beside the toy chest and set down a tray piled with sandwiches and several cans of soda. He had to step carefully around the sleeping form of Carly, still curled in a ball on the floor.

"Vesta, I—" he began, but his wife turned her face to the wall, ignoring him. The hand he stretched out in supplication fell again to his side. His weary eyes slid over to me. "Mrs. Tanner, I don't expect you to understand, but none of this was supposed to happen. I never intended anyone to get hurt."

"That's not what your résumé indicates." Erik moved to my side and slightly ahead in an obvious attempt to put himself between me and the gaping muzzle of Buddy Slade's handgun. "From everything I found out about your group, people always got hurt when you and your sidekicks showed up. Some of them ended up dead."

"That's not true! *We* were the ones who got beaten with nightsticks and gassed by the cops. It was a war! And it still is." In spite of everything that had happened, in spite of knowing the lives of his wife and his foster children were in serious danger, the zeal with which Bill Scoggins defended his cause remained undimmed. "Don't you people see what's happening? If we allow them to continue transporting weapons-grade plutonium and radioactive waste all over the country, we could all die! All it would take is one accident, one truck overturning or one railroad car derailing, and the whole planet could become uninhabitable for centuries! We have to stop them."

"And how does lying down in the road in the middle of the Savannah River Site save the planet?" I wanted to grab him by the throat and shake some common sense into his fanatic's warped brain. Beside me, Erik felt the tension gathering in my muscles and laid a restraining hand on my shoulder. "How does killing us advance your cause?" I hissed into his face, praying the children were too occupied with the video to pay us any attention. "Can you do it, Bill? Can you stand by and watch these kids die? Do you have the balls for it?"

I ripped my arm out of Erik's grasp just as Buddy advanced into the room, the gun leveled in the direction of my chest. "Hey, what's goin' on? Cut the chatter, girlie. Come on, Bill. The boss wants us downstairs."

For a long moment Bill Scoggins and I held each other's eyes.

He blinked first. "No one's going to die. We just have to make a few arrangements, and then we'll be gone. We may have to restrain you, but no one here is going to get hurt." Again he looked toward his wife, her face still firmly averted. "You'll be okay, Vesta, I promise. I'll see you and the kids have everything you need to keep going."

Behind him, I watched the sneering smile curl Buddy's lip, and I knew that, whatever fate was in store for us, it wasn't the benign outcome Bill Scoggins believed in. They'd already killed—once that we knew of, and who could say how many other times that they'd managed successfully to conceal? They couldn't afford to leave all these witnesses behind. Buddy knew it, and so did I.

"Come on." Slade jabbed Bill in the shoulder with the barrel of the gun. I gave a fleeting thought to making a grab for it right then, but Buddy read my eyes and stepped back quickly. "No way, sweetheart. But I got to admit I like your guts for even thinkin' about it."

He backed out into the hall as Bill Scoggins turned to follow. "Answer my question," I called to him, and he stopped. "What did you hope to accomplish?"

"I guess it can't hurt to satisfy your curiosity. The whole world will hear about it soon enough."

I could tell Buddy didn't like this turn of events, but he didn't know how to keep Bill quiet. I saw him look over his shoulder as if hoping Jack Wilson might appear and tell him what to do.

"We made a deal with that guard, Singleton, to steal a small amount of radioactive material. He'd never be able to smuggle it off the grounds. Security's too tight. So we staged the protest to give him the cover to pass it to us. While the rest of us were getting arrested, Spotted Elk slipped away into the woods with the lead-lined container and disappeared into the night. Jack's a brilliant strategist. The plan worked perfectly."

"Then how come the guy ended up dead?"

"The stupid bastard got greedy," Buddy said from the hallway. "Wanted more than the price we agreed on." Again he cast a glance behind him. "Come on, Bill. We gotta get movin'."

"And Mercer?" I had to know how deeply in all this she was involved. In spite of everything, I still didn't know how much she could be trusted to tell the truth.

Bill Scoggins paused, his hand on the doorknob. "She didn't have any idea what we were planning. We just thought it was too good an opportunity to pass up, maybe being able to lay hands on a fortune. Our work requires a lot of money."

"Guess you'll just have to go back to knocking off liquor stores to finance your noble cause."

He bristled at Erik's contempt, but let it pass. "Mercer wouldn't show anyone the map until we were inside, and Jack soon realized it was useless without a GPS unit. None of the landmarks existed anymore. We would have tried again, but—"

"But we screwed up your plans," I finished for him. "I wish I could say I was sorry."

"You haven't stopped us, just slowed us down a little." Some of the true believer's zeal had returned to his voice. "When you see how easily this plague can be let loose upon the world, everyone will understand that we have to stop the insanity of producing endless piles of nuclear waste. They'll know we were right. Then maybe you can understand why all this was necessary."

This last was directed at Vesta who had turned to stare sadly at her husband. "Never," she said softly.

With a shrug, Bill Scoggins left the room, easing the door closed behind him.

Sarah laid a comforting arm across Vesta's shoulders, then motioned with her head for Erik and me to move closer. With her free hand she traced the outline of the octagonal window. "I've got an idea," she said.

CHAPTER
THIRTY

None of us liked Sarah's plan, but no one had a better alternative, so after minimal discussion, we set to work.

Vesta woke Carly and gathered all the children around her in the corner of the room farthest from the door. She popped open cans of soda and passed out sandwiches from the tray her husband had left behind, all the while murmuring in soothing tones and answering their whispered questions as best she could. Sarah cranked up the volume on the video, hopefully just enough to cover the sounds of our preparations without attracting Buddy's attention. Erik hadn't been certain he was still out there, but we couldn't afford to overlook the possibility. Outside, the weather gods seemed to be smiling on our enterprise, at least for the moment, as thunder rolled through the hills surrounding Toccoa and a steady rain continued to drum against the roof.

After Sarah and I pulled the mattresses off both the bunks and hauled them across the room to the window, Erik set to work on the old wooden slats beneath the springs. The veins stood out on his neck, and we could see the muscles of his back and shoulders straining against the fabric of his shirt. With one final heave and a muffled grunt, he turned triumphantly, the splintered board in his hand.

Crossing to the window, Erik gripped the blunt end of the slat while Sarah and I pressed the mattresses around him. At his nod, Vesta replaced the Winnie the Pooh tape with the one we had selected and herded the children with her directly in front of the door. As soon as the music began, she urged them into song. Five lusty little voices broke into a spirited, off-key rendition of, "There was a farmer had a dog, and Bingo was his name-o" while Erik smashed the window and Sarah and I did our best to muffle the sounds with the thick bedding.

Erik used a blanket wrapped around his hand to pull the last shards of broken glass from the warped frame, and a blast of cold air swirled into the room. The children, wide-eyed, faltered a little, but Vesta spurred them on into "John Jacob Jingleheimer Smith" as Sarah stepped into Erik's cupped hands. He lifted her easily into the opening.

Out on the steep roof, her hands still gripping the windowsill, Sarah paused. Our eyes locked for a moment, and I could only nod numbly in acknowledgment of her bravery. My mind flashed back to the trophies and medals strewn across her mantel. More than a decade had passed since she'd tightroped her way across the three-inch-wide balance beam and gripped the uneven parallel bars with chalked hands. Did she still have the skills? Could she negotiate the narrow edge of the roof in a mounting gale, manage to hold on to a rain-slick limb with fingers numbed by cold? Could she even make the leap?

I knew she read all my doubts in that brief second and dismissed them. Sarah Jane Tanner knew what she could do. With a quick smile, she was gone.

I rushed to join Erik at the window while behind us the concert of slightly off-key voices continued to ring out. Sarah had peeled off her heavy sweater, leaving only a thin, dark turtleneck. In navy blue leggings and socks, the only thing visible against the stormy sky was the white of the brand-new sneakers I'd purchased just a few hours before. Her own slick-soled loafers would have made her attempt impossible.

I held my breath as Sarah eased her way down the sharp pitch of the roof, sliding once on the wet shingles, but finally reaching the edge where she paused for a moment, gathering herself. The limb she had selected during her long study of the situation was farther along toward the side of the house. The thin branches which earlier scraped against the glass were much too fragile to support her weight.

"Bay?" Vesta's voice, overriding the laughter and giggling of the silly song now playing on the tape, startled me, and I whirled to face her. "What's happening?" she mouthed. "Did she make it?"

"Not yet," I whispered loudly, "but she's just about ready to try."

I turned back to see Sarah, standing then, poised on the lip of the roof directly across from a stout branch of the towering maple tree whose dead, brown leaves littered the front yard. Like a diver gathering herself before a plunge from the high board, she took a deep, calming breath, then launched herself into the air.

I wanted to close my eyes, but they were riveted on the flash of white as Sarah's feet left the shaky security of the roof. For what seemed like hours she hung, suspended in midair, her arms outstretched in what I now knew was a quixotic, impossible attempt to save our lives. Sarah would die, horribly, impaled on a branch. Or worse, shattered on the broken pavement three stories below, her bones splintered, her organs crushed . . .

"She made it!" Erik's choked cry of triumph brought me back from the nightmare scenario I had been unconsciously creating while my eyes had recorded the amazing truth of his exclamation.

"She made it," I echoed him, the sound somewhere between a sob and a shout. I turned to Vesta and the kids, still singing away at the top of their voices. "She made it," I said again.

Even with the branches and limbs stripped of their colorful leaves, it was still impossible to see clearly where Sarah had landed. I tried to pick out the shoes, but could not, even against the stark, bare trunk of the huge tree. "Can you tell . . . ?" I began, my fears for her once again tightening my chest, when headlights bounced across the night and dipped to a stop in front of the house.

"It's them," Erik said softly as the sounds of doors opening and slamming drifted clearly up to us through the gaping window.

Where was Sarah? My partner and I exchanged looks of panic and again strained to discern her form amid the tangled branches and blowing rain. Surely she had not fallen? We had heard no cry. But what if she'd injured herself? What if she'd landed wrong and even now hung suspended just above Jack Wilson's returning henchmen? Sarah had to have been as aware of them as we were, poised as she was just over the Jeep.

I prayed she had made it safely, that she would keep her head down until they had moved away from her. And then I prayed she'd drop to the ground and run like hell for the nearest cop.

The bad guys were back, and time was running out.

For what seemed like a very long time, nothing happened. Erik maintained his vigil despite the cold rain and bitter wind blowing into the room, but could not be certain when—or *if*—Sarah had climbed down to safety. Their mission accomplished, the children had been wrapped in blankets and resettled on the mattresses in the corner farthest from the broken window. Carly had again drifted off into innocent sleep while Vesta crooned to the others huddled around her on the floor.

I stood with my ear pressed against the door, straining to make sense of the muffled sounds drifting up from downstairs. I desperately wanted to inch the panel open just a crack, to see if Buddy Slade still patrolled the hallway, but I was afraid to do anything to cause him to reenter the room. The longer Sarah's escape remained undetected, the better chance we all had of surviving this nightmare.

At least that's what I kept telling myself.

When I finally heard the heavy tread of booted feet on the uncarpeted steps, it was almost a relief. I signaled Erik, who left his post to join me in the far corner. We positioned ourselves in front of the children. Vesta eased Carly onto the floor and rose to join us. She clutched my hand as the door slid open.

Jack Wilson recoiled at the blast of cold air that greeted his entry. It took him only a moment to take in the significance of the gaping window and the fact that there were now only three of us standing to face him. Behind him, Bill Scoggins looked questioningly at his wife, who lifted her head and stared back at him in calm defiance. It may only have been my imagination that a brief glint of admiration flitted across his eyes before Buddy Slade roared from the hallway.

"The bitch got away? How—? God damn it, she's dead! I'll kill the—"

"Shut up, Buddy." Jack Wilson spoke with a quiet intensity that quelled his hired gun in midsentence. "Bill, go make sure the package is loaded in the truck, then send Harry and Spotted Elk on their way. They'll need to get out of the area as quickly as possible. Tell them I said to wait three days, then meet us at the scheduled rendezvous point. They'll know what I mean."

"What about . . . ?" Bill stumbled on the words, unable to complete the thought.

"Don't worry. I'm not going to harm your wife and children. You know me better than that, old friend. Get your things together, and I'll meet you outside. I don't think we have much time."

Scoggins raised a hand, in supplication or farewell I couldn't be sure, but Vesta turned her face away from him once again. "Be well," he said before turning and edging past Buddy Slade toward the stairs.

"What about me? What about Mags and Nilla? You gonna tell us about this rendezvous place, or are we just supposed to look out for ourselves?" Buddy whined, the gun still held rigidly in his hand as he moved into the room.

"You and your friends have been well paid," Jack Wilson answered, "despite your having screwed up every assignment I gave you. By killing Singleton and trying to kill Mercer, you've made it impossible for us to complete our mission. I suggest you take your money and get as far away from here as possible. And consider yourselves lucky."

The cold imperiousness of his voice held us all spellbound as he turned to face his lackey, his hands buried deep in the pockets of his heavy suede jacket.

"Ain't you forgettin' somethin'?" Buddy Slade stood his ground under Wilson's hard stare. "I'm the one with the gun. And I ain't goin' nowhere until I get somethin' more for my trouble. Seems like me and the girls done all the dirty work, and now you and your Injun friends think you can just waltz outta here with the goods. You tell them I think I'll just take that 'package' off your hands."

He waved the muzzle of the gun for emphasis, but Jack Wilson appeared unmoved. "Listen to me carefully, you little piece of prison garbage," he began, again in that same, dead voice. "If I wanted to, I could take that gun from you right this second and shove it up your scrawny ass. And if, by some miracle, you did manage to shoot me first, my friends would be all over you in a heartbeat. And if you somehow eluded them, there are a hundred more who would hunt you down and kill you."

I could almost smell the fear rolling off Slade. He stood unmoving, as if the penetrating glare of Jack Wilson had literally nailed him to the floor.

"And when *they* found you, you would beg them to shoot you." He took a step forward, and I held my breath in anticipation of the explosion. But it was Buddy who flinched,

Buddy who moved back slightly, and I knew Jack Wilson had won. "Over the centuries my people have developed very interesting ways to kill their enemies. Just because we wear blue jeans and baseball caps doesn't mean we've forgotten the lessons of our ancestors." Another step forward, and Slade was backed to the doorway. "I wonder how you'd hold up to having your ears cut off and your scalp lifted while you're still alive and screaming. And that would be just the beginning. There are other body parts you might find it even more painful to lose."

The gun wavered in Buddy's hand, then he turned and pounded down the steps. We heard the slam of the back door.

"I apologize for that, Vesta. I hope the children haven't been unduly traumatized."

I think she surprised herself as much as the rest of us when she said, very calmly, "Go to hell."

Jack Wilson accepted the rebuke with a smile. "Now," he said, turning to me, "if you'd be so good as to come with me, Mrs. Tanner. I think we should be on our way."

Erik bristled, taking a step toward him, when Wilson pulled the handgun from the pocket of his jacket. "I know, young man, that you feel honor-bound to protect the women and children, but believe me it's unnecessary. Bay will merely be a guarantee of our safe and unmolested getaway. Once we're clear of possible interference, I'll let her out at some backwater truck stop or gas station. I promise you no harm will come to her."

"You can't know how reassuring that is," Erik began, when Wilson cut him off.

"It's her or one of the brats, take your pick."

"I'll go," I said, stepping around Erik.

Jack Wilson gripped my upper arm with his free hand and backed us toward the doorway.

I never heard the sound of their feet on the stairs or the *click* which must have preceded the shot, but I read the mixture of panic and relief on Erik's face a split second before the deafening explosion filled the hallway, and Jack Wilson crumpled at my feet.

CHAPTER THIRTY-ONE

Winter had definitely come to the upstate, although December 21 was still a couple of days away. In spite of a brilliant sunrise, clouds had moved quickly to darken the hard blue of the morning sky, and thin flakes of snow drifted occasionally out of the heavy overcast.

The Judge insisted on coming. As I tucked an extra blanket around his legs, I had to smile. Lavinia, who vehemently and loudly protested the insanity of his decision to tag along, had nonetheless managed to resurrect his stained, insulated hunting coat and hat from some long-forgotten closet. Huddled in his wheelchair in the narrow turnout by the Ellenton historical marker, he looked like a grizzled child sent out by an overprotective mother to play in the snow. Aunt Eliza, her bent form swaddled from head to foot in layers of sweaters and scarves, stood chatting quietly with my father while my companion and I fidgeted, stamping our feet and blowing frequently into our hands.

Sarah had surprisingly declined my offer to share in this denouement to the bizarre events of the past few weeks. She would instead, she told me, spend the day decorating the Christmas tree with her kids, celebrating the joy and wonder of the season. It was hard to argue with her decision.

I, too, was celebrating, but for a vastly different reason. The call that morning, just as I was preparing to leave the house, had nearly brought me to my knees with relief and gratitude. Angie's excited voice announced that the infection had finally yielded to the most recent drug treatment. Dolores would live. Conquering the staph also meant they had a better than even chance of saving her leg. There was not a gift Divine Providence could have offered me more precious than the thought that one day I might step into my house to be greeted by the sounds of Dolores humming softly from the kitchen.

The sound of an approaching car snapped me back to the task at hand. I recognized the gleaming grille of Erik's black Expedition a moment before he flipped on the turn signal and eased the SUV onto the loose gravel behind the Judge's van and the nondescript brown sedan with Department of Energy decals affixed to its doors.

Mercer Mary Prescott hopped down from the passenger side of the Expedition, her hands stuffed in the pockets of her heavy wool jacket. Erik Whiteside, carrying a black instrument about the size of an electronic organizer, walked to the back of the SUV and pulled a metal detector from the rear compartment.

"Where's Cat?" I asked, checking the back seat of the vehicle and finding it empty. "Is anything wrong?"

Mercer and Erik exchanged looks. "She wasn't feeling well this morning," my cousin offered, her voice small in the cold, damp air.

"Another 'aberration'?" I knew it sounded snotty the second it was out of my mouth, but the subject of what to do with Catherine Prescott had been occupying a goodly measure of our discussions over the past few days. The Judge and I felt strongly she belonged in some sort of secure facility, at least until she could be re-evaluated by professionals—for her own safety, if for nothing else. Arrayed against us was her daughter's unshakeable belief that an institution was the worst possible place for Cat.

She had found an unexpected ally in Erik, who cocked an eyebrow at me and scowled. "Merce and I decided it wouldn't be a good idea for her to come all the way out here. She's resting."

Merce and I? I thought. *Hmmm. Interesting.* I left contemplation of the implications of this new alliance to another time and turned to the one member of our little expedition unknown to the rest of the group.

"I'd like you all to meet Don Rumpler." Our liaison with the Department of Energy nodded and shook hands as I made introductions. He was dressed impeccably in a beautiful gray suit, darker gray dress shirt, and gun-metal tie. The black wool of his overcoat matched the deep ebony of his skin.

"Pleased to meet you all. I'd just like to say, for the record, that I personally opposed the Secretary's decision to agree to this endeavor. Nothing personal, young lady," he added, acknowledging Mercer's frown. "But, as the department's chief of security for this district, I'm distinctly uncomfortable about civilians prowling around the facility."

"We appreciate your concerns," the Judge said, sitting up a little straighter in his wheelchair. "However, your Secretary felt it was a small enough price to pay for the disaster my daughter and her friends succeeding in averting. If those madmen had been able to make their getaway, the consequences for all of us could have been"—he paused for emphasis—"catastrophic."

When the local sheriff department's sharpshooter had dropped Jack Wilson in his tracks, the terrifying possibility of a "controlled" plutonium release by the New Earth Defense Network collapsed along with him. In addition, Buddy Slade had unknowingly run from Wilson straight into the arms of the tactical unit, and Harry and Spotted Elk had been intercepted as they attempted to flee. The lead-lined container with its potentially deadly stolen cargo was found sitting innocuously in the back seat of the Jeep.

Jack Wilson's shoulder wound would heal long before he and Bill Scoggins came to trial, the outcome of which should have been a foregone conclusion. However, not surprisingly, an entire phalanx of attorneys representing various antinuclear groups had offered their services, and there was talk of a plea bargain. Mercer still faced charges, but Law Merriweather was working on a deal of his own, based on the premise that my cousin had been more dupe than willing participant.

The only ones not netted on that terrifying night were Slade's sisters in crime, Margit Carlessen and Carmen Bonilla. Although he'd been quick to name them, the two girls had apparently disappeared before authorities could raid their apartment. Which meant that Dolores's attackers were still out there, free and unpunished. Erik and I were determined to do something about that if the police failed to come through.

". . . catastrophic," my father reiterated, to make sure our guard dog from the Savannah River Site got the message.

"I realize that, sir." Rumpler shifted uncomfortably, his black tasseled loafers making crunching noises in the gravel. I hoped he wasn't planning on trekking into the woods in those shoes.

"Well," the Judge said, waving Mercer to his side, "let's get on with it."

All eyes turned to my cousin. Mercer Mary Prescott pushed her scraggly bangs up out of her eyes and hesitated, milking the moment for all it was worth. Then, with dramatic flair, she pulled her right hand from her pocket.

Apparently I was the only one to guess at the significance of the old curling iron, the one I had so carelessly tossed aside as I'd rifled my cousin's duffel bag on that rainy night the police came to take her away from Presqu'isle. No wonder she had risked coming back to us, in spite of her fear of Jack Wilson and the feds. In my cousin's mind, her entire future, as well as her mother's, had been in the possession of the enemy.

My gloved hands made soft *plopping* sounds as I brought them together in acknowledgment of her cleverness. Mercer used her teeth to pull off her white mittens, then carefully unscrewed the metal end and extracted a thin roll of paper from the hollowed-out handle.

"We're right here," she said, unrolling the miniature map and placing it in the Judge's lap. We all moved around behind the wheelchair to peer over his shoulder. "And this is where Erik figures the ruins should be." The thin, dotted pencil line covered only about half an inch to the northwest of where we stood.

So Erik was already privy to Mercer's most closely held secret. In a matter of just a few days, a stranger had gained the trust she felt unable to grant to her family.

"What's the scale?" I asked.

Erik spoke just behind me. "It's hard to tell, exactly, but it shouldn't be more than half a mile from here."

"How'd you pinpoint it, son?" The Judge shook his head. "I've looked at a lot of maps and plats, but I don't think I could figure out how to nail down one specific spot like that."

Erik tapped the gadget he held in his gloveless hand. "It wasn't easy. The problem is that, before the world got around to setting a standard for cartographers, establishing the prime meridian at Greenwich and all that, every country had its own system for determining longitude. Back when this was drawn, ours was based on the Naval Observatory in Washington, D.C. It took some doing to find someone who knew how to convert these old coordinates into modern terms. A professor from the University of Colorado has a Web site with tables on it. After that, it was just a matter of feeding the info into the GPS unit here. It'll lead us to the proximate location. And then we'll have to rely on this baby." He patted the handle of the metal detector as if it were a faithful old dog.

He gestured toward the thick stand of trees lying directly in our path, and I wondered how "straight" the journey would prove to be.

Over his ridiculous protests, I settled the Judge and Aunt Eliza in the van with the heater going full blast and the thermos of coffee Lavinia had insisted we take along resting on the seat between them. How he thought he could negotiate the rough terrain in his wheelchair escaped me, but he was still ranting about my high-handedness when Erik, Mercer, and I shouldered our shovels and set off into the woods.

As our watchdog, Rumpler apparently didn't feel it was up to him to dirty his neatly manicured hands.

Erik took the lead, his eyes on the GPS unit as it guided us through the trees. We had to detour frequently to avoid boggy spots and dense thickets of thorny bushes, but eventually we ended up back on track. Behind us I could hear Rumpler muttering under his breath. I hoped he at least ended up with ruined shoes and soggy pants legs.

About twenty minutes after setting out, Erik stopped, and we moved up to join him. "This it?" I asked. Despite my certainty that this was a fool's errand, I couldn't help catching a little of the excitement which radiated from Mercer Mary Prescott as she clutched my partner's arm and gazed around her.

It wasn't exactly a clearing, but it was evident the trees and vegetation were much smaller and sparser than in the section of the woods we'd just crossed. As Erik paced, studying the instrument in his hand, Mercer crouched to spread the map out on the ground. I knelt down beside her. "I think the house would have been facing east," she said, "to keep the afternoon sun in the back. According to this, then, the cemetery should be somewhere over in that direction." She pointed past where Erik stood, surveying the area.

"Cemetery?" It was the first time Rumpler had spoken since we'd started out. "No one said anything about a cemetery to me." I saw the implications dawn in his hooded brown eyes. "Hey, you aren't digging up any graves. That wasn't part of the bargain."

We all ignored him, and I rose to begin my own perusal of the weed-choked ground. "There's a ridge here," I said, kicking at the almost imperceptible rise with the toe of my boot. I stepped up onto it and realized that it continued in pretty much a straight line. "I think this might be the remains of the foundation."

Mercer and Erik rushed to join me. We followed the outline of Perdition House until the fourth side became swallowed up by the encroaching trees. Again my partner consulted his GPS, then the paper my cousin held up for him. "I'd say it can't be too far in this direction. These crosses here on the map undoubtedly indicate where the cemetery was."

Fifty yards or so into the thick stand of loblolly pines we literally stumbled across the first pieces of broken, scattered headstones. Erik tucked the GPS unit into his jacket pocket and clicked on the metal detector.

"I'm going to work a grid, so I want each of you to take a corner of this open area and stand there to help keep me on track."

He motioned each of us into position, Rumpler grumbling as he stumbled over the uneven ground. Then, headphones in place, Erik began a slow, rhythmic sweeping, back and forth, across the dry, brown grass and bracken. Mercer fidgeted, literally hopping from one foot to another in anticipation. And again, despite holding out little hope of the success of this wild goose chase, I caught some of her excitement.

Twice Erik stooped, alerted by the detector. Mercer and I rushed to his side, loosening the hard packed earth with our shovels, only to rise disappointed, once with a rusty spike and the second time with what appeared to be the broken head of an ax.

Finally, when his sweep had taken him to within ten feet of our established perimeter, I saw the slow smile spread across his wind-chapped face as he slid the earphones from his head and held them out to Mercer. Even from that distance I could hear the insistent beeping.

The small, raised gravesite, its bricks crumbling, but intact, had been overgrown by wild holly and hawthorn. The marble slab, though cracked and splintered, still bore a few of the moss-encrusted letters carved into its surface: L c S c r R c ux .

"Lucy Spencer Robichoux," Mercer whispered. "It's her."

"Who?" Rumpler's voice seemed loud in the hushed dimness

of the graveyard. I hadn't realized he'd followed us.

"My fourth-great grandmother," I answered, awed in spite of myself at the miracle of having found her resting place.

It had taken very little time, once Aunt Eliza, Mercer, and I applied ourselves to the clues left in Isabelle Chase's final letter, to come to the inevitable conclusion that the family treasure had been secreted in Isabelle's mother's crypt. Aunt Eliza had been wrong in assuming Isabelle had been out of her mind with grief and worry when she addressed that letter to her dead mother. She knew perfectly well Lucy Spencer Robichoux had passed away some two years before. It was her attempt to record the hiding place so her daughters could retrieve the treasure without revealing it to outsiders, should the paper fall into the wrong hands: "*Unto Him I commend myself and my children, and unto you I entrust the guardianship of our family's future.*"

"Would you mind giving me a hand, Mr. Rumpler?" Erik had pulled on leather gloves and was working his hands around the largest piece of the broken marble.

Rumpler took a step back and looked over his shoulder, as if help were just beyond the trees. "I . . . I don't think I should do that," he stammered. "And neither should you. This is federal government property, operated by a private corporation." He seemed to gain confidence as he fell back into his comfortable bureaucrat's jargon. "We—*you*—are only here as a courtesy. I can't countenance your destroying—"

"I'll get it," I said, cutting him off. I joined Erik in trying to lift the heavy slab, but we were unable to budge it.

In the end, Mercer, Erik, and I used the shovels as pry bars. While Mr. Civil Servant watched in horror, we finally managed to move the cover enough for Erik to shine his flashlight into the depths. There was no smell of decay, only the bittersweet odor of damp, loamy earth. *Ashes to ashes, dust to dust*, I thought as Erik pulled the crumbling leather pouch from the grave. Rotted strips of cloth, some still clinging to the remnants of delicate, yellowing lace, disintegrated as the contents spilled out upon the ground. How ironic, I thought that the sun should choose that exact moment to break free of the clouds and cast a brilliant light upon the dull glow of tarnished silver, dirt-encrusted coins, and moldy gems.

CHAPTER
THIRTY-TWO

I clutched the lapels of my camel's-hair coat against the sharp wind that whipped around the corner of the huge building and sliced right through the thick wool. Somehow, this wasn't how I'd imagined it—soft white flakes drifting down from a lowering sky, the continuous honking of a hundred horns of every pitch and resonance, a tight layer of smoke and fumes that seemed to hang just a few feet over my head.

No, I told myself, not what I'd imagined at all. Maybe it was the paintings which made one expect riotous mounds of pastel-tinted flowers, and bell-skirted ladies in wide brimmed hats and parasols. Blame it on Monet.

I shooed away another hovering taxi driver and scanned the teeming sidewalk. I was ready to give up, to seek again the warmth of the train station, when, above the sing-song wail of a police siren, I thought I heard my name.

I turned, thinking perhaps I had been hallucinating, when it came again. "Bay! *Ici!* Over here!"

He was bent slightly, his gait slow and strangely halting, and he'd lost at least thirty pounds, but there was no mistaking the smile. Or that slight indentation at the chin, nearly lost in the gauntness of his haggard face, or the light in the depths of his steel-blue eyes.

"Ah, *ma petite,* you did not know me. It is no wonder. I am much changed."

"Not at all," I said, and meant it, moving naturally into his tentative embrace.

For a moment we stood there before the Gare du Nord, travelers parting and reforming around us, smiling to themselves as they passed.

"*Joyeux Noël,* Darnay," I said, against the smooth curve of his cheek.

"Merry Christmas, my darling," he murmured back, as the bells of Paris began to peal.

ABOUT THE AUTHOR

Kathryn R. Wall wrote her first story at the age of six, then decided to take a few decades off. She grew up in a small town in northeastern Ohio and attended college in both Ohio and Pennsylvania. For twenty-five years she practiced her profession as an accountant in both public and private practice. In 1994 she and her husband Norman retired to Hilton Head Island.

Wall is Treasurer of the Southeast Chapter of Mystery Writers of America and is National Publicity Chair of Sisters in Crime. She is also a founding member of the Island Writers' Network.

She is the author of nine Bay Tanner mysteries: *In For a Penny*, *And Not a Penny More*, *Perdition House*, *Judas Island*, *Resurrection Road*, *Bishop's Reach*, *Sanctuary Hill*, *The Mercy Oak*, and *Covenant Hall*. All the novels have achieved both commercial and critical success, and all take place in and around Hilton Head Island and the surrounding South Carolina Lowcountry.

visit Kathryn online at: www.kathrynwall.com

LaVergne, TN USA
12 November 2009
163941LV00004B/22/P